Deed of Glory

Deed of Glory

Alan Evans

HODDER AND STOUGHTON
LONDON SYDNEY AUCKLAND TORONTO

British Library Cataloguing in Publication Data
   Evans, Alan, *1930*
   Deed of glory.
   I, Title
   823′.914[F]   PR6053.V13

   ISBN 0-340-28539-7

*Photoset by Rowland Phototypesetting Limited, Bury St Edmunds, Suffolk.
Printed in Great Britain for Hodder and Stoughton Limited, Mill Road, Dunton
Green, Sevenoaks, Kent by St Edmundsbury Press, Bury St Edmunds, Suffolk.
Hodder and Stoughton Editorial Office: 47 Bedford Square, London WC1B 3DP.*

I have received help from many sources while working on this book and my thanks go to:

Mr. K. V. Crook of *Punjabi*.

Captain A. C. D. Leach, D.S.C. of *Churchill*, Dr. George Gray of *Burnham*, Len Storey of *Newark* and Lieutenant W. W. Griffiths of *Castleton*, all ex-USN destroyers.

Admiral Sir Mark Pizey, GBE, CB, DSO, DL.

Leslie Grace and George Millar.

Eric de la Torré, 'Cab' Galloway and the St. Nazaire Association.

Frank Brown and David Niven for translations.

M. Fernand Guériff, of St. Nazaire.

Mr. Fred Davie and Sgt. Barry Jenkins of Small Arms Wing of the School of Infantry.

Mr. D. Buckley and Vospers Shiprepairers Ltd., who now operate the King George V dock.

David Warner of Harwich dockyard.

Navy News; Airborne Forces Museum; Imperial War Museum; National Maritime Museum; Public Records Office; Naval Library; Naval Historical Center, Dept. of the Navy, Washington DC; and last but by no means least the staff of Walton-on-Thames Library.

But, as always, any mistakes are mine!

Contents

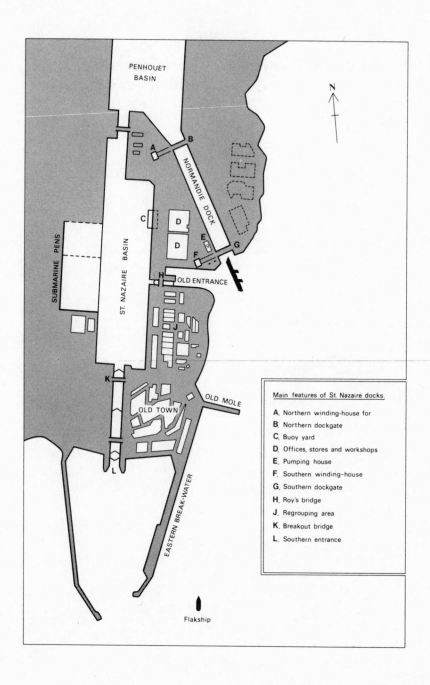

PENHOUET
BASIN

N

NORMANDIE DOCK

A

B

SUBMARINE PENS

ST. NAZAIRE BASIN

C

D

D

E

F

G

H OLD ENTRANCE

J

K

OLD TOWN

OLD MOLE

L

EASTERN BREAK-WATER

Flakship

Main features of St. Nazaire docks.

A. Northern winding-house for
B. Northern dockgate
C. Buoy yard
D. Offices, stores and workshops
E. Pumping house
F. Southern winding-house
G. Southern dockgate
H. Roy's bridge
J. Regrouping area
K. Breakout bridge
L. Southern entrance

"A deed of glory intimately involved in high strategy."
Winston Churchill of the Raid on St. Nazaire.

1

Saracen

Thursday, 20th June 1940, was a day of high summer with a blazing sun in a clear, blue sky. In the forenoon Lieutenant John Ward stood by B gun mounting forward of the bridge of the Tribal Class destroyer *Saracen*, bound for St. Nazaire. Her crew were at action stations as she entered the broad estuary of the Loire in the wake of her sister ship, *Punjabi*. Ward wore his steel helmet pushed to the back of his head so he could more easily use the glasses that hung on their strap against his chest. He was in shirt-sleeves, jacket discarded, but even so sweat ran down his face and he could feel the sun's glare reflected from the gun. At Narvik too, despite the bitter cold, all the guns had radiated heat like that – then, however, it had come from firing. Now the guns were silent, the ship quiet save for the steady pulse of her engines and the hum of the fans.

Ward was twenty-four years old and very tall with thick, black hair and brows, dark eyes and a bent nose. The scar left by the wound he had got at Narvik was weathered now and hardly noticeable, a thin line from mouth to ear on the right of his face.

He considered himself an average, run-of-the-mill naval officer and lucky to be such because he had only just scraped into Dartmouth and had passed out of it narrowly, despite dubious reports and comments: "Must learn to control his temper", "outspoken to the point of insubordination", "high spirits and exuberance should not be allowed to interfere with his studies." He had kicked over the traces in a reaction against his father's constant lecturing on the Perseus Group and its workings. His father had given his life to the huge group of companies but Ward had different ambitions.

11

At sea he did better. He learned to curb his temper and competing in the Navy boxing championship helped there, teaching him the controlled use of force. A big stoker bent Ward's nose and should have won the championship because he was a better boxer, but Ward hung on and in the last minute landed a knock-out punch. He realised that had been luck, but also that if he had not hung on he would not have had a chance to get lucky. That was another lesson. He grew up, but a devil still lurked behind his black eyes, in the hard stare or glint of humour that went with his slow grin.

In the summer of 1939 *Saracen* came home after a year off the coast of war-torn Spain, rescuing refugees from both sides. He suggested to his father, "It would be a good idea if you shifted every factory out of the cities into the country."

"That would cost a fortune!"

"It'll cost more than that if a war comes, Dad, from what I saw of the bombing in Spain."

"You could be right. So pack in the Navy, Jack. If war comes I want you in the business."

Ward shook his head. "Sorry. Just these two weeks' leave and I'm off again."

His father eyed him with exasperation. "I thought this naval game was just to pass the time until you started real work!"

Ward had spent the last year of this naval 'game' on a wartime footing, ready to fight for his life. He said patiently, "I always told you I wanted to go into the Navy."

"But not *stay* in it! Be reasonable, Jack. You'll be the one to take over the Perseus Group when I retire, and you need to get in some experience."

"Geoffrey is the best-suited –"

"Your brother is an accountant, business-trained and I have a good deal of respect for him. But you're the one with flair. You must run Perseus –"

Ward said, "No."

They had a row then. Ward did not want to quarrel

because he was fond of his father, but he would not give an inch.

"Then you won't get another penny out of me, you bloody idiot!"

"I've taken nothing for years – not since I went to sea!"

He walked out of the house and spent the rest of his leave in Paris. He had planned to, anyway. He even had the girl lined up . . . And at the end of his leave he went back to *Saracen* – and to war.

Saracen canted gently under helm as she followed a bend in the buoyed channel. Ward wiped the sweat from his forehead with the back of his hand, lifted the glasses and set them to his eyes. St. Nazaire was an evacuation port for the British Expeditionary Force, the troops being lifted from here as others were taken off from Dunkirk. Although the German army was not so close here as at Dunkirk, and was said to be more than thirty miles away, the *Luftwaffe* was present. St. Nazaire lay six miles from the sea and still distant from Ward by nearly five but a pall of smoke clearly marked the position of the town, and black specks circled above it like flies over a corpse.

The estuary was wide, the navigable channel running close to the flat western shore. The sun set it shimmering in heat-haze and Ward, glancing over his shoulder, saw another shimmer above *Saracen*'s funnels from their hot breath. The new paint on the forward funnel, covering some of the scars of Narvik, caught his eye.

The girl had asked, "Do you paint?"

The party was at Aunt Abigail's house in Chelsea that was always full of artists, writers, musicians, or phoneys. Ward reckoned they were phoneys for the most part, talking, posing, wearing weird clothes. Fair enough. They thought he was weird too, if their glances meant anything.

He answered, "Yes."

"Oil or water-colour?"

"Oil." He thought there was oil in the Admiralty paint and he had given a hand at slapping on plenty of that in his time. But then he said, "I'm only kidding." And explained because he liked the girl.

He was going to see her again some time, if he got back from this trip, which didn't seem all that likely: they were bombing the hell out of St. Nazaire at the moment.

He had been odd man out at the party, just as he was in his mother's family. He had no desire to paint, sculpt, or compose like cousin Mark. He had a voice that would carry in a gale but was not tuned to sing grand opera in the cities of the world as did barrel-chested Uncle Daniel. Ward's mother was a concert pianist: she had taught him as a child and he had tried very hard because he loved her, but they were forced to admit that while he might play a useful pub piano he would never appear on a concert stage.

He did not want to. He watched his family from the side-lines, with respect for their talents and amusement at some of their eccentricities. They regarded him, hulking and somewhat sinister, with perplexity. He just wasn't like them at all.

The party had been to celebrate the safe return from Paris of Patrick, Aunt Abigail's only child. Abigail Ward, once a ballerina, now was a widow and owned a chunk of London. Her husband had gone in with his brother, making the Perseus sports car in the years just before 1914. He had survived that war only to die at the wheel of a racing car when Patrick was still a boy. Understandably therefore, if foolishly, she doted on Patrick. A tall, slender youth, he had lived a life of idleness until suddenly he announced that he wanted to be an artist and the place to learn was Paris. His delighted mother sent him and supported him generously. Ward found Patrick rude, sarcastic, infuriating, but always had a feeling that this was an act and that Patrick would turn out all right at the end and when he was ready. Patrick got very drunk at the party, spoke to no one and walked out early. There was some criticism of his bad manners, though not by Ward. Aunt Abigail was upset. Then, the next morning, she telephoned Ward only hours before *Saracen* sailed for St. Nazaire to tell him tearfully that Patrick had joined the Army. "Some awful county regiment, *infantry*."

Ward's reaction was that if the Army needed Patrick then the war must be going very badly. He thought now, grimly, that it was. Most of the B.E.F. had been shipped out of St. Nazaire but many would never leave. Astern of *Saracen* lay the wreck of the liner *Lancastria*, her masts sticking out of the water of the estuary. Five days ago the liner had been bombed. She sank in thirty minutes with the loss of thousands of lives. There had been survivors, however, and some of these were still in hospitals ashore. There were also hundreds of Polish soldiers who had just arrived in St. Nazaire. The destroyers *Punjabi* and *Saracen* had been ordered to bring them all out.

Ward lifted the glasses again and the mile-long boulevard to the west of the town came up in sharp definition. The aircraft overhead were clearer now and he thought they were Heinkels. Where bombs fell more smoke balled up from the pall hanging over the town and a battery of Bofors guns was firing from the boulevard. He could see the smoke and flame, pale in the sunlight, at their muzzles.

The Heinkels drifted away, shuffled into formation and shrank into black specks again. The Bofors battery ceased firing, were hooked on to the towing trucks and rolled away along the boulevard. A ship waited in the St. Nazaire basin to take them aboard. Ward swept slowly with the glasses from west to east past the outstretched arms of the breakwaters guarding the locks and basins within. *Punjabi* and *Saracen* were following the deep water channel that ran on past the breakwaters and to the east of them. Now Ward could see over the stone pier that was the Old Mole. Beyond lay the dock built by the French to take the liner *Normandie*. It was one of the biggest docks in the world, the massive gate was open and all seemed intact. The Germans would probably use it soon.

Ward lowered the glasses. No 'probably' about it. *Saracen*'s captain, Lieutenant-Commander Julian Gates, had told him that the French were seeking an armistice.

15

Surrender would mean that Germany ruled this coast right down to the border with Spain.

Punjabi and *Saracen* berthed in the Normandie dock and Gates told his first lieutenant, "We want a landing-party. A good killick and a couple of men, one of them able to drive a lorry, and borrow an S.B.A. from the doctor." A sick berth attendant might well be needed to bring off wounded. He thought a moment, then added, "Send Jack Ward up to lead the party." That was no random decision. In Gates's experience, Ward could be relied on. Any officer could get into trouble but Ward got out of it too. He had shown that knack in Norway and it might be needed here.

The chosen killick, Leading Seaman Jenkins, rasped, "Here, you, Tracey! And Mackay! Come wi' me. Landing-party under Mr. Ward."

Mackay was eighteen, Scottish and new to the ship. He muttered to Tracey as they followed the leading hand, "Ward? Isn't he the big, bad-tempered looking –"

Jenkins threw over his shoulder, "Don't go by looks! He's a lovely bloke if you treat him right, just don't get across him. Now get a move on!"

Ward climbed to the bridge and reported to his captain. Gates carefully filled his pipe and sucked on it to test the draw. "Don't want to hang around here too long. Any sign of those Poles?"

"That looks like them, sir." Henderson, the navigator, pointed to a distant column of troops marching through the dockyard towards the ships.

Gates grunted, "Good. Got that map?" Henderson passed it to Ward, a well-worn road map of the area. Gates said, "A job for you, Jack. *Punjabi* is sending parties for most of the wounded from *Lancastria* but one lot is our baby. There are four or five chaps in a hospital outside the town." The stem of his pipe traced across the map and stopped at a pencilled circle. "There. You've got a killick

16

who can drive, so requisition a lorry from that lot at the end of the quay and bring those wounded back – quick. We understand Jerry is still some way off but his bombers aren't, so we won't want to sit here much over a couple of hours. Anything else you need to know?"

"No, sir." That was enough to be going on with.

Gates said, "Good God! They've brought their bloody bikes!"

Ward looked back over his shoulder and saw that the Polish infantry were wheeling their bicycles along the quay.

Ward belted a pistol around his waist, donned his battered cap in place of the heavy steel helmet, found his little party, and led them at a fast walk towards the lorries at the end of the quay. There were demolition parties busy in the port; a detonated charge *thumped!* and a distant crane leaned and fell. Ward looked along the length of the great dock. This would take any battleship in the world. Surely they would destroy it too and not leave it for the Germans.

Leading Seaman Jenkins was Welsh, dark, wiry and pugnacious. Like the two seamen he carried a slung rifle. He glared at Tracey when the young seaman ventured, "Didn't you say you'd been to France before, sir?"

Ward nodded, "That's right." They had talked when they shared a watch in the quiet of the night. "I was on leave in Paris for a couple of weeks not long before the war." That had been after the row with his father, a bitter memory especially now that his father was dead.

Tracey grinned. "That would be a bit different."

Ward had been there with a girl. He had not looked up Patrick in Montparnasse because a little of Patrick went a long way. He and the girl stayed in a small hotel near the Champs-Elysées and for most of the time the only other guest was an elderly Frenchman speaking carefully correct English. He was an engineer and stayed at that hotel whenever he came to Paris. He told Ward and the girl the places they should see. Sometimes they took his advice and always found it good. He even lent them his Renault to

17

drive out into the country. The two of them spent one afternoon under trees by a stream on a day as hot as this; but it had been cool and hushed in the dappled green shade . . .

Ward said, "Yes, it was different." He came back to the thumping of the demolition charges, the marching Poles, the jumble of army trucks ahead, and all of it under a sky smeared by smoke from the fires set by the bombing. One truck stood apart from the others, a three-ton Commer and it looked remarkably clean. A soldier stood to one side, scowling at it, a cigarette dangling from his lips.

Ward asked him, "Are you in charge of this truck?"

The soldier answered without turning, "For about five more bloody minutes."

Jenkins barked, "You're talking to an officer!"

That swung the soldier around. In one practised movement he nipped out the cigarette, came to attention and saluted. "Driver Gibb, T., sir!"

Ward returned the salute, "Easy."

Gibb relaxed and apologised. "No offence meant, sir, but I'm chocker, right up to here." He lifted his hand, flat, to the level of his neck to show how fed up he was. "I've looked after her like a baby, brought her over only a couple of weeks ago and now I've got to ditch her in the drink."

Ward asked, "Is it roadworthy? Will it *go*?"

"A-one. Not much juice, though. Where d'you want to go, sir?"

Ward showed him the map. "That hospital."

Gibb nodded. "I know it. I've been driving all round here for the past week. Only thing is, I've got orders to get aboard a ship."

"So have I. With a party of wounded from that hospital."

Gibb hesitated, then: "Can't leave the poor bleeders." He grinned, "Anyway, your ship won't go without you, sir, so I'm sure of a lift home." Ward was far from certain of that but Gibb was going on, "I'll take you straight there. It's only about a ten minute run. If you get in the front and your lads hop in the back —"

18

The journey took longer because they had to detour around streets blocked with rubble from the bombing. Parties of men and women were digging in the débris, pulling out survivors. Ward frowned as he watched them. His father had not survived. When *Saracen* returned from Norway in May 1940 she went into the dockyard and Ward to his home. His father had been killed in his office by a bomb during a daylight raid and buried the week before.

Ward comforted his mother and talked to his younger brother, Geoffrey. They walked on the lawn behind the house, Ward with his hands dug comfortably in his pockets, Geoffrey limping along with the stick that a bad fall when climbing in Wales had condemned him to. He didn't let it cramp his style, though: the many things he could still do he did to the utmost.

Ward said, "Father reckoned you couldn't run the Perseus Group."

Geoffrey shrugged, "He would. He never let me try, always made it clear who was the blue-eyed boy."

"And after I told him what to do with the job?"

"He didn't believe it; said you'd come back. 'Give him another year to get it out of his system and see sense.' "

"Because he didn't like losing an argument or anything else. He chose to forget I'm on active service these days. We're all the same. That's why you've got your bloody back up now."

Geoffrey glared at him, then laughed, "Look who's talking!"

That's better, Ward thought. He said, "I'm no business-man, and Dad knew it. He'd have given you the job pretty soon. Look, we all know the old boy paid top salaries to put the best men in the driving-seats of every company in the Group. They run themselves. In the beginning, interfere as little or as much as you like. You're the accountant. Feel your way . . ."

Geoffrey prodded the turf with his stick, thinking. Ward pushed him, "So there you are! Now, d'you think you can do it?"

Geoffrey hesitated, "Well – maybe I can . . ." He paused, frowning.

Ward heaved an inward sigh of relief. That was good enough. He said, "Well, you'll bloody well have to – my movements are likely to be pretty erratic from now on. I suppose I'll have to remain titular head, chairman of the board or whatever, but I'll give you all the authority you need."

"And advice?"

"If you want it."

Geoffrey muttered, "I think I will. One thing, to start with: Willcox sent me a letter by hand, all mysterious, saying the government wants us to set up a whole new factory, not for wireless but R.D.F."

"So?"

"I don't know what it *is* yet, for God's sake!"

Ward did and another word for it was radar. He grinned, "They'll explain. Take the contract because we need that stuff. Anything else?"

"Not at the moment." Geoffrey looked thoughtfully at Ward. "The old boy always said you were good at taking a decision."

Ward thought that was rubbish; in this he just happened to know the Navy would need radar.

Geoffrey went on: "He also said you were a throw-back to old Captain Matthew."

That startled Ward. "Bloody cheek! He was a pirate."

That was probably untrue. No one had ever openly accused Great-Great-Grandfather Matthew Ward of piracy. He came home after the American Civil War with a lot of money and there were rumours he had run contraband to the southern states, but Matthew never said how he made the money. He used some of it to set up a marine engineering works with his son in charge and two engineers from Clydeside. He called it the Perseus Engine Works after the ship in which he made his stake. Inside of a year the business was making money and Matthew was sick of it. He went out to Singapore and never returned, was lost at sea ten years later. His widow and son prospered, first of a line of hardworking, astute business people. The interests of Perseus now ranged from heavy engineering to radio, to hotels and a Scottish estate.

Ward thought he might have inherited Matthew's itch to go to sea but that was all they had in common, except that Matthew had been a very tall man with black hair and eyes with a hard look as they stared at you out of the old photograph. Anyway, nobody knew much about Matthew. The family weren't secretive about him, but he was rarely discussed.

Ward stirred in his seat beside Driver Gibb. They had been on the road for twenty minutes. Now they turned off the empty country lane winding between dusty hedges and entered the drive of the hospital. The roof of the building showed above trees and they followed the drive that curled around the trees and ended in a circle of gravel. Farther on, past the end of the building, was another copse and a cart track disappeared into it. Gibb turned the Commer on the gravel and braked it at the foot of the steps leading up to the open doors.

Ward got down from the Commer and passed through the doors, his men at his heels, their boots clumping on the polished wooden floor of the hall within. They halted and stood still, suddenly hushed. Nuns glided along the quiet, sun-striped corridors. An elderly woman that Ward took to be the Mother Superior came from an office into the hall and Ward explained his errand in halting French. Neither she nor her nuns showed any surprise at their presence and Ward decided they must have become used to armed men in heavy boots. There was no delay. He was shown to the wounded and his men started carrying them out on stretchers, lifting them into the Commer and making them as comfortable as possible. There were four: three soldiers and a seaman, all of them pale and ill but all eager to go.

In the Mother Superior's office she handed Williams, the S.B.A., four sets of written notes, one for each case. Williams scratched his head over them, the Mother

Superior explained and Ward tried to translate. It was some minutes before Williams said, "Right, sir, I think I've got the hang of them."

Meanwhile at the front of the building, the loading done, Tracey looked towards the hospital and asked, "What's the French for urinal?"

"Never you mind. I'm not having you getting lost in there. The place is like a rabbit warren." Jenkins jerked a thumb at the trees filling the curve of the drive. "Nip in there." And as Tracey trotted away, "Get well in and out o' sight! This place is full o' nuns and we don't want your John Thomas causing an international incident!"

Driver Gibb asked, "Where's your big feller?"

"The old girl is briefing him and the S.B.A."

"Hope he doesn't take too long over it."

"He won't. He's as keen to get back to the ship as the rest of us." Jenkins swung up into the rear of the truck and said to the men inside, "Won't be long now, mates."

Gibb climbed into the cab as Ward appeared with Williams in the doorway of the hospital, a flock of nuns behind them. He and the S.B.A. came quickly down the steps, putting on their caps, and at the foot of them Ward turned and saluted, then walked around the rear of the truck. "All aboard?"

Jenkins leaned out over the tailboard and hauled Williams inside. "Only Tracey to come, sir. He's gone to relieve himself." He opened his mouth to bellow for the rating then said, "Here he comes." He gave a snort of laughter. "He must ha' thought we were going without him. Never seen him move so fast!"

Tracey ran across the yellow, sun-seared grass from the trees, head back and legs pumping furiously. Ward started towards the cab then halted as Gibb started the engine. Tracey was waving. He was close and gravel spurted from under his boots now; Ward could see his gaping mouth and wide eyes. Tracey came up and panted, "I couldn't shout in case they heard me, sir! There's Jerries down at the gate, I think!"

There was a moment of stunned silence then Jenkins broke it, "You *think*! What d'ye mean, you bloody *think*?"

Tracey explained simply, "I've never seen one before, not really, just in pictures."

Ward stared down the drive to where it curled away around the trees. The Germans were supposed to be thirty miles away. Tracey must be mistaken, but – "Are they coming up here?"

"No, sir. Stopped on the road."

"How many?"

"A lot. A dozen. Maybe more. I didn't count them. I'd just – finished and then they drove up."

Ward said, "Show me." He told Jenkins, "The rest of you wait here."

He ran to the trees with Tracey. It was cool in their shade and they ran in that coolness for some thirty yards, then Tracey flapped a hand. Ward was already slowing and edging aside to take cover behind a tree. They were not at the edge of the wood yet, still in its shelter, but he could see the drive where it ran down to the gateway and through to the road. A truck was stopped on the road, its cab and open body just showing above the low wall. The body was filled with seated troops in green-grey uniforms, their carbines standing between their knees. There looked to be a score of them and one manned a light machine-gun mounted on the roof of the cab.

At the gate, ahead of the truck, stood a big, open Mercedes touring car, its dark, bluish-grey paintwork showing through the film of dust that coated it. Two soldiers with carbines sat in the back, another at the wheel. Like those in the truck their tunics were open at the neck, they wore forage-caps and on the right breast of each was a spread-winged eagle in silver. A fourth man was stepping down from the front of the car and stretching. He looked as tall as Ward, who saw the officer's silver piping on this man's forage-cap.

Tracey whispered, "Are they Jerries, sir?"

Ward nodded. They outnumbered his little party by five

23

or six to one. Then there was their machine-gun. And their car was parked across the gateway like a cork in a bottle, with Ward and his men inside it.

Leutnant Franz Engel stretched his long frame and looked around. In the distance smoke hung over St. Nazaire; they had seen the Heinkels make their bombing runs. Here there was only an empty road and fields basking under the sun. A drive ran up from the gateway to curve around a belt of trees and behind them rose the roof of the hospital. Nothing could be more peaceful.

Engel, twenty-three years old, lean and bronzed, grinned down at the driver of the Mercedes. Pianka was a much older man, a veteran of the first war. He sat squarely and patiently behind the wheel. Engel teased him: "I don't see any resistance, any Tommies."

Pianka shrugged, "I still say we are too far ahead, Herr Leutnant. It is against orders."

"Against the letter, maybe, but not the spirit. Reconnaissance is a part of Intelligence." He and Pianka were Abwehr, Military Intelligence. "If you want to learn then you go and look." He leaned forward to slap Pianka's shoulder affectionately. "Don't worry, old soldier. The Tommies have gone back to England, the war is over and soon we will be home." Pianka shook his head and Engel prodded him with a long finger. "You don't agree? Spit it out."

"The French have asked for an armistice but the Tommies haven't."

"They will. They can't fight on alone. It doesn't make sense."

"They don't work things out like that."

"So?"

"Remember when we were in Spain two years ago?" That had been with the Abwehr, too. "Remember the bull-fights? The Spaniards said the bull was most dangerous when he was in his *querencia*, his own chosen place in the ring, and you had to get him out of there to kill him.

24

Now the Tommies have gone to their *querencia* and there are thirty kilometres of sea to cross to get to it."

Engel took off his forage cap and ran fingers through his hair. He looked down thoughtfully at Pianka then grinned and shook his head. He climbed back into the car and settled the Walther P38 comfortably on his hip. "Back up. We'll pay a visit to the hospital and see if they have any interesting patients. As for the war and the Tommies – we will see."

Pianka nodded, unsmiling. "That's right."

Ward had run back to the Commer, Tracey scurrying at his heels. He pulled himself into the cab and heard Jenkins call, "All aboard," as he yanked Tracey into the back of the truck. Ward panted at Gibb, "Turn her round . . ." And as the Commer lumbered in a circle he pointed: "Follow that lane!"

It was no more than a track, winding away between the trees at the side of the hospital. As the Commer swerved into it Ward said, "They're Jerries all right and they're coming up here."

The Jerries had in fact arrived. Jenkins, crouched by the tail-board of the Commer with the two seamen, rifles at the ready, saw the Mercedes appear around the curve in the drive. A second later a bend in the lane hid the Commer but not before Engel had seen it. He yelled and pointed: "*Tommies!*"

The hunt was up.

The Commer bounced and slewed over ruts. Ward's cap slipped forward over his eyes and he shoved it on to the back of his head. In the rear of the truck they clung on to the tail-board until the stretchers began sliding when Williams sprawled flat on the floor with his boots against the tail-board and his hands on the nearest stretcher, so steadying all of them, tight-packed as they were.

The Commer burst out of the wood and now the lane ran between high hedges. Gibb kept his foot down, swinging the Commer round the snaking curves, then for a hundred yards the lane ran straight. They flashed past a turning on the right and ahead was a yard and a house. Gibb tramped on the brake, Ward saved himself with a hand braced on the dash. Gibb jammed the Commer into reverse and Ward jumped out as the truck rolled backward, Gibb hanging out of his open door to see behind, steering with one hand. Ward sprinted back along the side of the Commer and on to the turning. It was clear enough now that the lane swung to the right here. He stood in the middle of the lane where Gibb could see him, waving the driver on but with one eye looking back in the direction of the hospital. Dust still hung in the air, kicked up by the Commer's wheels and it clung to the sweat on his face. The anger at being hunted was building in him, so when the Mercedes car swung around the bend a hundred yards away he found that, unthinking, he had drawn his .38 Webley from his belt and cocked it. He pointed it, aimed and fired as he had been trained on the firing range: squeeze, cock, aim, squeeze, cock, aim –

Engel saw the tall Englishman and the pistol, the reversing truck with rifle-barrels trained over its tail-board. Then pistol and rifles fired and the windscreen of the Mercedes starred. There was a rapid clanging as if the car was beaten with a hammer, it swerved across the lane and smashed into the hedge. Engel sprawled across the broken windscreen, petrol stinking beneath him. He pushed himself up with hands splayed flat on the hot metal and fell back into his seat. His ribs and stomach hurt and his nose bled, the salt of it in his mouth. Pianka lay collapsed and loose over the wheel. The two soldiers in the rear had been thrown out and were now crawling dazedly away from the car. It would burn and the tank was nearly full.

Engel shoved out of the car and ran unsteadily around the back of it. He had to get Pianka out. He grabbed the driver by the shoulders and started to drag him from the car then heard an engine revving. He looked over his shoulder. Ten yards away stood the tall Englishman. He was about Engel's age and he wore the uniform cap of the Royal Navy.

His pistol pointed at Engel and they stared for a long moment at each other across the narrow stretch of rutted, dusty track. Then the pistol lifted, its barrel pointed at the sky, and the tall man swung away. He trotted long-striding after the truck, climbed into the cab, and it pulled away into the side turning and was lost to sight.

Engel lifted Pianka in his arms and carried him up the lane away from the car. His own truck came rocking down the lane, halted and the troops spilled out of it. Engel bellowed, "Give a hand here! Medic!" The orderly came running with his satchel and dropped to his knees by Pianka. Engel muttered, "Take good care of him." He straightened and looked back at the Mercedes. He could still see the face of the British naval officer; he had read his death in it and he would never forget it. He took a deep breath of life.

Gibb asked, "Are they still after us?" He shot Ward an anxious glance.

"No." They would have to drag that car clear to allow anything bigger than a bicycle to pass.

Gibb blew out his lips in relief. "That scared the whatsit out of me!"

Ward had not been afraid and he thought that probably that was because it had all happened so quickly. That German officer had not been afraid either: he had glared defiance into the muzzle of the pistol when Ward had been ready to shoot him. Why hadn't he? Because the German was unarmed and helping an injured man? He had not thought it through at the time, had instinctively turned away, but he was glad now.

The lane ran into a road ahead. A car flashed across the opening as the Commer rolled up to the junction and the two of them in the cab caught a quick glimpse of a girl sitting in its back seat. Gibb said, "They're in a hurry." He turned into the road in the wake of the car as it fled away from them.

Catherine Guillard was in a hurry. The Germans were coming and she wanted to be in her own place in St. Nazaire. She had been visiting her aunt in Paris and had returned as far as she could by rail but there were no trains running after Nantes. A taxi-driver had agreed to take her to St. Nazaire but reluctantly and only for a large fare, paid in advance. Her smile may have helped. Her mouth was too wide for classic beauty but it turned up at the corners and she had green eyes, fair hair carefully curled, and make-up carefully applied. She was tall for a girl, long-legged and still gawky; she was just nineteen and a little too serious.

Her father, once a senior official in the port, had died a year ago. Her mother had died back in the twenties. Catherine worked in the port office as secretary to a head of a department. Her services were prized because she learned a great deal from her father and so was knowledge-able besides being quick and efficient.

They passed several abandoned army trucks and the taxi-driver said bitterly, "The English have run home and deserted us!"

Catherine kept silent. She knew that the French government was asking for peace terms and that the driver was right. Two nights ago, however, General Charles de Gaulle had broadcast from London, calling for French volunteers to carry on the fight: "The flame of French resistance must not be extinguished." Catherine thought he was right too but there was nothing she could do.

Then she leaned forward. "Isn't that a soldier?"

He was a British soldier in khaki and he staggered as he walked. In the car they did not hear the German aircraft until it boomed overhead then swept up, climbing and turning. Its single bomb burst on the road some thirty yards ahead, between them and the soldier. The driver braked, swerved and swore, Catherine braced herself with arms and legs against the back of the seat in front of her and the car skidded past the small crater in the road but then slid sideways into the ditch.

They crawled out, gasping and shaken. The aircraft had gone and the road was empty except for the soldier lying twenty metres or so past the crater, dust and smoke from the explosion drifting over him.

Catherine said, "The soldier is hurt."

The driver was working his way around the car, inspecting it. He did not turn his head, only grumbled, "He'll be dead. If not now, then soon."

Catherine swung away angrily. At school she had shown a facility at languages. Her German was correct but her English much better because she had travelled to England several times with her father on his business trips. During one protracted tour she went to school there for six months and learned to speak the language well. She also made British friends.

So now she ran down the road to the soldier. He sprawled face down, covered in dust, his rifle still looped by its sling around his arm. He had neither steel helmet nor cap. Catherine put down her bag, carefully disengaged the rifle and then turned the man on to his side. He was of middle height, sturdy, and heavy to move. She supported his head with one hand while she snatched the cardigan from her shoulders and wrapped it around her bag to make a pillow. She put it under his head and that was, she thought, all she could do; she knew nothing of nursing. But she tried to clean the blood from his head and face with her handkerchief. She looked up when she heard the truck, surprised to see it since she thought the British had all gone. The driver of the truck changed down, steered it past the crater in the road and halted beside her.

The man who got down from the cab was a British naval officer. He took off his cap and pushed a hand through hair black and rumpled. His face was smeared with sweat and dust. He took in the girl and the soldier and bellowed, "Bear a hand here." Then he crouched by the soldier, looked across him at Catherine Guillard and started ponderously, "Bonjour, Mademoiselle –"

She cut him short: "I speak English."

29

Ward said from the heart, "Thank God for that. We saw the plane dive and the bomb burst. It got him?"

"Yes. I do not know if he is wounded except for his head. I have not –" She searched for the word.

Ward supplied it: "– examined him. We won't, either. No time." He rose as Jenkins and Tracey came running with Williams. Ward told the S.B.A., "We'll get him aboard, then you can take a look at him."

The three of them lifted the soldier carefully, Williams with one hand keeping the improvised pillow in place, and laid him in the back of the Commer.

Ward turned to the girl, "Thank you, Mademoiselle."

Catherine stared at him. Did he intend to leave her on the road? She asked, "You are going into St. Nazaire?"

"That's right."

"Then you must take me, please. My taxi is finished."

Ward glanced back at the car. Finished was right; the front end was stove in. Presumably its driver would want to stay with it: he did not enquire. He did not want another passenger in the Commer, let alone two. Nor did he particularly want responsibility for the girl if they should run into Germans again. But could he leave her here? He hesitated, then said reluctantly, "All right."

But Catherine Guillard had noticed that reluctance. She answered him icily, "Thank you."

"You'll have to travel in the back."

"There is a seat beside the driver, surely!"

"I ride in the front." Because he was in command, and in case they met trouble, but he had no time for explanations. "In you go."

Jenkins and Tracey reached down hands to her and automatically she took them. Then she was inside and staring at the wounded on their stretchers. Ward shoved up the tail-board, jammed in the pins and disappeared. The girl thought him an arrogant boor. The cab door slammed and Jenkins said, "Better sit down, Miss."

She sat beside the soldier on the floor of the truck as it jerked forward. One of the sailors knelt and quickly examined the soldier. "Can't see anything except that bump on the noggin." He looked at Catherine: "Concussion."

"I understand."

Williams gave her a boyish grin, "One thing, we're getting a better class of passenger."

She smiled at him, realising he was as young as herself, that all the sailors were except that ill-mannered, black-haired officer. Her smile faded.

The Commer was travelling at speed now and in the back they swayed to its rocking. None of the wounded complained but Catherine's soldier opened his eyes, stared at her, then reached out a hand. She took it and bent over to listen to his muttering. He was delirious. At times he thought he talked to his mother, at others it was a girl's name that he spoke, several girls. Catherine held his hand, talking quietly, trying to soothe him.

They were in the town, travelling more slowly, then bumping over the railway tracks of the dock area. The Commer halted by the side of the Normandie dock, sailors appeared at the tail-board and a petty officer shouted cheerily, "All right! Let's be having you!" And: "Mr. Ward! Captain wants to see you on the bridge, sir!"

The tail-board swung down and the wounded were taken off. The soldier was first and Catherine went with him. She held the pillow under his head and he gripped her hand, eyes still fixed on her face. He was carried up the brow, along the deck and down narrow, steep stairs. Catherine knew she was showing an immodest length of leg but that could not be helped. She was hot, tired, thirsty and the cotton dress clung to her as if wet.

They took the soldier to the wardroom and laid him on a leather-covered bench. Catherine sat with him. There were four English nurses there, all from *Lancastria*. She gathered from the nurses' talk that the sick-bay was already full of wounded from hospitals ashore which was why the survivors rescued by Ward were being brought down to the wardroom. One nurse gently prised the soldier's fingers loose and took over the job of comforting him while another brought Catherine a cup of tea. She drank it gratefully. It was good to sit quietly for a few minutes, head back and eyes closed, the hum of the fans and throb of machinery not unpleasant.

Ward was on the bridge. His captain asked, "Enjoy your run ashore?"

"It made a change, sir. We got them all, anyway."

"Any trouble?"

"A bit." Ward told him about it while Gates watched the brow taken aboard. *Saracen* cast off, then went astern. As she did so one last Polish soldier ran along the dock and jumped down on to her fo'c'sle. Henderson, the navigator, said, "Good God! He must have broken every bone in his body!"

He had not; only both legs and he counted himself lucky to get away on the last ship out of St. Nazaire.

Saracen swung stern first out of the Normandie dock and turned to head down-river. Gates, intent on conning his ship, tossed at Ward, "Well done. When did you eat last?"

"Breakfast, sir."

"Well, nip aft and get rid of that artillery you're wearing then grab a quick bite."

"Thank you, sir." Ward dropped down the ladder from the bridge. First he must see Jenkins, make sure he and the men of the landing-party were fed – and Driver Gibb. He was hurrying aft when the girl appeared and stared disbelievingly at the receding shore. Jack Ward also stared disbelievingly. "What are you doing aboard?"

Catherine turned to look up at him. "I came with the wounded man. He needed me. You should have told me you were sailing. Put me ashore, please!"

"Out of the question." *Saracen*'s captain would not return to the dock nor lower a boat just to set one girl ashore.

Catherine's patience had been sorely tried by this young man. Her chin lifted in anger and she demanded, "I insist –"

The klaxons blared, drowning her voice and Ward saw the aircraft, black silhouettes sharp against the blue. They flew in from the west, racing low over the estuary with the descending sun behind them so that he had to narrow his eyes to see they were single-engined Messerschmitts. He grabbed the girl by the shoulders, swung her around and shoved her in at an open door. *"Get below!"* Then left her as *Saracen's* guns opened up.

He ran forward along the port side, shouldering through the Poles crowding the deck. Then the enemy machine-guns fired, a long, ripping burst and up on the bridge he saw a lookout fall. A Messerschmitt passed low overhead with a bang and a howl, tore away over the water. His ears ringing, he climbed to the bridge. At the head of the ladder he halted, sick and shocked. That long enemy burst had done its bloody work here. The captain and most of the bridge staff were sprawled and still, only the signal yeoman and one of the lookouts moved dazedly.

Ward fought down his sickness and moved across the bridge to the voicepipe. The ship had to be conned and there was no one else to do it. "Coxswain?"

"Sir?"

It was a relief to hear that deep, west-country voice from the wheel-house. "Mr. Ward here. The bridge is a mess. What about you?"

"All right, sir. A bit deaf." From the hammering on the steel deck above him. But the coxswain took comfort from the calm tone of the young man on the bridge. Ward would cope.

"Port ten."

"Ten of port wheel on, sir."

Ward conned *Saracen* for only the time it took for the first lieutenant to be told and to come quickly forward. The bridge filled up with a new staff and the casualties were taken gently below. Gates, wounded in shoulder and leg, was carried to his bunk because the sick-bay was already crowded. Others went to the mess-decks. Ward became

33

navigator for the rest of the voyage; Henderson, his friend, was dead.

They were not attacked again.

Saracen berthed at Plymouth. There were ambulances waiting on the quay for the wounded and trucks to take away the Polish infantry, but the first man aboard was a rear-admiral. He was small, seeming shrunken under the big cap but he came quickly up the brow and saluted, very straight in the back. To Ward, who returned his salute, he said, "I'm looking for French subjects. Any aboard?"

"Only one that I know of, sir, a young lady."

"Where?"

"In the wardroom, sir."

"Thank you."

The Poles crowded on the upper deck gaped at the little admiral. His uniform was immaculate, brilliant with gold braid and he made a startling contrast to the drab infantry. When he strode aft they opened a lane for him so he did not falter.

Ward reported to the first lieutenant up on the bridge and he said wryly, "Company already and the beds not made. All right, Jack. Look, our people ashore want a verbal report on our state straightaway. You do that. Tell 'em I want to be here when the skipper's taken ashore to the hospital. I'll see to your admiral."

When Ward returned the ship was empty of her passengers, and the admiral. That night in the last slipping moments before he slept Ward thought he was glad they'd got the wounded and the Poles out and that he was sorry about the girl. God alone knew when she would see her home and family again. And the Normandie dock, one of the biggest in the world and now the Germans had it. Should have done something about that . . .

It was a thought often to return to him in the months ahead. He would bombard his superiors with ideas for improvements in equipment and tactics but always he would return to worry at the problem of St. Nazaire.

*

34

In Massachusetts, Joseph Edward Krueger, sole owner of Krueger Boatyards, locked the front door of his house and deposited the key with a neighbour. His bag in one hand and jacket swung over a broad shoulder he walked away from the house and down to the cab that waited for him. His wife was dead, and for the moment he was done with the boatyard and the house. He felt neither excitement nor exhilaration. When you have survived the war of your youth you do not hasten eagerly to another in your middle-age. You think about it quietly until you decide what is the right course and only then do you close up your home and book a passage for Liverpool, England.

He looked back once at the house, then turned to face his uncertain future.

On that same eastern seaboard but far to the south a ship patrolled the warm waters off Florida in the evening of her days. Her name was U.S.S. *Buchanan* and she was a flush-decked, four-funnel destroyer built for a war long past, the war of Krueger's youth. Unlike him she was strictly too old to fight another war but she would have no say in the matter. This country of hers was neutral, yet some of its sons were already at the war or headed for it, like Krueger, and her time would come.

2

"Our necks in a noose . . . !"

Ward served in *Saracen* until she was torpedoed and sank in the North Atlantic in late 1940. After his survivors' leave they drafted him, because he expressed a preference for small ships, to M.G.B.s, Motor Gunboats working out of Harwich. He said that was not what he meant at all, loudly and continually, but he served six months of long winter nights in the boats. He learned a great deal about them in that time, frightened some E-boats and had some terrible frights himself. He made a lot of friends and left with regret when his requests were finally answered and he was sent to a destroyer.

He served in her through the summer of 1941, escorting convoys from Liverpool to mid-Atlantic where they would hand over to the escort force from Nova Scotia and take their U.K.-bound convoy back to Liverpool. He was her first lieutenant and twenty-six years old when he was called to the Admiralty for an interview. He went with optimism and some apprehension. He thought his record was good but not spectacular.

The commander said, "You like small ships."

"Destroyers, sir." Ward wanted that straight from the beginning this time.

The commander nodded and said, "Well, we're giving you a command." And when Ward came down from the clouds he added drily, "This one is to learn on."

She was H.M.S. *Boston*, one of the fifty old U.S. Navy destroyers transferred to the Royal Navy in September 1940 in exchange for a lease of bases. They were known as 'four-stackers' or 'packets of woodbines' because of their upright four funnels. They were called a lot of other things, too.

Ward went to her at Sheerness knowing he would have his hands full but ready for anything. In his cabin he talked to his first lieutenant, also new to the ship. Joseph Edward Krueger was a lieutenant of forty-two with a wartime commission in the R.N.V.R., wide-shouldered and solid, taciturn but with an easy smile. And he was American.

Ward knew something of Americans. Not long before he went to *Boston* he had spent a weekend at Claridges with a party of them – and his brother Geoffrey. Ward went along because he was major shareholder in the Perseus Group, chief of the clan, and because Geoffrey wanted him there. He still leaned on Ward, knowing the decisions to make but needing reassurance. The meeting was to hammer out a number of deals between the American corporations and the Group. They worked long hours into the night but ended well pleased on both sides and the leader of the Americans told Ward, "We like a guy who comes straight to the point." Ward had just returned from one convoy, was due to sail on another and had been just too tired for circumlocution. Going back to the war did not exactly appeal but he preferred it to Geoffrey's world and blessed the day he talked his brother into running the Perseus Group.

He needed to know about this particular American, Joe Krueger, however, and started, "How long have you been aboard?"

"Just a coupla hours ahead of you, sir."

"Krueger." Ward asked, "Is that a Dutch name?"

"German. My grandfather emigrated to the States in the 1860s. We used to talk it back home when he was alive." And Krueger asked, "Does it bother you, sir?"

"No. Mountbatten's father had a German name till he changed it in the last war. I trust Mountbatten."

Krueger said solemnly, "I guess he'd be real pleased to know that."

Ward grinned. "The blokes will probably call you Fritz behind your back but if they don't it will probably be something worse, seeing as you're first lieutenant."

Joe smiled, "They did in my last ship."

"Which was?"

"Another ex-U.S. four-stacker, like this. When I first came over from the States they asked me what service I had so I told them. When they heard I'd done a hitch in the U.S.S. *Buchanan*, in 1919–20 they said, 'O.K., you know four-stackers, so you get one.'" He paused, then said quietly, "I got to like her. Shame."

"What happened to her?"

"Struck a mine and sank."

"Many lost?"

"All of the engineroom on watch; they never had a chance. The warrant engineer was a good friend of mine, nice guy." That was said with regret but no emotion; you could not mourn friends for ever. In that vein Krueger reminisced, "We used to talk engines. I ran a boatyard before the war and we worked with all kinds of engines – mostly for power-boats like your M.G.B.s or Jerry's E-boats."

"You're an expert?"

"I guess so," Krueger paused, then corrected himself, "I am, sure. That's not some big-mouth talk because I was twenty years in the business and in that time you get to be an expert or go broke."

Ward said drily, "So they drafted you to destroyers."

"Well, I knew something about them, too."

That was Ward's cue. "I'm told this one isn't the happiest of ships. Any idea what's wrong with her?"

"After two hours? No, sir."

Ward grinned, "Suppose we go in at the deep end. Is she ready for sea?"

Boston was a long, narrow ship. She rolled in the Thames estuary and Joe said, "She'd roll on a wet towel." Also she had twin screws sticking far out of her stern and a guard built on either quarter so she would not damage those screws when coming alongside. In consequence she was not easy to manoeuvre – as Ward found out when he tried his hand on the first day they went to sea, with Joe Krueger at his shoulder murmuring suggestions. While a conventional destroyer could turn on her heel, *Boston* handled like a big ship with a turning circle of a thousand yards or more. To follow the course changes of a more modern ship, sailing in line ahead, *Boston* had to anticipate them by several seconds. Ward said, "What you really need on this bridge is a crystal ball."

Krueger ruefully agreed. "That's about the size of it."

You could laugh or cry so they laughed. Then Ward looked around the bridge and walked out to the wing to peer forward and aft. He returned to his place behind the screen and said to Joe Krueger, "Well, now we know what's wrong with the ship: nobody else is laughing. We've got to change that."

In the following weeks Ward exercised *Boston*'s crew at every possible moment in every evolution he could think of and timed them with a stop-watch. On their first night back in Sheerness, he cleared lower deck and read the lesson according to Ward, standing on the mounting of the 12-pounder aft and glowering down at the faces below. "I can't say we're the worst destroyer crew in the world because I haven't seen them all! For the same reason I won't be able to boast some time in the future that we're the best. But when I meet another captain, *any* captain, I'll look him in the eye and think, 'Your ship's no better than mine!' Because you've got it in you! I've seen it before and I see it now. Between us we can make this old girl work!" He paused for a moment to let that sink in. He was not one for making speeches but he believed what he'd been saying and the men watching him knew that. "All right. Now we'll hold a wake for the cock-ups of today and start again tomorrow."

That night he met with the watch ashore in the back room of a pub. They tried to drink it dry and Ward sat at the ancient piano and hammered out everything from 'Roll Out the Barrel' to 'We'll Meet Again', with many dubious stanzas in between.

When they were alongside or went ashore Ward demanded a first-class turn-out and strict adherence to dress
regulations. God help the man – or officer – with shoes
that did not shine or a wrinkled jacket or jumper. At sea it
was different. There only practicality counted. When the
sun was bright Joe Krueger wore a baseball cap and in bad
weather a fur hat with flaps over his ears.

Ward looked at it and said, "Good God!"

Joe eyed Ward's brilliant orange oilskins, and said nothing. He knew the reason: so any man on deck could see
his captain on the bridge. For dry weather Ward had a
jacket and a duffel coat dyed the same colour and for the
same reason.

They went to Liverpool on convoy duty and worked out
of there for a month then were sent back to Sheerness and
the Channel. In November 1941 *Ark Royal* was finally
sunk, after several false German claims. Less than two
weeks later the battleship *Barham* followed her. In December Italian frogmen sank *Valiant* and *Queen Elizabeth*,
though both were in the harbour of Alexandria and would
be salvaged – in time.

And in December the Japanese bombed and torpedoed
Prince of Wales and *Repulse* and attacked Pearl Harbour.
Ward went to Krueger's cabin and found Joe sitting on his
bunk staring at a group photograph of officers aboard
U.S.S. *Buchanan* in 1920. They wore tunics buttoned tight
up to the neck and small caps set square on their heads. Joe
looked very young in the photograph. He looked old now.
Ward said, "I'm sorry, Joe."

Krueger muttered, "I knew some of the guys in those
ships at Pearl, fellers who had stayed on in the navy and
made captain or better."

"Are you going back?"

Joe thought about it, then shook his head. "It's the same
war and I'm already fighting it. I'll stay with the ship."

From then on, mostly in quiet moments on the bridge or
over a game of chess as *Boston* lay in port Ward learned
rather more about his first officer. In the winter of 1920 Joe

had left the U.S. Navy and a promising career because his wife had contracted polio. "I went to work ashore," he said, "on account of that way I could spend a lot more time with her. It was tough getting going at the start but we stuck it and somehow managed to ride out the Depression." He paused. Ward did not ask but Joe said, "She died in the summer of 1940. So I came over here. Thought about it and it seemed like a good idea."

Ward agreed with him: his coming had been a very good idea.

The ship, *Boston*, had been given to Ward to 'learn on'. He learned about the ship and her crew and they learned about him. *Boston* did not change but her reputation did: it became one for sound, efficient, hard work; she could be relied on. The ship herself still broke down frequently, was old and awkward and needed continual nursing, but every man aboard from Ward to the youngest seaman was devoted to her and determined to make her work. That, and the hardship of just living aboard, bound them.

Hardship? She was flush decked with hardly any flare so in bad weather the sea came inboard and flooded the mess-decks knee deep. Fresh water, on the other hand, was always short because the condensers could not cope. The galley oil-stoves were drip fed and could not be used in bad weather so the men ate cold bully beef for days on end. Even when the stoves worked the food still had to be carried forward along the upper deck from the galley amidships and so was cold anyway . . .

The list was endless.

Yet she became a happy ship. They were one family. In that bad winter they celebrated three marriages and no less than eleven christenings. They celebrated Christmas and Ward and his officers toured the mess-decks. Ward and Krueger possessed the caution of experience but some of the young sub-lieutenants accepted too much of the navy rum pressed on them and were obliged to retire early. The rum was issued neat because water was in short supply.

Also they mourned three dead. On a bitterly cold day,

41

Thursday, 22nd January 1942, Ward brought the body of the third of their dead and the shell-pocked *Boston* into Sheerness.

Now Rear-Admiral Quartermain waited for him.

Boston, back from convoy duty, lay alongside the quay, her engines stilled, her bridge, wheelhouse and chartroom pocked with holes from cannon shells and splinters. A party aft were rigging the gangway but already the bosun's mates were piping for liberty-men to fall in. They were gathering in the waist in their number-one suits, collars washed and re-washed to achieve the pale, pale blue of the veteran seaman – whether the wearer was forty or eighteen years old. They waited to be inspected by the officer of the watch and given their leave chits and railway warrants.

For one watch there were two days' leave, forty-eight hours. Ward also was going on leave. As commanding officer he had the right to go, but he did not always take advantage of it. More than once he had sent off Bailey, the warrant engineer, instead, because he was a middle-aged reservist with a large family, and because he had a hell of a life with *Boston*'s old engines, at sea or in harbour. But since this time she was in for work on her steering, Bailey would have to stay for that and Ward was going on leave.

A wireless was playing, Joe Loss and his band, singing coming from the galley amidships. Ward caught Krueger's eye. Like any close family, officers and crew knew each others' strengths and weaknesses. Krueger would have a quiet word with a few of the liberty-men before they went ashore, regarding their condition when they returned. They would listen, those few. They might still stagger as they came aboard but they would not be late nor carried back insensible by the shore patrol. Everybody knew Joe Krueger was nobody's fool, but fair, and it was due in large part to him that *Boston* was a happy ship. He was first lieutenant and, with Adams the coxswain, he saw to the day-to-day running of the ship. Always ready to 'bawl a man out' – his expression – when necessary, he was equally ready to listen sympathetically to a tale of bad luck. And then to do something about it, calling on Ward if need be.

There were buses waiting on the quay to take the liberty-men to the station and their trains. Ward and Krueger had arranged that. There was also an ambulance, summoned by a radio signal, as *Boston* had closed Sheerness, to take a wounded man to hospital. Now, instead, it would take away a dead man. *Boston* had no doctor. Gulley, the sick berth rating, had fought for the man's life, but in vain. He had died half an hour before they berthed.

The bosun's pipes sounded the 'still' and all on deck stood to attention, Ward at the salute, as the body was taken ashore. Then the pipes shrilled again and once more the deck swirled with activity. Ward relaxed and rubbed at the black stubble on his chin. He had been on the bridge without a break for twenty-four hours. He told Krueger, "She's all yours for a couple of days. I'll sleep aboard tonight and give you my address in London before I leave tomorrow."

Krueger was running his eye along the lines of liberty-men, inspecting them, picking out faces. Now he nodded approval and turned. "O.K. sir."

"Just don't forget she's mine." It was an old joke.

Joe made the ritual reply, "I saw her first." He had, by two hours. Now he said, "Not sticking my neck out, sir, but have you got anything fixed in London?"

Ward shook his head, "Just a bed, maybe a show, a beer or two." There had been several girls since the one at Aunt Abigail's party, brief attachments that were severed as the war moved him – or ended in flaming rows. He realised now that he was probably to blame for most of those but he hadn't thought so at the time. If there was no girl at the moment, that was due to lack of opportunity. 'It's not the women what kills you, it's the chasing after them.' He grinned at the old saw. Only now he didn't even get the chance to do the chasing.

He could not go to Aunt Abigail's house in Chelsea because it was a bombed ruin and she was living and working at a hospital in the Midlands. She had written not long ago saying her painter son Patrick, now in the Army, was somewhere in Scotland and doing a lot of work on landscapes –

Joe Krueger broke into Ward's thoughts: "Oh-oh! We have company!"

The yeoman and one of his signalmen were working on the bridge but paused now to peer as a silver-grey Daimler rolled slowly along the quay below and halted by the gangway. A Wren was at the wheel and she got out quickly, opened the rear door and stood at the salute. Ward thought, "Good figure, nice legs – a popsy."

The signalman muttered, "Cor! Look at that!"

And brought a growl from the yeoman: "Never you mind. Keep your eyes inboard and get them flags stowed proper."

Joe Krueger said, "Oh, boy! An admiral!"

A rear-admiral, the broad and narrow gold rings on his sleeve making an impressive flash of yellow as he climbed from the car and settled the cap with its gold-crusted peak on his grey head. He said something to the girl and she smiled.

Ward slid down the ladder to the deck and strode aft as the admiral made for the gangway, walking briskly and very straight in the back, a briefcase in one hand. Ward was waiting for him as he stepped aboard to the piping of the bosun's mates manning the side. Ward returned his salute and the admiral said, "Quartermain. You're Ward."

"Yes, sir." Ward searched his memory. He had seen this man somewhere –

Quartermain supplied the answer: "Saw you in June 1940. You were in *Saracen* when I came aboard at Plymouth. You hadn't shaved then, either. Now, where can we talk privately?"

"My cabin, sir."

Ward led the way forward past the rigid line of liberty-men. He knew what they were thinking: that the sudden arrival of a flag officer could mean a change of orders – and a drastic change in their plans. Quartermain knew it, too, and without breaking step he rasped, "You can stop worrying! I haven't come to cancel your run ashore!"

He halted outside Ward's cabin and ran his eyes over the damage to the bridge and wheelhouse. "Um! More work for the dockyard."

"Yes, sir."

"What action?"

"We ran into Dirty Bill last night –"

Quartermain's head jerked around: "*Who?*"

"Dirty Bill – an E-boat. Apparently he has a damned great skull-and-crossbones painted on his bridge. We didn't see it but a coaster in the starboard column did."

"Get him?"

"No. The coaster was in the way. He gave us one quick burst that did this lot, then ran like mad. We'll get him though, if he stays as busy as he's been the last few weeks." That last was not boast or threat but said with flat determination.

"Um!" Quartermain said, "We really want an E-boat captured, not sunk. We'd like to take it apart and find out how it ticks."

Ward thought there was damn-all chance of that and he'd happily settle for Dirty Bill at the bottom of the North Sea. He did not say so.

E-boats were nearly forty yards long, carried two 21-inch torpedo-tubes and a pair of 20mm cannon. Their three big diesel engines could push them along at better than forty knots and they were claiming a lot of ships.

His cabin was right under the bridge and held a bunk and a settee, both secured to the bulkhead, a desk and an armchair. *Boston* had just come in from sea so the armchair was still lashed to the settee. Ward slept on the settee in bad weather because he was often thrown out of his bunk. The armchair kept him wedged in place. Now he cast the chair loose and set it on the deck for the admiral. Quartermain sank into it and tossed his cap on to the desk. He was a dried-out little jockey of a man with a sharp-featured, brown, leathery face, silver hair neatly brushed and grey eyes.

"I'm from Combined Operations. Whatever I say, you'll keep under your hat."

"Yes, sir." Ward sat on the settee, scratched his stubble.

Quartermain took a folder from his briefcase and flipped it open. "This scheme you dreamed up for an –"

"– for an attack on St. Nazaire, sir?"

Quartermain's brows lifted, "You expected this?"

"Only when you said you were from Combined Ops. I've put up a few ideas but they were mostly on escort work. St. Nazaire was the only one that would interest Combined Ops; I've always thought it would be a job for them."

"Why did you pick St. Nazaire?"

"When I was there in 1940 I thought the dock should be put out of action."

Quartermain sniffed, "You took your time about saying so."

Ward, nettled, answered, "I was a junior lieutenant and I assumed my seniors would have that kind of thing taped. Also I was pretty busy, first on convoy –"

Quartermain broke in testily, "Yes, I know all that! And don't get snotty with *me*, sir! Now – what finally started you working out this lot?" He banged the folder on his knee.

Ward wondered, should he apologise? But Quartermain was waiting, sharp-eyed and impatient. To hell with it. He said, "*Bismarck*. When we sank her she was headed for St. Nazaire because that was the only dock outside Germany that could take her and repair her damage. Now there's *Tirpitz*. I hear she's commissioned and gone to Norway. She could be there because, after that commando raid on Vaagso a few weeks back, Hitler thinks we might be planning to invade Norway. Or she might intend to go raiding, attacking the convoys, slipping out into the Atlantic as *Bismarck* did. But if so, then she'd have a hell of a job getting back for repairs with the Home Fleet in the way, so before she starts the Germans will want to be sure of a dock outside Germany and that means St. Nazaire." He paused, then added, "We don't want her raiding, sir."

Quartermain said grimly, "We agree on that, anyway. So?"

"So close St. Nazaire. It took me a long time to work out how to do it because the only special knowledge I had was what I remembered of the place from one afternoon. I had to dig for the rest and I started off thinking of using a submarine. I wasted a lot of time on that before I decided on an attack by fast, small craft through the undefended shallows, carrying assault troops and demolition engineers."

Quartermain grumbled, "We thought of a submarine, too. No go." He leafed quickly through the folder, then closed it. "Quite a scheme. Imaginative, well-thought-out. A good idea . . ." His voice trailed away and his thin fingers tapped the folder.

Ward thought, "They're going to do it!" He said, "Thank you, sir. It's kind of you to say so."

Quartermain continued as if Ward had not spoken: "– but we've got a better one."

Ward's elation drained away. "Oh!" Then he asked, "Are you sure, sir?"

Quartermain glared at him, "Sure? Of course I'm sure! So is Mountbatten! D'ye want to argue with *him*?"

"No, sir, only –"

"Only – what?"

"I'd like to know about this plan that's considered better than mine. Can I be told, sir?"

"No."

Ward had expected that. He still had not finished: "I'd like to volunteer for it, sir."

"Why?"

"It was my idea and I'm not keen on sending somebody else to do the dirty work."

Quartermain snorted, "Rubbish! It's *not* your idea. And besides, this war isn't being run to satisfy any officer's craving for action. Anyway, we've picked our men." That was not in fact strictly true but Quartermain had other ideas for Ward: "Still, I might want you for another raid. Are you game?"

"Yes, sir." No hesitation. "What would it be?"

"None of your business. I'll tell you when you need to know – and that may not be for a long time."

"Will I lose *Boston*, sir?" That would hurt.

"No."

Ward was relieved, but wondered what this prickly little man intended for him.

Quartermain thought that the reports he'd had of Ward spoke of him, among other things, as abrasive. Fair comment. He shelved that, turned back to the main purpose of his visit and said, "One of the major faults in your plan is the lack of information on the construction of the dock gates."

"Sir?"

"You say large charges should be laid to blow them up but it seems you don't know much about explosives."

"No, sir."

"Neither do I, but we have people who do. Those gates are a hell of a size, ten times the height of a man and thirty-five feet thick, so to blow them up the charges have to be the right weight *and* in the right places. There'll only be one chance, no question of going back and lighting the blue paper again, therefore knowledge of the construction of the dock gates is vital – but we don't have it. We're trying to build up a picture from the information we *do* have but it isn't very good." Quartermain took a breath, then asked, "Do you have details of the construction of the dock gates?"

Ward shook his head, "I only saw them that one time in 1940."

Quartermain hid his disappointment and said only, "Um!" Ward had been a pretty forlorn hope, anyway. And the word from St. Nazaire was that the information would not come from there: the French who had worked the dock gates had been deported to Germany and German engineers did the job now. Geneviève had said so and she was one of his best agents.

Ward waited, listening to the sounds of the ship around him, cheerful voices on the upper deck; they were going on leave. The wireless was still playing, distantly, but Joe Loss had finished and that sounded like a Fats Waller record. Ward was a fan but Fats' countryman, Joe Krueger, had a collection of records in his cabin ranging from Beethoven to Rachmaninov and including some of Ward's mother playing Chopin. Joe had been awed when he learned one of his idols was the mother of his young captain.

Finally Ward said, "I don't mean to point out the obvious, sir, but there isn't much time. This has to be a winter operation. St. Nazaire is six miles from the sea so you need a long winter night for time to approach under cover of darkness and get out again before it's light. We're nearly into February already, and the nights will be too short after the end of March."

Quartermain nodded, "If it comes off, and ignorance of the dock gates is only one of the obstacles in the way, then I agree it must be by the end of March." He was silent a moment, scowling, then: "Churchill says the whole strategy of the war turns on *Tirpitz*. The threat of her breaking out keeps a large force of our capital ships tied-up in the north and there's still no guarantee they could keep her from the convoys – and our lives depend on them. Stop the convoys and this country starves. So we have just ten weeks to shut St. Nazaire or it's our necks in a noose." He stood up, jerking the creases out of his jacket as if shaking off the mood and reaching for his cap. "Where did you intend spending your leave?"

Ward noted the use of the past tense. "London, sir. My home is in Northumberland and that's too far to travel with just two days." In wartime, with train services disrupted or delayed, the journey alone could take at least twelve hours.

"Good. I want you to come to London tomorrow: Richmond Terrace, just off Whitehall. Ask for me after lunch and we'll show you what we've got and see if you can

49

add to it, possibly put a few more pieces into the jigsaw." He moved to the door. "And remember, keep your trap shut."

Ward stood on the deck of *Boston* and watched the little admiral stride jauntily to his car.

Ten weeks. Or our necks in a noose.

Quartermain was back in his office in Richmond Terrace in the late afternoon. He spent some minutes standing at his window staring out at Whitehall and the Cenotaph, the headstone for a million dead. The Navy lost eighteen thousand at Jutland alone and Quartermain had known many of them. That was twenty-odd years ago and now there was another generation of young men at war. He had thought he was done with war. It was a bloody business in which some things had to be left to chance, calculated risks but never taken lightly.

He thought back over his interview with Ward, comparing the man he had seen with what he had previously learned of the young lieutenant. Quartermain was sure Ward would do. Strong, quick, no genius but with a good head on him and able to think on his feet. A good man in a boat. If the job called for a boat – and that was not yet known – then Ward was the man for it. No ties. That was important. When all the avoidable risks were cleared away this job would still be dangerous.

That last word reminded him and he turned back to his desk and the telephone, asked for the number of the office in Baker Street. "Maurice? James here. The matter we discussed at lunch the other day . . . Tonight? Good. Thank you." He replaced the receiver.

So they were bringing Geneviève out tonight. That too was a risk, but unavoidable since he needed to see her, had questions to ask and instructions to give, and his radio contacts were far too fleeting.

He shifted uneasily at the thought, got up from the chair and paced the room, pausing to open the door and look at the Wren at the desk outside. He growled, "Is everything all right? Your quarters? No problems?"

"No, sir, thank you."

He closed the door and resumed his pacing. So far they had only lost one aircraft and the agent it carried since they started these pick-ups and deliveries, but he would know no peace of mind until Geneviève was safe. And they had ten weeks, no more than that. If they failed and *Tirpitz* broke out into the Atlantic . . . He swore, loud enough for the girl outside to hear and wince.

The next day, Friday, Ward travelled up to London in a crowded train. These days the trains were always crowded, just as London teemed with uniforms: French, Dutch, Polish, Australian, Canadian . . . He thought that soon there would also be Americans. He booked in at the small hotel he had first used because it was cheap, when living on his pay as a sub-lieutenant. He still went there out of habit and because it served him well enough. He was not looking forward to his afternoon with Quartermain. He knew nothing of how docks were built and felt he would make a fool of himself. If all the experts had already done their best it was a fat lot of good asking him to wade through the papers. He was the captain of an escort destroyer, and that was a job he knew. He was not fitted for this intelligence caper.

Richmond Terrace stood on the Thames embankment, close by the river that led to the sea, as befitted the headquarters of Combined Operations. There was a sand-bagged sentry post at the entrance and a soldier stand-ing on guard. The sandbags were daubed with the white paint that had broken out all over London and every other British city and town, on steps, kerbs, corners of buildings and in lines down the middle of the roads, all to help people groping their way through the black-out. The sentry wore a steel helmet and a respirator case of khaki webbing strapped on his chest. He stood rigidly at ease but as Ward approached he snapped to attention, shouldered the Lee-Enfield rifle and cracked his flat right hand on the stock.

Ward returned the salute as he went in. A messenger took him to Quartermain who glanced at his watch and grunted, "Good of you to come." Ward thought wryly that he had little choice. Quartermain said abruptly, "I'll be busy all this afternoon but the RAF'll look after you." And he sent Ward on his way to the office of a pipe-smoking squadron-leader.

There was a table with one bulky file resting on it. The squadron-leader sat Ward down before the file and said, "Don't write anything down, old chap." Then he left Ward to it, went back to his desk and his pipe.

The file was labelled CHARIOT: Ward found it alternately fascinating, then bewildering in its technical complexity.

He had the facility to scan a page of a balance sheet and absorb its contents instantly, a gift remarked on by his father, but he took his time with this file. He worked his way through it twice to be sure, then sat back and stretched despondently, realised the afternoon had all but gone.

The squadron-leader said around his pipe, "Any luck?" And when Ward shook his head: "I thought I saw you hesitate once – and look back in the file."

Ward hesitated now. "Well . . . there was one name, Peyraud, one of the designers. I knew a Peyraud before the war, met him in a hotel in Paris in 1939. He was some sort of engineer."

"Oh? What sort of chap? What was his full name? Where did he come from?"

"His first name was Alain but I don't know where his home was."

"Which hotel was it, then?"

Ward told him and thought back: "He was around sixty, grey-haired, about six feet tall and thin." The squadron-leader waited but Ward said, "That's all, sorry."

"Ah! Well, anyway, it was worth a try. No stone unturned and all that." He escorted Ward to the front door and shook his hand. "I understand you're having a spot of leave. Good show!"

Ward jammed his cap on his head and stalked up Richmond Terrace into Whitehall. He felt his failure keenly, remembering the capital ships lost by the thinly-spread Navy in the last few weeks, six including *Ark Royal*. The gaps they left must be filled but the only ships available had to be kept in the north instead, because so long as St. Nazaire was open to *Tirpitz* she might break out into the Atlantic and that threat had to be guarded against. So St. Nazaire must be shut, and quickly.

Ward strode on up Whitehall, his spirits lightening. There was a crisp coldness to the air after the confines of the Headquarters building. The land lay in the grip of winter and there were piles of swept, dirty snow at the sides of the road, but the sky was clear and a winter sun shone, without heat but with cheer. Ward looked up at it and thought, About time you showed!

On the corner ahead of him a man was selling the early edition of an evening paper, thin because newsprint was in short supply. A car slid past Ward, stopped at the kerb just short of the corner and a girl got out of the back and went to buy a copy. As Ward came up he took in that she had long legs, walked well on the high heels and had saved or somehow wangled silk stockings, a rare luxury now in this war of shortages and rationing. Blonde hair bent over her purse as she got out change and handed it over. The face lifted as she turned back to the car. Cheeks stung to colour by the cold, a wide mouth, green eyes –

Ward said, "Good God! You!"

The girl halted – of necessity since he stood in her path – and looked up at him, startled. He saw that and apologised. "Sorry! But aren't you –" He paused, realising he did not know her name, then went on, "Didn't we bring you back to England in *Saracen*? From St. Nazaire?"

"Yes." She smiled, then her eyes flicked away. Ward followed the direction of her gaze and saw the driver getting out of the car. He was tall, a young man about

Ward's age, dressed in a rumpled blue suit and his eyes were watchful. The girl said, "It's all right."

The man nodded, ducked back into the car, but remained watchful.

The girl turned back to Ward. "I – regret. It is a car from my work. Yes, I remember you brought me. I was angry because I did not wish to come." But she was smiling now.

"Er – yes." He recalled her anger and that he had been short with her, in fact bloody rude. He said awkwardly, "I wanted to explain my reasons but I didn't get the chance." That was not entirely true. He had been busy but the truth was he had forgotten about her until too late when he found that she, like the Polish infantry, had been taken ashore.

She shook her head, "I understood, after a little while, that it had not been possible to take me back."

She did not seem to be bearing a grudge. He held out his hand, "Jack Ward."

She shook it, "Catherine Guillard."

He said, "So you stayed. And you have a job."

"Yes."

She did not explain and he thought that she probably worked in Whitehall for one of the Ministries, and this was one of their cars. He grinned, "Hush-hush, eh?"

"I am sorry?"

"Hush-hush." He explained, "You're not allowed to talk about it." The phrase was a commonplace but she was foreign and this scrap of vernacular must have escaped her.

Catherine nodded, "Yes."

"All right, we won't talk about that, then."

"We are going to talk?" She looked up at him in solemn surprise.

Were they? Well, he was on leave, he had nothing else to do and now that he looked at her she was quite a pretty girl. She was older, poised, the gawkiness gone. "Of course. Look, I know I've apologised and you've been good about it, but I want to make it up to you. How would you like to go out for a bite to eat tonight, and some dancing?"

"Well –" Catherine hesitated. It was a long time since

she had gone out to dinner with a young man and she had not forgotten this one, so tall and with the black eyes under the black brows. The eyes were not hostile now, he was not scowling and looked like a man who might smile easily, but otherwise he was just as she remembered him. He was possibly a shade leaner and that made him appear even taller. His features had hardened and she did not recall so many wrinkles at the corners of his eyes, but the scar –

Ward misinterpreted her hesitation: "You're not married or anything?"

Catherine smiled, "No. Are you married – or anything?"

"Good Lord, no!" Anyway, this was different: he owed the girl a dinner and that was all there was to it. "So you don't need to worry about that."

She had been worried about something else but instead she said, "I do not have a wardrobe."

"Nobody dresses up these days." But she would surely know that. He said, "You look fine to me now."

"I do not look fine." She was bundled into a heavy coat against the cold. "I have a dress but it is not formal."

Ward rode over that objection, "The dinner won't be formal. So you'll come? Great! I'll pick you up around seven. Is that all right? Where do you live?"

She told him and then turned to the car. "Now I must go."

He handed her in, closed the door and lifted a hand in salute as the car pulled away. Its registration was civilian, not official, so he concluded it was some vehicle her Ministry had requisitioned. He walked back to his hotel because he wanted the exercise. He did not think once about Quartermain or CHARIOT.

He called for Catherine Guillard on the stroke of seven that evening at her address in a quiet row of houses behind Baker Street. As soon as the taxi stopped the girl came out of the house and closed the door, so she had clearly been waiting in the hall and looking out for him. She wore a dress

55

with a coat open over it: both were simple but new – and obviously very expensive. Ward wondered at that and the silk stockings. Usually the people of these islands were drab because clothing was restricted in style and cut, as well as being rationed. Had she some sort of black-market wangle? Or a boyfriend in the trade? Anyway, it was none of his business.

He thought she seemed nervous and so he said, "Very nice!"

She smiled at that, "Thank you."

He took her to the Dorchester. The Perseus Group owned some big hotels but this one belonged to the McAlpines. There were people in the restaurant who knew Ward as they had known his father, one of them a man from Shell, another from Vickers. The menu was impressive until you read the cautionary notice that a meal was restricted to three courses and only one of those a main course. The whole country was on short commons, one pound of meat, four rashers of bacon and a two-inch cube of butter – to last a week. Everything else came in the same meagre portions. The maximum price for a meal was five shillings but restaurants like that at the Dorchester were allowed to make a house charge of six shillings to cover linen, bread rolls and so forth, and a half-crown for dancing. Ward calculated that with drinks and the taxi fare later he wouldn't get much change from a fiver. He grinned. He could afford it. He had still not spent a penny from the Perseus Group. He had enough without that, if only because he so rarely got the chance to spend his naval pay.

He and Catherine talked easily. In fact he did most of the talking, though he did not notice it at the time, mainly about *Boston* and her crew but carefully, without giving away any secrets.

Catherine smiled, "You are proud of her."

He shrugged and grinned. "She's a cantankerous old bucket, sometimes, but we've got a good ship's company and my Number One, that's the Joe Krueger we were talking about, is a terrific bloke."

All he learned of Catherine was that she had a room in the house behind Baker Street and he supposed it was a block of flats or a hostel for girls working in the Ministries. She did not talk about her family and home in France and he understood that could be painful for her. She was curious about his own home on the Northumberland coast.

They danced a lot, Ward adequately, the girl very well. At the start of the evening she was reserved, watchful, but by the end they were laughing together. He decided she was a very pretty girl and watched to see the turn of her head and her smile.

So when he took her home in the taxi he tried to kiss her but she stopped him, firmly. "No. Please."

That set him off-balance. Did she think he would try to seduce her in a taxi? Then he remembered this girl was alone in a foreign country. He knew little about her but liked her and wanted to know more. Fat chance of that, and he said without hope, "I don't suppose you could get a day off tomorrow?" Saturday was a working day.

She asked, "You go to your ship tomorrow?"

"Not till late. And there's a train at six in the evening."

She thought a moment, then: "I could see you tomorrow afternoon."

That cheered him up. "Fine. Where and when?"

"Here." The taxi had turned off Baker Street and stopped outside her house. "At two?"

"I'll be here on the dot."

He handed her out of the cab and watched as she rang the bell. The door opened. There was a curtained blackout cubicle just inside and he caught a glimpse of the shadowy figure of a man. Then she turned to wave and the door closed behind her.

He went back to his hotel happy. He had enjoyed himself and without Catherine he might have spent the evening alone. It was a bit of luck meeting her.

The next morning he paid his bill and left his case behind the desk at the hotel, arranging to call for it in the evening.

57

He lounged about in the hotel, read the papers, drank coffee, lunched at twelve-thirty, and then set off impatiently to walk the mile-and-a-half to Baker Street.

Reading the papers had brought his mind back to the war – and CHARIOT. Quartermain had told him flatly he could not join it – even if it took place. It had to, he was certain of that. After the sinking of H.M.S. *Hood* with the loss of a thousand men, the Navy had taken its revenge and sunk *Bismarck*. But what if *Bismarck* had escaped into St. Nazaire and made repairs, had lived to continue her Atlantic marauding, or if *Tirpitz* now broke out, sure of a haven in St. Nazaire? The Atlantic convoys, Britain's lifeline, were stretched thin already, the U-boats dangerously close to cutting them off altogether. It was no wonder Churchill had suggested that the whole strategy of the war hinged on *Tirpitz* . . .

Ward was scowling when he reached the house behind Baker Street but the sight of Catherine soon took his mind off the war. She ran quickly down the steps to meet him, shrugging into her heavy winter coat as she came. They walked and talked and this time she did her share, chattering of France before the war. Some of the shop windows in Oxford Street were boarded over, the glass blown out of them in the bombing. Others were criss-crossed with adhesive tape to prevent them shattering from blast and the girl peered in, eagerly curious.

They sat for a while in Hyde Park. Air-raid shelters were sunk in the ground and a battery of anti-aircraft guns poked their long snouts out of sand-bagged gunpits. Beyond the bare branches of the trees the fat-bellied barrage balloons floated over London, silver-grey against the cold blue of a winter sky. Ward and the girl laughed a lot that afternoon and they stayed out so long that he had to hail a taxi to take her home. He had enjoyed himself immensely and he told her so as he stood with her outside the house, the early winter dusk around them.

She smiled at him, "It was nice. I have not been so happy for a long time."

"I'd like to see you again."

"No arrangements, John, no letters." She said that firmly.

He wondered if she had written to another man and then got the telegram: "Regret to inform you . . ." This war was almost as bad for the girls waiting at home as it was for the men at sea. He said, "All right. But next time I get leave –"

She stopped him then by kissing him, hard. He was not expecting that but put his arms around her and she leaned against him. After a moment she pushed free and walked quickly to the front door, it opened and he again glimpsed the figure of a man in the entrance lobby. She turned and waved, he saw the pale blur of her face and then she was gone.

He climbed into the taxi and went back to his hotel. The bar wasn't open but he tipped the porter generously to fetch him a large whisky. The bribe, and his uniform, worked wonders: whisky was a rare luxury these days. He needed a drink. He did not want to go back to sea so soon. He knew that as soon as he got leave again he would seek out Catherine Guillard.

The porter returned soon afterwards and Ward gulped the last of the whisky, expecting to be told his taxi waited to take him to the train. The time was nearly five-thirty. But the porter said, "Telephone for you, sir."

It was Joe Krueger's deep drawl that came over the wire: "Glad I caught you, sir. You have a reprieve. The old girl won't be ready for another twenty-four hours, and luckily they've put back the sailing of the convoy by that amount because they're waiting for a couple of ships to complete loading. How's the furlough?"

"Terrific! Thanks, Joe."

Ward told the porter, "See if you can find me a room for tonight." Once that was arranged he took a taxi and drove to Baker Street.

He paid off the taxi, pushed the button of the bell and heard it ring, muffled, inside the house. After a moment the door was opened by a man, tall and broad, heavily built, possibly in his forties. The black-out curtain of the cubicle hung down behind him but was not completely closed and a chink of light lit him, dimly.

"Yes, sir?"

"I'd like to see Miss Guillard, please."

The man hesitated. "She isn't here, sir."

"Oh!" That was a disappointment. Ward tried again. "Do you know where she's gone? When she'll be back? Did she leave a telephone number?"

"No, sir."

The street was silent and so was the house. The man stood like a rock, unmoving, one hand behind the half open door, waiting to close it. Ward was suddenly uneasy. There was something bloody funny going on here. "What is this place? And who are you? That girl came in here barely two hours ago and I want to see her or be sure she's all right." There was quiet determination in his voice.

The man was still a moment longer then held the door wide. "You'd better come in, sir." He closed the door behind Ward, pulled aside the blackout curtain and led the way into the hall beyond. "If you'll wait a moment, please, sir."

The hall was dingy, lit by a single light hanging low over a desk at one side. On the desk was a telephone, a small clock with a busy tick and a bell push that the man thumbed. Ward did not hear the ring but a second man entered immediately from a door at one side. He was younger than the first, thin and stooping. The first one said, "Gentleman wants to see Miss Guillard."

The young one said, "Lieutenant Ward?"

"Yes. But how – ?"

The young man turned away. He picked up the telephone, dialled, waited, then said, "Lieutenant Ward is here, asking for Miss Guillard." He listened, then: "Yes, sir." He put down the telephone and looked at Ward. "Will you take a seat, please?" He gestured to a solitary straight-backed chair by the wall.

Ward asked, "How do you know who I am? And where's Miss Guillard?"

He got only the patient answer, "If you'd like to make yourself comfortable, it'll only be for a few minutes."

"*What* will only be a few minutes? What's going on? Has something happened to her? An accident?"

Patiently again: "I'm afraid I can't tell you anything, Lieutenant, but someone else is coming who will."

Ward did not sit down. The hall was about ten yards long from the blackout curtain to the foot of the stairs that lifted up to a landing. He paced the hall, back and forth. The young man stood at the foot of the stairs and the older one by the curtain that covered the front door. Now Ward could see that the younger one was in charge and the other was a guard. A *guard*! Ward checked in his pacing at the thought. Why a guard, in the hostel where Catherine lived? He did not ask, certain now that these two would not answer. He went on pacing, worried and puzzled, anger building in him, while the clock on the desk ticked away the minutes.

Finally he heard a car draw up in the road outside and the young man said, "If you'd like to go out, sir." Ward looked at him from under black brows and the young man took an involuntary pace backward and said quickly, "It's my superior. You'll have to talk to him."

Ward said deliberately, "If this is some smart-Aleck trick to get me out of here I'll damn soon get in again, and God help the pair of you when I do." He pushed through the curtain and the guard followed cautiously, opened the door and let him out, closed it behind him. Ward stood in the street once more, blinking in the darkness. A big car, its colour indeterminate in the night, was drawn up by the kerb. Its hooded headlights glowed and the engine ticked over softly. He crossed to it and saw a Wren sitting at the wheel, facing stiffly to her front. Then the back door opened and from inside the car a voice said, "Get in." He recognised the voice's owner: Rear-Admiral Quartermain.

Ward said, "I came here to see a Miss –"

"I know. Get in." The voice was still quiet, not curt but demanding obedience. Ward climbed in beside Quartermain and closed the door. The car moved ahead and he saw a glass partition separated them from the Wren at the wheel.

Quartermain said, "I haven't much time because I'm on my way to catch a train to Glasgow, but you deserve an explanation. You've been seeing Catherine Guillard. You were supposed to be going back to your ship tonight but instead you went to that house to see her –"

Ward broke in angrily, "*Boston*'s sailing was put back for another twenty-four hours so I came around to the house! I only took the lady back there a couple of hours ago but some tough who answered the door this time said she's gone out and he wouldn't tell me anything else! Who the hell are they in there? *What* are they?"

"I can't tell you that. Except that they hold in their hands the lives of the men and women who stay in that house." In fact they were men of the Strategic Operations Executive, the organisation that ran secret agents in occupied Europe. Their headquarters was in Baker Street and the house was one of several in which agents stayed. Quartermain went on, "Anyway, she isn't there now."

"How do you know? Where is she?"

Quartermain said quietly, "When Catherine Guillard landed in this country in 1940, I recruited her. Inside a fortnight she was back at her job in St. Nazaire, carrying on her normal life – but working for us as well. We've sent a lot of people back; she was one of the first. Yesterday she came to Richmond Terrace to see me – and afterwards bumped into you outside."

It took time to sink in, for Ward to accept it. He supposed Quartermain meant that Catherine was some sort of agent, presumably working with the French Resistance. He asked, "Isn't that – dangerous?"

Quartermain answered with bald truth, "Always." He remembered her recent report on a Hauptmann Engel of the Abwehr who was in charge of counter-espionage, and a certain Herr Grünwald, an officer in the Gestapo. Dangerous. Very.

Ward asked, "Can I see her?"

"No."

"You've already trusted me with secrets, for God's sake! Do you think I'd put *her* at risk?"

"No, but you can't see her. I sent her back to France tonight."

3

Engel

The moon hung high in a sky sprinkled with cold stars and strung with cloud shredded by the wind. The big meadow lay in a bend of the Loire river and had been used for landings before. The three men who came to it in the night knew it of old. It was well away from houses and roads, was approached by a long, narrow, rutted track down which they pushed their bicycles. The grass was short, the ground firm and this night hard with frost, level and without rocks. There were no high trees around it. Thus a Lysander could set down no matter what the direction of the wind might be. Finding such a field had not been easy, but necessary. And worth it.

Henri, the leader, was a man of thirty-odd, not tall, not broad, unobtrusive. One of his companions was an agent going out and the other was his young assistant, Jacques. They halted and stood still with only their heads turning, holding their breath and listening to the night until Henri said, "Good." They moved then, passing from the lane through a gate into the meadow, walking through the wet grass and pushing their bicycles to the low copse in the corner of the field. They leant the bicycles there and Henri looked at his watch. It had taken them an hour to reconnoitre the outskirts of the field and ensure that no German patrol lay in ambush. Now time was short. He said softly, "Hurry it up! Jacques?"

"I'm ready!"

His assistant unloaded three wooden stakes from the crossbar of his bicycle. Jacques was barely eighteen and fumbled in his haste and excitement.

Henri and Jacques walked out into the meadow, leaving the third man behind them in the shadows. Henri pointed downwards, Jacques rammed one of the stakes into the earth and Henri lashed a pocket torch to the top of it. They turned away and walked up-wind, Henri steadily counting his paces.

A hundred and fifty metres up-wind of the first stick Henri pointed again, Jacques pushed in a second stake and Henri tied on another torch.

They turned, walked out to the right for fifty metres, and set up the third stake topped by a torch.

Henri looked at his watch again and said, "Right. Get him."

Jacques dashed away with the eagerness of youth, heading back for the man they had left waiting in the copse in the corner of the meadow. Henri walked back to the first stake. The three stakes formed an inverted L and Henri stood at the bottom end of it, looking up the meadow, feeling the wind on his face and listening to the thump of his heart.

Before the war he had worked for his father, selling and repairing farm tools. In 1939 he joined the army and in 1940 was wounded. He was in hospital in the south, that part of France not occupied by the Germans, at the time of the surrender. He was bitterly outspoken about the débâcle, but not for long. The British recruited him and from then on he held his tongue. They spirited him away to England, trained him as a wireless operator and in the late spring of 1941 parachuted him back into France with his wireless in a suitcase.

He held documents showing he had spent a long convalescence in the south before returning in 1941. He took over the agricultural repair business from his ageing father, and trundled about the roads of France in the same Renault van he had used up to 1939 and which had been ancient even then. Because of his work he had passes into all the restricted coastal areas. His father was dead now, and he had no other family. He had not used the van tonight because repairers of farm tools did not make calls at night. And besides, a bicycle was quieter and more easily hidden.

The network, SPINSTER as it was known to London,

was a small one, consisting virtually of Catherine Guillard and Henri, her wireless operator, or 'pianist'. The boy Jacques carried messages sometimes and was eager to do more. Henri had recruited him when doing a job at the farm where Jacques lived, but had his doubts about the boy. Jacques was devoted, loyal and they believed brave but he was also young, impatient and melodramatic. They called for him when he was needed and he had the telephone number of a bar in St. Nazaire where he could reach Henri in an emergency. And that was the network. Catherine wanted it small and so did Henri: the bigger the network, the bigger the risk.

Between them Catherine and Henri carried out occasional sabotage, cutting telephone lines or blowing up sections of railway track, minor damage that could be repaired in a day or so but that was grit in the German war machine, nevertheless. Far more importantly, they sent information.

So far they had killed no one. A German officer, Feldkommandant Holtz, had been killed in Nantes, just upriver from St. Nazaire, but they had no part in it, had known nothing of it. They believed, however, that the death of one German officer had not been worth the hostages shot in reprisal. They knew the time would come when the British and Americans invaded and that then they would have to use their hidden weapons. It would be their duty then, but now their duty was to survive, to watch and to inform London of what they saw. London had ordered Henri to meet tonight's outgoing agent at a rendezvous and bring him here. He had never seen this man before and probably would not again.

Jacques returned bringing the agent, who was wrapped in a thick overcoat and carried a bulky briefcase. His breath, like theirs, steamed on the cold air. They waited, listening, softly stamping their feet, hands jammed into pockets.

Jacques said, "He's late."

Henri answered, "Only a few minutes. He'll be here.

They're good, those airmen." He thought, But – suppose flak got them? Or a night-fighter? With Geneviève aboard? He started to pray.

Then Jacques, youngest and with the sharpest hearing, said, "He's here!"

He trotted away up the meadow, heading for the other torches. Now they all heard the low mutter of the engine and Henri's head turned, fixing the source of the sound. He pulled his own torch from his pocket and flashed it in that direction, the morse letter H for Henri.

The aircraft was suddenly there, sweeping low and black towards the meadow. Henri flashed his callsign again and the signal-lamp below the fuselage of the Lysander winked in reply. The plane circled the field, its high wings, angular and strutted, silhouetted against the night sky. Henri switched on the torch on its stake beside him. Its reflector had been removed so it shone all around and not just upwards. At the top of the field Jacques lit one torch then sprinted across and lit the other.

The Lysander came in with landing lights burning, their glow spilling over the field and slipped over Henri's head, so low he could see the extra fuel tank under the fuselage and the spatted wheels. The engine note dropped, it touched down and he heard the thump of its wheels. It ran on towards the other lights and halted between them. The landing lights were switched off and in the sudden darkness the Lysander was almost invisible. Then its engine note rose again as it turned and taxied back to the bottom of the meadow, turned again and stopped close to Henri and the outgoing agent, pointing up-wind.

Henri saw the head of the pilot in the cockpit inside the transparent canopy and ran in with the agent as the rear part of the canopy was slid back. The plane's passenger climbed out and down to the ground. Henri pushed the outgoing agent up the steps leading into the fuselage, shoving him up into the tiny after-cabin before passing up his briefcase. The canopy slid shut and the beating tick-over of the Lysander's engine quickened. The little aircraft moved forward, picked up speed with wings rocking on the uneven terrain, was airborne – was gone, leaving only a receding drone.

Jacques was collecting the stakes and torches. Henri gripped Catherine's arm and urged her towards the copse. "It is good to see you. Good. How was it?"

"Interesting." She thought of Jack Ward. "Very." Then she added, "We have a job."

"We've had a job for this last year!" He glanced at her, "But this is special?"

Catherine nodded. "I can't tell you what it's all about because I don't know, but I have instructions. They take precedence over everything else. It's work for us both."

Henri shrugged, "So?"

"They want us to find a man. An engineer called Alain Peyraud."

"Where do we look?"

"They don't know. Before the war he often stayed at a certain hotel in Paris. I think someone in Paris is checking on that; London will let us know if anything is found there."

"Sometimes I think they are mad," Henri grumbled. "One must have a place from which to start a search."

Catherine said, "I think I will be able to tell you that – after I've been in to work on Monday."

Henri said, "Be careful." He was concerned for her, not for himself – even though if she were taken then his life would hang on her silence.

Catherine said quietly, "I will be careful. The sooner I am back at work and living my normal life, the safer I will be. That is our security – the daily routine. We must not change or they will suspect us. I will work hard as I have always done and I will also treat the Germans as I have always done."

They walked on and into the copse. Henri said, "You take Jacques' bicycle. It's lighter than the other."

Catherine smiled. "The young man is still eager?"

"He is still young. If he is lucky he will grow older."

As John Ward had grown older. Catherine pushed the bicycle to the end of the track and rode off into German-occupied France.

That was in the early hours of Sunday morning. On the Monday she went back to her work in the dockyard office at St. Nazaire.

On Monday evening Hauptmann Franz Engel was returning along the quay to his place of work by the St. Nazaire basin. Across the water lay the huge caverns of the U-boat pens with their roofs of ten-foot thick, reinforced concrete. They were shadowed in the gloom of evening and in their dark interiors glowed the dim lights burnt by the watch-keepers on the boats.

Engel was very tall, very lean and straight. He had been posted to St. Nazaire in October, after being wounded in Russia. He swung one leg stiffly, and as he crossed the timbers of the bridge over the Old Entrance to the basin his boots beat out a dot-and-carry-one rhythm. His destination lay two hundred yards further on, between the basin and the Normandie dock. There was a long terrace of work-shops and offices and near the far end of it, sandwiched between warehouses, stood a grubby, three-storied build-ing. It was one of his offices. The other, where his clerks and his staff worked, was a mile away in a fine building in the new town, on the Boulevard Albert, close to the office of the *Kommandatur* in the College of St. Louis and looking out over the wide sweep of the estuary of the Loire. He saw his staff, and papers, when he had to, but he preferred to use his rooms here on the quay by the basin. Everyone else preferred things that way, too.

Work in the yards was not over for the day but there were a few clerks and other staff on their way home. Some of them used the road along the side of the basin, the way Engel had come, crossing the Southern Entrance to the basin by the swing bridge and so going on into the town. He saw the Guillard girl in the trickle of men and women. He was not surprised that she had finished work early. She was personal assistant to a department head who said proudly that Mlle. Guillard worked twice as fast and twice as accurately as anyone else. And because of her knowledge of the dockyard and its workings she was of far more value than any secretary only trained to type and file papers.

Engel stood in front of her and saluted. "Guten Abend, Fräulein."

"*Monsieur.*" The girl answered him coldly and in French. Her German was good. It was not as fluent as Engel's French but good enough for her to interpret when German officers visited the yard. She spoke it then as part of her duties but would not use it now, Engel knew.

No matter. He had a reputation here and it was not for amiability and courtesy. Nevertheless, he smiled at Catherine Guillard and asked pleasantly, in French, "I trust you enjoyed your weekend?"

"I spent some days in Paris. I have an aunt there who is elderly." The answer came curt.

Engel knew the girl visited that aunt at irregular intervals. He also knew she was curt because he was a German and she hated him. He was pleasant to her, despite her hatred, for the simple reason that he liked her. That had not kept him from his duty. Catherine Guillard held a position of some minor importance so he had checked on the existence of the aunt in Paris, vetted the girl herself and even kept her under surveillance for some time. There was nothing to cause even a breath of suspicion: his instinct told him she was all right and his instinct rarely failed him.

"Paris is a beautiful city. I envy you." He stepped aside and saluted again as she walked past him and on towards the bridge.

Catherine's heart thumped, as it did on every encounter with Engel. He was dangerous and she had told Quartermain so. Hauptmann Engel was the one who had seen at once that the gates of the Normandie dock were a temptation to sabotage, who had set up the surveillance of the engineers who operated them and who had neatly swept up the gate operators when they attempted their first act of sabotage, just before they could carry it out.

But it was Grünwald of the Gestapo who had interrogated and deported them.

Engel walked on to his office. A sentry stood at the door, wearing on his chest the metal gorget of the *Feldgendarmerie*, the Military Police. He saluted and Engel lifted a hand smartly to the peak of his cap as he entered the building. Inside was a hall, uncarpeted, and stairs led up from it to the two floors above, both of them empty as Engel wanted them. He liked the quietness, and the sense of space.

On the left of the hall a door led to the guardroom where an N.C.O. and six men of the *Feldgendarmerie* were always on duty. They supplied the sentry, and men when Engel needed them in a hurry. The door was shut, was never left open, and the men inside were never noisy.

Engel passed through a door on the right of the hall and into his office. He took off the high-peaked cap and dropped it on his desk. His office windows looked out over the basin to the U-boat pens but the curtains were drawn now and the lights lit. Another desk with a typewriter stood against one wall, close by the fire where an orderly now knelt, stoking it with huge lumps of coal. That desk was used by Private Pianka, who now lay sleeping on a bench by the door. Engel ignored him and the orderly and went to a cupboard behind his desk. He unlocked it with a key on his chain, took a bottle from a row inside and poured cognac into a tumbler. When it yielded a bare inch of golden liquid he swore, then hurled the empty bottle past the orderly's ear to burst against the wall like a grenade. He opened another bottle. The orderly, pale and staring, scurried out like a frightened rabbit.

Engel terrified him. That kind of incident and the opinions Engel expressed of the Führer and various generals, openly and loudly, had convinced the entire German garrison at St. Nazaire that he was mad.

Pianka woke when the bottle burst, sat up and rubbed at his square face. Then he stood, tugged down on his jacket and at once the green-grey of his uniform settled neatly on his body. He was stolid, unimaginative and faithful. A puckered scar from a shrapnel wound narrowed his right eye, giving him a sinister appearance that was totally misleading. He was forty-eight years old and still a private.

Without his cap, his hair showing iron grey and his long face lined, Engel might have been Pianka's contemporary rather than twenty-three years his junior. He manoeuvred his body into the armchair and lifted his stiff right leg to rest its booted foot on the desk. The leg ached, as it always did. The knee was held rigid, locked with a metal plate but he was very lucky to have kept the leg at all. In Russia, where butchery passed for surgery, he had been leading guerilla columns behind the Russian lines and the pitcher had gone too often to the well. Pianka, his driver then as now, had brought him out, Pianka with a dressing over his eye, Engel with his leg splinted to a rifle.

Engel sniffed at the cognac, sipped, drank, sighed and reached out for the bottle.

Pianka said, "Go easy on that stuff."

Engel ignored him and refilled the glass. He lay back with eyes half-closed, his long body relaxed, the ache in his leg easing. He thought this was the best part of the day, when he could take a drink quietly. Later Pianka would drive him to the Officers' Mess where he would eat dinner, alone.

They heard a car draw up outside. Pianka, eye to a crack at the side of the curtains, said, "It's that shit, Grünwald."

Engel did not stir.

Grünwald entered, walking quickly, brisk, efficient. He was a short man, in his early thirties but running to fat that was not quite hidden by the carefully tailored dark grey suit. He was freshly shaved, his hair parted, oiled and brushed smooth. He halted before Engel, frowning portentously. "I've not yet had a reply to a memorandum I sent to you a week ago."

Engel gave no sign of hearing him and Grünwald said, on a rising note of anger, "It concerned matters affecting our common duty."

Their common duty was to stamp out French Resistance but they had not succeeded. There was a sporadic but continuous succession of minor acts of sabotage, telephone wires and railway lines cut. Engel had plotted the incidents on his map and was convinced the Resistance cell was in St. Nazaire. He reflected now that the very word *sabotage* was a French invention, dating from the railway strike of 1910 when they ripped out the cross-ties, the '*sabots*'. They were at it still.

Engel was Abwehr, Military Intelligence, specifically counter-espionage. Grünwald was Gestapo, and confined to secret police duties. But Engel knew Himmler wanted the Gestapo to take over from the Abwehr and run the whole counter-espionage operation, and was pressing the Führer for this. Admiral Canaris, head of Abwehr, was fighting him but Engel believed that Canaris would lose because Hitler and Himmler were two of a kind. God help them all, he thought, when Himmler makes the rules.

That day had not yet come, however, so Grünwald made a great show of cooperating with Engel. Engel, on the other hand, cooperated only when he had to, and made that clear. It was a rare event.

Now he murmured, "Duty? The only memo I saw was about an office. I'm not a billeting officer so I sent it on."

Grünwald said impatiently, "I spoke to the General about the empty floors above here. He said we must settle the matter by agreement."

"I have settled it. I'm in possession."

"That is not good enough. I need at least one of those floors for members of my staff."

"One? And what about the basement?"

There were cells in the basement. Grünwald scented negotiation and agreed, "It would be useful."

Engel shook his head. "No, it wouldn't. There's no bathtub." One of the Gestapo methods of interrogation was to plunge the victim's head under water until he was on the point of drowning. Repeatedly. Until the answers came. Engel detested all such methods.

Grünwald slid away from the subject. "My staff has increased in recent months, I need further accommodation and this building —"

Engel's boots slammed to the floor and he stood up. Grünwald started back from the towering figure but Engel said only, "I'm hungry."

Grünwald ignored that and persisted: "I want a definite answer on the matter."

Engel put away the bottle and locked the cupboard. "All right. I am definitely going to eat." He paused, watching Grünwald, who stood thin-lipped and glaring. Engel said, "You want a serious answer, so I'll give you one. I think it's incredible that a man should be building a little paper empire when we're living in the middle of a hostile population, we're at war with Britain and Russia — and now, with America in the war also, two or three million Americans will be over here in a year or so to help all the others beat the hell out of us. And you want another office." Engel walked to the door, flicked at the light switches and strode down the hall. Grünwald was left in the firelit gloom with a grinning Private Pianka. The Gestapo man muttered angrily under his breath and hurried after Engel. Pianka chuckled, locked the office and followed.

Grünwald's Mercedes was outside, a black and gleaming monster. Lights glowed inside it and showed Leutnant Horstmann sitting at the wheel. He was Grünwald's aide, tall, blond, muscular, and handsome. Engel thought he would look fine on a recruiting poster and that was all he was good for. He was a wooden-head, but clever enough to keep clear of the Russian Front or any other front. In the back of the car sat Ilse, Grünwald's wife. She was only twenty and when Grünwald first brought her from Berlin she had been sulky and sullen, but she had settled down now and seemed happy enough. She wore a fur coat, open to show her dress and her long legs. The dress had a low neckline and, as Engel saluted, Ilse leaned forward, gave him a wide smile and let him see into the valley between her breasts.

Engel grinned sardonically. As far as he as a person was concerned it meant nothing: the girl simply couldn't help herself. Then Grünwald stood before him, tugging on his gloves. Horstmann started the car and Grünwald said savagely, "We will talk again, Hauptmann Engel!"

His voice was barely audible above the noise of the engine but Engel heard it and the menace in it. He said, "We will not. Listen, Grünwald, because I won't tell you again – I wangled this office for myself in order to get away from the *Kommandatur* and you and a few more bastards like you. I keep it. You shut up and build your empire elsewhere. Now go to hell."

Grünwald did not answer, Engel's cold blue eyes stifling speech. He found himself in the Mercedes and across the bridge and into the town before he could recover. Then he told himself there would be a day of reckoning. And meanwhile . . . Meanwhile he would bide his time and make his plans.

He told Horstmann, "I have work to do. Drop me at the *Kommandatur* and take my wife home. Then go and eat. Fetch the car for me in two hours."

Pianka said, "He's dangerous."

Engel nodded. "Very."

"What if he finds out about his wife and her pretty boy?" Pianka opened the door of the ramshackle old Citroën that Engel used. Grünwald's Mercedes looked what it was: official. The Citroën could have been driven into town by a farmer and that was why Engel used it, to see without being seen.

He climbed into the front passenger seat and settled the stiff leg. "Let us hope he doesn't. At least, not till we're ready. Ilse is our – what was that word Rudi Moller used?"

"Moller? Your friend the *Schnellboot* captain?"

"That's right. And the word was sheet-anchor. It can

save you when the storm breaks. Ilse is our sheet-anchor."

And both he and Pianka knew only too well that the storm was building.

4

Landscape with Figures

Ward took his ship to sea in the forenoon of Monday, 26th January. The convoy formed up off Southend in two long columns: only two because the channel swept clear of mines along the East Coast was narrow. *Arundel*, *Boston*'s sister ship and the senior, was far ahead, leading the twin columns. Ward, as usual, tagged on at the rear as whipper-in.

He stood at the front of the bridge, hands jammed comfortably in the pockets of his bright orange duffel coat. Another day, another convoy. A yellow sun in a heavy sky that could hold snow; it was cold enough and would be a sight colder further north. Forty-eight hours from now they would be opening the Firth of Forth.

Forty-eight hours: his mind switched back that length of time to Quartermain in the gloom of the car, saying, "I sent her back to France." There had been silence then. It was hard for Ward to grasp that the fair-haired girl with whom he'd walked and talked that afternoon would be in German-held France that night and in mortal danger.

Quartermain broke the silence, carefully dispassionate: "I don't like discussing personal matters but I must. You've only known this girl for a few hours. It isn't serious, is it?"

Ward shook his head. "No, sir. I just – like her. When I found I had an extra day I thought I'd take her out for the evening again and I was going to look her up next time I was in London."

"Um!" Quartermain lifted his wrist to eye his watch and muttered, "I'll be cutting it fine . . ." To Ward he said, "I can't tell you to forget her, though it might be as well if you did –"

"I won't." Ward looked round at the admiral. "If you get

a chance – I don't know how you people operate – I'd like you to tell her so, and that I'm keeping my fingers crossed for her."

Quartermain thought about it, not liking the idea, finding it unprofessional. Still – "It might be possible." He would go no further. Wireless messages were of necessity brief because long transmissions invited pin-pointing by German radio direction finding stations, capture and death. But a few words like that might mean the difference between despair and hope, particularly to a young girl under continuous strain, a reminder that there was another world where sheer survival did not depend upon acting a part.

The Wren dropped Quartermain and his suitcase at Euston then took Ward back to his hotel. He did not know the workings of Quartermain's mind, had only that grudging: "It might be possible." He drank a few beers in the bar, tried to read but could not concentrate, tried to sleep but lay wide-awake. The next day he went back to his ship.

Now he crossed the bridge to the port wing and looked back along the narrow length of *Boston*. There were gunners servicing the two 20mm Oerlikons mounted on the port side by the second and third of the four funnels. The rapid-firing Oerlikons were a vital part of *Boston*'s armament. When the Admiralty took over the fifty 'four stacker' destroyers from the United States Navy for escort work they had drastically revised their armament. Three of the original 4-inch guns were ripped out along with nine of the twelve torpedo-tubes. Now each destroyer carried a 4-inch gun on the fo'c'sle, the two Oerlikons either side, three 21-inch torpedo-tubes abaft the funnels and a 12-pounder high-angle gun in the stern. This last, together with the Oerlikons, could be used for anti-aircraft defence.

It was not a fearsome set of teeth but all the Navy could spare. Ward wished they had taken out the last three torpedo-tubes and given him another pair of 20mm guns. The tubes had not been used and it was the opinion of the men of the 'four stackers' that they never would be, while the Oerlikons were in action on every convoy. The gunners worked quickly about them now, hands deft on the oiled machinery. The keenness of their eyes and the speed of their reactions might mean the difference between life and death for many aboard this ship.

Once *Boston* was clear of the Thames estuary Ward would order the guns to loose off a few rounds, to make sure everything worked correctly and so that the gunners could get their hands and eyes in. There were reports that an E-boat, possibly Dirty Bill, had sunk another ship off Cromer last night. The E-boats worked out of the Hook of Holland.

Joe Krueger said, "Starboard column's wandering a bit, sir."

"Send 'em a smoke signal."

Impassive as an Indian, Joe replied, "No fire, sir, and my blanket's below." He took all the old jests without a blink. He would point out, and with truth, that his New England accent was closer to that of the BBC than those of the crew with its leavening of Geordies, Scots, and Cockneys.

Ward turned forward, lifted the glasses to his eyes. "We'll run up and chivvy 'em." He stooped over the voicepipe. "Starboard ten. Fifteen knots."

"Starboard ten . . . ten of starboard wheel on, sir. Revolutions for fifteen knots."

Ward straightened as *Boston* heeled under helm, turning to head out to seaward of the starboard column and then scurry up its length, herding the ships into better station. They were bound for the Firth of Forth. Ward frowned thoughtfully. Quartermain had gone to Scotland but to the West Coast. Cousin Patrick, too, was in Scotland – somewhere. What had his mother said? Working on landscapes?

Had Patrick wangled himself a job as an artist for the Army? Odd. But Patrick was always an odd one, sarcastic, irresponsible, idle. He stood about six feet but Jack could hardly remember Patrick standing. He was more usually slumped in an armchair or lounging against a bar. He once said to Jack, "You're welcome to the Navy, old man. It

79

beats me what you see in it. There are easier ways of
making a living, if you have to, which I do not. I suppose
life is like an ocean liner, really. There are the earnest
toilers, chaps like yourself, to make the thing go. And there
are the passengers of which I am one; first class, thank
God.''

Ward grinned at the memory and his eyes flicked over
Boston's rust-blistered length. No passengers here, first
class or otherwise.

He stooped again over the pipe, "Meet her. Steer oh-
seven-oh!''

"– course oh-seven-oh, sir.''

The little steward brought Ward his lunch, bully beef in a
sandwich and coffee in a beer-stein. The coffee machine
worked twenty-four hours a day and was the one advantage
of these ex-U.S. destroyers. Ward bit into the sandwich
hungrily. The coffee itself was excellent, by courtesy of Joe
Krueger; the foreman of his boatyard sent him a parcel of
American goodies every two weeks. Ward drank from the
stein. A garishly painted pot with a handle and a lid, he had
bought it from a pawnshop in a moment of inspiration and
now his coffee stayed hot and free of sea spray.

He swallowed, "Port ten. Steer oh-five-oh.''

"Port ten, steer oh-five-oh . . . Ten of port wheel on,
sir.''

Ward heard the yeoman tell his signaller, "Get the loud
hailer and have the lamp ready." They would be needed to
herd the strays back into line.

"– course oh-five-oh, sir.''

Boston was foaming up the seaward side of the starboard
column – and there was the *William Henry*, wandering all
over the bloody place as usual. Ward said, "Make to
William Henry: 'Keep better station.'''

He chewed the sandwich and thought again of his cousin.
Patrick's mother said he had been changed when he returned from France. "He's kinder to me, more thoughtful,
quieter. But sometimes when he looks at other people he
seems so . . . *hard*.''

That didn't sound like an artist who was working on landscapes . . .

Patrick's legs ached as they drove him up the last man-killing lift of the hill. The blue-brown and green sweep of it, patched with drifts of snow, was blurred by the sweat that ran, stinging, into his eyes. The rim of it was still distant against a high blue sky, clouds torn into white streamers on the wind. The Bergen rucksack dragged at his shoulders and the nine pounds of the Thompson submachine-gun weighed more like ninety.

He saw his platoon commander go down into the heather, a few yards ahead and to his right. Patrick followed suit, plunging down into the soaking bracken, then working up through it to the crest, moving on elbows and knees with his belly on the ground, the Thompson cradled in his forearms. The valley opened before him and he halted, huddled down below the crest, only his head showing in its rolled khaki comforter. He panted like a dog, looked behind him for the other eight men of his section, saw not one of them but knew they would be working up through the bracken on either side of him, with the other two sections of the platoon beyond.

He faced forward. This wasn't a halt for a rest. They'd stopped because Madden's lot needed time to play their game down in the valley. A different exercise, quite separate from his own platoon's. Captain Peter Madden had a gang of around twenty that trained on their own. He was a nice guy and a tough nut.

Patrick craned his head and saw how the hill dropped to the valley bottom where a river ran, then lifted to a road on the opposite slope. An armoured car, carrying the insignia of the 'enemy', showed at the head of the valley and started to trundle down the road. In about half a minute, Patrick thought, when he changes down for that bend, they'll hit him.

He reached down for the long commando knife and used its razor's edge to cut away the long strip of khaki serge that

81

some barbed-wire had torn from his trouser leg. He slid the knife back into its sheath on his thigh and reflected that it was a change from a palette knife, just as this whole caper was a far cry from sitting at a sun-shaded table on a Paris pavement. He'd written to his mother that he was doing a lot of work on landscapes and that was true enough because he painted still, but most of his work was done like this. Maybe he could write and illustrate a book: 'Through the bracken on your belly with Bergen and Tommy-gun'.

It had its compensations. The hills of Ayr were spectacularly beautiful. He drew and painted them when he could. Their curves were subtle and sensuous. They did not, however, remind him of Sarah. Miss Benjamin's curves were warm and moved. He went to her in Glasgow when he could, which was not often, but he managed to find time, among other things, to draw her.

"Not like this!"

"Just like that," he told her. "Keep still."

"You'll get me arrested. Bloody artist. *Are* you really an artist?"

He had to admit he did not look the part. He was a soldier now and his hair was cut short. He had always been slender, though big-boned, but this last year or so he had grown muscle and it moved lumpily on back and shoulders. His hands, too, were broad and hardened, the pencil seeming fragile in such a grip. But when he showed her the sketch – "Hey! That's – that's marvellous! I . . . no . . . no, Patrick! What're you doing? Patrick, *please* . . . Hell, I wanted to keep it!"

He'd torn up that first one and all the others. "They're not right. When I get it right you can keep it. Come here."

Sarah Benjamin. Christ! What a girl! And a husband commanding a desk in London. Sarah said he was being unfaithful to her – "and what are you laughing at? Patrick, you're a *bastard*!" She meant that.

A voice called quietly from the bracken. "Any moment now, Corporal."

"Right, sir," Patrick answered. He had pulled Corporal

a month ago, after the commando raid on the Norwegian port of Vaagso. There'd been talk of a decoration but only one man had seen him clear the house of Germans and that man had died. Now they were training in house to house fighting, and his platoon was on its way back from the abandoned village up on the moors through which they stalked and bombed their way.

There came the dull *whuff!* of an explosion, dirt and smoke lifted in front of the armoured car and it swerved aside, ran off the road and halted. Now Madden's men rose out of the bracken, the khaki suddenly lifting from the dark green and brown carpet. Some ran straight to the armoured car with their weapons trained while others stayed at the side of the road, facing back the way the car had come or towards the end of the valley, on guard.

They were training with particular urgency and no one knew why except presumably the mysterious little admiral who often came to see them.

Now that the action down in the valley was over Patrick shoved up to his feet, following his officer's lead, looked for his section and saw them coming after him. As he ran down the hill towards the road there was another car now, a khaki-painted Morris. Patrick's attention was concentrated on where he placed his running feet; put a foot wrong on this ground and you went arse over tip. But he saw a small figure in a dark blue uniform get out of the Morris.

The river. Patrick ran into it, waded as it rose to his thighs then up around his chest. Half the platoon were swimming now; he was one of the tallest among them. They splashed ashore a hundred yards up the valley from Madden's lot and the armoured car, climbed to the road and formed into a body while still on the move, three files with the officer at their head, the sergeant and the two corporals in rear. They doubled down the road, the water from the river-crossing dripping from them, their rubber-soled commando boots thudding on the concrete.

Patrick thought that he saw more water than did cousin

Jack in the Navy. He was often sarcastic about Jack, but that was only because he was secretly in awe of him. Jack always knew what he wanted to do and did it. He had long been a remote figure, different, standing back and watching the rest of the family. Geoffrey had described how, in the summer of 1939 when Jack came home from Spain, his father had thrust the crown of Perseus at him and Jack had thrown it back. There'd been one hell of a barney, but Jack had walked out on his birthright and never looked back. Hard, our Jack. If you taunted him into stating his faith he would talk simply of tradition, loyalty and duty with that look in his eye that said he believed in them and if you didn't like it you could go to hell.

These days Patrick believed in them too. The war had focused his mind and he had learned quickly. The Commandos had no use for the cynical, nor for the carelessly reckless, because neither could marshal the inner discipline needed to accept the demands imposed upon them.

Patrick knew the men ahead depended on him, and he on them. He was a painter, an artist, but he was also a soldier.

Quartermain asked Captain Madden, "Well, Peter? How did it go? It looked good from where I was."

Madden had joined the Durham Light Infantry in 1938 as a private, a Territorial weekend soldier. Now he wore the three cloth stars of a captain. His webbing equipment of belt and ammunition pouches was damp and smeared with mud where he had worked through the bracken, and he carried a Thompson submachine-gun.

"Pretty well, sir. We made a landing from the sea just after midnight and then a forced march until it started to get light. We carried out the final approach under cover, laid and wired the charge and went to ground."

Quartermain nodded approval, then his eyes settled on the platoon coming up the road at the double.

Madden's gaze shifted to the Morris and, disappointed, to the A.T.S. driver. When he and his men were training in

Landscape with Figures

Devon, Quartermain had often driven down from London in his Daimler, the pretty little Wren at its wheel. Now, up in Scotland, Madden did not see her so often. He shrugged and turned back to Quartermain. "Any news, sir? Of what we're training *for*?"

"Not yet. When the time comes, *if* the time comes, I'll tell you. You need to be ready for anything. You may go in by sea or by air, ambush a vehicle, blow up a house or capture a boat. Don't be impatient, Peter. Action will come soon enough, even if it's not this pet scheme of mine. That one could be this year, next year, some time, never." He paused. "Or next week."

The sodden platoon swung past him, breath steaming on the air, boots thudding on the road. They faced their front and only the corporal at the rear of the right-hand file turned to look at him. There was something familiar, Quartermain thought, about the tall, dark-browed figure.

He watched them go. Dusk was falling and a fine rain driving on the wind. He turned up the collar of his bridge coat. He had seen that look before, quite recently, but he couldn't for the life of him think where.

85

5

E-boat Alley

None of those East Coast convoys was good that winter but some were worse than others.

In the two weeks following Ward's visit to London *Boston*, with her sister ship *Arundel*, shuffled between Sheerness and Rosyth. They escorted a convoy north, spending two nights at sea then one in port before taking another convoy south. They saw no E-boats but during that time other escorts were in action and Dirty Bill was reported sighted on two occasions. On both of them the convoy she attacked lost a ship.

At Rosyth *Boston* played football against *Arundel*'s team and won 3-2. A leading stoker announced his engagement to a stunning girl in Edinburgh. Everybody wondered what she saw in him and made ribald suggestions. He had 'sippers' of the rum ration of the entire stokers' mess-deck and that night another leading stoker had to stand his watch. On one convoy northward the coaster *Mary Donaldson* struck a mine and *Boston* towed her into Sunderland in a near-sinking condition with six dead aboard her. On the return run south, as the convoy entered the Thames estuary, *Boston*'s steering engine jammed, she swung sharply to port and tried to ram a ship in the starboard column. Only a rapid series of orders from Ward to the engineroom turned her, using main engines and screws. It had happened before and Ward knew it would happen again. But this was his ship and he lived with that little weakness as he did with all the others.

And, as Joe Krueger often said, if with more hope than confidence, "Well, she never lets you down when it really matters."

Boston's engineers set the steering right with sweat and

swearing. That was on Friday, 6th February. They lay all
night in Sheerness and sailed on the forenoon of Saturday
with a northbound convoy.

And some were worse than others . . .

At midnight, off Great Yarmouth, Krueger came on to the
bridge. "How does it look, sir?"

Ward, leaning with arms crossed on the bridge-screen
and peering into the night said, "All behaving themselves.
Good station-keeping, well closed-up and no stragglers.
Hardly surprising really – they know what it's like round
here."

"Sure." This stretch of the East Coast convoy route, from
south of Smith's Knoll to the mouth of the Wash, was a
favourite German hunting ground and known as 'E-boat
Alley'. Which was why Joe Krueger added, "I've taken a
look around. They're all on their toes." He was talking now
of *Boston*'s gunners and look-outs.

Ward nodded. "E-boats are supposed to be afraid of
destroyers." Because of their high speed and heavier armament. *Boston* had the armament but not the speed.

"Yeah?" Joe thought about it, then said, "They hide it
pretty good."

Ward grinned. Below him and forward of the bridge the
four-inch gun was closed-up for action, its crew huddled
behind the shield to gain protection from the cold and
warmth from each other's bodies. The sea was calm and
that would suit E-boats. *Boston* still rolled but not much,
and the gunners behind the shield only had the sea washing
around their ankles occasionally. That was a mercy. The
four-inch was known on the lower deck as the submarine
gun because in heavy weather it was as much under water
as above it.

That triggered a thought and Ward said, "We had a
signal just before you came up, a weather forecast. It's
going to turn dirty before morning. Make sure everybody
knows." So that everything movable could be lashed down.
"And rig the life-lines."

"Aye, aye, sir." Krueger went away.

White water spilled back from the stem along either side of the bow, an edging to the black fo'c'sle. Beyond it were the two columns of ships, twenty-eight in all but most of them too far ahead for Ward to see. *Arundel* was up at the head of the convoy and a Fairmile motor-launch out on either wing, again unseen. They were good little boats but mainly there to rescue survivors if need be. They were no match for E-boats.

Ward could make out the nearer ships, the black bulk of each under its trailing smoke. The tanker *Missouri Star* was too far up the port column to be visible but he could see her with his mind's eye. Long, low in the water and heavy with oil, she was the most valuable ship of the lot. But all were valuable because they carried the cargoes that an over-stretched railway system could not. One coaster would carry more than a dozen long freight trains.

The columns headed north at eight knots but *Boston* was making twelve because as tail-ender she swung from column to column, shepherding, coaxing ships back into station if they erred. It was a quiet night and Ward could hear the pinging of the Asdic from its compartment at the back of the bridge. The R.D.F. compartment was back there, too; Krueger, like all the Americans, called it radar. One of the sub-lieutenants was in there, peering over the operator's shoulder at the cathode ray tube. The Warrant Gunner, Huw Phillips, 'Phillips the Guns', stood at the other end of the bridge by one of the two rangefinders. He wore the hood of his duffel coat pulled up over his head and his eyes glittered inside it like those of some mad Welsh monk.

Charlie Barnwell, the signal yeoman, rotund and red-faced, was out on the starboard wing with one of his signalmen, watching the ships ahead. Charlie held the signal-lamp ready. Then there were the lookouts on either wing and the bosun's mate standing at the back.

Krueger returned to the bridge, took up a position a pace from Ward's left shoulder and they stood in companionable silence. They had long since bridged the gap of two thousand miles and twenty years between their backgrounds. They were both seamen. They did not agree on everything but they got on very well.

After some minutes Ward pushed back from the screen and walked out to the starboard wing to stretch his long legs. He looked astern because that was often the way the E-boats came, from astern and seaward. The R.D.F. should pick them up but sometimes didn't. Then – one second there was nothing and the next second all hell let loose. He told the lookout, "Keep your eyes skinned. We don't want a dark stranger bearing gifts."

"Aye, aye, sir."

Ward turned back across the bridge. Bearing gifts . . . he remembered Quartermain and the gift the testy little admiral had hoped for: help with CHARIOT. He wondered if they had made any progress in their search for information about the dock gates. Then he remembered Catherine who was in occupied France now. He walked on, out to the port wing. Catherine was in more danger than he was. At least he had his friends and his own people about him while she –

"*Boat-bearing-red-six-oh!*" The yell came from aft. It jerked Ward's head round and he saw the gunner of the port side Oerlikon in black silhouette, arm outstretched and pointing, swinging the gun itself on to the bearing like another pointing finger. Ward traced the line of it out into the darkness, picked up the streak of white water that was bow-wave and wake, then the long, low, swift-sliding smudge of black that was the boat.

The port lookout was calling a bearing and the rating at the rangefinder chanted the ranges. Phillips passed them on to his guns: "– bearing red six-oh, one thousand –"

Ward was back at the voicepipe, stooping over it. "Full ahead both! Port ten!"

"Port ten . . . ten of port wheel on, sir. Full ahead both." That was Leading-Seaman McCudden at the wheel. His skinny body would be hooked awkwardly over it like a question-mark but he was a good helmsman, second only to the coxswain.

Ward was certain that it was an E-boat out there to port. It was making thirty-odd knots, three times *Boston*'s speed, four times that of the convoy, and was running too flat in the water to be a British motor torpedo-boat or gunboat: they lifted their bows high, planing over the seas when at speed. He threw at Phillips, "Fire!"

But the E-boat struck first and a gun hammered rapidly out in the night, the muzzle flashes making one wavering flame. Phillips barked into the P.A. microphone, his voice echoing out of the speakers, and the four-inch slammed close under the bridge, then the rapid banging of the port-side Oerlikons. The first round from the four-inch was starshell, aimed to burst ahead of and above the E-boat but its blue-white, shivering glare gave Ward only a glimpse of the stern of the enemy. She had turned and was tearing out to run up the outside of the port column.

She was gone, and *Boston* headed after her.

"Midships!" Ward straightened from the pipe. The guns had ceased firing, their target lost in the night and the blaze of the starshell blinding them all. But it had shown up the enemy and now everybody knew roughly where he was. All the ships in the convoy were aware that an E-boat was attacking from astern and from the inshore side. They would be looking –

There was a second long lick of yellow flame out on *Boston*'s starboard bow, stamped on the vision for a second, then gone. The port column of the convoy lay there and the muzzle-flash looked to be a half-mile up it. A good long way, but the E-boat could easily be there by now.

Ward ordered, "Starboard twenty."

"Starboard twenty . . . twenty of starboard wheel on, sir."

Boston was heeling to run up outside the port column on the trail of the E-boat. "Meet her . . . steer that." Guns were firing all along the port column now. Every ship

90

mounted a twelve-pounder aft for her own defence, Lewis
guns as well. He saw that some of the ships in the starboard
column were also firing. At what? Another E-boat out
there? *Boston* was steadily working up speed. Now there
was tracer from the Lewis guns on the ships ahead, stitch-
ing looping lines of light across the night, converging lines
that marked just about where the E-boat must be – unless
they were all shooting at shadows. But a yell came up from
the four-inch and Phillips bawled in reply, "*Commence!*"

So the layer of the gun on the fo'c'sle had the target in the
layer's telescope mounted on the gun. The four-inch fired
out over the bow but Ward closed his eyes before the flash
and opened them afterwards, not blinded. He lifted the
glasses that hung on his chest. He did not see the shell fall
but there on the starboard beam were the black boxes of
ships against the skyline, sliding slowly aft one by one as
Boston head-reached on them. Then, looking forward
again, he saw it, a distant, white ribbon of wake running up
to a blur of moving, thicker darkness that had white wings
to it. That would be the sea flying back in spray from the
German's bow.

Ward told Phillips, but loud enough for all on the bridge
to hear, "She's fine on the starboard bow. Seen?"

"Seen, sir!" Phillips bawled down at the gun, "Bearing
green five! One thousand!"

Ward thought the E-boat was closer than that but the
barrel of the gun swung fractionally, the layer searching,
then steadied. He closed his eyes again a split second
before the flash could blind him, felt the concussion of air
from the gun's firing, lifted the glasses and looked out
again. He found the white furrow and bent his knees to call
into the voicepipe, "Starboard ten!" He still stared through
the glasses.

"Starboard ten . . . ten of starboard wheel on, sir."

Boston heeled under helm and Ward watched the curve
in the white furrow ahead: the E-boat was turning towards
the convoy. To fire torpedoes? If so, then they would know
about it soon enough.

91

Krueger said, "They've stopped firing in the starboard column."

So they had lost whatever they had seen, if they had in fact seen anything. This E-boat was still closing the convoy, well within torpedo range but not faltering. Did she have torpedoes? Or had she been laying mines and simply decided to shoot up the convoy as a bonus? *Boston*'s guns were now pointed at the convoy and Ward ordered, "Check firing!" An error in setting the range might drop a shell on one of their own ships. That was not the way to make friends.

Phillips bawled, "*Check! Check! Check!*"

It was time to cancel *Boston*'s turn to starboard. But – Ward said, "She's going through." He switched his eyes from the E-boat, sought and found instead the ships ahead of her in the port column. He waited, then: "Meet her."

"Meet her, sir."

"Steady. Steer that." Ward straightened, knees flexing to balance him as *Boston* rocked back to an even keel. He looked again for the E-boat but did not find it. "Where the hell has it gone?"

Krueger answered, "Ten on the port bow."

Ward looked out on the bearing, caught just a glimpse of white water and the flying, low black silhouette, then the guns of the port column opened up again and the tracers flew in at the E-boat. He saw her firing then, prickling with flashes. She was tearing in on the column of ships ahead of her – and so was *Boston*, about a thousand yards further south. Ward lowered the glasses. "Tell the port-side Oerlikons to be ready."

"Aye, aye, sir," answered Phillips.

Ward gave all his attention to the ships seen over his bow. They were steaming at eight knots and, as near as he could estimate it, about a cable's length between each ship and the next. Two hundred yards sounded a big enough gap but it could easily dwindle. In the darkness, split by gunflashes, threaded by tracer, and under the stress of a sudden attack, a ship could easily veer off course and another could close up on it. The gap might still be big enough if you hit it exactly right. If you did not –

Krueger called, "She's gone through!"

Ward let his glasses hang on their strap as the firing and the tracers ceased. The gunners aboard the ships of the port column would be desperately swinging their pieces round to meet this new threat from starboard.

Silence on the bridge. The ships that had been just silhouettes in the middle distance were now right ahead and rushing up at *Boston* out of the night. There was an old 'three-island' tramp, the wells between the fo'c'sle, super-structure and poop stacked with some form of deck cargo. The gun on her poop was swinging around. Astern of her was the long, flat-iron hull of the *Missouri Star*, low in the sea with the oil in her, superstructure set right aft.

Christ! They'd closed up! Either the tramp had lost way or the tanker had made up on her. The gap between was less than a cable, terrifyingly less. Ward ordered, "Port ten!" He wasn't turning back now.

"Port ten! . . . ten of port wheel on, sir!"

Boston heeled but only briefly. Ward said, "Meet her . . . steer that." Now her bow pointed at the superstructure of the tramp and *Boston* seemed set to ram her. The neck of sea that separated them shrank with every second and the hull of the ship ahead inched agonisingly slowly forward across *Boston*'s closing bow. Ward watched that inching progress, the shrinking gap between them and the other gap between tramp and tanker. The crew of the four-inch gaped at the poop of the ship coming at them, then back to peer up at Ward on the bridge.

The stern of the tramp loomed over them and *Boston* swept past so close that on the bridge they saw the gunners on the tramp's poop standing frozen. To starboard the bow of the *Missouri Star* charged in as *Boston*'s three hundred and fifteen feet of hull slipped through the chink in the port column. Just. The Torpedo Gunner, standing right aft by the 12-pounder in *Boston*, watched the fat bow of the tanker run in on him then slide past *Boston*'s stern like a great slamming steel door.

The bridge came to life as the port look-out shouted, "Boat! Red seven-oh!"

In the channel between the two columns of the convoy they saw the E-boat. Her cannon marked her as she fired at the ships of the port column. Once inside the convoy she had turned to race south so now she was broad on *Boston*'s port bow, a bare five hundred yards away and coming on at thirty knots or more. In the night, and seen bows-on, she looked like the end of a black pencil in the V of silver spray thrown up by her stem.

The port side Oerlikons opened fire, their rapid hammering seeming laboured against the background ripping of the machine-guns. The E-boat skidded around and her foreshortened silhouette lengthened as she ran away across the channel. The fire of the Oerlikons followed, the 4-inch slammed and the flames from the E-boat's cannon were joined by another flame, vertical but bent on the wind by the speed of her. She did not stop or alter course, but ran on, tearing between two ships of the starboard column.

Phillips shouted exultantly, "Hit her!"

She was on fire, no doubt of that. Ward ordered, "Starboard ten!" to turn *Boston* south and head back between the ships to her station at the tail of the convoy. Her guns were silent now but those of the starboard column were firing. As *Boston* turned Ward watched the E-boat. Her cannons had ceased firing but she was pursued by tracer, then that also stopped and there was only the trailing tongue of flame to show her position. Seconds later that, too, disappeared into the outer darkness.

Ward ordered, "Midships . . . steer that."

The R.D.F. reported, "Contact bearing oh-eight-oh! Going away. Looks like that E-boat, sir."

Huw Phillips grumbled, "Lot of bloody good that is! It's when they're coming *in* we want to know, not when they're going out!" Then, brightening: "Hey! Didn't we give that bastard a shock when we nipped through the convoy and jumped out on top of him!''

Charlie Barnwell, the yeoman, muttered, ''Not as big a shock as it gave me.''

There was a shifting of all of them on the bridge as the tension eased and Joe Krueger said, ''I'll take a walk around.'' He left the bridge.

Ward got up in his chair. His mouth was dry and he called, ''Bosun's mate!''

''Sir?''

''See if you can get some coffee up here, please.''

''Aye, aye, sir!''

The bosun's mate brought up the coffee, Ward's in his stein. It was hot and strong and he sipped it gratefully. Joe Krueger returned to the bridge, claimed a steaming mug and cradled it in his gloved hands. Ward asked, ''Any problems?''

Joe shook his head, ''All O.K., sir.'' He swallowed a mouthful of coffee. ''There was some crowding in the heads when you took us through the convoy.''

Ward shrugged. ''It probably looked a lot more dangerous than it really was.''

Krueger knew very well how dangerous it had been and mentally lifted his hat. If Ward had not got it exactly right and the tanker had charged into *Boston* the old four-stacker would have been cut in half and gone down like a stone, and most of her crew with her. Besides which the *Missouri Star* would have been holed, and would probably have sunk also. He said, ''They're getting around to liking it now. It's a hell of a story to be able to tell when you're safe ashore in some pub.'' He paused a moment, thinking about it, then: ''But if it's all the same to you, sir, I'd prefer you didn't do it again.''

Ward thought, *Not if I can bloody help it*. Aloud he said, ''I'll bear your advice in mind, Number One.''

Boston ranged out to the starboard column, inspecting, returned to her station then swung out to port to edge up along the outside of the convoy. All was quiet again. There was the faint *pinging* of the Asdic and a soft chinking and rattling as the bosun's mate collected the empty mugs. The look-out reported a light off the port bow and Mason, the navigator, took a bearing to it. That was the next buoy in the series marking the inshore limits of the swept passage.

It would be starting to get light soon; time now to look forward to that, and to breakfast. The galley stoves would be working in this moderate sea so it would be a cooked meal. There had been a forecast of bad weather but it had held off so far. This was still good E-boat weather –

There came a rumbling explosion from ahead in the convoy and a leaping tower of flame that soared and was gone in the blink of an eye.

Instantly Ward was at the voicepipe: "Full ahead both!"

"Full ahead –"

The second explosion came with a monstrous flame that climbed and did not subside but widened at its base. Krueger shouted, "The tanker!"

Boston was closing the *Missouri Star* rapidly: she was stopped and already settling, ablaze along her entire length. Ward asked himself: Torpedoed from inshore? The less likely alternatives were that an E-boat had got into the middle of the convoy or that the torpedoes had carried from outside the starboard column. With the glasses he swept the darkness ahead and inshore, then returned to the tanker. It filled his vision, the hull barely visible just beneath the flames and smoke that hid derricks and super-structure, flames that lit the sea for a quarter mile around.

At that moment the E-boat ran through the edge of the circle of light. She was moving fast and heading south, and passed between the blazing *Missouri Star* and *Boston*, a bare cable's length from the destroyer's bridge. The German's guns were firing at the coaster astern of the tanker as it swerved to pass the sinking ship. Ward saw the heads of the men on the open bridge of the boat and the gunners at the cannons. He also saw quite clearly the insignia painted on the side of the bridge abaft the bow-mounted torpedo-tubes: a skull and crossbones.

Boston's starboard Oerlikons were firing. Ward ordered, "Stop starboard! Hard astarboard!" Stopping one screw would bring *Boston* around more quickly, not in an attempt to chase the E-boat because he knew that was hopeless, but to give the Oerlikons a few more precious seconds before they lost that elusive target. He had to look out for the ships swinging out of the port column of the convoy to pass the tanker, and for the Fairmile motor-launches that would be hurrying up to look for survivors –

Krueger said savagely, "Did you see it? That was Dirty Bill! The *bastard!*"

"I saw it." The look-outs had been yelling since the boat first showed. Ward pointed at the light inshore. "He was lying the other side of the buoy." Lying in ambush, hearing the noise of gunfire from the south as the first E-boat attacked, waiting patiently for the convoy and the last hour of the night when men were tiring, their concentration strained and their reactions slowed. Watching the convoy pass, knowing that the escort destroyers would probably be at the head and the tail of it, picking his target. Casting off from the buoy and moving slowly ahead with his engines throttled back to a low rumble, closing unhurriedly to make a perfect kill.

Ward said into the voicepipe, "Midships. Half ahead both." Then he raised his head and his voice to order, "Stop the chatter!"

His command cut through the angry muttering of the others, silenced it. The Oerlikons were also silent, the E-boat gone into the darkness. Ward took *Boston* wheeling back to her station at the rear of the convoy that had now passed north of the burning tanker and the *Missouri Star* fell astern, one of the launches still circling her in the faint hope that there might be survivors.

There was a scowling quiet on the bridge, resentment against odds that were so loaded against them. Long hours of darkness . . . two destroyers guarding more than thirty ships . . . Ward thought ruefully that the oil had come three thousand miles only to be lost on this last homeward stretch. And the men? The men with the guts to sail aboard a floating bomb like the *Missouri Star*, how many of them had died? How many other ships were lost this night, off this coast or out in the Atlantic?

And how many more would be lost if *Tirpitz* came out?

He shivered in the dawn chill. The sun was just under the rim of the world and its blood-red glow washed across the heavy bellies of the clouds.

There was the glow of a false dawn behind him from the still blazing tanker.

There were only seven weeks left in which to mount CHARIOT.

The weather deteriorated rapidly that day and it was blowing a full gale when they turned up the hands of the morning watch on 9th February. Their hammocks swung in a close-packed line a foot above the tables in the dim-lit, thunderous cavern of the mess-deck and the breaking of the seas on the fo'c'sle two decks above sounded like the beating of a great drum. The deck under the hammocks was awash, a foot deep in water that surged forward and aft, starboard to port as *Boston* pitched and rolled. It was an evil-smelling gruel because the working of the ship in these heavy seas leaked fuel oil out of the tanks and into the mess-deck. Scraps of food, dropped clothing, books and caps floated in the greasy scum.

The men worked themselves out of their blankets. They had turned in 'all standing', duffel coats and oilskins wrapped around their legs for warmth. They squirmed like contortionists in the hammocks, the deck-head close above, dragging on first their coats, then their oilskins and finally their seaboots that hung from the hammock hooks.

They grabbed the rails above their heads and swung their bodies down out of the hammocks until they stood on the deck with the seawater washing around them. The bulky, misshapen, steadily cursing figures held on to tables, stanchions, anything secure as they worked their way hand-over-hand along the mess-deck.

The first man up the ladder opened the hatch, the wind howled around it and the sea fell in. It cascaded over the first man then down over the others following him. They climbed out on to the upper deck just abaft the bridge, clamped gloved hands on the life-lines and waded through the seas sweeping the deck, headed for their stations.

Ward watched them from the bridge. The light was growing and he could identify some of the muffled figures by the way they moved. There was no sun, just a dull grey light between leaden sky and mountainous seas. And all they got for it, he thought, was an extra sixpence a day 'hard lying' and the pride of being able to boast when ashore, "Small ships, me!"

He turned to face forward. The convoy ahead was being tossed about like paper boats while *Boston* rose and fell with the sickening speed of a mad lift, so that first he was looking down on the ship just ahead and then he was peering up at a wall of water towering above him. *Boston* did not always lift enough: too often the waves broke and fell on her fo'c'sle, tons of seawater hammering down with force enough to send a shudder right through her. It was weather like this that had been known to smash the bridges in these old four-stackers and kill the men on them.

The yeoman shouted against the wind, "*Empire Journey*'s signalling, sir!" Then he read out the stuttering flashes from the freighter: "Will-we-make-Forth-by-end-of-war?"

The convoy would be very late into the Firth of Forth. *Empire Journey* was a big, new ship and in spite of the weather could make twice this speed if left to herself. Conforming to the convoy's crawl at the speed of the slowest ship was irking her master. Ward shouted, "Make: 'Affirmative. Which war?'"

He saw Krueger grin, Charlie Barnwell laughing as he lifted the lamp to send the reply.

There was no moaning aboard *Boston*, but plenty of swearing. They groused too, because 'you had to grouse to keep a good job.' Except that it wasn't really their job –

nine-tenths of *Boston*'s crew were civilians who had signed on for 'hostilities only'. There were butchers, bakers, clerks – a score or more of trades and one telegraphist who spent every spare moment studying for a degree in chemistry.

Ward thought he was damned lucky to have them. He was different and things weren't the same for him. This *was* his job; he had chosen it. He supposed he was rich. So what? He grinned. He was cold, hungry, wet, unshaven and unwashed. He was captain of *Boston*, shabby, cantankerous, a bitch in bad weather – and that too was what he wanted.

It was as well he did not know that he was soon to lose her.

The watches changed and the convoy crept northward. Night fell and in the mouth of the Forth when *Boston*'s crew thought they were home the engines of one elderly coaster gave up the struggle. While the rest of the convoy plugged on *Boston* went through the laborious process of passing a tow and then hauled the cripple into port.

Boston was alongside her own berth just before midnight, her engines finally still, the ship at rest. There were no baths aboard her so Ward stood under a hot shower to ease the chill and ache out of his bones. Even this was a luxury only obtainable in port. At sea when Ward washed he did so in a basin and by halves. Strip top half, wash, dress, strip lower half . . . so that if he was called to the bridge he only had to drag on half his clothes as he ran.

He fell into his bunk. Inspection and reports showed no damage to *Boston* that rendered her unfit for sea, but they had no sailing orders so they might have all tomorrow night in, too. Sufficient unto the day, however; he turned over. Catherine Guillard . . . Quartermain . . . the red glare of the burning tanker . . . that bloody E-boat, Dirty Bill . . . CHARIOT?

He slept the sleep of exhaustion.

6

"Enemy in sight!"

Joe Krueger came to Ward in his cabin. "Wireless signal, sir."

Ward took the sheet from him and read it. ADMIRALTY TO BOSTON REPEATED C. IN C. NORE, C. IN C. PORTSMOUTH, COMMODORE HARWICH. PROCEED FORTHWITH TO HARWICH AND REPORT TO COMMODORE HARWICH TO COME UNDER DIRECT ORDERS CAPTAIN D21.

Ward said, "What the hell?"

Joe scratched his jaw thoughtfully. "Twenty-first Flotilla. I thought they were based at Sheerness, making sweeps across the Channel? Captain Pizey?"

Ward nodded. "That's right."

"So what does he want with us? He's a torpedo man, isn't he? You reckon something's up?"

"Could be, Joe. Could be." But what?

Boston joined the 21st Destroyer Flotilla at Harwich on 11th February. The six destroyers swung to their buoys off Parkstone quay in the river Orwell. When *Boston* was secured to her own buoy her motorboat was lowered and Ward crossed to the leader, *Campbell*, to meet the man who commanded the flotilla. Mark Pizey, the Captain (D), was a man of middle height who looked shorter because of his breadth of shoulder. With Ward he was cheerful, brisk and welcoming. In his cabin he said, "Take a seat! Good to see you! How's *Boston* these days?"

Ward lowered his long frame into the chair. "We think she's in pretty good shape for an old lady, sir."

"Well, there are no spring chickens in this flotilla." Not one of his ships was less than twenty years old. Pizey grinned. "Do you think *Boston* might frighten *Scharnhorst*?"

Scharnhorst! Ward blinked, cleared his throat. "Well, she frightens me, sometimes."

Pizey liked that and roared with laughter. Then: "Well—" With that word the conversation became serious and Pizey said, "We are part of Operation Fuller . . . As you must know, *Scharnhorst*, *Gneisenau* and *Prinz Eugen* are down in Brest and have been for some time. Admiralty think they are going to try to get back to Germany, making a quick dash through the Channel under cover of darkness. If they do, then we are to be really a sort of longstop. What with submarines lying off Brest, mines being laid by submarines, aircraft and minelayers, Bomber Command and Swordfish torpedo-bombers set to make strikes, M.T.B.s – well, in theory they won't get as far as us. But *if* they do, then maybe –" He let that hang for a moment, then finished, "So we'll be ready. And that's why I'm glad to see your torpedoes."

Ward took the point. He was not a torpedo specialist like Pizey, but he was well aware that in a destroyer attack with torpedoes a 'zone' was essential. The chances of scoring a hit on a single target with one or even three or four torpedoes, were minimal. By the buckshot principle, however, the more you fired, in a 'zone' to cover the target, the better were your chances of a hit. *Boston* could add three torpedoes to Pizey's 'zone'.

By that evening Ward had also taken the point about being ready. The flotilla had steam up and was ready to slip at five minutes' notice. Pizey had his six captains aboard *Campbell* for the meeting he held every evening to discuss all possible eventualities and how they should be met.

Ward contributed little, but asked several questions and learned a lot. Pizey had joked about his first appointment as a sub, how his new captain greeted him: "He glared at me and said, 'Your predecessor was a bloody fool so I got rid of him!' I thought I would be next!"

There was laughter. But Ward thought it might well be a parable, for him to hear and digest.

The forenoon of the following day, a typical February day with lowering clouds, driving rain and a rising sea, found the flotilla exercising individually off Orfordness. Ward stood on the bridge of *Boston*, balancing against her savage pitch and roll, wiped rain and blown spray from his face and said, "Beautiful morning, and doesn't she love it."

Joe Krueger answered placidly, "I guess it'll be worse before it gets better."

"Thanks for them cheering words." Ward lapsed into silence. 12th February. And now only six weeks were left in which to mount an operation against St. Nazaire. He had heard nothing from Quartermain but, of course, he would not. The admiral had already told him plainly that he would have no part in CHARIOT.

"Signal from *Campbell*." Joe Krueger's quiet voice jerked Ward back to the present and he needed to be on his toes. The other ships of the flotilla were exercising individually but *Boston* was carrying out evolutions in company with Pizey's ship, *Campbell*. For the obvious reason: since the Captain (D) wanted to find out what kind of ship and captain he'd acquired, Ward and *Boston* were now performing under his watchful eye. Any mistake would be seen – and pointed out forcefully. Pizey wanted his captains ready for anything.

The Captain (D) did not suffer fools gladly – ready for anything meant just that. It was now five minutes short of noon and throughout the morning Pizey had been dreaming up situations for *Boston* to deal with, ranging from dive-bombers through attacking E-boats to a U-boat surfacing right astern. Now Joe muttered, "What'll it be this time? Prepare to repel cavalry coming over the bow?"

Ward grinned. "With your Colonel Custer at the head of them, I expect."

But Charlie Barnwell the signal yeoman was reading the flickering light: "Exercise-ends-signal- VA Dover-Enemy-battle-cruisers-passing-Boulogne-speed-about-twenty-knots-proceed-in-execution-of-previous-orders. Follow-me."

Joe Krueger said, "Oh, boy!"

Campbell was already turning. Ward stooped over the brass mouth of the voicepipe and ordered, "Port fifteen."

The voice of C.P.O. Adams came hollowly up the pipe from the wheelhouse. "Port fifteen . . . Fifteen of port wheel on, sir."

"Meet her . . . steady." *Boston* was on a course to fall in astern of *Campbell*. "Steer that."

"Course oh-five-oh, sir."

Ward paused a moment, picturing the coxswain below. The buzz would not have reached him yet. Ward said, "We've a signal reporting German battle-cruisers in the Channel, Coxswain. We have to stop 'em." Or try to.

Silence. Then Adams said, "Bloody hell!" And Ward knew it would be.

Joe Krueger was waiting with another signal from Pizey. This one was wireless, calling in his flotilla and ordering a course for Number 53 buoy, that lay twenty miles east-south-east of Harwich.

Ward handed it back to Joe, thought about it and said, "Jerry's pulled a fast one, sailed in the night and taken his chance on this passage through the Straits in daylight."

Krueger chewed his lip. "What about the submarine ring? The M.T.B.s and bombers?"

Ward said grimly, "It sounds to me, Joe, as if we've been caught with our trousers down." But when he switched on the loudspeaker his voice, echoing through the ship, was cheerful. "We've just heard that *Scharnhorst* and *Gneisenau* are out and we're going after them. It'll make a change from Dirty Bill; they're a bigger target."

He switched off, turned away and told Joe, "I'm going to look at the plot."

In fact there had only been one submarine and the German squadron had slipped past her. From then on a succession of errors and mischances allowed them to steam northwards unobserved for several hours, until belatedly sighted by a Spitfire patrol.

Ward dropped down the ladder, ducked in at the door of

the chartroom abaft the wheelhouse. Mason the navigator stood by, curious, while he leaned over the chart, measuring, calculating times and distances. Enemy speed only twenty knots and this flotilla working up to twenty-eight. He could feel the vibration running through *Boston*'s hull.

Down in the engineroom Bailey, the Warrant Engineer, watched his gauges and muttered, "Come on, you old cow. Don't pull any of your bloody tricks now. Please!"

Ward climbed back to the bridge and Mason followed, ventured, "When d'you think we'll be in action, sir?"

Ward snapped, "How the hell would I know!"

Mason turned away, startled.

Krueger glanced sidewise at Ward, now back in his place behind the screen. Ward caught his puzzled glance and knew the reason for it. He said quietly, "We won't be going into action because if I'm right we'll miss them. Oh, I know – if we could keep this up and if their speed stayed at only the twenty knots reported, then there'd be a chance." He eyed Krueger. "But if you were in their position would you be content with twenty knots when you could make a damn sight more?"

"Like hell I would. I'd pull all the stops out." Joe stared out over the bow at *Campbell*. "What do you think he'll do?"

Ward shook his head. "I'm damn glad it's Pizey's decision and not mine."

The seven ships of the flotilla were formed in two divisions, the first led by *Campbell* with *Vivacious*, *Worcester* and *Boston*, the second by *Mackay* with *Whitshed* and *Walpole*. They hammered along at twenty-eight knots, all the old ships feeling it and *Boston* worst of all. Their course was from buoy to buoy marking the channel swept of mines. They looked for those buoys and made sure of each one because death lurked outside them. And beyond the minefield, far to starboard, *Scharnhorst* and *Gneisenau* . . .

The steward climbed to the bridge and staggered forward to the screen. He was the youngest, and smallest, rating aboard. At Christmas he had made the rounds of the ship in Ward's jacket and cap, the jacket hanging on him like an overcoat and the cap balanced on his ears. Now he wore oilskins like a tent and they ran with seawater from his passage along the deck. He brought sandwiches in a tin and Ward's stein filled with coffee. The other officers would take it in turns to eat in the wardroom but Ward would not leave the bridge. He would not lose much thereby. In this weather, the galley could not operate so there would only be sandwiches and coffee for all hands.

The yeoman said, "*Campbell*'s signalling, sir." Ward saw the flags run up to *Campbell*'s yard then break out to stream on the wind. The yeoman had his telescope to his eye and the signalman stood at his side with pad and pencil poised. Charlie Barnwell read the flags: "Alter-course-in-succession-oh-nine-oh-degrees."

Ward stood at the voicepipe, holding its brass bell-mouth in both hands. Charlie Barnwell reported, "Executive, sir!" but Ward waited. The flags were whipped down from *Campbell*'s yard. *Campbell* turned, *Vivacious* seconds later as she followed in the leader's wake, then seconds later still, *Worcester*. And *Boston* with her bigger turning circle had to alter course that little bit sooner to come around and fall in astern of *Worcester*. Ward gauged it with a practised eye. While *Worcester* was still turning he ordered, "Starboard twenty!"

"Starboard twenty, sir!"

"Twenty of starboard wheel on, sir!"

Ward watched *Boston*'s head come around, cutting inside the white track left by the destroyers ahead. "Meet her . . . Steady . . . Steer oh-nine-oh!"

". . . course oh-nine-oh degrees, sir!"

Boston settled neatly astern of *Worcester* once again and Ward thought, Distance about right . . . Might need to increase revolutions a fraction if the rest start to pull away from us. God knows what the chief'll say then – he must be sweating and swearing already. Wait and see.

Joe Krueger said, "*Jesus!* Now we know how he figures to do it!"

Ward grinned wryly at him, "As I said, I'm glad it was his decision, not mine."

Pizey was cutting the corner by taking his flotilla through the minefield. He would be in time to engage the enemy, or he could lose every ship in his command.

Ward said, "From now on anyone on the upper deck not actually engaged on duty will lie down with his head inboard." If they struck a mine that precaution might possibly save a few lives. He used the end of the towel, wound around his neck inside the bright orange duffel coat, to wipe spray from his face. *Boston* was shipping green seas over her bow as she rammed into them at nearly twenty-eight knots. The waves broke around the 4-inch gun and foamed against the bridge. Ward added, "So long as they don't drown lying on the deck."

Krueger said, "That could be." And he passed the order on over the speakers: "– with your heads inboard – where weather permits!"

Ward asked, "Pilot – how long before we clear this lot?"

"The minefield?" Mason answered, "About an hour, sir."

Ward slid up into his chair and settled comfortably. It was important that anyone on the upper deck should be able to see him there, relaxed and unworried . . .

Soon afterwards *Walpole* signalled to Pizey: "Unable-maintain-speed-bearings-running-" *Boston*'s yeoman spelt out the signal.

Krueger said, "There but for the grace of God . . . I seem to recall you said something about *if we can keep this up*."

Ward scowled at *Campbell*, watching for Pizey's reply. "From past experience of this ocean greyhound of ours I'll be surprised if –" He left it unfinished but reached out to rap on the wooden rail.

Joe followed suit: "We're coming up for a boiler-clean, I guess?"

Ward answered, "But not due. The chief did a silver

nitrate test yesterday. No sign of the dreaded condenser-
itis – yet."

The condenser distilled seawater into fresh water for the
boilers. If it failed, and frequently it did, the silver nitrate
test on a sample of the water produced would turn that
sample cloudy if the salt content was too high. Steaming for
any length of time with salt water in the boilers would clog
them.

Pizey ordered *Walpole* to return to Harwich. On *Boston*'s bridge they watched her turn out of line and set a
course for home. "And then there were six," Ward murmured.

"Leader's signalling again, sir!" That was Barnwell. "Air
alert, bearing oh-seven-oh, sir!"

Ward ordered, "Action stations! Air alert!" The klaxons
blared and he shouted above them, "Anyone see anything?"

All of them on the bridge were searching the sky with
glasses, but there was no answering report. Ward was not
surprised. Visibility was only about five miles and the
aircraft could be seven or eight miles away and still hidden
by low cloud. *Campbell* would have picked it up on her
radar. She had a special 286 P set for that purpose. Her 271
set, like *Boston*'s, would only locate surface targets.

Krueger had put on a steel helmet, was holding out
Ward's. He took it, handed his cap to the signalman. "Stow
that for me." He jammed on the helmet and settled the
strap under his jaw.

"Aircraft bearing red three-oh!" The yell came from the
port lookout. His bearing was measured anticlockwise
from the bow, and coincided roughly with the radar compass bearing. Ward saw the plane now, dropping out of the
cloud base, and grunted agreement as voices chorused,
"Junkers 88!" It was turning to fly a course parallel to the
flotilla and discreetly out of range of the guns.

Ward lowered his glasses. Krueger followed suit, recited
sardonically, "Twinkle, twinkle little goon, all your bud-

dies will follow soon." The Junkers, starting on a wide, circling patrol around the flotilla, would be sending a wireless signal to bring up others. Joe added, "I'll lay aft, sir."

He slid down the ladder to his position in action, in command of damage control, and Ward watched him make his way aft, holding on to the life lines already rigged for the promised worse weather to come. Even as it was, the sea bursting over *Boston*'s side swept her deck to cream around Krueger's sea boots.

"Leader's signalling, sir . . . Aircraft alert bearing oh-seven-five!"

Another one, the first now flying down the starboard side of the flotilla. Again they waited, swept the clouds with their glasses. The port side 20mm Oerlikons were training forward while those to starboard were following the first Junkers.

"Aircraft bearing red two-oh!" The lookout and Phillips the Guns bawled it together.

Ward's glasses twitched around and he found twin specks, held them, then lowered the glasses. Two more 88s. Would they wait for more? No. The first 88 was circling around the back of the flotilla, just appearing now far off *Boston*'s port quarter and turning in – the silhouette changed from side to front view. The other two were coming on, making for the head of the strung line of ships.

Ward lifted the telephone and spoke to Rickman, the sub commanding the guns aft. "Engage the bird coming in astern."

"Sir!"

Campbell opened fire, followed a split-second later by *Vivacious* and *Worcester*. Bursting shells made dirty smudges on a dirty sky, pocking it around the two Junkers. They kept on, still high, sometimes lost in wisps of cloud. Then *Boston*'s little armament added its clamour to the din. Ward swung round to sweep the sky astern of *Boston*, saw the first Junkers cruising in, bursts from the Oerlikons and the 12-pounder aft all around it, the bombs falling.

109

The Junkers tilted on one wing, swung away to port then climbed unscathed towards the clouds. The bombs burst in a row a cable's length from the port side. Bailey in his engine-room would hear the concussion of their bursting but not close enough to worry him. Nor Ward. He turned forward, saw spouts lifting from the sea to starboard of *Campbell* but again well clear, the other two Junkers racing away and climbing into cloud.

Phillips bellowed, "Check! Check! Check!"

The guns ceased firing, their targets gone. Instead there came the brassy tinkle as empty shell cases were kicked across the deck and over the side. The immediate danger had receded. Now they remembered the other that was with them still as the flotilla raced eastward through a charted minefield. A destroyer's skin was thin and a mine would blow the bottom out of *Boston*.

". . . Air alert! Bearing oh-eight-five!" Charlie Barnwell read the signal flying from *Campbell*'s yard.

Again the searching of the sky and the yelled sighting report. A flight of three Junkers, but 87s this time, Stukas with their inverted gulls-wing configuration. Old enemies, becoming too old for this war. But they weren't the only ones getting too old, and they were still killers. Ward glanced around the deck of *Boston* then at the destroyers ahead. *Boston* was still making twenty-eight knots. He touched wood again.

The flight of Stukas split up and came howling down on the flotilla. They were making separate attacks and one of them chose *Boston*. Ward heard the bang of the 12-pounder aft and then the rapid hammering of the Oerlikons. He spoke into the voicepipe, "Starboard twenty."

"Starboard twenty . . . Twenty of starboard wheel on, sir."

Ward straightened, shot a quick glance astern and sky-ward. The Stuka was pointing right at him, wings and nose a flat W as he saw it head-on, the bomb hanging underneath between the spatted wheels. One of the Oerlikons was quickly on to it, the 20mm tracer arcing up, flame pale in the grey light of day but marking the path clear enough to the Stuka. The pilot was not liking it, letting the bomb fall early and turning away with the underside of the aircraft showing, the 20mm shells still stitched to it like a trailing thread. And now there was smoke streaming from the Stuka – Ward swung back to the compass and the voicepipe. *Boston* was heeling to the turn. "Meet her . . . Steer one-double-oh!"

"Steer one-double-oh! . . . Course one-double-oh, sir!"

The bomb burst off the port beam, too far away to be counted even as a near miss and they had *Boston*'s turn and the Oerlikons' good shooting to thank for that. *Boston* was straightening, the Stuka sliding away, streaming smoke in a thin trail but levelling off low over the sea and heading for the rain-blurred horizon.

"Check! Check! Check!"

The guns ceased firing.

Ward ordered, "Port twenty." To bring *Boston* back into line after that swerving turn out of the path of the bomb.

"Port twenty . . . twenty of port wheel on, sir."

Krueger climbed the ladder and stepped on to the bridge. "We breathe again." The sky was clear of aircraft.

Ward ordered, "Meet her . . . Steady. Steer oh-nine-oh."

"Steer oh-nine-oh . . . Course oh-nine-oh, sir."

Boston was back in the wake of *Worcester*, the undamaged flotilla still crashing on at twenty-eight knots. Ward said, "Not yet. We'll breathe in ten minutes." They would be out of the minefield then. "But softly."

Certainly *Boston* had so far clung to the skirts of the hurrying old ladies ahead of her. But you never knew, you couldn't make a bet.

Krueger was touching wood again.

At 1430 they were clear of the minefield and Ward swung back to the chartroom but a minute later was called out again to the front of the bridge by the yeoman.

"Signal from *Campbell*, sir. Course oh-seven-five." And as the hoist was whipped down from *Campbell*'s yard: "Executive!"

Ward stooped to the voicepipe, watching *Worcester* ahead as she heeled under helm. "Port ten." He turned his head to tell Krueger, "Judging by the chart we could meet them inside the hour; it'll depend on their speed."

". . . ten of port wheel on, sir." That was Leading Seaman McCudden at the wheel now. Ward had told Adams to stand easy as soon as the minefield lay astern. He would be needed again, soon.

"Meet her. Steer oh-seven-five."

Boston's bow was again splitting *Worcester*'s wake, its foam washing around the forward 4-inch and sliding aft. Ward looked out at the humping sea, lowering clouds and shrinking horizon. They had said it would get worse. It had – and it wasn't finished yet. Visibility was poor, and worsening. That might be all to the good. If you were facing a superior force and you couldn't attack at night then maybe bad weather was the next best thing in the way of cover.

1445. Another air alert. The aircraft dropped out of the cloud cover and turned towards the flotilla. Ward switched on the speakers and said rapidly, "*Check! Check! Check!* Hold your fire. Aircraft friendly! Aircraft friendly!"

He switched off and watched the aircraft, a Hampden, coming up astern of them.

Then Charlie Barnwell the yeoman said, "Bloody *hell!*"

The Hampden had dropped a stick of bombs, some falling just astern of *Mackay* and hurling spray over her guns' crews.

Ward said, "Maybe we should have hoisted battle ensigns. Shown him the red, white and blue."

The yeoman answered, "Got 'em handy, sir."

Ward nodded, but the Hampden could not see them in this visibility and they would not hoist battle ensigns until

Pizey did. When they saw the enemy. *If* they saw the enemy. He looked at his watch. 1447.

Phillips groaned, "Oh, Jesus, *no!*"

The Hampden had circled away but now was returning. Ward tore his eyes away from it long enough to order again: "*Check! Check! Check!* Friendly aircraft!"

The bombs shrieked over *Boston* to fall very close to *Worcester*, drenched her in tall pillars of dirty seawater. This time when the Hampden turned away it kept going, followed by cursing. Phillips was breathing deeply: "One thing, sir, our lot were a bloody sight more accurate than Jerry's."

That took the heat of anger out of the moment. It was also true; the single Hampden had come closer to hitting than had any of the Germans. Ward said, "He was looking for the enemy and thought he'd found them, so we could be close. We might get more of that."

Half an hour later they were still thrashing eastward. The weather had further worsened – and the visibility. Rain had now reduced it to three miles, sometimes less. The sea was higher and the forward 4-inch – the submarine gun – was living up to its name, its crew clinging to it as the sea washed around their legs.

Ward asked Mason, "What's our position?"

"About twenty-two miles west of the Hook, sir."

That was the Hook of Holland. Ward thought that by taking the bold course and cutting across the minefield they might just have made it. Any minute now Pizey could give the order to spread out to search for the enemy . . .

Ward had never commanded in a destroyer action. He had been at Narvik but was then only responsible for his own job, his own part of the ship. Now he had a command. He had to do it with *Boston* and her company of a hundred and forty-six men.

They had to do it with him, trusting him.

All right. There was a first time for everything as the bishop said to the actress. Do things by the book but be ready to tear the book up if you had to.

113

Watch Pizey like a hawk.

The yeoman called, "Leader's signalling!" A lamp blinked rapidly from *Campbell*'s bridge and Charlie Barnwell read, "R.D.F.-contact-bearing-one-four-five-degrees-nine-miles. I-intend-to-close-the-enemy-and-attack. When-enemy-is-engaged-ships-will-attack-independently."

Ward shouted over his shoulder as he dived aft to the chart: "Acknowledge!" He found Mason already laying off the bearing and they did the sums together.

Back on the bridge Ward told the yeoman, "Keep your eyes on *Campbell*."

"Aye, aye, sir." Patiently; he and the signalman spent their entire time watching every one of the ships for a signal.

Krueger said, "The coxswain is back at the wheel, sir."

Ward nodded. "Looks as though we're all right on this course to intercept. If we turn to meet them too soon we'll lose ground. *They* must have been making about twenty-seven knots to be in the position they are now."

Pizey's flotilla was on a converging course ahead of the enemy but if he turned too soon he would be *astern* of the enemy by the time he sighted them.

He ordered no change of course.

The yeoman muttered to his signalman. "Get them battle ensigns bent on and ready."

Krueger had gone aft and Ward used the speaker system to tell his crew: "We may be in action in less than thirty minutes. The enemy is about nine miles to starboard. The ship hasn't let us down and I know you won't let her down."

He turned to Stewart, the Asdic Sub who would man the torpedo sight on the bridge. "We'll be engaging to starboard. Tell the T.G."

"Aye, aye, sir." Stewart picked up the phone to the tubes aft to tell the Torpedo Gunner.

Ward spoke to Bailey down in his engineroom. "All she's got if I call for it, Chief, even if it shakes her to bits."

"Aye, aye, sir. But she's near busting herself already."

Those last minutes started leadenly but accelerated. In what little time there was you thought of what you were about to do, *not* of your chances of survival. Ward knew the huge armaments of the capital ships, *Scharnhorst, Gneisenau* and *Prinz Eugen* and that they were well screened by big, fast destroyers. That was enough to be going on with.

"Aircraft green five-oh!"

And that too was enough to be going on with. It was a Junkers 88 and it flew across the stern of the flotilla, the guns following, not firing because the range was too great. And it flew on, out of sight.

That report was the first of many. Some were enemy, Messerschmitt 110s and Heinkel 111s but there were also Beauforts, Hampdens and Spitfires. Some of the enemy attacked the flotilla while others fired recognition signal flares – four red balls in a diamond pattern – presumably to identify themselves to ships they imagined were friendly. Some of the British aircraft did not attack the flotilla but others did. And then Phillips bawled, "Gunfire! Green seven-oh!"

Ward lifted his glasses and looked out on the bearing. There were gunflashes, also the rising fireflies of tracer directed at aircraft and no doubt now who was firing. Though they would certainly have seen it aboard *Campbell*, he bent over the compass then told the yeoman, "Make to leader! Gunfire bearing one-five-oh."

Boston's signal was acknowledged. Then another hoist ran up to *Campbell's* yard and broke out. The yeoman read, voice lifting, "*Enemy in sight . . .*"

Ward did not listen to the bearing, knew where the enemy lay, already held their flickering fire in his glasses and – He ordered, "Hoist battle ensigns!" He thought he saw . . .

There they were! At first just a long scattered line of low silhouettes: E-boats forming the portside screen and inside them the destroyers. Ward wondered if Dirty Bill was among the E-boats. The ships beyond were hidden in

115

smoke, from the flak thrown up by the screen as they put up a barrage against attacking aircraft, and from the funnels of the destroyers. Flame from the flak cut the smoke and then there was more flame beyond. From guns. Two battle cruisers suddenly showed as monstrous, insubstantial shadows in the mist then came up clear in the lenses. Not sharp, because rain and bad light furred their edges, but clear enough, big enough.

Campbell was heeling under helm, turning in on a course to attack. Pizey had said 'attack independently' but *Vivacious* and *Worcester* followed *Campbell* around and so did Ward: "Starboard twenty!" He had time, just, for one picture to be stamped into his memory, of the three destroyers ahead crashing through the big seas, attacked by enemy aircraft, battle ensigns streaming in the wind, every gun flickering with muzzle flashes and jetting smoke. Then *Boston* herself was heeling, sweeping around in a wide, threshing turn to settle into line astern of *Worcester*.

The forward 4-inch was in action now, submarine or no, engaging the screening E-boats. The ammunition number rammed the round home with his gloved fist, the breech closed, the gun fired. The trainer at his wheel was steadily traversing the gun to starboard each time it reloaded, until it fired one last round to starboard, right on the beam, then swung forward to point over the starboard bow once more as *Boston* crashed through the screen.

Ward was not using his glasses now, did not need them. The rating at the rangefinder was reading the range to the battlecruisers. Ward could not hear him above the din but Phillips was repeating them in a parade-ground bellow, "Four thousand! . . ." Two nautical miles. Water spouts straddled *Campbell*, great columns of seawater hurled into the grey sky. The flotilla was under fire from the 11-inch main armament of the battlecruisers and a hit from just one of those shells could finish any one of them. And *Boston* drove on, bow in the white wake of *Worcester*. Ward was no different now from a captain of Nelson's day. All the myriad responsibilities of command were put aside save

116

one, and that to bring his ship into action with the enemy.
That responsibility lay on every man aboard, from stokers
to coxswain. They were there to drive this worn old ship
into torpedo range of the German battlecruisers.

If they survived.

Campbell was executing a fine zig-zag, leaning first to
port, then to starboard as she swerved to evade the enemy
salvoes. *Vivacious* and *Worcester* were doing the same and
Ward copied them. "Starboard ten! . . . port ten! . . ."

Now *Boston* was straddled, as the other three ahead of
her had been. Over the racket of the Oerlikons and the
slamming of the 4-inch had come the ripping roar of
plunging salvoes and huge watery towers had lifted first
astern and then to port. Phillips intoned the shrinking
range, "Three-five-oh!"

Thirty-five hundred yards. How long was Pizey going to
hold on?

Campbell was turning to port, heeling, *Vivacious* following. Ward bent over the voicepipe, eyes on *Worcester* and
beyond her the giants shrouded in smoke from more
salvoes. He was aware of the Oerlikons ripping away aft.
Boston was still under attack from enemy aircraft.

Worcester was not turning. Hadn't she seen the signal?

Ward ordered, "Port twenty!"

"Port twenty . . . twenty of port wheel on, sir!"

Boston swung out of *Worcester*'s wake and settled instead in that of *Vivacious*, trailing a little where the gap had
been left in the line but there was no help for that. *Boston*
was giving all she had just to keep station. Even with the
last ounce he had warned he might demand from Bailey,
she could not haul up closer on the other two.

A salvo howled in to burst astern and Ward turned
quickly to see the white-topped towers collapsing, falling.
He looked out over the beam to the battlecruisers, then
forward to see the torpedoes leap from *Campbell* and an
instant later from *Vivacious*. Stewart, at the torpedo sight,
shouted, "Torpedoes fired!"

They plunged into the sea from the triple tubes on

117

Boston's deck. Now Pizey's flotilla had to get out – if they could. Now that the job was done and the torpedo 'zone' no longer needed, the formation was breaking up. Proceeding independently the ships would offer three separate, smaller targets rather than one big one. *Campbell* had turned north-east and *Vivacious* north-west. Ward held *Boston* on course, splitting the angle between them. The three ships fanned out, the distances between them rapidly widening. Ward looked astern over the starboard quarter and caught a glimpse, no more, of the enemy squadron before a rain squall blotted them out.

Had the torpedoes scored a hit? He didn't know.

The weather had gone from bad to worse since they started the attack and *Boston* was shipping green seas both forward and aft. He had seen nothing of *Mackay* and *Whitshed* for ten minutes or more. He looked for *Vivacious*, then *Campbell*, but they, too, had disappeared into the mist and rain. He asked, "Anyone see anything of the others?"

"No, sir," repeated around the bridge. *Boston* plunged on alone over an empty, gale-swept sea.

He spoke into the voicepipe, "Revolutions for twenty knots."

"Twenty knots. Revolutions for twenty knots passed, sir."

There was no sense in shaking the old girl to pieces rushing blindly northward. *Boston*'s speed fell away and at twenty knots she rode a little easier – which in her case meant not quite so badly. She still shook throughout her frame, rolled and pitched and shipped the big seas inboard, but at least she wasn't battering herself to death.

The port look-out bawled, "Gunfire red nine-oh!"

Ward swung left, trained his glasses to port and picked up the long yellow flashes in the murk, made out a ship there.

"Port twenty!"

Boston turned and headed towards the firing – that ceased. The 4-inch was trained out over the bow, waiting the order to load but it was not given. The ship was *Campbell*.

Ward ordered, "Make: 'Where is the enemy?'"

The yeoman read the answer, the light flickering from *Campbell*'s bridge: "Have lost contact with enemy destroyers course north-east. Follow me course two-seven-oh."

The two British destroyers headed westward and a few minutes later were joined by *Vivacious*. Five minutes after that they came on *Worcester*, stopped and on fire, life rafts and men in the sea alongside. The other three destroyers stopped to pick up survivors.

Later *Worcester* got under way but was capable of only eight knots. Meanwhile a signal from the C.-in-C. Nore ordered the other destroyers to return to Harwich. *Mackay* and *Whitshed* had now rejoined and the five steamed for home at twenty knots.

They passed the Landguard fort at the mouth of the harbour half an hour before midnight, refuelled, took on ammunition and torpedoes and landed wounded. *Boston* had no wounded and Joe Krueger shook his head in wonder. "She's hardly got a scratch on her that we didn't start with, apart from the weather damage. Boy! Were we lucky! Shelled by battlecruisers and bombed by two air forces, theirs and ours."

Ward sucked at coffee, hot and strong, the stein held in both hands: "Understandable."

Krueger nodded. The bad weather, mist, and the mêlée that the battle had become, all made for confusion. "The fog of war, all right. And I've never seen so many airplanes! M.E. 109s and 110s, Junkers 88s, Wimpys, Whirlwinds – and the rest. I'm damn' sure we fired on a couple of friendlies. Don't think we hit 'em though, thank God."

"How is it below?"

Krueger shrugged. "Standard bad weather state. We had sea washing a foot deep in the mess-decks before we pumped her out."

"Tell the galley I want a hot meal for every man before we sail."

"I got the cooks started on that, soon as she was stable enough to light the stoves. It won't be exactly *cordon bleu* but the guys will eat."

In the galley the cooks cursed: "Dried eggs, dried milk – the only thing they can't dry out is this old cow!"

But *Boston*'s crew ate – just.

The flotilla sailed at 0330 and at 0645 were on patrol again off the Hook of Holland. It was believed, or hoped, that one of the three battlecruisers had been damaged and was still limping home. Daylight air reconnaissance dashed that hope and at 0943 the flotilla was ordered back to Harwich.

On *Boston*'s bridge Mason asked, "What's the date?"

Krueger answered, "February thirteen."

Mason said lugubriously, "Unlucky for some."

Ward thought, Unlucky for us. *Scharnhorst, Gneisenau* and *Prinz Eugen* had escaped. The enormity of it struck him like a slap in the face. An enemy fleet had steamed through the Channel in broad daylight.

His first reaction was anger and the black rage burned inside him but he shut his mouth on it. There was silence on the bridge. After the work and the meal as the ship lay at Harwich, there had been a brief release of tension, relief at having survived. Now that was gone and there was only gloom, anticlimax. Ward had to control his anger because his men deserved better than that.

He said, "Pass the word for the coxswain." And when Adams came to the bridge Ward told him, "My congratulations and thanks, Coxswain. You did a terrific job. I'll be saying the same to the Chief and everybody else aboard but I wanted you to know now."

"Thank you, sir." That came flat.

"You don't look too happy."

"I'm choked because the bastards got away with it, sir."

"So am I. But it wasn't your fault or Pizey's or any other

of the men who tried their damnedest. You can pass *that* word *now*! I'm bloody proud of the lot of you!"

He succeeded in raising their spirits but wished he could raise his own.

When *Boston* picked up her buoy a boat was waiting to come alongside. Curiously, it brought Quartermain.

Ward took the wiry little admiral to his cabin under the bridge. This time the steward had contrived to unlash the armchair from its bad weather station against the settee. He had also set out a bottle of gin. Ward offered Quartermain the chair and mixed him a pink gin, took one for himself and sat down on the settee. He lifted the glass: "The sun's over the yard-arm and I think we've earned this one. Cheers, sir!"

"Cheers!" Quartermain sipped at the gin, ran it around his mouth, swallowed. He watched Ward empty his glass and set it down, sigh and rub a hand over the stubble on his chin. Quartermain asked, "How d'ye feel?" Knowing very well, having been over the course himself and more than once.

Ward shrugged. "Glad to be alive. Sorry we didn't get one."

"Ready to go again?"

"Any time. All we need is topping up with fuel."

Quartermain nodded, "Unfortunately, the chance has gone."

Ward said, "We've only seen or heard bits of this operation and you probably know a lot more, sir." He finished bitterly, "From our point of view it looks like an almighty cock-up."

Quartermain swallowed the rest of his gin, shook his head at the offer of another, stood up and began to prowl restlessly about the cabin. "It's not my area, but I suppose I know a bit more. There'll be an enquiry, of course. You did all that was possible and Pizey did bloody well. So did the Swordfish torpedo bombers and a lot of people here and there. I think the enquiry will show up a succession of

121

misunderstandings and some bad luck. But Jerry will be crowing because he's sailed a fleet through the Channel in broad daylight. By God! but he'll make some capital out of *that*! I'm told that when the First Lord informed the P.M. they'd got away with it, Churchill said just one word: 'Why?' "

Ward said, "Why they got away with it? Or was he asking their reason? Was he asking why they've gone north?"

Quartermain halted in his pacing. "What do you think?"

"It could be just that the Air Force was making it too hot for them in Brest. Or Hitler wants to stiffen his naval defences in the north and the Baltic. Or perhaps he intends *Scharnhorst*, *Gneisenau* and *Prinz Eugen* to join up with *Tirpitz*. If that lot sets out raiding –" Ward did not finish, did not need to. The damage that could be wrought by such a force set loose in the Atlantic to attack the big, slow, vulnerable convoys, would be enormous. "It's the same threat we've talked of before, only now it's worse. They must still expect to have to fight a major action, sooner or later, and then they might well need a dock outside Germany that could take a ship of their size. And that brings us back to St. Nazaire."

Quartermain did not blink, his face remained expressionless.

Ward asked, "What do *you* think, sir?"

"I think – your last suggestion could be right. It's a possibility we can't ignore."

"So what about CHARIOT, sir?"

"Going forward, but we still need to know about the dock-gates. And we still need a ship for it."

"A *ship*?" Ward stared. "Surely to God, sir, and with all due respect, the Navy can find one ship!"

"Not so easy. We need every one, particularly of this kind. The plan demands a destroyer and the Admiralty is proving very reluctant to part."

Ward was reminded that Combined Operations possessed very little; such ships as they needed for operations they had to beg or borrow. He stood up in his turn and prowled over to a scuttle, peered out at what little he could see of *Boston*. Part of his mind immediately turned to the work he wanted done before she went to sea again.

Quartermain guessed at the train of Ward's thought. *Boston* was the young man's first destroyer command and he was proud of her. The admiral remembered that feeling, too, though he had experienced it over twenty years ago. He thought that Ward was less serious, less impatient and intense than he himself had been – but probably none the worse for that. Or was he judging himself too harshly? He liked this young man. He said drily, "Suppose they picked your ship, just took it away?"

Ward swung around, startled, then grinned. "You had me worried for a moment, sir, but I don't think this old girl would be up to a job like that."

Quartermain shot him a sharp glance, suspicious. How much did Ward know or guess? "Like what?"

"Fighting her way into a defended port, landing troops, giving them covering fire and fetching them out again."

Quartermain relaxed. Ward did not know how they planned to use the destroyer. "You're right about that . . ." He lifted his cap from the table.

Ward asked, "Is that all you came to see me about, sir?"

"No. I've had word of a friend of yours and she's well." That was over a week ago, just a curt report that the station, Geneviève, was still operating. It was three weeks since Quartermain had sent a wireless signal to the circuit in Paris asking them to obtain Peyraud's address from the hotel near the Champs Elysées. A day later they reported the hotel had been requisitioned by the Germans as an office and swarmed with them. So now everything depended on Geneviève, with her contacts at the St. Nazaire dockyard office.

Ward thought, Catherine. He asked, "She's – well? Can you tell me any more, sir?"

"Her safety depends on silence." Quartermain hesitated, then told what he could for Ward's comfort. "She has the advantage of running a very small team. The bigger the team the greater the chance of one of them being detected. The disadvantage of a small team, of course, is that there are fewer people to do the work." He finished definitely, "That's all I can tell you."

He was relying on Geneviève to locate Peyraud and expected to hear from her very soon because she knew the urgency. Good news or bad? Quartermain could only hope.

Ward said quietly, "Thank you for that much. I'm glad she's . . . all right."

Quartermain turned to the door. "I have to go."

As his boat took him ashore he looked back at *Boston*, filthy from foul weather and gunsmoke, a hardworked, worn, old ship. But ready to go again. He picked out Ward's tall figure on her deck. If the news from France was good then he could have a task for him. Until this evening he hadn't been certain of the man, but now he was. That, really, was why he'd come: he'd needed to make up his mind.

His thoughts returned to the events of the last twenty-four hours – and the past months, a succession of defeats and losses and now they needed a victory. CHARIOT had to go through – and succeed.

But it was a very risky, very dangerous business.

7

A Dirty Game

The Germans in St. Nazaire were celebrating the escape of the battlecruisers through the Channel and there were many impromptu parties, one of them at the *Kommandatur*. Engel knew of it though he was not invited. He would not have gone, anyway. But he celebrated, sitting in his office across the basin from the U-boat pens, his chair pushed back and booted feet up on the desk. Although it was still early in the afternoon one glass of cognac was already warming his belly, another stood on the desk, and he watched it, savouring it in anticipation. The typed orders lying on the desk were also good news though they left him only six weeks, till the end of March, to break the Resistance in this area. He had a couple of ideas . . .

Pianka hunched over the typewriter, punching at it with two thick fingers as he copied the report Engel had scrawled in pencil on a pad of message-forms. Pianka, too, was celebrating with cognac, a glass of it balanced dangerously close to the vibrating carriage of the typewriter. He paused to straighten his bent back, lifted the glass and toasted: "The Navy!" He tossed back the cognac and scowled at Engel. "That was a hell of a thing they pulled off, you know? They really rubbed Churchill's nose in it!"

Engel said, "That's right. I'm proud of them." He was. This was a good day.

Pianka turned back to punching the typewriter and grumbled, "Your writing is bloody awful! Every day it gets worse! Takes me all my time to read it! *Hell!*" He swore as he hammered out his mistake and started the word again. Engel took no notice, nor did he move when a car pulled up outside except to take his new orders from the desk and button them in the pocket of his tunic. Pianka shoved back his chair, listened to the familiar tick-over of the big

Mercedes and made his habitual announcement, "It's that shit, Grünwald."

Engel did not answer. A moment later Grünwald entered, wearing his expensive dark grey suit with a long leather trenchcoat thrown over his shoulders like a cape. He said, "I got a message that you wanted to discuss something and I happened to be passing, so –?" Making the point that he had not come here at Engel's bidding.

Engel thought. You're trying to save your precious dignity but Pianka has the name for you. You'd lick my boots if it would take you another rung up the ladder. When I look at you and remember the men I left in Russia I could vomit.

Grünwald muttered, "What the hell's the matter?" Engel's cold glare had unnerved him. He smiled sourly. "Cheer up, Hauptmann. This is a great day!"

It was no longer a great day, not even a good one. Engel decided to get things over, to play his greedy little fish and land it. He said, "Admiral Dönitz will come here soon. We don't know when, but he will come to inspect the U-boat pens and see how the building of the new ones progresses."

Grünwald shrugged his shoulders inside the leather coat. "So? This is known."

Engel said, "Usually he spends the night at the Château Beauregard outside the town but I think it would be a generous gesture on our part, in view of the Navy's triumph today, if we were seen to make a gift to the admiral of a suite here, where he could stay and look out over the basin to his U-boats in their pens."

Grünwald watched him suspiciously. "You say 'we'. How am I involved?"

"The suite would be on the floor above this. Afterwards that floor and the one above it would be yours."

There was a gleam in Grünwald's eyes but he was still suspicious. "What do you want in return?"

Engel lowered his boots to the floor and limped across to the window, stood looking out at the Mercedes and the handsome Aryan features of Horstmann behind the wheel. Engel said, "I don't like traitors but they have their uses. I understand that there are disaffected Englishmen who can be infiltrated into the prison camps as captured RAF flyers and that they then supply the guards with information on the prisoners' escape plans."

Grünwald nodded. "That is so."

Engel went on, "We know that some RAF men who are shot down are smuggled out of this country by the French Resistance before we get to them. The French have a network for this purpose. We know there is a Resistance organisation here in St. Nazaire but so far we haven't been able to find it. Therefore I want you to go to your masters and borrow one of these traitors to pass himself off as a British airman needing help."

Grünwald said softly, "I see! And we will work together on the operation?"

Engel thought, As long as it suits you. He said, "Of course. Well, is it a deal?"

Grünwald hesitated. "This suite for the admiral, it would be a gift from us both?"

"Naturally."

The Gestapo officer frowned. "There is the question of his safety when he spends the night here. There is possible danger from the Resistance; remember Feldkommandant Holtz?"

Holtz had been assassinated in Nantes, just up-river from St. Nazaire, in November. French hostages were shot in reprisal. Engel had not been involved in that and was glad. He nodded. "I have not forgotten. And I don't think you need have fears for the admiral." He explained what he had in mind.

Grünwald smiled unpleasantly. "Very well. For once we are in agreement; it is a good plan!"

Engel watched from the window as the still smiling Grünwald strode out to the Mercedes and Horstmann drove him away, doubtless to the *Kommandatur* and the free drinks. Engel turned and limped back to his desk, lifted his glass and took a long, gulping swallow, coughed and sighed.

Pianka, still hunched over the typewriter, said, "I don't trust that bastard."

"Neither do I." Engel refilled his glass. "Is your lady friend, what's her name – the housekeeper at Grün-wald's – still keeping her eyes and ears open?"

Pianka looked at him sideways. "Fat Anna is not my friend. She and Grünwald are two of a kind; she reports and I pay her. That stud Horstmann is round there every chance he can get and Anna says the slut is waiting for him like a bitch in heat. It's all typed, dates, times, details, and locked in my drawer."

Engel sighed again. Intelligence could be a dirty game sometimes, but when you played it with people like Grün-wald it stank to high heaven. He was glad, however, that he had a card up his sleeve: the day would almost certainly come when he'd need it.

Engel left his office in the early darkness of that winter day and Pianka waited for him in the Citroën with its shaded headlights glowing dim because of the black-out. A cold wind blew in off the estuary, the rain slanting on it. In the buoy yard across the road the buoys brought in for maintenance glistened blackly. As Engel reached the car a girl came walking quickly along the road that ran by the side of the basin and past the office of the Abwehr, heading towards the bridge and the town. She wore a raincoat belted at the waist, the collar turned up and a scarf covering her hair. As she came up Engel recognised her despite the gloom and lifted a hand to his cap in salute: "Mam'selle Guillard." She nodded, not looking at him and did not break her stride. He said, "A moment, please."

Catherine Guillard halted. "A moment only, if you please. It is raining."

"Yes. In Intelligence we know everything." The joke did not amuse her. She watched him coldly. He shrugged. "Perhaps I could give you a lift. Because of the rain."

"No, thank you. I prefer the rain."

"You do not like us Germans."

"You have no business here."

Engel could understand her reaction. Nevertheless – "I mention your dislike because in the course of your duties you show it." One of the girl's duties was to interpret when the dockyard dealt with the Germans: she spoke their language well.

"I am always correct." Her eyes held his, unflinching.

"Correct, yes, but formal, distant, cold. And that could bring you trouble from . . . certain people."

"Is that a warning? A threat?"

"A warning, not a threat. I do not speak of myself. There are others." Like Grünwald. Engel's leg was hurting, and his tone hardened, "I think you are entitled to your opinions but it is unwise for you to make them so obvious. I am not suggesting warmth, just neutrality. For your own sake."

"Very well, I will try." The girl turned away, then back: "Thank you." She turned again and went walking on along the side of the basin.

Engel climbed into the car. Pianka let in the clutch and said, "A tough nut, that one." Then, as they passed the girl walking quickly through the rain, the coat flattened against her, he added, "Nice legs, though."

"You're a lecherous old bastard," Engel told him and Pianka grinned. Engel knew his old friend was nothing of the sort. He rubbed his stiff leg and wished the summer would soon come so that this aching would ease a little. He liked the girl. That had not stopped him from vetting her because of her work in the dockyard office and he had kept her under surveillance a couple of times when he had the men to spare. Her life was an open book: no family in St. Nazaire, no lover, just a few friends or acquaintances. She bought on the black market occasionally, but who didn't? He liked her because there was a freshness, directness about her, honesty. And after talking to Grünwald . . . He growled at Pianka, "Hurry it up! I need a drink!"

129

Catherine watched the car until it disappeared into the darkness. She was breathing quickly and not because of walking into the wind and the rain. She was afraid of Engel. Not as she was afraid of Grünwald; that was a shuddering inside, a gut-churning fear of his hands on her body. Engel she feared because he was brave and clever. She knew she had to be very careful with him.

That Friday evening, as every evening, Catherine went to a café near her apartment in the Rue de Saille. It was her habit to take a glass of wine and talk with the proprietress, an old friend, for an hour or so. It was almost time for her to leave when Henri entered. He had not showed up for several days and she'd been very worried. Not only for him: time was slipping by and she knew the urgency of the matter.

He carried an old shopping bag with food in it that he had bought while visiting farms, servicing their machinery: butter, cheese and eggs. He sold these to the patrons of the café; this was a regular business. He looked very tired tonight but he grinned when he came to sell some eggs to Catherine Guillard.

He had found Peyraud. That was all he told her then – that and the place name: Le Havre.

But the following day, Saturday, when they met on the train to Le Havre, he told her the whole story, the clacking of the wheels giving them privacy.

Catherine, in the dockyard office, had obtained the address of the engineers who built the dock. Their office was in northern France and Henri went there. He found the Germans in control, and he had to wait some days before he could be sure of a safe man to contact. When he did take the plunge he had luck. The man he approached, very casually, in a bar at the end of the day's work, proved to be a senior clerk. When Henri asked about Peyraud the man looked about him nervously. "You want M'sieur Peyraud?"

"That's right. It is a personal matter."

"The office has no papers for M'sieur Peyraud, the Germans took them."

"The Germans! Why?"

"He refused to work for them and resigned." The clerk glanced around again to make sure they were not overheard. "You understand, I agree with him, I do not want to work for the Germans but I have a wife and children. You are Resistance?"

Henri shook his head, "I just want to talk to Peyraud."

The clerk smiled crookedly, "You are wise, trust no one. I will find out what I can. Tomorrow at this time – here?"

The next evening, he gave Henri the name of a village to the north of Le Havre. It was not Peyraud's address but it was known in the office that he had bought a house in that vicinity.

Henri drove there in the rattling old Renault and toured the area for days, ostensibly looking for work. Because of his business at St. Nazaire he had a pass for the coastal zone. It was a country of forests, secluded hamlets and lonely, hidden houses. The people were suspicious of a stranger asking questions.

Now Henri's shoulder nudged Catherine as the train rocked and he grinned at her. "I thought I was going to spend the rest of the war up there, but in the end I found the place. It's nearly twenty kilometres from the village they told me about, there aren't many people up there and the old man only bought the house in the summer of 1939 as a place to retire. He hadn't lived there much because most of the time he was away working on some harbour or dock, so only a few of the locals knew of him. He came back in September 1940 and in March of '41 the Germans moved into the house. He's a prisoner there. I got all this from the people we're going to. Jean Boilet runs the sawmill. Nobody lives near them and they're safe."

Catherine glanced at him. "They know?"

"Just what we are. Not where we're from or what we're doing."

The less people knew the less they could tell . . .

131

Catherine Guillard woke with the dawn in the Boilets' house that Sunday morning and went down to the big kitchen where Henri had spent the night. The household was already stirring, and they drank bitter *ersatz* coffee and ate crusty bread with Jean the woodcutter and Madame, his wife. Woodcutter was an old-fashioned term. Jean owned the sawmill built next to the house, felled trees from the forest, then cut them into timber.

Afterwards Catherine and Henri climbed the stairs to the room at the top of the house and settled down to work. The room was small and bare save for two chairs. They sat side by side and some three feet back from the open window so the sun would not reflect from the lens of the telescope and give them away to a German patrol. It was a bright sun in a hard, blue winter's sky. It gave no heat but nor did it breed mist or heat-shimmer; the air was crystal clear. They had brought the telescope with them – it opened out to a length of a third of a metre, but closed to a cylinder only four inches long and thus was easily concealed – and they took turns with it at the open window.

They looked out over a shallow valley, thickly wooded with here and there the silver flash of sunlight on a stream that wandered down the floor of the valley to reach the sea through a gap in the cliffs a mile away. A bit more than a mile away, across the valley and standing in the open near the edge of the cliffs, was a sandbagged emplacement above which lifted a metal dish of some sort – it was hard to determine what it was. The ground dropped away from the emplacement down to a big house, surrounded by a wall, that stood in a clearing not far above the stream. A road ran up from the south along the cliff tops, descended into the valley, crossed the stream by a hump-backed stone bridge and ended at the gate leading to the house. There was only one other clearing and that lay a quarter mile inland of the house and on the same side of the stream. Because it was a fine day Jean had taken his three cows across the stream to graze there on the last of the winter's grass.

Henri held a map spread on his knees while Catherine

A Dirty Game

made notes on a pad. Henri muttered, "This map's a good twenty years old but nothing's changed – except that thing on the cliff-top." He lifted the telescope. "Jean says there is a machine-gun post on this side of the gully, overlooking the beach but I can't see it. Maybe we can get him to pin-point it for us."

He slowly traversed the telescope. "Just the one sentry on the gate that I can see. And one on the cliff-top by that thing, whatever it is." He shifted the telescope from one sentry to the other. They wore soft field-caps, not helmets, and the blue-grey uniforms of the Luftwaffe. The one on the cliff-top strolled slowly, rifle slung over his shoulder. The other, at the gate in the wall where the drive led up to the house, leaned with his back against a pillar, rifle propped against his leg and its butt on the ground. It was too far for Henri to make out expressions, but: "They look bored stiff."

Catherine murmured, writing neatly, carefully: "Jean estimates between forty and fifty men and he says at night there are two sentries patrolling the house, one inside the wall and another outside it. He has seen their torches. Also there is wire about ten metres outside the wall and all around. And more wire across the gully, just above the beach. We must check."

Henri caught his breath. "There he is!" He passed the telescope quickly and as Catherine snatched it: "He's just come out of the side door, walking around to the front."

The images blurred as Catherine swept with the telescope, seeking, then hesitated and were still. The old man was tall, wrapped in an overcoat that hung below his knees. He wore a beret and his hands were gloved. Accompanied by a sentry who had come with him from the house, he walked steadily but not slowly down the side of the house and turned right to cross in front of it. At both sides of the house evergreen trees grew inside the wall so the wall itself was barely visible. When he reached the line of trees on the seaward side of the house he turned left and walked down

133

along them, turned left again to cross in front of the gate with its sentry, then finally left again up to the house.

He walked around that square, possibly forty metres each side, again and again. At first he was followed by his guard, but after two or three circuits the guard stopped by the sentry at the gate and just watched the man walking.

Henri said, "He moves pretty well for his age."

But the old man had slowed to a weary trudge by the end of thirty minutes. He stopped and looked back at the two soldiers by the gate and one of them lounged over to him. Together they walked slowly up the side of the house and entered at a door there.

Henri had the telescope and he muttered, "He's back in the same room; I saw him then."

"Above the side door? Where the Boilets always see him at the window?"

"That's right."

"According to Madame Boilet there is only that one room above the kitchen." Jean's wife had worked in the house before the Germans came. "Look." Catherine turned the pages of her pad to the sketch she had drawn to Madame's instructions. Henri lowered the telescope, peered at the plan and nodded, then set the telescope to his eye again.

They watched through the day but in the early winter evening Jean went to fetch his cows and Catherine walked with him. Henri had wanted to go in her place but she refused: "I want to see for myself."

Catherine and Jean walked slowly down through the forest to the stream and crossed the wooden bridge, built there by his grandfather. They came to the clearing and the cows moved slowly, curiously, to meet them. Jean stayed with them but Catherine paced quickly, counting, around the field, then wandered down the middle of it, looking at its surface. She stopped at the end nearest to the old man's house, hidden from her now by a quarter mile of forest, and looked back up the slope to where Jean waited with the cows. The wind blew cold in her face; she checked its direction with a long strand of cotton and nodded her satisfaction.

It was dusk when she returned to the house, and time she and Henri left for St. Nazaire. Jean had a flat-bed lorry he used for delivering timber. It was loaded now and he would take them to the nearest railway station. He said, "It is in order because my customer needs the wood at once and I cannot deliver tomorrow, so it must be today." That was in case they were questioned when passing out of the coastal area. Henri had his official pass while Catherine was his girlfriend, out for a day in the country.

As the lorry hammered along Catherine asked, "We will return on Saturday. That is possible?"

"It is possible." Jean asked no questions.

And in the clattering train, before they came to Nantes and parted to make their separate ways back to St. Nazaire, Catherine told Henri, "We must ask London for a pick-up because there are plans and maps, far too much information to send by wireless. Ask for it as soon as possible – by Lysander or off the beach, we'll set it up for either."

Henri scratched his head. "What's so important about that place, about that man?"

"I don't know." Nor did she try to guess.

During that week they made their transmissions and were answered, London asked questions and gave instructions. On Tuesday reception was bad and Henri received little, on Wednesday nothing at all. But on Friday London confirmed the time and place of the pick-up.

On Sunday Henri travelled north for fifty kilometres to a small cove on a lonely stretch of coast. The night was good and dark, the sky overcast with a drizzling rain falling. Henri huddled at the foot of the cliffs and stared across the short stretch of beach at the sea that washed it. There was little surf and that also was good: a dark night and a quiet sea.

He checked his watch. When it showed the arranged time

he flashed the torch out to sea, waited one minute then sent the signal again. He waited another minute, growing anxious now, lifted the torch again, then paused. There was something . . . It took shape as a dinghy carrying two men, and when Henri saw the splash of oars he rose, trotted down to the sea, and waded in. The man at the oars stopped rowing and the little boat bobbed on towards Henri, the way coming off it. He reached out with one hand to fend it off, with the other held out a slim package the size of a paperback book. The man in the stern of the dinghy grabbed the package, Henri pushed the dinghy away and the man with the oars turned it, pulled out to sea. When Henri regained the beach and glanced over his shoulder the dinghy had gone into the night, silently back to the motor gunboat from which it came.

The next morning, as Catherine left the Rue de Saille to walk to her work, she passed Henri and he nodded, "B'jour!" So she knew the pick-up had gone to plan.

Quartermain knew it before the day was out because the package was in his hands. He studied its contents at his desk in Richmond Terrace for some thirty minutes and then made his decision. He would risk a desperate gamble. He drafted a signal to 'Geneviève' and it was sent that night at the scheduled time when the pianist in the field would be listening in.

Henri received it. He sat on the bed in his apartment, the suitcase open beside him, the wireless aerial strung around the room. Reception was good and he only had to ask for one block of figures to be repeated. He decoded the signal, sent an acknowledgment, and walked round to the café where Catherine Guillard went each evening. He carried the old shopping bag and sold its contents of cheese and eggs as usual. Then he sat at a table alone and read his newspaper. As Catherine passed on her way out she paused by him and they made casual conversation. Then Henri said quietly, "It came."

Catherine stared at him. So soon? He said, "One night starting with the twenty-seventh. The BBC will send a

136

message on the night they will come. 'François mend the nets.' They want a guide and I said I'd do it."

Catherine said, "We will talk again." She left the café, went to the church and prayed. Usually these days she prayed for the safety of a man she loved but hardly knew, but tonight she prayed for the soldiers her information might bring to their deaths.

From where he lay in the big bed Patrick could see the branches of the trees waving outside the open window, and could hear their rustling, and the rain, and the quiet creaks and groans of the house in the night. It was a tall old house, in a shabby Glasgow street, and Sarah's flat was at the top of it. She had said, "Just like your authentic artist's garret."

The fire had been banked with coaldust so that it would stay in until morning but that time was close now. A glow showed where an ember burned through the dust and the fire spat softly as rain fell down the chimney. He heard a check and change in her breathing and knew she was awake.

"Patrick?"

"Mmm?"

"Are you going away?"

"Don't know." But he had a strong suspicion. Nobody else in the troop seemed to share it, nobody knew anything but he had a feeling –

"Is that why you sent the paintings away?"

"Not really . . ." There'd been a dozen paintings, unframed, and some sketches. They had followed him around from barrack to billet for the past year and recently he'd kept them here in Sarah's flat. "I just thought I'd accumulated enough. Besides, this dealer in London keeps pestering me, and he pays good money, too. At least, he did for the other one I sent him."

That was true as far as it went. But Sarah was right – he had also sent them to London because of this feeling that an operation was in the wind. The money the dealer had sent him before he spent on visiting Sarah and on Sarah herself, on paint, brushes, canvasses, all of them hard to find after two years of war and bloody expensive. His mother no longer sent him cheques because he returned them. He lived on his pay like the rest of his troop, and what his paintings brought. He could paint: he knew that now. Before the war he hadn't been sure . . . When you're surrounded from the day you're born by artists of one kind or another it's easy to assume you're an artist too, when really you're just a talker. So he'd pretended he wanted to go to Paris to learn to paint when in fact all he wanted was to get away to see if he *could*. He had no doubts now. He was an artist. He had also been trained to kill a man with a knife or his bare hands but he got more money for the painting.

Sarah said her husband in London sent money to her and she returned it because she wanted nothing from him, was finished with him. She asked for nothing from Patrick, either. He thought she was fond of him as he was of her. He didn't know about love, that was something else again and pointless anyway, because –

Sarah said, "You'll go away, though. Some time. Probably soon."

"Probably."

A week ago, just after *Scharnhorst* and *Gneisenau* slipped through the Channel the spry little admiral had come up to Ayr and Madden's lot left for Salisbury Plain that same night – for 'specialised training'. Patrick wondered what the hell they were up to. He wished it could have been his lot the admiral had asked for. *Boston*, he knew, had been with the destroyers that attacked the battlecruisers. The ten-man section of a corporal's command was enough for him to worry about, but cousin Jack captained a ship with 150 men aboard and drove her at *Scharnhorst*. And that *was* responsibility to make you shudder . . .

Sarah slid over on top of him, propped on her elbows her breasts lightly brushing his chest. "We'd better make the most of what time we've got, then."

After the running battle in the Channel *Boston* was detached from Pizey's flotilla and returned to escorting the east coast convoys with *Arundel*, who signalled: "Welcome home. How is your steering now?"

That harked back to the jammed steering-engine of three weeks before and *Boston* steaming in circles. Ward answered, "Good in a roundabout way. We love you, too."

So they went back to work.

The weather was not so bad, the ship not quite so wet. They were twice attacked by E-boats but if Dirty Bill was one of them he was not identified and they did not lose a ship. But the memory of the blazing tanker lingered.

A signalman and a cook received letters telling them their girls had found another: the signalman was sunk in gloom but the cook mightily relieved. The joint wake and thanksgiving was held in a pub in Sheerness and became riotous but the shore patrol was not called. And when cook and signalman came back to the ship singing, the coxswain met them at the side, shut them up, dressed them down and sent them peaceably to their hammocks.

On the evening of Wednesday, 25th February, Ward brought his ship into Sheerness for a boiler-clean and six days' leave for, almost, all hands. He had not thought of CHARIOT or Quartermain for some days but the admiral had not forgotten him. Five minutes after *Boston* berthed the telegram was brought aboard.

8

". . . it should be quite a party."

Ward wondered what the hell it was all about this time. As the train puffed and sighed into Salisbury Station he looked at his watch and saw it read ten past one. Only ten minutes late; that wasn't bad at all for a wartime train. The telegram from Quartermain had been uninformative, to say the least. It had read: Report Salisbury 26 February ETA Station 1300.

He had told no one, remembering Quartermain's instruction, "Keep your trap shut!" Joe Krueger and the others thought he was headed for his home in the north. As he should have been, instead of down here to look at files or some damn thing for Quartermain's benefit. It had been a waste of time in Richmond Terrace and he was willing to bet it would be a –

He was out on the platform and the Leading Wren was saluting him. He returned the salute, recognising her. Dark hair and eyes, nice legs, nice figure, nice smile: Quartermain's popsy. He said, "Has he sent you to stop me getting back on the train?"

The smile widened at that and the girl said, "Admiral Quartermain sent his car to fetch you, sir."

"Same thing."

Ward walked with her out of the station and asked, "Would you tell me your name? So I don't have to call you Leading Wren Thingummy?"

"Jenny Melville."

"How do you like working for the admiral, Jenny Melville?"

"Very much. I want to stay with him."

"Good job?"

"Not always." Sometimes it's bloody, she thought. Sometimes you learn more than you want to.

140

They came to the silver-grey Daimler and Jenny Melville opened the rear door for Ward but he only threw his bag in. "D'you mind if I sit in the front? I hate talking to people's backs."

"Why, no, sir."

He joked, "Besides, it feels as if I'm going to a funeral when I sit in the back of this thing."

The girl did not laugh.

She drove north out of Salisbury, headed for Amesbury and then turned on to the Devizes road.

They talked of the war and the girl asked about *Boston* so Ward told her about the cook who had celebrated the breaking of his engagement and various other stories and made her laugh.

Once he asked, "Do you know what all this is about?"

"I'm not allowed to say, sir," and the laughter was gone.

The sky darkened and the rain started to fall. At Tilshead she swung the big car off the road and into the camp at the top of the hill. They were stopped at the gate, but only briefly; the sentries knew her. Jenny Melville drove through the camp and out on to the empty ranges beyond.

They drove in silence now. The girl seemed to be worried about something, her smile gone and her lower lip caught in her teeth. Ward thought Salisbury Plain was a less than cheerful sight this afternoon, an empty, barren, blasted heath. Not quite empty, though – there was an army truck pulled in at the side of the road ahead of them and standing on a knoll near the road was a small, dark-coated figure under a black umbrella.

Jenny Melville halted the Daimler behind the truck. "There you are, sir."

"Thank you."

The clouds were low over the plain. It was raining heavily and steadily now, driving on the wind. Ward climbed to the top of the knoll using one hand to hold on his cap and stood beside Quartermain. Rain ran off the back of the admiral's umbrella in a small waterfall. He looked

141

around as Ward squelched up and grunted. "Um! You got here then. Good."

"Good afternoon, sir."

But Quartermain had turned away and was gazing out over the plain. A house stood about two hundred yards away, very old and ramshackle, the roof almost gone and the windows just gaping holes. There was still a door and it was shut. About thirty yards from the door a line of white mine tape was pegged out round the house on the long, tussocky grass. On higher ground three or four hundred yards beyond the house was an old bell-tent, while below it, and left, was a sandbagged machine-gun emplacement.

Midway between the house and the knoll, and facing the house, were two men lying behind a Bren. Movement drew Ward's eye. A quarter mile away a group of soldiers had risen from cover in the grass and gorse.

Quartermain said, "Commandos."

There looked to be a dozen or more but as Ward watched the party split into two. A small group of four headed away towards the bell-tent, while the rest made for the house. All moved at the double.

They carried submachine-guns and Ward thought, Thompsons? They slogged up the slope over the heavy ground towards the house and tent at a fast trot. The small group deployed and dropped flat about fifty yards from the tent. Most of the large group bellied down along the white line of the mine tape but three ran on, circling wide around the front of the house. They passed the Bren and finally dropped into cover close to the head of a shallow valley, little more than a fold in the ground, that twisted away across the plain. They were about thirty yards from the sandbagged emplacement.

Quartermain looked at his watch. "Forty seconds to go." Without turning he said, "We've found your Monsieur Peyraud who helped build the dock at St. Nazaire and we're going to bring him out. He refused to work for the Nazis and now he's held prisoner in his own house. We struck lucky there – the Nazis would probably have carted him off to jail if they hadn't needed a body of men in the area for another reason . . . Anyway, we want Peyraud to come of his own free will so we need someone who can gain his confidence quickly. Remember, we are talking of a man of sixty-seven, in good health but woken in the night by gunfire and finding himself faced by armed strangers. He needs to see a friendly face, someone he knows and can trust – or be persuaded to trust."

Quartermain looked at his watch again and muttered, "Ten seconds." He was silent a moment, then: "Your record shows you have your faults and my own experience is that you have a temper and directness of approach that can border on insubordination. But you also have sincerity and I think Alain Peyraud would trust you."

Ward stared at him, unable to believe this was real. He was supposed to be on leave in Northumberland, not standing in the wind and cold rain of Salisbury Plain, being asked to land in occupied France. Was Quartermain serious?

Suddenly the Thompsons before the house, the tent and over by the sandbagged emplacement burst into racketing life. Four of the men lying before the house rose and ran like sprinters across the open ground, crouching and weaving. The Bren in the foreground was firing short bursts over their heads and Ward thought, Christ! They're using live ammunition!

The four plastered themselves against the wall of the house, one either side of the window, one either side of the door. The two flanking the window each hurled something into the house through the empty frame. Seconds later the grenades exploded in a double *thump!* The men by the door kicked it in and charged into the house while the other two rolled in over the window-sill. Those left at the mine tape now ran across, crouching under the fire of the Bren. Two broke away to belly down, one at each corner of the house, but the others ran straight inside.

There was firing inside the house. Ward saw, through the holes that had been the upper windows, the men appear in

143

the rooms there. Grenades burst and the Thompsons hammered for half a minute, then the men poured out of the house again. They moved, spread out and independently, in short rushes, first back to the mine tape and then making a wide circle around the back of the house. Two of them dragged or half-carried between them a third man who seemed unable to run and stumbled continually. Quartermain said, "He's hobbled. Just a half yard of rope between his ankles but it keeps him down to an old man's speed."

The other party were falling back in similar fashion from the bell-tent, now bombed flat, and the two groups met some two hundred yards from the side of the house farthest from the door. They had circled it. Now they went on together and were met by the three at the head of the valley. The sandbagged emplacement had been bombed and smoke still drifted from it. They all withdrew down the valley, firing back at the house. When they were lost to sight the overlapping chatter of the Thompsons still came rattling back across the plain to where Ward and Quartermain stood.

The Bren ceased firing, then the Thompsons.

The two men at the Bren stood up. One of them lifted the gun, the other the ammunition box, and they trudged back to the road and the waiting truck.

The others reappeared at the head of the little valley, moving in a loose double file, an officer at their head and a sergeant at the tail. They slogged at the double across the plain, heading for the house.

Quartermain nodded satisfaction. "That's the fourth time they've done it." He turned his head to look up at Ward. "Well? What about it? Will you go?"

"Yes, sir." After all, he reckoned he had started it, sending them in search of Peyraud.

"Just like that. Do you know what you're in for?"

"No, sir." But, after the exhibition just seen, he had a fair idea.

Quartermain sniffed. "You're a mad bugger. Fortunately there are a few more about. Come and meet them."

144

He started down from the knoll. Ward followed, heard squelching behind him, glanced around and saw Leading Wren Melville trailing them. She wore rubber boots and Ward wished he'd brought a pair; his own feet were soaking.

The commandos were drawn up rigidly before the house but as Quartermain approached he bellowed, "I'm not talking out in this bloody rain! Get 'em in the house, Peter!"

The officer barked an order, the ranks broke up and the commandos entered the house. Quartermain and Ward followed them. The wind whistled through the broken windows and rain dripped through holes in the floor. The commandos stood in a loose half-circle. Quartermain found a dry square yard, let down his umbrella and shook the water from it. Jenny Melville took it and stepped back discreetly.

Quartermain said, "Good afternoon, gentlemen!"

An answering murmur came back. There was a smell of wet khaki serge, sweat and oil and cordite. Ward thought these men carried about them all the stenches of war but one: blood. Would that come soon? The light was fading. Their eyes watched the admiral but they would flicker briefly, curiously to Ward.

Quartermain said, "You will be fully briefed tonight but as you've probably guessed, today's exercises were in preparation for a particular raid and I'm going to tell you something about it now."

That created a little stir and quick exchanges of glances. Quartermain waited for it to subside then went on: "First of all, this is Lieutenant John Ward. He's going with you. John, this is Captain Peter Madden, Lieutenant Tim Gregson, Sergeant Beare . . ." He reeled off the names of all of them without hesitation and finished: ". . . Sergeants Dent and O'Donnell."

Ward thought it sounded like a lot of chiefs and not many Indians: three sergeants in a party of fifteen? Technical men, maybe? His eyes switched from face to face around

145

the half-circle, meeting the eyes measuring him. Captain Madden looked confident, a cheerful, don't-give-a-bugger-for-anybody sort of bloke he thought he could get on with –

"Mr. Ward was brought here at short notice." Quartermain scowled an apology at Jack. "I heard a week ago where Peyraud was held and knew the type of operation this would be because Jerry has a *Freya* radar close by the house. Reconnaissance Spitfires have been over a few times to take a look at the *Freya*, so we have aerial photographs of the area, we know how the raid has to be made and I was able to bring Peter and his men here for training. But it was only the day before yesterday that I received enough detailed information to order the raid – and to send for you."

The little admiral looked around the waiting half-circle. "Your objective is to rescue an old man, an engineer, from a house on the French coast. But we *don't* want Jerry to realise we've taken him or that the raid was made to get him. For some time we've been planning another raid by a company of the Parachute Regiment to capture parts of a new German radar, the *Würzburg*. They're going tomorrow night, and so will you. We know all about the *Freya* by the house but attack it anyway, so Jerry will think that you, like the paras, went for the radar. In today's exercise it was represented by the bell-tent.

"The area for several miles around the house is heavily wooded and unsuitable for a parachute drop. It is considered the casualty rate would be unacceptably heavy. So instead you will be in the hands of your pilots. There is only the one landing zone, a clearing a quarter mile inland of the house, about as long as a football pitch and not quite as wide."

Pilots? Ward wondered what aircraft could land in that small clearing – a Lysander? But he thought they only carried a couple of passengers and you could hardly land six of the things . . .

He listened to Quartermain: "A French Resistance man will mark the zone and meet you to act as guide. You will bring him out because that area would be a death trap for him if you left him. While there is a track from the L.Z. to the Freya there is no track through the forest to the house and that is the reason for the guide. Speed and surprise are essential, and you won't have time for map-reading your way through close country at night. The German garrison billeted in the house to guard the *Freya* and our engineer, and to man a pill-box overlooking the beach, totals fifty or more. You will need to neutralise the pill-box because landing-craft will lift you off the beach."

Quartermain paused a moment to let that sink in, then: "So – attack the Freya, burn the house to the ground and bring back that man. Surprise and speed. You have my confidence, gentlemen."

The commandos marched back to the road and the truck, climbed aboard. Captain Madden stood by the tailboard and Ward stopped beside him on his way to the Daimler. He had a question he needed to ask but Madden spoke first. He took off his helmet and ran fingers through wiry hair, a middle-sized, compact young man of about Ward's age and he grinned, "Well, if it all goes to plan it should be quite a party. What do you think?"

Ward answered from long experience, "It's a bloody certainty it won't all go to plan."

Madden nodded cheerfully and winked. Ward realised the wink was not intended for him, turned and saw Leading Wren Jenny Melville holding open the door of the Daimler for Quartermain, saluting as he climbed in. She returned Madden's wink then abruptly became solemn as she found Ward's gaze on her. She still held the door open – for him, he realised.

He turned quickly back to Madden and asked his question: "How do we get there?"

Madden told him in a word and Ward said, "Jesus Christ!"

9

The Raid

Sergeant Archie Dent was just three hours short of his twenty-first birthday and he wondered seriously, though he was not a serious young man, if he would make it. He sat in the pilot's seat of the eight-man Hotspur glider and stared out through the perspex canopy at the night. The runway of Thruxton airfield was desolate under the moon, a black tarmac desert. The Blenheims that had been the first aircraft to land there in 1941 had burst three tyres on the rough concrete so it had quickly been tarmacked.

It was a fine, clear night. The weather men reported, however, that much of France was covered in snow. There were fourteen Whitleys lined up at the end of the runway, all the bombers running up their twin Merlin engines and creating a thunder in the night. Twelve carried men of the Parachute Regiment, their mission to capture vital parts of the *Würzburg* radar at Bruneval, north of Le Havre on the French coast. The two remaining Whitleys were each to tow a glider, one piloted by Sergeant Dent, the other by Sergeant O'Donnell. Captain Madden and six commandos were packed into O'Donnell's glider, Lieutenant Gregson and six other men, including Ward, into Dent's.

The Hotspur was thirty-nine feet long with a wingspan of forty-six feet. It sat very low, on short oleo legs, and Dent in the pilot's seat had his boots no more than three feet above the runway. Between Dent and the bomber ahead of him the tow snaked widely, slack on the tarmac. The wash from the Whitley's propellers was enough to set the Hotspur, a flimsy craft of wood struts and plywood, to violent juddering.

The headroom inside the glider was only five feet at most; the hull measured three and a half feet across at its widest point. There was a door on the right and forward,

another on the left and to the rear. Lieutenant Gregson sat
in the nose, just behind the pilot. Three of the other six sat
sideways facing the right hand door, the other three faced
that on the left. The doors were just crude panels, three
feet high by two wide and fastened in place with knock-off
catches. There were tiny portholes, about four inches in
diameter, but cut in the roof so that the men could only
glimpse the star-scattered sky.

Every man aboard was strapped into a Sutton harness,
webbing straps coming down over his shoulders, others
round his waist, all fastened at the navel with a locking-pin.
Dent and Gregson in the nose wore flying suits against the
cold while those in the hull sat on sleeping-bags, others
spread over them. The seats were low and they sat with
their knees under their chins.

This would be only Ward's second flight in a glider and
he swore it would be his last. He had been given one quick
trip earlier that day – "to get the hang of it", Madden had
said. In fact the flight had been to see if Ward became
airsick. He had not. He had learned how to get in, and out,
and he wanted to know no more. He hated being shut in
this crowded box, unable to see what was going on, or to do
anything about it. Madden and the others were full of
confidence. Ward's thought was that as this jaunt had to be
attempted then the sooner it was over and done with the
better.

The others. He wished there had been more time to get
to know them but he thought he knew enough. Last night at
the briefing and again today they had all studied the aerial
photographs and the maps, questioned, argued, listened
and learned, committing the information to memory.
Ward remembered now the description of Wellington's
men – 'not tall but deep in the chest'. That fitted these
commandos in the Hotspur with him. Sergeant Beare was
the biggest with a wrestler's build, broad and long-armed
with huge hands. He was also the only regular soldier
amongst them. The others had been Territorial soldiers –
part-timers – or had volunteered in 1939. Jimmy Nicholl

was the smallest, dark and very quick. The other privates, Lockwood, Driscoll and Baldry, Sergeant Dent the pilot and Lieutenant Tim Gregson, all were men of average build. They were a cheerful lot but they all had a reassuring aura of contained toughness. Tim Gregson, in particular, gave a man confidence; between them he and Peter Madden could pull this off.

If anyone could.

Dent licked his lips. Not long now. He squinted as the lights of the flarepath glared into life. One by one and in quick succession the twelve Whitleys carrying the paras took off, then the thirteenth, towing O'Donnell's glider, raced along the runway and lifted into the night sky. Dent thought, Unlucky thirteen. He crossed his fingers for O'Donnell, then took a deep, steadying breath. Here we go!

The Whitley ahead of him lumbered slowly forward, the snake of the tow straightening astern of it. Dent saw the ground crew signal to the bomber's pilot that the slack was taken up and the pilot opened his throttles. The Whitley ran away and the Hotspur juddered after it, speed increasing rapidly until they were past sixty knots and Archie felt the lift, heard the rear-gunner in the power-operated turret of the Whitley, voice squawking through the intercom to his pilot and down the line that ran along the tow into Dent's earphones: "Matchbox airborne!"

Now the Hotspur was flying above the Whitley that was still on the runway, they were off the ground and out of the slipstream and the juddering was gone. Seconds later the Whitley lifted off, climbing, and the Hotspur climbed with it, above and behind at the end of the tow. When the Whitley levelled off, Dent eased forward on the stick and the Hotspur dropped below the bomber, bucketing a mad instant as they passed through the slipstream, then riding smooth and still.

Archie Dent checked his few instruments: airspeed, altimeter, turn and bank, "angle of dangle". You had to keep the angle of the tow right or be battered in the slipstream. The levers that operated the flaps were down by his left knee and the tit to release the tow, a ball the size of a billiard ball, was in reach of his left hand. Across the cabin stretched the rope fastened to the clips holding the perspex canopy; pull that and the canopy came free, leaving the cabin open.

He could just make out the tow stretching up to the Whitley, three blue lights on the trailing edge of each wing. He could hear the roar of its engines and see the cigarette glow of their exhausts.

He settled solidly down into the seat. This was going to be a long trip, his longest by far.

It could well be his last.

Ward sat with his left shoulder against the plywood bulkhead that separated him from the pilot's cabin. He worked his wrist up from under the covering sleeping-bag and held his watch before his face. They had been flying for only ten minutes.

On his right sat Sergeant Beare, sleeping, as were most of the others. Young Jimmy Nicholl's head rested on the sergeant's broad shoulder. Further back in the hull a light glowed: Lockwood, a farm labourer before the war, was reading with the help of a pocket torch. Ward had caught a glimpse of his book before they boarded the Hotspur, Hemingway's *For Whom the Bell Tolls*. He thought it an unfortunate choice of title.

How could Lockwood read, the rest of them sleep, with what lay ahead? He looked out of the tiny porthole above him, at the bright, moonlit sky. It was bitterly cold and he was glad of the sleeping-bag, and the airborne troopers' smock they had given him along with close-fitting helmet and gloves. A Thompson gun hung on its sling against his chest and the Verey pistol in a pocket of the smock was a pressure on his hip. Madden gave him a short course on the Thompson at Tilshead, and asked, "Are you sure you've never handled one before?"

Ward answered, "Never." But he knew from grouse-shooting days with his father that he was a natural shot.

Now he wondered about Krueger, *Boston* and her crew, all of them on leave. He should have been on leave too, and that thought summoned up memories of his time with Catherine Guillard.

He stared across the narrow cabin, lit only by the tiny portholes in the roof, and forced himself to concentrate on the business in hand. He mentally checked over the details of the operation. Again. And again.

When they were over the sea Dent and O'Donnell jettisoned their oleo landing gear because, to shorten the landing run, they were going to land on the wooden skid beneath the nose and hull of each Hotspur. It was a beautiful, clear night with a moon. Archie Dent reckoned visibility at four miles and prayed they would not meet night fighters. He tried not to imagine German cannon shells tearing through the plywood skin of the Hotspur.

The flight went on.

They had been airborne over two hours when Archie heard the voice of the rear-gunner in the Whitley: "Hallo, Matchbox! Skipper says enemy coast in five minutes!"

Archie straightened in his seat and took a fresh grip of the stick. At the briefing they'd said that enemy radar, if it picked them up, would see only one 'blip' for both Whitley and glider, and that by the time the glider cast off the tow they would be inside the minimum range of the radar. Thus they would land undetected and Jerry would think the Whitleys were on a routine bombing raid. The briefing had been understandably reticent, however, on the subject of what would happen to them during the time that the enemy radar was tracking them, be they represented by two blips or two hundred . . .

Archie put that thought to one side and repeated the rear-gunner's message to Lieutenant Gregson who rapped on the bulkhead behind him, alerting the half-dozen in the hull.

Ward woke to his rapping, surprised that he had slept.

He gave Beare a nudge and the others came awake as Beare passed it on. Lockwood's torch clicked out and the book was put away. They stripped off the covering sleeping-bags and kicked them out of the way. They were ready.

The rear-gunner reported, "Skipper says enemy coast in sight!"

Whatever relief Archie Dent might have felt was short-lived. A flash lit the perspex dome and his head jerked, his eyes narrowed against the glare that was instantly gone, instantly repeated again and again and interspersed with the regular *crump! crump! crump!* of bursting flak. The radar had indeed been tracking them, the guns lying in wait. He saw the bursts well out to starboard but the sight gave him little joy for he knew that the other Whitley was out there in the middle of them. He prayed for her, but in vain.

He watched the tongues of flame mark her. Then she was falling, sliding away towards the sea. She was still under some control, her dive shallow but her end certain. Now, suddenly, she was a ball of fire. Then the rear-gunner's voice squawked in his ear, "LZ in sight right ahead! Pull off now!"

Archie yanked at the tit and felt the kick as the tow was released. The Whitley lifted above him and pulled away ahead, flying on inland to keep up the pretence of a routine bombing raid. He gave all his attention now to the night before him, saw a distant pin-prick of light on the ground and gently adjusted his course.

All was silence now. The guns had ceased firing, the Whitley droned away into the distance, and there was only the whisper of the windrush as the Hotspur slid softly down the moonlit night.

Gregson asked, "See it?"

Dent used his left hand to pull off the headphones and drop them. "Seen."

Gregson sounded cool and Dent thought that he was going to be a good man to have along on a crazy show like this.

The guiding light was gone, masked by the forest inland as the glider descended.

The white line of phosphorescence that was the sea breaking on the shore drifted up towards him. On either hand were grey cliffs with the black throat of a gully between, at the bottom of it a thread of silver, the stream winding inland. He was sliding above the gully now and he could see lights again, three of them now, one closer than the other two. They were in a clearing and he could make that out, the moonlit ground white with frost or snow, surrounded by the black-patched treetops.

It wasn't much of a landing ground. A bit longer than a football pitch they'd said at the briefing, forty yards wide, and a stream at the end of it.

He had to get the Hotspur down before the first marker light and stop her before the other two. They'd said the wind would be right on the nose and there was a lift of the ground up to the lights before it dropped away to the stream. It had sounded bad enough at the briefing, but up here in the dark, trying to bring the glider in as low as he dared over the trees, holding her nose up so she was just short of stalling – this was murder.

All around was the forest. He had to put her down at the lights or she'd be a bloody wreck.

And only one chance.

He put the nose down, the Hotspur seemed to fall over the black wall of the trees and he was looking at the white ground coming up at him. He shuddered at the thought of smashing in on the fragile nose, his legs inside it. He hauled back desperately on the stick, pulled up the nose then let it drop again, just holding her from stalling. The first light rushed up at him and now he stalled her deliberately, heaved hard on the first lever and got half-flaps, then the second lever, full flaps. The Hotspur hung for a second nose up, he saw the light just ahead of the port wing and he knew they were low, almost down –

The glider slammed on to the earth.

The silent flight was ended and the night full of sound

now, a slamming, ripping and tearing as the Hotspur skidded across the frozen ground and Archie fought to hold her down, hold her straight, and somehow stop her. There were no brakes. Snow flew back like spray as the nose ploughed through it. Blackness lifted like the waving arms of a great Indian goddess and he recognised the bare branches of a tree at the instant he saw the silver of the snow-covered earth falling away. He yelled, *"We're goin' in the drink!"*

In the black coffin of the cabin Ward heard the yell as all of them were jolted and tossed about, secured though they were in the Sutton harnesses. There came one monstrous blow on the hull and a cracking and crunching of timber and the Hotspur slewed, fell sideways – and stopped, lying on its port side.

Into the sudden silence the voice of Sergeant Beare barked, "Out!" They pulled on the pins of the harnesses and they fell away. Beare snapped off the clips on the right hand door and kicked it out. He followed it quickly, Thompson gun held ready. Jimmy Nicholl went next, then Ward. The door on the port side was crushed against the earth, so the other men squirmed out after him.

The night was still. It seemed the ruse had worked and they had not been seen. The Hotspur lay under the spread branches of trees and sideways-on to the stream that ran only feet away. Above him on the bank the commandos threw themselves down in the carpet of snow and peered out into the clearing. Sergeant Beare loomed with the stocky figure of Dent, the pilot, behind him and Ward asked, "Where's Mr. Gregson?"

Dent answered, "Bought it, sir." He explained: "We hit a tree. Branch smashed in that side of the canopy, ripping it off, just missed me but hit Mr. Gregson."

Ward asked, "Are you sure he's dead?"

"Yes, sir." That was Beare, and he added, "No sign of the other glider either. God knows where they finished up."

Dent started, "I saw the other tug –"

A voice above them called, "Somebody comin'!"

Beare snapped, "Hold your fire! That could be the Frog we're meeting!"

He started up the bank and Ward went with him, the pair of them halting below the crest so they could just see over it and out into the clearing where the snow was cut in a broad furrow by the Hotspur's skid. A figure trotted towards them through the snow, awkwardly because of hands held high. A youth by the look of him, light on his feet, not tall. He wore trousers tucked into the tops of boots and a dark, short overcoat buttoned to the neck, beret clapped on his head.

He slowed to a walk as he came to the shadow of the trees and Ward took a step forward so he could be seen. The figure halted and the challenge came breathlessly high: "British?"

"*Oui!*" Ward answered and walked forward.

They met under the snow-clad branches of the trees and in the filtered moonlight Ward looked down into the face of Catherine Guillard.

For a second he was speechless, then he burst out in astonishment, "Catherine!"

The girl was no less surprised: "John?"

Then anger brought from Ward, "Are they all bloody mad, sending you on a job like this?"

"No, John! They did not know it would be me and I had no choice. There are only two of us who could handle this, who know the ground, the details, what has to be done. The other is my wireless operator and he can't be risked; he argued, inevitably, but without him there is no communication with London. So it had to be me."

Ward still stood tight-lipped and Catherine said quietly, "Anyway, it is very little. I waited near here in the house of friends –," but alone because the Boilets had gone away to escape suspicion, "– listened to the BBC until the message came. Then I set the lights and now I guide you. And afterwards I leave with you. It's really very simple."

And if the raiding party failed to escape? Ward knew the

orders and he was not so certain that Quartermain had never suspected Catherine Guillard would be involved in this way. They were playing for high stakes and an agent was an agent. But she was looking up at him and here in the snow and under the cold moon there was a current between them and she reached out to touch his arm.

Beare muttered, "We've got to be moving, sir. Would you like me to take charge?"

His black bad temper spoke for Ward, "No, I bloody well wouldn't!"

Beare thought, I hope the big bastard knows what he's doing.

Ward stared out over Catherine's head into the field beyond, fighting down the rage, thinking coolly again. There was still no other glider. He turned to Dent. "What were you saying?"

Archie Dent answered, "I saw the other Whitley go down in the sea, sir. Didn't see anything of the Hotspur."

Ward took it in. Gregson was dead and probably Peter Madden and all his party so Ward was left with the handful of men around him and Catherine Guillard. He was aware of Beare and Dent watching him.

He said, "Sergeant Dent, when we get closer you'll take one man and do what you can with the *Freya*. Steal a bit if possible but shoot it up anyway. The idea is to make it look as if this raid was aimed at the *Freya*. Remember?"

"Yes, sir." Dent glanced round. "I'll take Baldry. All right, sir?"

Ward nodded, "Time?" He looked at his watch.

Dent checked his: "Twelve twenty-five."

"Agreed. Give us till fifteen minutes from now to get into position. That'll be twelve-forty. But if you hear firing down here before then, you can start right away. Any questions?"

"RV afterwards, sir?"

Ward told himself he should have thought of the rendez-vous but he had been concentrating on the immediate first decision.

157

Dent prompted, "The original, sir? First bend in the gully down from the bridge?"

The bridge was seaward of the house and might well have a sentry: but with any luck they would be out of his sight round the bend in the gully. Ward nodded.

Beare asked, "Pill-box, sir? Line of retreat?"

The plan rehearsed on Salisbury Plain had been for one small party to take and hold the pill-box at the head of the gully and so keep the escape route down to the beach open for the others. Ward said, "We'll have to take that when it comes. We're short-handed as it is." He saw Beare nodding reluctant approval.

Ward looked round at them, cast a glance back down the slope to the wreck of the Hotspur where lay the body of Tim Gregson, then faced forward. "Move now."

The men in front of him rose to their feet and Ward led the way forward with Catherine Guillard. Behind them came Jimmy Nicholl, then Lockwood, Driscoll and the broad figure of Beare bringing up the rear. Dent and Baldry followed for a while, then headed out where Catherine indicated, making for the track leading up the slope to the cliff-top. Ward could not make out the *Freya* there but the wooded crest was an unmistakable hump against the night sky.

Catherine and the file of men moved steadily through the forest, following a path hidden beneath the snow that crunched softly under their boots. They glimpsed the moon-bright sky through a lacing of branches but under the trees it was dark. Ward's breath streamed like smoke in the crisp, cold air. He realised he was breathing quickly as if he had run a race, knew this was due to tension and tried to control it, breathed more slowly and deeply.

He wished to God that Catherine was safe, somewhere else, anywhere but here, but they needed her. By leading them right to the house she was gaining the element of surprise and a chance of success.

But it was still a bloody mess.

What else could go wrong?

What could go right, now, with the already small force reduced to less than half?

When the first flak burst Peter Madden thought his glider was hit. It bucked and shuddered, but then it still flew and he realised the bursts were ahead of the Whitley that towed them. The glider was only being shaken as it passed through the turbulence the flak created. He sat behind O'Donnell in the nose and over the pilot's shoulder he could see the Whitley silhouetted against the flashes. Then, as O'Donnell juggled with the controls to hold the Hotspur steady, Madden saw flames wink into life on the dark silhouette. They showed as tiny slivers of orange light on the port wing, then the starboard, but the slivers grew to wide, trailing tongues almost before he could blink.

He reasoned that both engines must have been hit. She was going down. If both engines had been hit then the rest of her would probably be holed like a colander. The pilot was still flying her – she was in a shallow dive, as if under some control, but he could not save her. Madden waited for instructions, some message, but none came back along that fragile line from the flaming, falling wreck.

He shouted at O'Donnell, "Let go!"

The pilot jerked at the tit and the towing-line fell away. He eased the stick to port and the Hotspur slipped out of the track of the Whitley, then eased it back and the Hotspur steadied, flying free. For seconds he was blind because the blazing aircraft had destroyed his night vision, then the Whitley struck and the fire was blotted out as she buried herself in the dark sea below.

O'Donnell held the stick with one hand, snatched off the earphones with the other and tossed them aside. "Bloody caper, this is!"

Madden asked, "See anything? Know where we are?"

O'Donnell shook his head, then: "There's the coast!"

Madden saw the white line of breaking surf below and

ahead. They were flying at eighty knots. O'Donnell said, "And there's the cliff!"

It lifted before them like a grey wall and it seemed they would smash into it. Then O'Donnell got lift from some blessed thermal and the Hotspur soared, swooped up over the edge of the cliff and skimmed on above the snow-covered trees that ran below like a black, foam-flecked sea.

And in the bright moonlight they could see no gully or silver thread of a stream, no lights, no clearing. Peter Madden said, "Turn north." He was sure they were too far south.

O'Donnell answered, "North, sir."

The Hotspur tilted as it turned, losing altitude, then settled again into level flight but now the trees below looked dangerously close, seemed to be reaching up to tear at the belly of the glider.

O'Donnell warned, "We'd better find a hole soon."

But the forest stretched away endlessly, ready to rip the Hotspur apart – and the men inside her.

Then Peter Madden pointed. "Look! Down there!"

It was a break in the trees, possibly a road or a track running through a clearing, a ribbon stretched straight and white against the mottled white and black shadows of the gorse or bracken on either side. The clearing looked poss-ibly wide enough, definitely not long enough, but they had nowhere else to go.

Madden said, "Take it!"

O'Donnell was already easing left on stick and rudder, then pulling the stick back to him, touching right rudder. He was lining her up, straightening her, steadying. They were low and slow, near to stalling. He swallowed and thought that if the bloody wind was right then they just might – The track was under them, the Hotspur's skid nearly rubbing. There were trees on either hand, set back across a score of yards of clear ground, and close ahead. In the space of a heartbeat he wondered what the ground and the track were like under the snow, then they were down, the Hotspur bumping and lurching, swaying and screeching as the ruts of the track tore at her.

O'Donnell fought to hold her steady and straight, kept her from cartwheeling but could not hold her on the track. She slithered off into the open ground and bucked across it on her belly. The trees loomed up but first there was undergrowth. Snow spurted over the canopy, but they were slowing, the bushes acting as brakes. One wing caught and held briefly, the Hotspur spun around full circle on its skid and the other wing was sliced away on the trees. They ground to a shuddering halt.

For a long moment nobody stirred. Then, realising they were on the ground and alive, they moved as one.

O'Donnell pushed up the perspex canopy and he and Madden climbed free of the wreckage. The men were scrambling out of the cabin, deploying to form a defensive perimeter, and Madden listened a moment, head on one side. There was the sighing of wind in the trees, a rustling as his men bellied down at the edge of them, but no sound of German armoured vehicles tearing up the road – not yet. Madden moved quickly along the line of men, asking softly, "Everybody all right?" O'Donnell followed him and they found no man missing or even injured.

O'Donnell muttered, "It's a bloody miracle."

Madden agreed with him. But he still had problems. He did not know where the other Hotspur was, or where his objective lay. He did not know where *he* was and he would not find out standing here.

"Move!" He started out northwards along the track, trotting in the powdery snow at the side of it, the Thompson held two-handed across his chest. He only had the faintest of instincts to guide him. The men rose and followed him in file, O'Donnell at the tail.

They double-marched though the close-crowding trees that told him nothing for ten minutes. It was an eerie experience. They were still shaken by the Hotspur's landing and now they were running along a lane through moonlit forest in a land hushed, snow-covered – and held by an enemy who might be hidden in the forest alongside, watching, coldly choosing his moment. Or around the next bend in the track.

Suddenly, ahead of them, a village lay in a clearing, a mere scattering of houses with a church standing at their centre. Madden halted his party. There was no light to be seen, not a sign of life – but he thought he knew where he was. He turned back along the track and into the trees, took out his torch and the map from the big pocket on the leg of his trousers. He had studied the map a hundred times before, committing its features to memory and he was sure about this village but still he checked that there was no other exactly the same. There was not.

He pencilled in his route then led his men past the village, flitting like shadows under the spread branches of the trees. A dog barked once, and a second time, the sound carried clear on the frosty air, then there was silence again as they left the village behind them. Now they ran in a shallow valley, the forest on one side, a stream on the other, and that was when they heard the crackle of small arms fire and saw its red winking far down the valley, above the trees, on the wooded crest of a hill.

That was their objective and it was still all of a mile away, across strange country, treacherously snow-covered and in the dark.

As Peter Madden and his section had crawled out of their wrecked Hotspur, Catherine Guillard was leading Ward and his men through the forest. The journey took time because Catherine stopped frequently to check that she was on the right path. She had reconnoitred this route by daylight and now it was night.

Finally they came on a break in the forest and Ward stood with the girl under the last of the trees. The forest curved away to the left and right, the trees describing a great circle. To his right a stream, a tributary of that running in the valley bottom, wriggled out of the forest, meandered along its edge and passed within yards of him.

A path ran along the far bank of the stream and beyond stood a stone wall. Inside that enclosing wall, in the middle distance, lifted the dark, angular mass of the house, its roof silver under the snow and the moon.

Catherine pointed left and said, "The gate is that way – and one of the guards." She had to raise her voice to be heard above the rushing stream. It ran fast and brawling in winter spate and Ward knew it would be cold.

The stream and the house, the trees, the snow and the moonlight, all made a Christmas card scene. Just inches from his face, however, festoons of barbed wire, sagging and rusting, looped from tree to tree. The German garrison had used the trees as fence posts to run their wire. It jerked now as Lockwood worked on it with cutters. The others were spread out along the edge of the forest and Beare stood at Ward's shoulder, head turning slowly as he surveyed the ground.

The last strands of wire parted and trailed in the snow. Catherine made to move forward but Ward's hand on her arm stopped her. He said, "I can see the house. You stay here." She would be, just possibly, safer there. "Join us afterwards. When we get out." If they got out. "Wait at the bottom of the valley." He pointed. "Beyond the bridge and out of sight of it."

Catherine opened her mouth to protest, thought better of it. Their eyes met briefly, then Ward climbed away down the bank and waded into the stream.

The water was icy cold and the tumbling race of it deafened him. None of them heard the patrolling sentry. He walked around the bend in the path some thirty yards away and halted. He wore a coalscuttle helmet, carried a rifle over one shoulder and after a second of staring immobility he fumbled to bring it into action and yelled a warning.

Beare and Nicholl fired at him with their Thompsons, but he ran back around the bend in the path. They could hear him still shouting, and now an answering voice. Then a whistle shrilled.

Ward splashed out of the stream, looked back and saw the commandos coming after him, lifting their boots high out of the dragging water as they pranced across the stream like horses.

He turned and ran at the garden wall, barely six feet high, swung easily on to the top and down on the other side, then waited there, only seconds, for the others. Now he could see all of the house, the moonlight glinting on blacked-out windows, a door open at the front and a man on the steps outside it, yelling down to the guard at the gate. Ward heard the clatter of a Thompson, distantly, from beyond the house, and saw the flicker of muzzle-flashes on the cliff-top where the *Freya* stood. Then there was a fusillade of rifles and Thompsons. Clearly Dent and Baldry had stirred up a hornet's nest.

Driscoll was last to swing over the wall. Ward led all of them, running crouched in its shadow to the trees that lined the side of the house and went on to meet the rear wall. They were planted in two rows, seeming to be an evergreen windbreak. The shadow under their branches was as deep as that by the wall and Ward straightened as he ran. He had wondered what else could go wrong and now he had his answer. The cat was out of the bag and surprise was lost. Now all they had to rely on was speed.

Beare, pounding through the snow, overtook Ward as they reached the end of the house. The gable wall of it was dark but they could see a ground floor window and the side door they sought. A window above was curtained but a chink of light showed. That should be Peyraud's room –

Beare panted, "Want me to make a recce, sir?"

"No!" Speed. They had to gamble on it. "Straight in!" Ward swerved towards the house, running across the open ground towards it but now they were out of sight of anyone at the front. He brought up against the door and fumbled for the handle.

Beare rasped, "Stand clear!" He was ready with his Thompson to smash the window and Lockwood stood on the other side, a grenade in his hand, finger hooked in the pin. But Ward got the door open and burst in, throwing it wide. He was in the kitchen, long and narrow with a huge table seeming to fill it. A banked up stove at one side showed a warm glow and a kettle stood on top of it sending out a feather of steam. The glow shed a dim red light across the bare scrubbed floorboards.

A narrow servant's staircase ran up the opposite wall. Ward vaulted over the table and took the stairs three at a time. Beare went after him, cursing his recklessness, shouting back, "Lockwood! Driscoll! Hold here!"

Ward turned at the head of the stairs on to a narrow landing that ran the width of the house. A passage opened midway along on the left, presumably leading to the rest of the house. There was a closed door to his right.

Beare shoved past, Nicholl crowding behind him. They reached the passage and Beare peered around into it. A single lighted bulb hanging halfway along the passage showed open doors and at the far end a soldier, rifle in one hand, tunic in the other. He stood at the head of another staircase but he looked over his shoulder at their peering heads. Beare fired a burst, the spent cartridge cases leaping and bouncing from the walls to roll tinkling across the floor. The soldier disappeared and they heard him falling on the stairs, then shouting. Beare told Nicholl, "We can't check all those rooms so hold here!"

Nicholl dropped down, only his head showing to stare down the passage, his Thompson trained. Beare went to look for Ward.

Ward had found Peyraud's door locked, had braced his back against the opposite wall and kicked. The door shook and at the second kick splintered at the edge and swung inward. He caught a fleeting impression of a room crowded with solid, old furniture. There was light, partly from the embers of a log fire that glowed red through the fine white ash in the grate, partly from a small oil-lamp with a low flame, a night-light that burned on a table by the bed. The bed itself was large and Alain Peyraud was almost lost in it, a tall man still but shrunken a little with age now. He

165

lay propped on one elbow and blinked short-sightedly, startled, at Ward while his free hand groped about the table in search of his spectacles.

A burst of fire racketed outside in the passage. Beare entered, pushed past Ward and crossed to the window. He knelt there, peered out through a crack in the curtains and threw back over his shoulder, "Bloody lucky nobody was in that kitchen, sir. I reckon the door was open because the sentries on patrol nip in for a crafty brew now and then." He turned and eyed Ward reprovingly, then nodded at Peyraud. "Is this the feller, sir?"

Peyraud's head jerked around to peer in the direction of the voice while his hand still hunted for the glasses. He said with a high note of disbelief, "English?" Then he started as a single shot outside was followed by the hammering of Thompsons. Those below in the kitchen were muted but Nicholl's on the landing just outside the door was again deafening.

In the silence that followed the sound of German voices deep inside the house seemed thin and distant. Ward said, "British commandos." He stepped to the table and put the spectacles into Peyraud's scrabbling fingers. "I'm an officer of the Royal Navy. I hope you'll remember me: Jack Ward. We met in Paris in 1939."

Peyraud hooked the spectacles over his ears and looked at Ward, then sat up in bed and lifted the lamp to peer more closely at Ward's face. Finally he nodded. "I remember. We used to play billiards. You were with a lady, very nice."

There was another burst of fire and the *crack!* of a grenade exploding. Ward said quickly, "I haven't much time. We came here to take you to England. The Germans are using the great dock at St. Nazaire and we have a plan to put it out of action but we need detailed information about the gates and the dock. You built it; you can tell us. Will you come with us?"

Peyraud stared up at him, then said, "You mean – now? This moment?" Then he added, "But of course you mean now. You cannot delay."

"We couldn't warn you, couldn't get a message to you."
Peyraud nodded, but hesitated. "This is my home."

The Thompsons hammered again and Beare crossed to
the door, shot a glance at Ward that said "For Christ's sake
hurry it up!" He sidled out.

A grenade exploded close, so that they felt the shudder
of its blast in the room. Ward pressed. "Will you help us,
sir?"

Peyraud answered him. "I'm a prisoner here. They send
a guard with me when I walk outside and they lock me in
this room at night. If I am lucky they will keep me here but I
think they will lose patience and send me to a German
prison. I am an old man and that would kill me. So. You
need me, I will come." He threw back the covers and
swung his legs out of the bed, stood in woollen pyjamas
several sizes too big for him.

Ward heaved an inward sigh of relief. His orders were to
bring Peyraud out whether he agreed or no. That had not
been a pleasant prospect. "Thank you, sir."

Beare reappeared. "Driscoll can't see anybody at the
back yet but that won't last much longer. We've got to
move, sir!"

"In one minute."

And in one minute Peyraud, clothes dragged on over his
pyjamas with Ward's help, his overcoat still unbuttoned
and a beret clapped on his head, was hustled out of the
room and down the stairs. Beare picked up the lamp,
hurled it against the wall and saw its oil take light. At the
door he shouted to Nicholl, "O.K. Jimmy! Out!"

Nicholl wormed back from his position at the angle of the
corridor, rose, and ran down the stairs. Beare threw an
incendiary grenade around the corner to fall in the corridor, heard it burst and saw the leap of flame. He threw
another into the bedroom and then followed Nicholl.

Down in the kitchen Driscoll defended the outside door.
Behind him and on the far side of the room was another
door and Lockwood knelt there. He could see along a
passage to a hall where there was yellow light. He was to

hold this passage and thus the kitchen and the escape route. He was not to bring the enemy down here. German soldiers ran across the end of the passage but he kept still and did not fire. They sounded to be running out of the house. He set down two incendiary grenades, handily close to the wall.

He heard the trampling of feet on the stairs over his head, glanced round and saw Ward and a muffled, stumbling figure come down into the kitchen, then Nicholl. Lockwood turned back to the passage, just as a soldier appeared at the end of it. He wore no helmet but carried a rifle across his chest and he started cautiously down the passage. Lockwood let him come on then shot him down at point-blank range.

Dust fell from the ceiling as a grenade exploded on the floor above, then another. Rubber-soled boots pounded on the stairs and Beare jumped the last three steps down into the kitchen. Lockwood shifted his Thompson to his left hand, lobbed incendiary grenades down the passage into the hall then fired a burst after them.

Ward stood beside the outside door with Peyraud beside him. As Lockwood retreated Beare pointed at Driscoll and Nicholl. "Into the trees and be ready to cover us." And to Ward, "Then you, sir, and the old – gentleman. O.K.?"

Ward nodded. He noticed the slight hesitation in Beare's voice before he produced the word 'gentleman', and wondered what had been on the tip of his tongue before the sergeant had remembered that Peyraud understood English.

Driscoll and Nicholl slipped out through the door and ran crouching, zig-zagging across the white stretch of moonlit open ground, vanished in the black shadow of the trees. Ward waited, then followed them out, pulling Peyraud along by the arm. The old man skidded in the snow but Beare steadied him and started to hurry him across the open ground towards the trees. They were half-way there when three German soldiers ran around the corner from the front of the house. Beare pushed Peyraud and Ward towards the trees, stopped and pointed the Thompson. He saw one of the men go down then Driscoll and Nicholl opened up from the trees. Lockwood joined him and they fired together. A second man fell and the third ran back around the corner of the house. Lockwood said, "They must be bloody balmy, charging about like that!"

Beare agreed. "They must have thought we'd pulled out already. Off you go." And Lockwood ran towards the wood where Ward crouched with Peyraud in the shadow of the trees.

Together they watched the sergeant's arm swing, and an instant later yet another incendiary grenade burst inside the kitchen. The entire end of the house was an inferno. Of the human remains to be found there in the morning, who would think it important to prove that one of them was not Peyraud?

Beare arrived panting in the darkness under the trees, the others rose and they set off. They moved in single file again, winding between the trees, Ward, Nicholl, then Driscoll and Lockwood with Peyraud between them, finally Beare. Peyraud was puffing but keeping up the hurrying pace, lifted along on Lockwood's arm.

They circled the rear of the house. Through breaks in the trees Ward saw the flashes of firing still from the cliff-top where the *Freya* stood but he thought their intensity was diminishing. Dent and Baldry must have seen the house in flames and should be pulling back now. The fire was spreading, the whole roofline now a leaping, roaring blaze as the ancient timbers burned and sparks streamed upward with the billowing smoke.

They came on the track that ran through the wood from the house up to the *Freya*. Nicholl crossed, then Driscoll. Ward was about to follow when he saw figures against the dirty red light cast by the burning house. There were men on the track, close and coming quickly, their silhouettes jerking as they trotted up the shallow incline. Ward crouched and glanced behind him, saw Lockwood pull

Peyraud down then get in front of him, training his Thompson. The three of them faded into the shadows. Ward could see no one but he knew Beare was somewhere in the darkness and ready. He faced forward, leaned left shoulder against a tree and waited.

The men passed within feet of him and he counted them: six. He could hear their laboured breathing, see it smoking on the cold air. Two wore big coal-scuttle helmets but the others were bare-headed and one was without a tunic, wore only a shirt. They carried rifles across their chests and their faces were grey smudges as they passed one by one across the sights of his Thompson. He prayed that none of the commandos would fire. It would be one action they would certainly win, a perfect ambush at close range, but at the expense of giving away their position. They had to get Peyraud out, that was all that mattered.

The last of the soldiers disappeared up the track and Ward let out the long-held breath, Peyraud sneezed behind him and Ward twitched at the sound of it, thankful that it had come too late to betray them. He rose, hurried Peyraud across the track and saw Beare trotting after him. Ward moved deeper into the trees, to the head of the file again and they moved on.

The light of the burning house was always on their left hand as they worked around it. Ward reckoned they were getting close to the bridge that carried the road across the stream. Already Peyraud was wheezing and frequently stumbling. He was too old for this pace.

Ward saw moonlit open ground ahead and the line of the garden wall. He halted the file with an outstretched hand, moved forward alone. He stood at the wall, close in its shadow, found a foothold and was able to look over the top. Below and to his left lay the narrow stone bridge. Beyond it Catherine would be waiting. He heard the rush of the stream as it was funnelled and creamed into white water under the arch of the bridge. The road dipped down the opposite side of the gully from the top of the cliffs, crossed the bridge, then swung away to his left and inland towards the house. He could not see the house but the flames lit the sky. There was no sentry visible on the bridge but he could have taken cover. There was still sporadic firing from the direction of the house.

He retraced his steps, beckoned Nicholl and led the file on, moving right, away from the house and the bridge, until trees lifted outside the wall. They climbed it then, lifting the old man bodily and passing him down the other side, and went on into the cover of the trees. They were out of sight of the bridge. The gully, with the tumbling stream threading the bottom of it, was on their left hand now. It swung right and there Ward halted them again.

He waited, called softly: "Catherine?" A moment later she emerged from the shadows. Her eyes widened when she saw Peyraud, but she made no comment. The moon-light filtering down through the branches lit the planes and hollows of her face as Ward looked down at her. She gave him a quick smile.

Before them the cliffs stood against the sky on either side of the gully that lay below and in shadow, clothed thickly in bracken. And between the cliffs was the sea.

Ward's eyes lifted again, searching, and Beare's voice came low at his side, "I don't see it." He was talking of the pill-box, somewhere near the cliff-top across the gully. Ward shook his head, turned and searched instead the shadows under the trees. Beare said, "I've put sentries out but you won't see 'em from here."

Ward could not. There was only Peyraud sitting in the snow with his back against a tree, Catherine crouched beside him. Ward joined them. Peyraud was breathing quickly, raggedly, his head back against the tree and face up-turned as he fought for breath.

Ward said softly, "Monsieur can rest a little." He touched the girl's arm. "Catherine?" He led her back to where Beare stood looking out across the gully and asked her, "Can you show us the pill-box?"

She shook her head. "I only came as far as the house." And Jean had been unable to pin-point the machine-gun nest.

171

Ward nodded. "All right. Will you wait with the old man?"

"Yes." Then she added, "I think Monsieur Peyraud is not well. I think he has not eaten well and, being a prisoner – We must not go so quickly."

Beare's head turned at that. Ward said, "We may have no choice. He can rest now but it won't be for long."

The girl nodded. "I understand." She went back to crouch by Peyraud.

Beare muttered, "We'll carry the old feller if we have to. No sense in taking him back to snuff it."

No sense at all, they needed Peyraud alive and well. Aside from that, Ward knew he would have to answer to himself for the old man's life. He said, "Dent and Baldry should have been here by now." If they had broken off the action at the *Freya* when the house was set alight. If they were alive.

Beare grumbled agreement. "They're late."

There was no question of waiting for them, let alone seeking them. Ward and his party had to get away with Peyraud – if they could. He said, "We'll give the old man a minute to get his breath back." And he hated to abandon the other two.

Catherine was fighting fear. She had steeled herself to set up the landing lights, meet and guide the raiding party. She had not, could not have imagined the rest of it, the ear-battering din and the dark terrors of her journey alone through the forest to this place.

She whispered words of encouragement to Peyraud but she watched Ward where he stood with Beare. She had gathered that half the raiding force had been lost. At the time she hadn't considered the significance of that: only now did she realise the enormous odds faced by the handful of men around her. She and Henri had counted the German garrison and put it at fifty – or more. These few men had successfully attacked that garrison and seized Peyraud . . . but now they had to make their way down to the beach under the eyes of the men in the pill-box, somewhere high on the opposite slope. And the responsibility to get them through rested on Ward.

He said, "The pill-box. We know it covers the beach and we know we can't get off while it's functioning so we've got to shut it up. If it covers the beach then we have to assume it *doesn't* cover the gully. So one party goes after the pill-box while the rest start down the gully. We can't hang about here."

Beare nodded. "Jerry'll start moving out from that house soon and he'll come this way. I'll take Nicholl and fix the pill-box." He pressed: "Time's about up, sir."

Then he grabbed Ward's arm and pulled him down, pointed. Ward saw movement in the shadows under the trees, a hand flapping a signal. Beare whispered, "Driscoll! He's heard something!"

The German section they evaded as it passed on the track? Ward could hear movement now, the soft crunch of boots on snow and an irregular scraping. Then a voice called softly, hopefully, "Arsenal?"

The voice was Sergeant Dent's, and immediately Driscoll gave him the other half of the pass-word: "Rangers!"

A shadow advanced through the trees. "Thank Christ, you're still here! Baldry's copped one!" The shadow became two men, Dent struggling along with one arm around Baldry's waist, Baldry's arm across his shoulders. The pilot was half-carrying the commando whose legs floundered as he walked. Beare took him and laid him down with his back propped against a tree. Dent, sweating, wiped a hand across his face. He said, "Top o' the right leg. I put a dressing on it best I could. Had a hell of a job getting him down the hill!"

Beare lowered his head over the leg, peering, and Baldry asked between gasps, "Is it – all right?"

Beare answered, "Could've been worse. A few inches higher would've spoiled your dirty weekends. The dressing looks O.K." He straightened and turned to Ward. "I think we've got to move, sir."

That they had. Apart from those dead in the house there were fifty-odd Germans hunting them now. Ward gave his orders and they moved out.

Beare and Nicholl, making for the pill-box somewhere up on the other side, went down towards the stream while Ward led the others in file along the steadily descending side of the gully. He could hear the grunts of pain as Baldry was humped along between Dent and Lockwood in the middle of the file, the puffing and stumbling of Peyraud, clinging to Catherine Guillard's arm. Driscoll was at the tail and watching for any pursuit.

They had covered two hundred yards when a challenge came from high across the gully, a hoarse bellow. Ward threw himself down in the bracken, thinking, They've spotted Beare! But when the machine-gun flickered across the gully he heard the *whip-crack!* of bullets passing close overhead. He and his party were the target.

He turned on his side, worked the Verey signalling pistol out of the pocket of his smock and loaded it. As he did so he shouted, "Sergeant Beare! They've brought at least one gun out of the pill-box to cover the gully! I'm going to draw their fire and give you a chance to get up there! The rest of us will push on to the beach!" They had to get Peyraud to England.

His shouting brought another sweeping burst from the machine-gun but the tracers were still high. Then Beare's voice came back, "Right! Move fast an' keep your head down, sir! You're a big target!"

Yet another burst, but again over Ward so they still hadn't fixed Beare's position. Ward pointed the pistol at the sky, fired, dropped it and grabbed the Thompson. The Verey light burst brilliant red, high above the beach and drifted slowly down. That was the signal to bring in the landing craft, and it might distract the machine-gun for long enough . . .

He pushed up and bolted down the hill towards the stream. He ran with long, leaping strides, neck-or-nothing. The stream came up towards him and he heard the *whip-*

crack! again, behind him now but very close. When only yards from the stream he stumbled, slipped in the snow, fell forward and rolled over the bank to plunge into the icy water.

He crashed in feet first and up to his waist, spray bursting around him. He waded frantically forward, arms swinging wildly to give him momentum, the current pushing at him and rocks turning under his boots. He could see the machine-gun now, flickering up on the side of the gully and he flailed desperately towards the cover offered by the far bank, threw himself into it.

He crouched there panting for a few seconds, getting his breath back and his wits together. One hand was twisted in the wet stems of bracken bordering the stream, the other held up the Thompson. He kept his head down as Beare had told him. "You're a big target!" Ward knew it. When he broke from cover again he would move as fast as he could but this time, struggling up the side of the gully, he would be slower. Maybe last time the steep fall of the ground had saved him. Maybe next time the machine-gunner would set his sights correctly. Ward was a seaman, not a soldier, and knew he was not trained for this.

He waited as the gun fired again and the burst kicked a trail of spouts along the surface of the stream. When it stopped he would go.

Maybe he would never see Catherine again.

The gun fell silent. He kicked up, scrambled out on to the bank and started running, bent over and weaving, waiting for the bullets. But instead there came a long ripple of muzzle-flashes high along the hill's crest, the separate bursts blending into one rattling clamour. It was punctuated by the *thump* of grenades and he saw them bursting below the crest where the machine-gun fired – or had fired. It was still silent.

Beare's voice bellowed up the gully, "Cease fire!" In the hush that followed he called, "Arsenal?"

"Rangers!" The answer came from the top of the slope. Ward halted, panting, and saw men appear there, dropping like bouncing balls down the side of the gully towards the stream. He thought, *Peter Madden! Thank God!* Everything would be all right now.

He turned and went down to the stream again, waded across, scrambled up the bank and Dent appeared above him, helped him over the edge. A Thompson fired close by and the pilot warned, "Keep down! Jerry's up at the top o' the gully!"

Ward crawled into the bracken. The firing was heavy now, from the pursuit at the head of the gully and the British falling back towards the beach. He asked, "Where's the old man?"

"That French bit took him away. Soon as you set off they started crawling under cover of this stuff." Archie Dent flicked at the bracken and it shed snow in glistening powder. "Lockwood took Baldry. Driscoll's just up the slope a few yards." He called, "O.K. Mike?"

"O.K."

Ward heaved himself up. Driscoll sprawled in the bracken a few yards away, Thompson at his shoulder. There were flashes of small-arms fire from the forest at the head of the gully but they seemed pale against the red glow from the blazing house behind them. The raiders were filtering back on both sides of the stream, moving singly in short rushes from cover to cover. Ward saw Beare make a short run then sprawl again to fire up the gully.

Ward copied him.

They fell back to the beach, moving singly. Ward left Archie Dent and Driscoll to hold a position just above the beach while he went down to it. The mouth of the gully was closed by barbed wire but a gap had been cut by Lockwood. He passed through to the beach.

There were two landing-craft, a cable's length offshore and steadily butting in. They must have seen the flames from the burning house and already been closing the beach when Ward fired the Verey light. The Brens mounted aboard them were firing, sending tracers sliding in high flat arcs towards the head of the gully. Ward stood with his boots on shingle, one arm wrapped around Peyraud. He glanced across the old man at Catherine and said, "Just a few more yards." The words were meant for both of them.

The first landing-craft grounded and the ramp splashed down. The section of infantry aboard streamed ashore and raced up the beach to form a defensive screen. Ward set Peyraud and Catherine on the ramp and shouted to the seaman at the head of it. "Take good care of him! He's what we came for!"

"Aye, aye, sir!"

Ward turned and trotted back up the beach. He crouched by the kneeling lieutenant commanding the defensive screen and watched as the raiders came through one by one. At the last came Beare with Nicholl – and Peter Madden.

Beare lifted a hand as he passed and growled, "Bloody good stuff, sir."

Ward went with Madden down to the boats. Peter looked exhausted, still breathed heavily and sweat ran down his face despite the cold. He said, "Dropped more than a mile away. Had to double most of it. Bloody nuisance. Where's Tim Gregson?"

Ward told him and Peter said sickly, "He was engaged to a girl in Bristol. Cracking girl." He fell silent then.

They were aboard the landing-craft, the screening infantry withdrew, the ramps were hauled up and the boats went astern, the Brens still raking the gully. Ward sought out Catherine and Peyraud where they sat right aft and sank down beside the girl.

Archie Dent's voice came disembodied out of the darkness: "Here, it's my birthday!"

Silence, then Ward said, "Many Happy Returns."

Dent answered, "Not of that bloody lot!"

There was laughter in the boat and Ward joined in, over-loud, reaction gripping him.

They had done it. Peyraud with his vital knowledge was on his way to England. Ward thought about Peter Madden and his party, who had saved the whole enterprise from disaster because without them Ward's little band could never have captured the pill-box before the pursuit caught up with them. Madden and his group had run, at night, for a mile through strange enemy-held countryside, had carried their arms and equipment, and had fought a decisive action at the end of it. Ward thought commandos were amazing men. And one of them, Sergeant Beare, had said, "Bloody good stuff, sir."

That was something to be proud of.

And Catherine Guillard. He glanced sidewise at her and saw her face turned up to him, the quick smile. He had thought he would never see her again. But now . . .

The note of the engine changed, Ward got up and helped Peyraud to stand, extended a hand to Catherine. They were closing the M.T.B.s waiting to take them aboard and hurry them home. He would be able to send a radio signal from the M.T.B.

They were a step nearer St. Nazaire and the great dock.

Quartermain went to the Admiralty in the early hours of the morning and paced the subterranean corridors until the signal came through. It was one laconic codeword that told him the operation had been successful. He heard it with relief but nothing more. He knew it was just another step along the way and there was still a long hard road ahead.

10

"Were you so sure?"

The M.T.B.s put them ashore at noon in a narrow creek on the Hampshire coast, near Southampton. The creek lay hidden from curious eyes in a shallow valley, at the head of which stood a big, solitary house. It was a bleak, deserted place on that winter day. They landed on a wooden jetty, at the end of which several vehicles were parked: an army three-ton truck, several cars, three ambulances. On the jetty waited doctors and medical orderlies, a general and several other officers, some with the red tabs of the staff, some naval. There were two civilians dressed sombrely in dark overcoats – and Quartermain in a bridgecoat with its collar turned up against the wind. He stared disbelievingly at Catherine Guillard with Ward's arm about her, then said, "Good God!"

The M.T.B.s departed for their base at Portsmouth. Peyraud and the wounded were taken to the ambulances and whisked away to hospital – but not before Quartermain had spoken words of thanks to the men, and a welcome to Peyraud. "We are very glad to see you in England, Monsieur. We need you." A captain of Royal Engineers went with Peyraud.

The general and his aide climbed into one of the cars and Madden paused at the door to look across at the Wren waiting by Quartermain's Daimler. Madden winked at her and she smiled, then quickly opened the doors for Quartermain, Catherine and Ward. The cars and the truck carrying the commandos drove only as far as the house and halted before its door. In pre-war days it was a country hotel but now it was run by the Army, its natural seclusion reinforced by miles of barbed-wire fencing and patrolling guards. A sentry stood at the door. Catherine thought it dark and depressing.

179

Inside, on the ground floor, it still seemed a hotel with a large hall, an anteroom and dining-room, but the rest was given up to offices. A broad staircase led from the hall to the floor above which was a barrack, bare and austere, the right-hand wing holding rooms for officers, that on the left a dormitory and mess for other ranks.

Quartermain told Ward, "I'll see you later. First I'll have a word with the lady." He took Catherine away.

Ward ate in the dining-room with Madden and the other officers, then adjourned with them to a large room with maps tacked to the walls and a long trestle table with several officers seated around it. Ward and Madden made their verbal reports which a clerk took down in shorthand. Then the cross-questioning began. There were several murmurs of approval and the general nodded vigorous agreement. To Ward, weary and impatient, it went on interminably . . .

Quartermain led Catherine Guillard to a small room with a desk, a chair behind it and an armchair. He settled her in the armchair, sat down behind the desk and muttered absently, "I'll phone the Executive in a minute and get them to send some clothes for you." That was the Strategic Operations Executive, the secret organisation that 'ran' Catherine as an agent. "We were expecting a man. Why did you do it?"

Catherine explained, as she had to Ward, that she had had no choice. He accepted that: in this war men had no monopoly on danger. There came a tap on the door and a white-coated steward entered with a meal on a tray for them. They sat in silence until he had set it down and left.

Quartermain said, "The two civilians you saw are from the Executive. They will have a lot to ask you, starting today and going on tomorrow, but first have you anything urgent to tell me?"

Catherine nodded. "Something new – and very urgent. But first, can I have a sheet of paper and a pencil?"

Quartermain got them from a drawer and she took his place at the desk and sketched quickly. "You have plans of

St. Nazaire. This is the basin, here are the U-boat pens. Here is the bridge over the Old Entrance. Along this road are offices and workshops. The last building but one, here, about two hundred metres north of the bridge, is only occupied on the ground floor by the officer of the Abwehr, Hauptmann Engel, and a dozen of his men. But now the upper floor is being made into an apartment. Men of the Todt organisation are doing the work but the day I left they borrowed a carpenter from the dockyard. That evening he came to the office and said he'd overheard that the apartment was for Dönitz. He is to visit St. Nazaire and he will spend the night in that apartment."

She went back to the armchair and sank into it. She was very tired.

The admiral frowned. "He overheard? It is talked about openly?"

Catherine explained, "Everyone knows that Dönitz will come. He does from time to time, because of the U-boat pens. That is no secret."

Quartermain stared down at the sketch. This could be the chance they had waited for. There were enormous difficulties, not just those this girl could see but another complicating factor that she knew nothing about: CHARIOT. He asked, "When?"

"I don't know, but I think I can find out."

Quartermain shook his head. "No. You can't go back again."

"It is quite safe. My absence is explained. My chief granted me a week to visit my aunt in Paris. She is old and feeble, and real. I have done this before."

"Landing at night in German-held territory is never safe and once you are there you are always in danger." And the danger increased with the days; luck ran out. It had run out for other agents.

They did not argue. She was too weary and said simply, "I will return to France because she is my country. It is my right, and my duty."

They ate then, but poorly, the girl listless and Quartermain worried for her. Afterwards the civilians from S.O.E. came in and began their questioning. It was dark when they finished for the day, the lights on and the black-out curtains drawn. Quartermain took the sketch away with him.

Ward escaped when the debriefing was done, the congratulations and handshakes over. He looked for Catherine in the anteroom where there was a fire and a bar now, with a steward, but she was not there nor in the dining-room beyond. Another steward asked him, "Are you dining, sir?" Ward shook his head, went back to the hall and found Quartermain in the act of shrugging on his overcoat.

The admiral glanced around to see they were not overheard then said quietly, "You'll be glad to know that Peyraud has already told the captain of Engineers a great deal. All we want now is the necessary ship. That is difficult but Lord Louis is bringing pressure to bear." And Mountbatten could exert considerable pressure. Quartermain went on: "I understand *Boston* won't be ready for sea until Tuesday, so you still have a couple of days' leave. Will you go up to London tomorrow?"

Ward asked, "Is Catherine going?"

"No."

"Then I'm not. Where is she, sir?"

Quartermain picked up his cap and briefcase. "She's gone to bed. The girl is exhausted."

"I – hoped to see her."

The little admiral looked at Ward scowling down on him, "You will." He did not think it a good idea but it couldn't be helped. He tapped the briefcase, "I've got a copy of your report, and Madden's, in here. I've yet to read them but I've had a quick word with the general. You all did well, very well." He glanced at his watch. "I'm going to London now." To talk to the Executive about the girl. If she was going back then the sooner the better, so suspicions would not be aroused on the other side. "I'll be back for dinner tomorrow evening."

So Ward had a drink with Peter Madden then went to his

bed. It was narrow and uncomfortable. His kit had come down on the truck from Salisbury Plain along with that of the commandos and some steward had hung up his uniform. Ward threw the airborne forces smock and the rest of his filthy clothing into a corner. He was bone-weary but lay awake for some time, restless. When he finally slept he dreamt of the burning house and the machine-gun firing at him as he crossed the black water of the stream.

He was up and about early the next day but a steward told him Catherine was already with the two civilians: "Said they'd be in there all day, not to be disturbed and they'd let us know when they want coffee an' lunch sent in, sir."

Ward swore, ate breakfast and strode out of the house. At the gate the corporal on duty saluted and said, "'Morning, Mr. Ward."

"'Morning!" Ward had never seen the man before. Had the sentries been shown photographs of himself and all the others? He didn't know or care. He walked for miles through country lanes and returned along the Southampton road. He stopped at an old pub with a low, smoky ceiling, drank a pint of bitter and talked with the landlord. The pub was a small hotel: creaky passages and rooms with tiny latticed windows. When he got back to the house at noon there was a car waiting to take him to lunch with the C.-in-C., Portsmouth.

He swore again but there was no help for it. He went to his room and cleaned his shoes, looked in at the dining-room but Catherine was not there, climbed into the car and growled at the Wren behind the wheel, "All right, let's get it over with."

He spent the afternoon at Portsmouth. He was given a good lunch, questioned closely again about the raid and his account of it was heard with attention. It was impossible not to be pleased and flattered. Only in the car going back to the house did the black mood fall on him again. He sat in silence the whole way. It was snowing heavily now and the wipers flapped at the white curtain it laid on the wind-

screen. Despite the snow and his bad temper, as the car
ground up the gravel drive of the house he apologised to
the Wren with a rueful grin. "Sorry I was so bloody rude."

She was pleased. "That's all right, sir."

He started to get out of the car then paused, peering
through the darkness up the steps of the house. The sentry
in his waterproof cape was almost hidden in the shadow of
the doorway, but beside him . . . Ward said to the driver,
"Wait a moment, will you?"

He climbed out and walked to Catherine where she
stood on the steps, a coat around her shoulders, staring out
at the night and the snow. No light showed in the house
behind her but with his face bent close to hers he saw her
smile, then the corners of her mouth drooped again.

Ward asked, "Fed up?"

Her voice was low, husky, "I want to go from this place."

He wrapped his arm around her and led her to the car, its
engine still ticking over softly, opened the rear door and
said to the Wren driver, "Run us down the road, will you?
My responsibility."

The girl hesitated because it was against the rules, but
only briefly. "Very good, sir."

He climbed into the back with Catherine and held her
until the low gabled shadow of the pub loomed up through
the snow. The car stopped and he led her inside.

The room he took her to was close beneath the roof so
Ward had to stoop under the beams. Its floor tilted and it
was long and narrow with two armchairs before a log fire at
one end and an oak bedstead with a big feather bed at the
other. There was a tray on the table by the fire: a bottle of
navy rum, glasses, and a jug of hot water. The girl drank
water with the rum but Ward took it neat.

She asked, "When did you arrange this?"

"This morning. I told the chap here I was on a course and
my wife was coming down. He was in the Navy in the last
war – in big ships, but a nice bloke all the same."

She was quiet for a time, then asked softly, "Were you so
sure?"

"Were you so sure?"

"No." He looked at her over the glass. "Were you?"
But she only smiled and went to bed with him.

Later he slept quietly, one arm around her. She did not
sleep for a long time. She cried a little and was not sure
whether it was because she was happy or sad, because in
fact she was both. She finally slept with the tears still wet on
her cheeks.

When Ward woke it was dark in the room except for the
glow of the embers in the grate but his watch told him it was
morning. He eased carefully away from the girl and out of
bed, padded naked to the window, head bent beneath the
beams and pulled aside the blackout curtains. The room
was at the back of the house and he looked out over a mile
of snow-covered heath to the sea beyond. In that first light
it caught no glint of sunlight, was cold and grey.

He turned away and went to the fire, put logs on the
embers and crouched there watching the small flames climb
hissing on the wood. He could smell the resin in it. He
wondered if this with Catherine was a mistake? He must go
his way, and the girl must go hers. And yet, mistake or not,
it had happened because they both wanted it to.

Quartermain would be annoyed.

To hell with Quartermain.

He heard a stir behind him, turned his head and saw
Catherine awake, watching him. He rose and went back to
her.

That morning they borrowed wellingtons from the landlord and went walking in the snow, threw snowballs and
acted like children. Ward saw a warship far out to sea and
wondered if Mountbatten would get his destroyer in time
for CHARIOT. They were into March now. CHARIOT
had to go by the end of this month for the tide and
the darkness to be right. Time was running desperately
short.

He had telephoned from the pub the previous evening
and left a message at the house for Quartermain: "Tell him
Mr. Ward and friend are spending the evening out."

185

At noon he telephoned from the pub again and told them at the house to send the duty truck. The driver would have to get the permission of the orderly officer and he would tell Quartermain. More fuel to the flames. Ward shrugged. The truck came and at the house they had a drink at the bar then went in to eat a leisurely lunch.

They were alone in the dining-room for some time and when Quartermain came in they did not see him. He stood on the threshold, newspaper and briefcase under his arm, watching them. He said to himself, Damn, damn, damn! This was a complication he had not wanted. A half-blind man could see it, written all over their faces.

But when he went to them he only said, "So there you are . . . Sorry to interrupt but I must claim Catherine for some little time, things to discuss." He did not put down his briefcase but held out *The Times* to Ward. "You'll find that interesting. There's no mention of your doings, nor will there be. That way the Germans will think we're keeping quiet because the raid was a failure and we didn't capture the radar as the paras did at Bruneval."

He went off with Catherine and Ward opened the paper. The report of the Bruneval raid was there. Frost and his paratroopers had scored a spectacular success. The *Würzburg* radar was described as 'a radio location unit'. All the objectives had been achieved with relatively minor casualties – and prisoners brought back too. Ward read the news with grim satisfaction. At last, here was something to cheer about after all the defeats and failures of this winter.

He took the paper through to the anteroom and settled down in an armchair to read the rest of it. The Japanese were invading Java and there was heavy fighting in the Crimea. Noël Coward's *Blithe Spirit* was on at the Piccadilly.

A familiar name jumped out at him: "Patrick Ward: A rare, raw new talent . . ." The art critic was writing of a one-man show at a London gallery and for a *Times* man he was wildly enthusiastic. "This first showing of Ward's

work . . . a dozen paintings and sketches . . . outstanding
new talent . . . possible genius in khaki." That 'possible'
was the only hint of reservation.

Ward thought, Well, I'll be damned! Good for Patrick!

Quartermain took Catherine to the small room and settled
her into the now familiar armchair. "How are you?"

"Very well." She smiled at him, relaxed.

Quartermain thought about Ward but only said, "Um!"
This was a complication you might always get with people,
particularly young people. He could do nothing about it.
"Pleased with your clothes?" Catherine wore a pleated
skirt and a blue jumper. Quartermain thought she looked
very nice, also very English.

"They're lovely." In fact she thought the clothes boring,
even dowdy. The Executive had supplied them. She smiled
at him. "My own from France are upstairs. Your people
have laundered and pressed them. I'm very grateful."

"You take out only what you brought in – apart from the
money, of course, which the Executive will supply." He
tapped his briefcase.

"That is always useful."

Quartermain emphasised the point: "No presents. No
keepsakes."

"None." Catherine smiled for him again, "Don't worry.
I'm not a young, love-sick girl."

Quartermain did worry but did not say so. "Tonight. Are
you ready?"

"Yes." The girl said that without tremor or hesitation.

Quartermain unlocked the briefcase, took out a slim
folder and passed it to her. "Your instructions."

She opened the folder and began to read:

For Mlle Catherine Guillard, organiser of SPINSTER.
Operation: SPINSTER.
Field Name: GENEVIEVE.
Name on papers: Catherine Guillard.
(1) INFORMATION

We have discussed with you, thoroughly, the possibility of your returning to France to continue the overall mission which you were originally given when you left for that country in July 1940.

It is our joint understanding that nothing prevents your returning to the same area to carry out the same tasks.

(2) INTENTION

(a) You will return to the Field by Lysander . . .

Catherine read on to the end, then went back to the beginning. She read the instructions again and again until she knew them by heart while Quartermain stood at the window, staring out, unhappy.

The girl finally signed the instructions and passed them to him. He replaced them in the briefcase and said, "All pretty much as before, the movements of shipping and so forth. But Dönitz – you've told us where to find him, now we must know the night."

"That is understood."

Quartermain was silent a moment, then: "I don't want you to go."

"I know." She stood up, went to him and kissed him. "Will you do something for me?"

"Of course."

Catherine went in to dinner with Ward that evening. He had bullied, cajoled and bribed to get a bottle of wine from the steward and they ate a cheerful meal. Quartermain sat alone, pleading that he had papers to read and he spread them on the table for appearance's sake. But afterwards he went to their table and said to Ward, "There's something I want to show you. It'll take a couple of hours."

Ward stood and stooped over Catherine, "See you later."

"Au revoir." She smiled up at him.

He stroked a finger gently down her cheek and went away with Quartermain.

They drove to Southampton. It was raining now, the snow turning to dirty slush. German bombing had laid the city waste, whole streets razed to the ground, nothing left of the houses but a jagged frieze of stunted, broken walls. As they passed through the gates of the dockyard Quartermain said, "We're going to the King George V dock. Peyraud has confirmed that its construction is almost identical to that of St. Nazaire. He's pinpointed the places for locating demolition charges, and the commandos are already using it for training."

They stood side by side in the night, close by the dock, the bottom of it hidden in darkness like the pit. The water of the harbour outside was flecked with white where a breeze riffled it. The same wind drove rain into their faces and Quartermain muttered bad-temperedly and turned up the collar of his coat.

He said, "I know you are worried about the passage of time but set your mind at rest. Mountbatten has got his ship and CHARIOT is on. Look —"

He pointed towards the landward end of the dock and Ward saw men materialise out of the darkness. There looked to be a score of them, running in a loose file, making little sound because of the rubber-soled boots they wore, their legs topped with bodies made huge by the massive packs they carried. They were faceless, their features smudged with black, anonymous in the khaki battledress they wore.

They ran past Ward, their backs straight, their arms moving like pistons. He asked Quartermain, "How much do those packs weigh?"

"Around ninety pounds."

They had run the length of the dock, a quarter mile, and ran on now. One party went to the winding-shed that held the machinery for opening the dock gate, another to the gate itself.

Quartermain stirred. "You won't see any more now, not in this darkness. Come on." He started back the way they had come and Ward paced alongside. Quartermain said,

"They started doing it in daylight, then practised laying the charges blindfold, now in the night."

Ward asked, "Do they know what it's for?"

Quartermain shook his head, "No. They believe it's just one more course. They're giving it all they've got because they always do; nobody could work harder. But all they expect at the end of it is the satisfaction of having achieved another skill and, maybe, a few days' leave."

"Will they get it?"

"No. There isn't time."

They came to the Daimler, walking in silence. Ward had expected the admiral to be at least enthusiastic now that CHARIOT was definitely to go through, but he was morose and walked with hands deep in the pockets of his coat. Ward could see him scowling as he got into the car.

Ward followed and the Wren driver, Jenny Melville, closed the door. Ward said, "Thank you for telling me, showing me."

He bent his head to peer at the face of his watch. Quartermain saw the movement and said, "There's no hurry. You earned this trip, at least, after your fine effort on that raid. Besides, I had another reason for dragging you over here." Quartermain's hand came out of his pocket and he thrust an envelope at Ward. "This was her idea. She said she couldn't face a parting."

Ward took the envelope. That was all he could see in the gloom inside the car. He turned it over in his hands then put it away in his own pocket. "She's gone."

"Yes." Quartermain frowned. "I'm sorry. I can understand how you feel."

"Can you?" Ward turned his black stare on Quartermain. "I'd like to break somebody's bloody neck!"

He packed his kit at the house and caught a late train out of Portsmouth station. He was rejoining his ship. The train was as full as they always were and Ward stood shoulder to shoulder in a corridor jammed tight with weary sailors going home. Because of the blackout the lamp bulbs were painted blue and so were the windows except for one small circle in the middle of each pane to let passengers see the station when the train stopped – if it stopped at a station. This one did, sometimes. At other times it ground to a halt and there was nothing but blackness to be seen.

In the dim-lit, smoke-filled atmosphere Ward could barely make out the features of men only yards away. In the compartment behind him they sat sleeping, wedged together so that they swayed as one to the rocking of the train, as if in hammocks aboard ship. A sailor slept stretched out precariously on each luggage rack above the heads of his fellows. Some of the men were soldiers, and their rifles were stacked among the kitbags and packs that were crammed on the floor between their legs.

The train waited for long periods in sidings, leaving the track clear for freight trains to rumble slowly by. Somewhere a child cried fretfully, unceasingly. Ward leaned his arms on the wooden rail across the window, used them as a pillow and dozed fitfully.

They would raid St. Nazaire before the month of March was out.

Catherine had written words of love to him but now she had gone to France and he was going to sea again.

11

Dirty Bill

The night was dark and overcast and still, the kind of night on which you could expect an attack, and *Boston* was in E-boat Alley again. She slid her knife-edged stem through a quiet, oily sea making barely a ripple. They were hunting E-boats but it was Dirty Bill they hungered for.

Boston was alone. When she had left the dockyard after her boiler-clean she did not go back to convoy duty, but instead was sent patrolling. The change was welcome. Now *Boston* was not stuck at the tail-end of a convoy, itself a big, spread target and out in the middle of the channel swept through the minefields. Instead she crept along at the inshore edge of the channel, feeling her way from one marker buoy to the next. She showed no light, made no smoke and little bow-wave or wake. This particular tactic was Ward's idea; he could not forget how Dirty Bill had lain inshore of a buoy to launch her torpedoes at the *Missouri Star*. But this was their third night out: convoys had been attacked on each of the two previous nights and aboard *Boston* they had seen the far-off glow of starshell, heard the gunfire faint with distance and the muffled *thud!* of a torpedo striking home, but Ward and *Boston* had found nothing.

He thought, We need a bit of luck. He could feel that the tension on the bridge was slackening now because the night would soon be over and all the hours of patient searching had gone for nothing. He lowered the glasses and rubbed at his eyes. Try again in a minute. There were plenty of others searching, anyway, the two look-outs and Phillips the Guns, Mason the navigator and Joe Krueger in his fur cap. Tired or not, surely one of them would spot something? If there was something to spot.

192

Dirty Bill

When Ward had returned to the ship after the raid, Joe asked him, "Good leave, sir?"

"Very." Remembering Catherine Guillard. Then, flatly, "No."

Joe blinked at that sudden turnabout but wisely changed the subject. "See any shows?"

"One."

"Good?"

"I won't forget it."

He would not talk about it, could not, but instead told Joe about Patrick. On his way back to the ship Ward had a couple of hours to spare in London and sought out the gallery in Cork Street where Patrick's work was on show. It was crowded and he edged through from painting to sketch to painting. He had gone there curious; prepared simply to stare uncomprehendingly and give the experts the benefit of the doubt but instead he found that this was work he could understand. One painting in particular caught his attention: it was of a long, straight road, dusty under a bright sun. A car lay at the roadside, doors hanging open, abandoned, a burst suitcase beside it spilling clothing into the dust. A small boy stood in the foreground, his face dirty, eyes staring out of the picture. For Ward it was the sunken *Lancastria*, bombed cities, the blazing *Missouri Star*, the whole waste and misery of war set down in awful simplicity.

Others held him, like the one of soldiers on the march among snow-capped hills, their figures made tiny by the immensity of the back-drop yet each one vibrantly alive. The face of the leader in the foreground was strained with effort, dogged with determination: this man would never give up.

But at the end Ward went back to the boy.

He learned that every picture had been sold – and for prices up to a hundred pounds. That was getting on for two years' pay for a corporal. Patrick was on his way to being a financial, as well as an artistic, success.

And the rest of the family? One of Geoffrey's periodic

193

letters had reported, very briefly, on the progress of the Perseus Group. The context of those letters varied but there was always a request somewhere for advice or a decision – and Ward knew why. He himself had got out from under his father's wing when he joined the Navy and went to Dartmouth, but Geoffrey had stayed and worked under a man who always insisted on taking the final decision. With the habit of deferring so beaten into him Geoffrey was finding it hard to learn to stand on his own feet.

Another letter, from his mother at home in Northumberland, said she had just finished a four-week concert tour of army camps throughout Britain. Her brother, uncle Daniel was touring the States, singing Verdi and Rossini and complaining bitterly about putting on weight after leaving the rationing of England . . .

Ward lifted his glasses again, stared into the blackness. His own artistic career had stuck at thumping out 'Bless 'em all!' at ship's concerts in pubs ashore. He grinned. Still, he'd been right about Patrick. Those years in Paris hadn't been wasted. The grin slipped away. He'd been wrong about this bloody patrol.

Boston was closing the green-lit buoy that marked a wreck. There were many in this channel and Dirty Bill was responsible for a number of them. Ward ordered, "Starboard ten," to take *Boston* around the wreck.

"Starboard ten, sir."

There was quiet on the bridge.

Ward told the coxswain, "Meet her . . . Steer that." He straightened, now looking out towards France over the heads of the others on the bridge.

Catherine was there. She had returned there over a week ago.

He concentrated on his ship, conned her carefully around the wreck and back on her course to the next buoy marking the channel, but a part of his mind was with the girl. He had had no word from Quartermain. In the car that night he had talked to the admiral of killing – he had learned to keep the hatches battened down on his temper but had not succeeded then – and he'd meant what he said. If Catherine were harmed and there was one man somewhere who was guilty, then he would break – He checked there. Face to face, would he kill? On the raid to bring back Peyraud he had fired not at men but at threatening shadows in the darkness. In June 1940 he had looked over the sights of his pistol at an enemy – then had walked away. So –

"There's the next buoy. On the bow." That was Phillips.

Mason, the navigator, said, "Seen." He bent over the compass to take the bearing.

Ward picked up the distant winking light. There was a long way to go yet.

Phillips grumbled, "Not a bloody thing. If we go on like this we'll be back on escort work in a day or two, I'll bet you."

Joe Krueger said, "It can happen when you least expect it." He paused, then added bitterly, "Like Pearl Harbour."

He fell silent and Ward waited, the pair of them slowly sweeping the darkness ahead with their glasses. Then Joe went on, "This war with Germany, now, that was no surprise. I took a working vacation in Europe back in 1937, France, Germany – rubber-necking most of the time but I looked at a lot of powerboats and engines so that made the trip tax-deductible."

Ward took the glasses from his eyes and asked, "E-boats?"

"No, but I got to know the engines those beauties use. You catch one an' I'll make her go." Joe's teeth showed in a grin. "Anyway, I told you I spoke German with my grandfather back home, right? So the language there was no problem. I saw the torchlight parades and talked to people, listened to Hitler's speeches and I didn't need any translation." He turned to look at Ward. They were all quiet on the bridge, listening. "Around about then a lot of people still thought Hitler was a funny little guy with a Charlie Chaplin moustache, hooting and hollering and pounding a desk with his fist. I didn't think he was funny; I could see a war coming."

He faced forward and he and Ward lifted their glasses together. Ward swept from starboard to port. Cat's-paws of foam flecked a sea that was near flat calm. There was the buoy, and they were slowly, silently closing it – He saw the shadow as the look-out and Krueger spoke together: "*E-boat port side of the buoy!*" "*Boat red one-oh!*"

The E-boat lay just outside the little circle of radiance spilled on the sea by the lit buoy. It might have been anchored or even tied up to the buoy itself. Ward put his mouth close to the voicepipe: "Port ten!"

"Port ten . . . ten of port wheel on, sir!"

Ward said, "Coxswain! There's an E-boat about two cables ahead. You'll have to be quick down there when I give you the word!"

Adams' voice had an edge of excitement as it came up the pipe: "Aye, aye, sir!"

Softly, hoarsely, Phillips was passing orders to the guns: ". . . four hundred! Load!" Ward watched the low silhouette of the boat ahead, just an irregular slab of greater darkness on the sea, while below him on the fo'c'sle he saw the crew of the 4-inch shifting quickly around their gun.

The muffled *clunk* of the quietly closed breech came up to him as he ordered, "Meet her . . . steer that."*Boston*'s bow pointed at the low, black shape and she was closing it steadily, slipping over the surface of the sea like a shadow. How close could they get to the E-boat before her look-outs spotted them? Ward thought her crew might not be seeing too well in the night, their vision marred by the light on the nearby buoy. And they would not be looking for a ship coming from this quarter because they were hunting convoys that would be steaming out in the middle of the swept channel.

Ward said quietly, "Be ready with that light."

The rating manning the searchlight on the wing of the bridge acknowledged in a barely audible whisper.

Phillips' low, husky call to the 4-inch came: "Three hundred!"

If they could get close enough Ward would ram. *Boston's*
bow would cut through the E-boat like a knife through
butter or ride over her, grinding her under. There was a
stillness on the bridge as if they all held their breath. Then
diesels burst into life ahead and their roar came bellowing
back across the water. Ward, eyes fastened on the German, his hands cradling the brass bell-mouth of the voicepipe, mouth right over it, ordered, "Full ahead!"

"Full ahead, sir!"

Ward straightened quickly and shouted to guns and
searchlight: "Fire! Light her up!"

"*Fire!*" Phillips bawled it; no need for quiet now. The
E-boat was moving ahead as the 4-inch recoiled, the barrel
seeming to jerk back from its own muzzle-flash. The slam
of it firing and the crash as it burst came almost as one
because the range was so short. The two carbons in the
searchlight were crackling as the gun fired and struck arc
now, creating a point of intense light that the big, dished
mirror threw out in a dazzling beam that fell on the
E-boat just as the shell from the 4-inch struck and burst in a
flash of yellow flame aft of the low, open bridge. The boat
was barely 200 yards away now and the light showed her
stern tucked down in churning foam as the big diesels
gathered the leverage to hurl her forward. There were
figures on the bridge and at the cannon in the waist,
swinging it round to point at *Boston*. The white beam lit up
the E-boat for all its length and made plain the insignia
painted on the side of the bridge: a skull and crossbones.

"*Dirty Bill!*"

Ward was not sure afterwards if they had all yelled or
whether the words were only in his mind. At the time he
had only one thought: to destroy the E-boat ahead. *Boston's* engines were quickening but her responses were
slower and she had nothing like the manoeuvrability of the
E-boat.

Ward ordered, "Starboard ten!" To point *Boston's* stem
ahead of the E-boat, setting her on a course to intercept
and at the same time turning her so the port side Oerlikons

would bear. The 4-inch fired again and that shell went over, the plume of water lifting beyond Dirty Bill. The cannon of the E-boat was firing and so were the machine-guns. Tracer was flying, pale where it cut through the searchlight's beam but outside it like a string of shooting stars in the dark of the night. The cannon shells were striking or ricocheting, howling off *Boston*'s hull but, unresponsive as she was, her bow was still coming round in time to point ahead of Dirty Bill. The 4-inch fired. The E-boat was turning away but *Boston* was almost on top of her and the range down to a hundred yards. The 4-inch shell burst on the E-boat and her cannon stopped firing. There was a flicker of yellow in the waist of her and then a soaring pillar of flame.

She was already moving too fast to be caught and rammed but she had been hit twice at point-blank range and any second now the Oerlikons on the port side would bear, open fire and cut her to pieces. Ward ordered, "Meet her!" To straighten *Boston* on a course to chase after Dirty Bill but running off the E-boat's starboard quarter so that she would lie under the hammer of the port side Oerlikons. The fire aboard her and the searchlight's beam showed the cannon was manned again and –

"*She's not answering, sir!*" The coxswain's voice was agonised as it came up the pipe: "*She's jammed and I can't shift her!*"

Boston's bow was still swinging to starboard, turning further and further away from Dirty Bill.

Ward snapped, "Stop port!" That would straighten her but not soon enough and he couldn't chase an E-boat using one engine. He had only seconds to grab his chance before it was gone.

The gap between the old four-stacker and the E-boat was widening rapidly, had grown to more than a quarter mile already. The searchlight's beam still held the boat but now she seemed tiny and Ward could not make out the figures on her bridge. The fire aboard her was snuffed out. *Boston*'s port side Oerlikons got off only a very brief burst before her bow swung back with the stopping of the port screw to follow the E-boat, now right ahead – and disappearing into the night. The 4-inch fired at her shadow, and missed.

Ward conned *Boston* using main engines but his chance was gone: the E-boat fled and the searchlight lost it. For a few seconds more one of the look-outs thought he could see the white blaze of her wake but then he admitted it was gone. The guns were silent, the searchlight flicked out and darkness swept in.

Phillips the Guns swore softly, steadily. Joe Krueger groaned, "We had him! Like *that!*" He stretched out his open hand then closed it into a fist and slammed it on the bridge screen. He shook his head, face sour with disappointment. "I always said the old cow never let you down when it really mattered. Looks like I was wrong this time."

Ward stared after the vanished E-boat, the one he and his crew wanted most of all. The others on the bridge could vent their anger but he would not. At least they had mauled the E-boat and put her into dock so that she would be out of the battle for a while, would sink no ship. Surely that was some consolation? Ward thought it was not enough. His men and his country were taking the blows and too many of them: the losses at sea, the fall of Singapore, the escape of *Scharnhorst* and *Gneisenau* . . . They needed a victory. Europe, under Nazi oppression, needed a victory.

The importance of CHARIOT loomed larger every day.

Ward could not talk of CHARIOT and this was no time for a speech, and he hated them, anyway. Best to put the incident behind them and get on with their job. So he said only, "She didn't let us down; just bad luck." He took *Boston* limping home, steering by main engines and the screws because this time Bailey and his blaspheming engineers could not free the jammed steering.

Ward sat in his bridge chair as the watch changed on a clear, bright morning, his orange duffel coat wrapped around him. He thought that at least the night's action had robbed the E-boats of their waiting tactic – they would not care to try it again for several months, now that they'd been caught out. And meanwhile, the Warrant Engineer, after he'd finished swearing, had said they would be in the dockyard for a day or two while the steering was repaired. That was all right because Joe Krueger had some jobs he wanted done and so did Ward. And he wanted to see about *Boston* being painted; the battering of the winter seas had left her scruffy . . . And so he made his plans.

Until he saw the bow lift and there came the roar of the explosion as *Boston* struck a mine.

They tried to save her but fractured bulkheads gave way before they could be shored up against the inrush of the sea. She settled, listing only slightly to starboard and Ward listened stone-faced to the report of Joe Krueger, come filthy from below decks, then went to see for himself before he accepted the verdict. She sank in fifteen minutes. There was time to disarm the depth-charges and launch all the boats and rafts, to send off a wireless signal of distress and have it acknowledged, but *Boston* was awash for half her length when finally Ward stepped into the last boat to leave and was pulled away.

The ship sank sedately and quietly, except at the last when there were internal rumblings. Then she slid under, leaving only a stain of oil and a litter of flotsam. By a miracle no one was in the fore-part of the ship when she struck the mine and they had not lost a man. Even the two cats and the mongrel, pets of the mess-deck, were saved. As Ward counted heads and learned this with relief a part of his mind told him more coldly that he had lost his ship. More than that; the efficient human machine that was *Boston*'s crew would be broken up and drafted piecemeal to other ships who needed them.

A captain who lost his ship had to face a court martial. That should prove a formality and find him guiltless but its implications were hardly encouraging and still had to be endured. His career had not been spectacular and there were plenty of destroyer captains with solid reputations marked by decorations, first lieutenants with glowing reports who would be thought to deserve a command better than he. He was on the beach, without a ship of his own and God alone knew when, if ever, he would get another.

12

Phoebe

Catherine Guillard did not try to pump her chief about the
coming visit of Admiral Dönitz, nor did she attempt to
seduce a general, bribe an official or burgle the offices of
the *Kommandatur*. Only the first of those methods occurred to her, and she still waited; there were other ways of
finding out. Only two days after her return to St. Nazaire,
sitting quietly in the big room where the clerks worked, she
heard talk that the Todt workers who were building the
U-boat pens had been set targets for the twenty-sixth of the
month.

Then the following evening, waiting in the café for
Henri, she heard a group of German soldiers grumble
because their furlough had been postponed. They were to
have left on Friday the twenty-seventh but all leave had
been cancelled for that weekend. Henri and Catherine had
heard rumours of this but now it was confirmed – and with
it the date of Dönitz' visit. That night, at his scheduled
time, Henri called London on the wireless. The message he
sent was brief: 27-30-3.

The next day Catherine asked her chief for leave of
absence on the weekend of 27th to 30th March.

And in England Ward received another telegram from
Quartermain.

He strode with Joe Krueger rapidly along Richmond Ter-
race through drizzling rain at fifteen minutes to three on
Thursday afternoon. The telegram in his pocket read
REPORT TO ME LONDON 1500 MARCH 19 PRE-
PARED ASSUME COMMAND. ACKNOWLEDGE.
QUARTERMAIN.

It came the previous day to Northumberland, the comfortably large, old stone house built on the side of the Cheviot hills and looking out to the sea. It was not of the size or splendour some might have expected for the home of the ruler of the Perseus Group but Ward's mother liked it and had always refused to leave. She was delighted to see him and Krueger; when they were sent on survivor's leave Ward took Joe home with him and he talked music, Bach to Tchaikowsky, for hours with Ward's mother while Jack listened to Fats Waller. It was a leave briefly interrupted by Ward's court martial – held on Friday the 13th of March – but the board of five officers senior to him and chaired by a frosty-eyed post captain acquitted him with expressions of sympathy.

He showed the telegram to Joe: "Want a job?" And he warned, "It might be a bit unusual."

"So was *Boston*, sometimes." Joe did not have to think about it, already knew what he wanted: "Think you can wangle it for me?"

Ward said, "I'll have a bloody good try!" He was in no hurry to go back to sea but it was the life he had chosen instead of taking on the task of running the Perseus Group and it was still the life he wanted. He remembered *Boston* and her crew with pride.

Now Joe hunched wide shoulders and peered up through the rain at the barrage balloons floating over London. "I bet if they cut those wires this island would sink."

The sentry at the sandbagged entrance was as rigid and immaculate as before and Ward returned his cracking salute. Joe waited in the hall and a messenger took Ward up, handed his pass to the Wren and the girl smiled. "The admiral is expecting you, sir." She went quickly to Quartermain's door, tapped, and opened it: "Lieutenant Ward, sir."

The admiral sat behind his desk. There were two chairs facing him and Peter Madden rose from one of them as Ward entered. His khaki battledress was neatly pressed but his wiry hair, as always, looked as though he'd just run his fingers through it. "Jack!"

"Hello, Peter!"

203

They shook hands and Ward thought, So Madden is in on this; one point in its favour.

Peter said sympathetically, "Sorry to hear about *Boston*. I think I can guess how you feel."

No, he bloody well couldn't. But Ward, cap under arm, faced Quartermain: "Sir!"

"Um! Five minutes early. Shaved as well." Quartermain pointed at the vacant chair and when Ward was seated he went on, "I suppose you want to know what ship you've got . . . Well, it's not what you wanted. It's a Fairmile 'B' motor-launch."

The admiral paused and watched Ward for the familiar black glower but saw no flicker of expression. For a man just kicked where it hurts, he thought, he hides it well.

"But I think," Quartermain finished, "I can promise you a destroyer when this operation is over and done with . . . which should be a little over a week from now."

"Thank you, sir." For just a week Ward would captain a clockwork boat on the Round Pond, if necessary.

"Um," Quartermain said drily. "So long as you get your destroyer, you don't give a monkey's what the rest of this is about."

"Well –"

"All right. Peter knows all this but I'll put you in the picture. Last November we tried to capture Rommel. It was a gallant attempt and it failed only because of faulty intelligence. The raiding party did their job magnificently but Rommel wasn't where they were told they'd find him."

Quartermain was silent for long seconds staring down at the desk. Then he looked up. "We hope to be going after Dönitz."

Ward took a deep breath. Dönitz! He was aware of Madden watching him, smiling at his surprise.

Quartermain said, "Admiral Dönitz is commander of the U-boats, the expert in their deployment, a king-pin in the war against our convoys. His capture would be a nasty shock for Hitler and Germany. Peter and his men have been training for this for several months, though they did not know the objective. They are ready and proved that when you brought out Peyraud. We've only been waiting for the opportunity and now, perhaps, it has come. I am informed that Dönitz will be spending one night in St. Nazaire between the twenty-seventh and thirtieth of this month."

St. Nazaire? Had that information come from Catherine? Ward did not ask, did not know how much Peter Madden knew or was allowed to know. He saw Quartermain's eye on him and the admiral nodded slowly. Then: "We also know exactly where he will be in St. Nazaire on that night, in a house close to the Normandie dock. You will command a Fairmile motor-launch, put Madden and his men ashore and bring them, and Dönitz, back. That's stating it very simply."

By God, it was! Ward stared at Quartermain, mind racing as he recalled St. Nazaire and the dock, seeing the obstacles – and there were many. It was only a week away! But – "Which of those nights, sir? Because –"

He stopped short. Did Madden know about CHARIOT?

Quartermain shrugged irritably. "We don't yet know exactly which night and that's the big catch. CHARIOT goes in on the night of the twenty-eighth of March, so you sail with Commander Ryder or not at all. You can't go for Dönitz *before* because you'd alert the defences and CHARIOT would be rendered impossible. You can't go *after* because CHARIOT will put that entire coast on the alert and you'd never get near the dock, never mind Dönitz." He foresaw Ward's question and added, "Commander Ryder commands the naval force of CHARIOT while Colonel Newman leads the commandos who will be put ashore to carry out demolitions. The force is assembling at Falmouth and you go down today. You'll be fully briefed there and trained for the operation. When, *if*, I receive information that the exact night Dönitz will be in St. Nazaire coincides with CHARIOT, I will give you your final orders. The odds are three to one against, but I'm hopeful." He looked at his watch: "You've a train to catch. Any questions?"

A lot, but they would be answered at Falmouth. Now – "My first lieutenant, sir, I want him."

Quartermain's eyes narrowed. "Krueger? What have you told him?"

"Only that it would probably be an unusual job."

"Um!"

"He wants to go anyway, sir, whatever it is."

"Does he?" Quartermain frowned. "It says something for you, I suppose, that he's prepared to take a leap in the dark just because you're going."

"It says a lot for him that I want him, sir. He's a good man."

Quartermain shook his head. "The Fairmile has a crew."

"Joe Krueger is an expert on engines like those."

"She has an engineer."

"He speaks fluent German."

"Colonel Newman has a German speaker in his party."

"*We* haven't, sir." That was Peter Madden. "I think he could be useful."

Quartermain glared at the interruption. "Do you, indeed!"

Madden did not blink, "Yes, sir."

"Do you know him?"

"No, sir, but Ward –"

"If he's good enough for Ward then he's good enough for you? I see! Well, Lieutenant Krueger is a good officer but he's a veteran of the last war."

Ward said, straight-faced, "There are plenty of officers still serving who fought in the last war."

Quartermain swung on him, "*I* am behind a desk, I would remind you, not planning to go charging about in Occupied France! Krueger is forty-three and too old for that!"

Peter Madden said thoughtfully, "Newman is thirty-eight and I believe Major Copland is over forty." He glanced at Ward: "Bill Copland is second-in-command to

Newman." He looked back at Quartermain. "I wouldn't like to tell Major Bill he was too old."

Quartermain glowered from one to the other, then gave a bark of laughter. "Neither would I! All right. Your American is in."

The Fairmile 'B' Class motor-launch was 112 feet long by twenty in the beam with twin petrol engines giving her eighteen knots. There was an open bridge above the wheel-house, a 20mm Oerlikon forward and another aft. She had a pendant number but her crew called her *Phoebe*. Ward never found out why. Her crew comprised Sub-Lieutenant Jameson, R.N.V.R., Petty Officer Doyle, and ten ratings. Jameson was small, twenty and looked sixteen, while Doyle was twenty-six, bearded and fatherly. Ward thought they were a good bunch. *Phoebe* was one of sixteen Fairmiles being trained for CHARIOT but her crew, like those of the other fifteen, believed they were part of Commander Ryder's '10th Anti-submarine Striking Force'. Ryder had devised this cover because it was suspected that there was a German agent in Falmouth.

Ward assumed command of *Phoebe* on the morning of Friday, 20th March, and sailed within the hour to practise firing the Oerlikons at a target-sleeve towed by an aircraft. That was off the Eddystone light. On Saturday they embarked Peter Madden and fourteen commandos then sailed with the other launches, similarly loaded, to take part in Exercise 'Vivid'. The commandos came from the *Princess Josephine Charlotte*, the ship that had brought them from Scotland some days before. It seemed they had no connection with the 10th A-S Force except for this exercise, supposedly designed to test the defences of Devonport, in fact to be a rehearsal for the attack on St. Nazaire. That Saturday night the British defences worked very well and the attempted landing of troops by the launches went very badly. Ward, like the rest, found the glare of land-based searchlights made navigation difficult, and identifying features ashore was almost impossible. If

the St. Nazaire attack were to go like that, by the end of
next week they'd all be dead.

He stood grim-faced and silent as they left Devonport
behind to return to Falmouth. Joe Krueger was not so
depressed since he still did not know their true task – even
though privately he was sceptical of the '10th A-S Force'
story.

Peter Madden came to the bridge and stood in silence for
a minute or two then told Ward, "Well, last time the
rehearsal was fine and the operation went all to hell. Maybe
tonight's balls-up was a good sign." He was talking of the
raid to bring back Peyraud. Joe knowing nothing of it, was
puzzled, and nobody saw fit to enlighten him.

Ward only nodded. He was uneasy about using a motor-
launch for this job, did not like the idea of a petrol engine
and its explosive potential, but the Fairmiles were all they
could get. He was worried too by the effect of the lights.
But most of all the uncertainty gnawed at him: were they
going or were they not? Quartermain had a room in a hotel
in the town but Ward had not seen him since his arrival in
Falmouth when the admiral had given him his orders and
then left him to it.

The next day Ryder called the officers of the launches
together at his HQ in a house on the cliffs above Falmouth,
and briefed them for the attack. He had a model of the St.
Nazaire docks so that every man would know his objective
and where it lay.

He explained that the overall objective was to destroy
the great dock at St. Nazaire because it was the only one
outside of Germany big enough to take *Tirpitz*. If it was
closed to her she would not dare to venture into the
Atlantic. It was one thing to sail knowing she would have to
fight her way home but also knowing there was an alternative haven in St. Nazaire. It was another matter if that
haven was closed; then *Tirpitz* would be bottled up in her
home waters.

H.M.S. *Campbeltown*, formerly U.S.S. *Buchanan* and

twin to *Boston*, was the destroyer to be used in the attack. *Campbeltown* was to ram the dock-gate, then she and the launches would land commando demolition parties to blow up the machinery of the dock and other installations.

Afterwards Ward told Joe of their own particular objective. Joe said only, "Dönitz!" He was silent for a long time, thinking about this, and CHARIOT. Then: "Well, as I recall you did say this could be *unusual*." He drawled out the word. "I've heard about British understatement but this is ridiculous."

On Tuesday, 24th, they were off the Eddystone again for practice firing and it was dark when they returned to their berth at Falmouth. Quartermain was not there to meet them and he had sent no word.

It was a long time before Ward slept that night. Quartermain's information about St. Nazaire came from Catherine so if he received no information then it meant either that she had none to send – or she was unable to send it. That was not an easy thought for him to push to the back of his mind. Catherine . . .

That day her chief had called her into his office. "Ah! Mademoiselle. I see from my diary that you asked for leave of absence this weekend."

Catherine apologised for making such a request so soon after being away, but, "My aunt in Paris is very old and the winter is hard on the elderly. I wish to travel on the night train, that is Thursday night, and return on Sunday to be at my desk the next day."

"Ah! No. I regret, Mademoiselle, that is not possible. I may need you to interpret on the Friday. I am told to expect a German visitor."

Catherine persisted, "Surely, M'sieur, he cannot be so important, this visitor."

Her chief smiled, leaned over the desk and said in a low voice, "The apartment over the Abwehr office is to be complete for that Friday."

The girl's eyes widened. "Oh!" By now the purpose of that particular apartment was an open secret.

"Exactly. But, Mademoiselle, suppose you took the train on Friday night and returned on Monday?"

Catherine smiled. "Thank you, M'sieur, that will be just as convenient."

All the Fairmiles were to complete with stores on Wednesday, 25th. Those carrying demolition parties would also be loading three or four hundredweight of explosives and fuses.

Most of the stores for *Phoebe* were boxes of ammunition and grenades for the commandos and Peter Madden came with them. He was standing with Ward and Joe Krueger on the deck of the Fairmile where she lay alongside when Quartermain's silver-grey Daimler rolled along the quay and stopped beside her. He did not get out of the car, just wound down the window and crooked a finger. Ward and the other two went ashore and saluted.

Quartermain said flatly, "We had word out of France last night –" He paused.

Peter Madden prompted, "Yes, sir?"

Ward thought, That means she's still all right.

Quartermain said, "It's the night of twenty-seventh, twenty-eighth. That's the night *before* CHARIOT."

They were all silent for a moment, then Peter Madden said, "So it's scrubbed."

Quartermain took off his cap to run a hand over neat silver hair. He was carefully shaved, looked lean and fit, but tired. "For now. We just wait for another chance."

"We're not likely to get another as good as this." Peter Madden was not smiling now. Jenny Melville was at the wheel of the Daimler but he did not look at her. He scowled at the pile of stores on the quay. "This bloody lot will have to go back then."

Quartermain said, "No. Behave just like the others for the time being and carry on loading." It could be bad for morale if one launch unloaded again. "And don't say anything to your men. I'll do that, later. Now I'm going to tell Commander Ryder."

Jenny Melville drove the Daimler away as they saluted. They saw the rest of the stores taken aboard and then walked up and down the quay, three quiet men, bad-tempered with frustration. Once Madden kicked furiously at a wooden bollard and said, "Don't get me wrong, I'm not in a hurry to leave all this." It was a fine, sunny day, an early foretaste of spring. "I'm not a sort of khaki kamikaze, but when you train and wait for a long time, then the chance comes along and you lose it at the last by just one day, it's a let-down. I feel like biting somebody."

Ward grunted agreement.

They did not hear the return of the Daimler until it drew up alongside them and stopped. This time Quartermain threw open the door himself and stepped out quickly. He was smiling. "Ryder's decided everybody's ready, the weather's right, so is the tide at St. Nazaire, and hanging around twenty-four hours would only add to the risk of Jerry finding out. So he's going a day early."

Ward sucked in a breath then let it out. "Then it's on!"

Quartermain nodded. "You sail tomorrow. Original plan."

Peter Madden noticed Jenny Melville that time. He smiled at her but she looked away, anxiously biting her lip.

Quartermain said, "There's something I want to show you." They climbed into the Daimler and he took them up the hill to Ryder's headquarters in the house on the cliff-top. There he introduced them to the squadron-leader Ward had met in Richmond Terrace and pointed to some aerial photographs laid out on a table. Ward and Madden studied them, Joe peering over Peter's shoulder.

Quartermain said, "You'll see five ships lying close by the Old Entrance in the St. Nazaire basin."

Ward saw them, nodded, and the squadron-leader said, "To us they look like destroyers."

"The point there," Quartermain put in, "is that they

211

each carry three guns of 4- or 5-inch. That's another fifteen bloody guns!"

The squadron-leader used a pencil to point to a slim shape in the basin but just north of the Old Entrance. "And this looks like an E-boat."

Ward looked up quickly as Quartermain said, "Our information out of France confirms all of that. It is also that the destroyers go to sea and return by the Southern Entrance to the basin while the E-boat uses the Old Entrance."

The squadron-leader asked, "Anything sinister in that?"

Ward smiled. "Not really. The E-boat captain is the junior and so he'd have to wait to use the Southern Entrance until all the destroyers had passed through the lock, so he chooses the Old Entrance instead. The lock there won't take a destroyer but it is big enough for him. So when he comes home he makes his own way in without queueing up behind the others and he gets alongside quicker."

The squadron-leader's brows lifted. "Is that important?"

"If you have to take on oil, water, ammunition and stores before you can go ashore on the town – yes, it is."

"Ah!"

Ward stared at the photographs. "Peter and his men will have to pass that E-boat on their way to their objective." He glanced at Quartermain. "You said you wanted one."

The admiral shook his head. "One of the objectives of CHARIOT is to blow up the Old Entrance and the Southern Entrance, so there'd be no way of getting her out. Stick to *your* main objective."

Ward shrugged. He would rather have the E-boat than Dönitz because they would learn quite a bit from the boat but the admiral would tell them damn-all. It would be good propaganda to kidnap Dönitz but so would it be to steal an E-boat out of a German harbour. Furthermore, while the loss of Dönitz might impair the efficiency of the U-boat offensive, its fleet would hardly fall apart. The U-boats

212

would still have to be fought and beaten, one by one, at sea.

That night they embarked the commandos, secretly and under cover of darkness. *Phoebe* was ordered to ferry a detachment, one of several who would sail aboard *Campbeltown*, from the *Princess Josephine Charlotte* to the old destroyer. Afterwards they would take aboard Peter Madden and his men.

Ward stood on the bridge as *Phoebe* closed *Campbeltown*. The Devonport dockyard had converted her for the raid. Her two after funnels had been taken out and the two remaining cut with a rakish slant aft so in the night she would loosely resemble a German torpedo-boat, their term for destroyer, of the *Möwe* class. She rode high in the water because every pound of weight, equipment, fuel and water not essential to her part in this raid had been taken out of her. Her torpedo tubes and the 4-inch in the bow were gone, the 12-pounder had been moved from aft into the bow and she now mounted eight 20mm Oerlikons on "bandstands" set above the deck.

As they lay alongside, Ward requested permission to go aboard and it was granted. Jameson the Sub remained on the bridge of *Phoebe* while Ward and Joe walked the deck of *Campbeltown*. There was armour plating around her bridge and wheelhouse. More was riveted to the deck, but upright, four lines of it stretching forward and aft making low protective walls behind which the commandos would shelter on the final approach. The deck teemed with them now as they came aboard.

Campbeltown was changed but she was still enough of a twin to *Boston* for it to be an eerie feeling to walk her deck; this was *Boston* reborn. And for Joe the *Buchanan* of his youth. Ward and Joe Krueger stood in silence, remembering other ships, other faces in the night, many nights. Then Joe, aware of what lay ahead for his old ship, said abruptly, "I'm going back aboard." He walked away.

Ward understood, turned to follow him and came face-to-face with a soldier taller than most of the others. He was bulky with webbing equipment, grenade and ammunition pouches strapped about his body, and he carried a Thompson submachine-gun slung from one shoulder.

Ward stared, "Patrick!"

His cousin grinned at him. "I thought I might bump into you, sooner or later. I saw you buzzing about in a motor-launch a couple of times. You stand out a bit on that thing. I used to have one like it in the bath."

Ward said, "Don't be so bloody rude or I'll leave you to walk home." The launches were to bring back the commandos after the raid.

Patrick asked, "You're on this party?"

Ward nodded. Patrick *had* changed, by God! The languid man-about-town was buried in the past. This was a soldier, tough and competent, looking you straight in the eye. "I saw your exhibition."

Patrick said, "The best one wasn't there." He had finally painted Sarah and got it right, finished it the last time he saw her and left it with her. He had a letter from her in his pocket now, unopened, to be read later when he found time and a quiet place aboard this ship, probably not until they were at sea.

"There was one of a boy on a road . . ." Ward paused, not knowing how to put his feelings into words. "I never thought paint on a canvas could talk but that one certainly spoke to me."

Patrick hitched at the Thompson gun, settling it more easily on his shoulder. "Paris is – was – marvellous. I had a hell of a good time but I worked damned hard as well. I didn't take the war seriously till I woke up one morning and found I had to drive like mad for the coast to get out. We weren't strafed but we saw it going on a long way ahead of us. When we got up there the Stukas had gone and there was just this one car and the boy in the road. It was quiet as the grave. We took him on to the next town and left him at a convent. He never cried at all, never said a word."

Ward watched him, remembering the party Aunt Abi-

214

gail had thrown for her son's return. "So you got drunk."

"That's right."

"And then you joined the Army."

Patrick shrugged. "I suppose I'd have done that anyway. It seemed to be popular." And, with a flash of the old Patrick, "One likes to be seen where the best people are, you know."

Ward's own people waited for him. He said, "We'll try and have a drink afterwards."

Afterwards?

But Patrick only grinned, "Good idea, Jack."

CHARIOT sailed.

Ward conned *Phoebe* out of Falmouth at two in the afternoon of the next day, 26th March. There were the two escorting destroyers, *Atherstone* and *Tynedale*, and the attacking force: one old, obsolete destroyer, one motor-gunboat, one motor-torpedo-boat and sixteen Fairmiles. It was not an impressive flotilla with which to assault Hitler's European fortress.

Mountbatten had told Newman, the commando colonel, that he believed the commandos could get in and do the job but he did not expect many of them to come out again so any man could stand down if he wished. None did. Ward thought Mountbatten had been honest and must have enormous faith in the men to tell them that. But St. Nazaire was six miles inside the estuary of the Loire, so for six miles the little ships would be running between the banks of a river lined with waiting guns, alert and ready.

Ward had telephoned his brother Geoffrey before sailing and told him, "I want you to stay with Mother for the next few days."

Geoffrey was silent for a moment, then he said heavily, "I see. Like that, is it?"

"A bit hairy. Any problems at your end?"

"You mean the Perseus Group?" Another long silence but Geoffrey broke it, saying, "No. I can cope." It was a flat statement of fact, no doubt in his voice at all: Geoffrey was his own man. When he went on his voice was different again, fumbling for words. "Look, Jack, be careful. You're a great bloke."

"You're not bad yourself. Cheerio."

"Good luck!"

So – from now on Geoffrey would run the Perseus Group in his own way, right or wrong, and Ward was leaving no loose ends.

But it was a very odd feeling.

13

"Dönitz is there . . . !"

As the ships of CHARIOT sailed, Hauptmann Engel climbed into the front of his old Citroën and Pianka drove along the side of the St. Nazaire basin then across the bridge leading to the town. They bumped out from under the web of girders that formed the suspension of the bridge and Engel saw a group of naval officers, white jerseys showing at the necks of their blue jackets. He recognised some as U-boat officers and one who was not. This was the first time Engel had seen the captain of the *Schnellboot* ashore, though he had watched the boat pass in and out of the basin several times during the last few days.

So had Henri – and had told London.

Engel said, "Pull in here." Pianka obeyed and the Citroën came to rest beside the group. Engel poked his head out of the window and called, "Rudi!" Then as one of the officers glanced around: "What the hell are you doing here? The last I heard you were in the Baltic."

Rudi Moller, short and jaunty, grinned and stepped over to the car. "Since last September I've been working out of Holland but now they've sent us down here with Schmidt's Fifth Flotilla for a bit." He jerked his head at the basin and the five destroyers tied up there. Rudi added, "They probably thought we could do with a rest and they were right."

Engel studied him and saw the lines of strain on the young face. "Tough, eh?"

Rudi Moller shrugged. "A long winter and long nights. Most of the time you can't see what you're doing and when you can, the Tommies throw all kinds of stuff at you." He grinned. "But a couple of nights' sleep and I'll be as good as new."

"I've got an office and a bottle on the other side of the

basin, just along from where your boat is berthed," Engel told him. "Look in and I'll give you a drink." He nudged Pianka and the Citroën pulled away. Engel thought Rudi was looking older, edgier, worried behind the grin. The war was getting to him, as to all of them.

The Citroën headed north out of St. Nazaire. There was a damp chill in the air and Engel wore his long greatcoat and rubbed at his knee. After five kilometres he said, "Next on the right." And as Pianka changed down, swung into the turning: "That wood ahead."

They drove down a narrow lane between high hedges for 400 metres and passed no house, saw no one. The wood was dense, carpeted with undergrowth and the trees met above the lane and made it a green-lit tunnel. Pianka slowed to a crawl at Engel's bidding and they went on until they came to a gap in the hedge with a clearing opening from it. Engel said, "Here." Pianka turned into the clearing and stopped the Citroën. Only then did he see the man crouched at the gap in the hedge and keeping watch on the lane. It was Horstmann, Grünwald's lieutenant.

Another car stood in the clearing, a Renault as old and battered as the Citroën. Pianka muttered, "The little shit is showing some sense at last." The Renault looked anything but a Gestapo vehicle.

Grünwald himself stood by the Renault. He came forward as Engel got out of the Citroën and they met between the cars. Grünwald said, "I've got him."

Engel asked, "What do we know about him?"

"He's English. He came over in 1937, an admirer of the Party and the Leader, attended the rallies and offered his services. There was an idea he might be used as an agent in his own country but that had to be abandoned."

"Why?"

"Drink. One and he talks, two and he shouts. He was totally unreliable for that work."

"What about *this*?" Engel snapped sourly, "One wrong word and they'll bury him!"

"He'll stay off it," Grünwald assured him, "It'll only be

for a few days. He's not a drunk, not an alcoholic so don't be put off. He's good, smart and quite an actor. Besides, it fits – we shot down a plane only last night, and no survivors. He can do the job."

Engel asked, "Why? Why will he do it?"

Grünwald blinked at the question then stated what seemed obvious to him, "He wants to get on in the Party and the Service, like the rest of us."

Engel scowled at him, brooding and thought: Don't include me. Grünwald and this English traitor wanted money and power, by any means. They were two of a kind. He said, "He's one of your lot?"

Grünwald shrugged. "He's S.D., yes." S.D. meant *Sicherheitsdienst*, another name for Gestapo. "Does it matter?"

"Not so long as he knows this is my operation and that he is responsible only to me."

Grünwald looked surprised. "Of course."

Of course? Engel growled, "All right, fetch him out."

Grünwald called, "Turner!" He explained in an aside to Engel: "We had a pay-book for a Turner that fitted him."

The man got out of the back of the Renault and joined them. He wore the uniform of a Royal Air Force sergeant with the airgunner's badge, trousers tucked into flying boots. He was tall and thin, bare-headed, his brown hair cut short. He was handsome in the way that Horstmann was handsome, with well-chiselled features, firm mouth and chin.

Grünwald said, "He looks the part, yes?"

Engel had to admit he did. "Has he been briefed? Does he know his story and what he has to do?"

"Yes," and Grünwald added, "His French is poor but his German good."

Engel looked at Turner. "Let's hear it from the beginning." He flicked a finger at Pianka, "While he's talking you check to see if he's clean."

Pianka grabbed Turner and slammed his face forward against the car. Turner struggled, snarled an obscenity and Pianka stepped back, fist clenching.

Engel's hand lifted and the rasp of his voice froze both of them: "That's enough! Right reaction because our airman would not like being manhandled by a foreigner, but in the wrong language!" Turner's curse had been in German. "Get on with it!"

Pianka stepped forward and started his search. Turner said, in German accented but fluent, "We'd been on a raid, dropped our load and we were on our way home –"

Engel interjected, "Where is that?"

Turner glanced at him, "Let's say Southern England. That's all I'm telling you."

Engel nodded curt approval and Turner went on, "We ran into flak when we were near the coast, the kite caught fire and the skipper ordered us to jump. I came down in a field and looked around for the others but couldn't find them. The sea wasn't far away and I think maybe they dropped into the drink . . ."

While he talked Pianka checked him – thoroughly. He stripped Turner to the skin, even removing the flying-boots and the socks so that Turner stood against the car stark naked and shuddering in the damp cold. All of his few possessions, each item of his clothing was examined by Engel as Pianka threw them on to the roof of the car. He was looking for anything that might betray Turner as a fake but they were all genuine RAF issue.

At the end Engel nodded, "Good. Get dressed. Where is your flying-suit? Parachute?"

Turner grabbed at his clothes and said through chattering teeth, "I hid them under some bushes, close by a church, about a mile north of here."

Engel turned on his heel and limped back and forth across the clearing, thinking it over. Turner knew his part and if he played it well enough then the scheme had a chance of success. If he botched it – Engel limped back to the others, his stiff leg hurting him. He said, "You know

220

that if they see through you, then they will kill you. They'll
have to, because they daren't let you go."

Turner, dressed again and confident, said, "Don't
worry, I'll pull it off."

"Hide in the woods for the rest of the day. Move at night
and look out for our patrols. As far as they are concerned
you're a British airman on the run and we don't want you
caught or shot. You find out a name or a face of someone
who *counts* in the network, not just some errand-boy, then
you get that information to *me*. No one else. Is *that* clear?"

"Yes, sir. Understood. To you alone."

Engel was silent a moment. He did not like Turner but
the man was risking death so he said, "Good luck."

"Thank you, sir."

Engel nodded to Grünwald, limped back to the Citroën,
climbed in and Pianka drove out of the clearing. Horstmann lifted a hand to them as they passed but Engel did
not acknowledge it.

Pianka asked, "Where to?"

Engel did not answer, but asked, "What about Turner?"

Pianka shrugged, "I think he might do it."

"I didn't ask about his chances. What did you think
about *him*."

Pianka grimaced. "Another shit, like Grünwald."

Engel grunted agreement, "But we've got to use him.
He's our back-up if this other thing fails. There's a Resistance network and we have to smash it." He was silent a
moment, then: "Take me back to the office and we'll have a
drink to wash the taste away." And to ease this bloody leg.
"Tonight we'll talk to Horstmann. You get hold of him and
bring him to the office. It's time he started paying."

Turner hid in the wood through the afternoon. He found
another, smaller clearing away from the lane but close to
the edge of the wood so he could see if anyone came near.
He kept on the move, shifting about the clearing because it
was very cold and because he had nagging doubts. Not
because France was a strange land to him and he had barely

221

a few words of the language; that was in character for a British airman and all to the good. But suppose the French had checks no one knew of, and found out the truth? He tried to suppress the thought. Anyway, the stakes were high: if he discovered the name of the man Engel and Grünwald wanted that would bring him promotion in the S.D., he had Grünwald's word on that, and when the war was over there would be a job in England for him, a job like Grünwald's, with power, money and women.

When dusk fell he moved out of the trees and walked in the shadow of the hedges. In that way he had tramped around several fields before he saw a farmhouse in its yard, dark behind closed shutters. As he approached the bark of a dog and the rattle of its chain set his nerves on edge. He froze, peering, until he made out the dog straining towards him, claws scrabbling on the cobbles of the yard, the chain pulled bar-straight.

The door of the house opened and light from within silhouetted the figure of a man. Turner circled around the dog, walked up to the door and called, "I am an English airman! *Anglais!*"

They took him in. There were the farmer and his wife, both in their sixties, and one young man that Turner thought must be a grandson. The others called him Jacques. None of them spoke English but they fed him on thick soup and a hunk of bread with a bottle of red wine. He wolfed down the food but drank sparingly, remembering his orders. All the time the French talked among themselves but in low, rapid tones and Turner caught none of it. Although the old man and his wife seemed nervous, the young one, Jacques, was clearly filled with suppressed excitement. He seemed to be arguing some course of action but the other two shook their heads and repeated over and over, "*Demain! Demain!*"

Turner knew that much French; whatever Jacques wanted to do, his elders were insisting that he put it off until tomorrow. Turner could see their point; there would be German patrols and if one of them caught this excited young man there would be awkward questions asked.

The elders persisted and won. Jacques, disgruntled but still eager to please, took a torch, showed Turner to a barn with its loft piled with hay and gave him to understand he was to sleep there. Before he left, taking the torch with him, he produced a knife from somewhere inside his clothing and showed it to Turner. It looked to be a butcher's knife with a sharp-honed blade some six inches long, narrowing to a needle-point. Jacques put away the knife as quickly as he had produced it then laid his hand dramatically on his chest and intoned, *"Ami!"*

Turner, not to be outdone, seized the hand in both of his and shook it. *"Oui! Ami!"*

Left in the darkness of the loft he listened to Jacques's boots clumping across the yard and then the slam of a closing door. He laughed quietly. These French! Full of dramatics! Children!

He made himself a bed in the hay and settled down. He had made a good start and tomorrow he would build on it.

He woke with the first light to the sound of boots on the cobbles below. He crawled out of the hay to a little cob-webbed window and saw Jacques push a bicycle across the sunlit yard to the farm track, then mount it and pedal away towards the road. Clearly the boy had gone to get help. There was nothing to do but wait, so Turner crept back into the hay and slept again.

The old man brought food to him later; then, at mid-morning, Jacques returned and visited the loft briefly. He said, *"Ami,"* pointed out of the window at the sun then moved his finger across the sky. Turner nodded understanding: someone was coming to see him later.

It was late afternoon when Jacques hurried across the yard and called Turner down from the loft with urgent gestures. He led Turner cautiously to the house. The fine morning had clouded over and the kitchen was gloomy. As Turner entered it from the back of the house a young woman on a bicycle rode past the windows at the front. The

223

old man and his wife, sitting by the kitchen range, looked up anxiously. The dog's chain rattled, then its challenging bark turned to a welcoming whimper.

The young woman came into the kitchen. She stood across the scrubbed pine table from Turner, watching him as Jacques spoke to her rapidly. The old couple murmured greetings and disappeared into the next room. The girl eyed him critically.

Turner was disappointed. He had hoped for someone higher in the chain of command, not a messenger-girl on a bicycle. He remembered Engel's demand: 'someone who counts in the network, not an errand-boy.'

The girl said, "Please sit down."

Turner asked, "You speak English?"

"A little."

He laughed with feigned relief. "Thank God for that!" He pulled a chair up to the table. "I left school when I was fourteen and never learned any French."

Catherine Guillard put her handbag on the table, peeled off her gloves and laid them beside it. "I am sorry I could not come sooner." Admiral Dönitz had arrived that morning and she had been obliged to wait in her office in case she was required to interpret, but at lunchtime her chief had sent word that she would not be needed. He remembered that she wanted to go to Paris and she had his permission to leave work early. As she left the yard Henri was waiting for her, leaning casually by the gate. He slouched along beside her like any other workman but muttered uneasily, "Jacques telephoned. He's jumping for joy. He thinks he has a British airman out at the farm, but the man doesn't speak French."

Now she smiled warily at Turner and began her questions. "Where were you brought down?"

"I landed about five or six miles north of here . . ." He told his tale.

She interrupted once to ask, "What did you do with the parachute?"

"I wrapped my flying-suit in it and stuffed the lot under

224

some bushes." He described the place and she recognised it.

Turner finished his story and she asked him about his home. He rambled on for some time about the house in a London suburb, the local cinema and the pub, the shops. He was lucky then, though he could not know it; Catherine had stayed in the area with her father for a while before the war and recognised many of the little details.

She was satisfied. This Englishman was genuine – but still a problem. She said, "We can get you back to England."

"Great!" Turner grinned at her, delighted to discover that this girl obviously had more authority than he'd thought.

She held up a hand. "It will not be easy and it may take a long time. You must be patient. You will have to stay here for some days until we can make arrangements."

Turner shrugged. "You'll do your best, I know. And I'm very grateful."

"Jacques will look after you and I will send someone to help you as soon as I can. But we must be careful, you understand."

"Of course. I see that." He leaned his elbows on the table. "Jerry must be on the look-out all the time for blokes like me."

"He is." Catherine glanced at Jacques and said in French, "You must be watchful."

"I will. Depend on me." He was clearly proud of the trust she placed in him.

"I will speak with the old people now and ask them to keep this man for some days."

Turner understood little of this, but saw the young woman leave the room and Jacques go to the window and peer out, keeping watch on the track that led to the road. The girl's handbag still lay, with her gloves, on the table. Jacques' back was to Turner, who hesitated only a second, then stretched his hand out to the bag and eased open the catch. Inside was a purse, a jumble of oddments such as a lipstick, a notebook and pencil – papers. With one eye on Jacques' back he slid the identity card part-way clear of the others, enough for him to see the photograph, the name Catherine Guillard and the address in the Rue de Saille. He pushed the card back and carefully closed the bag.

He realised he was holding his breath and quietly let it out. Only now did he realise the risk he had taken, and it appalled him. In fact, however, it seemed that he'd had all the time in the world because he sat for another full minute before the girl came into the room and only then did Jacques turn around.

Catherine said, "I've asked them to let you stay in the house as much as possible – that way the time will not drag as it would in the loft." It was important that this young man did not become bored and restless. He would have plenty of waiting before he saw England again and they must try to make it bearable when they could.

Turner answered, "Thank you." He meant it. The loft was all right for sleeping but not for waiting through long hours, buried in hay to keep warm and listening to the rats.

Catherine explained all this in French to Jacques who listened attentively. Even so, she wished she did not have to depend on him. She would move the airman to another safe house as soon as she could, and meanwhile she had no alternative but to trust the boy. "You have the telephone number where you can contact Henri. He will be there every night while the airman is here. During the day he will call there often. If you need help or advice you must ask him. That is understood?"

"Perfectly."

Catherine decided she had done all she could. She rode away on her bicycle and Turner watched her go, content. He had only to wait for the night and then walk out of here. He was home and dry.

In the port of St. Nazaire, Engel was standing close by when Admiral Dönitz turned to Kapitän-Leutnant Herbert

226

Sohler who commanded the Seventh Submarine Flotilla and asked, "What will you do if the British attack St. Nazaire?"

"There are standing orders that cover the possibility," Sohler answered. Then he added, "But it is considered highly improbable."

Dönitz did not like that answer. "I wouldn't be too sure about that!"

In the late afternoon Henri cycled down from the town and crossed the Southern Entrance of the St. Nazaire basin by the swing bridge over the lock. He was no sooner over than the bridge was swung aside and the destroyer *Jaguar* slid out into the lock. The ships of Schmidt's Fifth Flotilla were on their way to sea. Henri watched for a minute then turned left away from the Old Town and the square. He rode along the side of the basin to a point about a hundred metres from the Old Entrance. The bridge over the lock there was also swung open and the *Schnellboot* was in the lock, going out to join the destroyers. Even had the bridge been closed he could not have crossed it this evening because there were sentries posted on the far side and the length of the quay beyond was protected for some 200 metres by more sentries at the end of it. That was the section where Hauptmann Engel's office stood.

Henri turned and rode back the way he had come. No one took any notice of him because the yards were at work and men were everywhere. A café stood close by the Southern Entrance and Henri propped his bicycle against the wall, took a beer to a table by the window. From there he could see the bridge across the Southern Entrance, and the road beyond leading around to the mile-long Boulevard and the *Kommandatur*. He waited until it was almost dusk and time for the blackout. Only then did the cars come.

There were two of them and they came into sight as they turned inland from the Boulevard. They drove steadily and Henri walked out of the café, climbed on his bicycle and set

227

off along the side of the basin as the cars turned on to the bridge. He was halfway to the Old Entrance when they passed him, moving more slowly now because of the men working on the quay, the leading car with its klaxon blaring to clear the way. As it passed he saw men of the *Feldgendarmerie*, Engel's military police, inside with machine-pistols. The second car slid by, twenty metres behind the first and he glimpsed a small figure sitting erect in the rear, a navy greatcoat and a great blaze of gold lace.

The cars swept on across the swing bridge over the Old Entrance, the sentries there saluting. Henri braked and dismounted. The cars stopped two hundred metres further on outside the Abwehr office. The tall figure of Hauptmann Engel stood at the front, saluting, and the sentries at the door presented arms. His guest in the long naval greatcoat stepped out of the second car and crossed quickly to the entrance, hand at the peak of his cap in acknowledgment of the salutes, and disappeared inside.

Henri turned the bicycle around and pedalled back along the side of the basin, crossed the bridge at the Southern Entrance and rode up the hill. At the Place Carnot he turned right into the Rue Henri Gautier where he had an apartment. He carried the bicycle upstairs and left it outside the door of his room. Once inside he locked the door, set up the wireless and sent a signal to London. They were keeping a listening watch and answered his second transmission.

He breathed a little easier after that. When they did not hear you, you had to keep sending, wondering all the time if the German radio-detection vans were receiving you and getting a cross-bearing on where you were – and that was bad for the nerves.

He packed the wireless back into its suitcase and went down to the café where Catherine spent an hour or so each evening. He waited until she was alone then he left the café but paused briefly at her table to say softly, "Dönitz is there and the destroyers have sailed. London knows."

Catherine nodded. "I asked for leave to go to Paris so I

228

must, for appearance's sake, but not until tomorrow and I will return the next day. While I'm there I'll contact the escape route to Spain for the English airman. You will keep an eye on Jacques meanwhile."

Henri frowned. "He's too young, too excitable and always acting, but I'll look after him. You take care."

He walked out. So he could call on Catherine tonight if he needed her, but tomorrow he'd be on his own. And this evening he had to sit at the end of a telephone line in case young Jacques had any problems. Also there was the British interest in Admiral Dönitz and the movements of the destroyers to be considered. He had no idea of the British plans, and did not wish to know them. But something was brewing – he could feel it . . .

He went to the bar where Jacques might call, ordered a beer and settled down at a table near the telephone. He borrowed a newspaper but could not concentrate on it. He was on edge. His unease was like the tension he felt in the torrid heat of summer before a storm broke. But this was a calm winter's night.

14

". . . we're ducks in a barrel!"

The night was dark under a clouded sky but they had the promise of a moon later. There was light enough for Ward, on the bridge of *Phoebe*, to see the long lines of launches stretching away into the distance astern. Joe Krueger, solid and calm, and Peter Madden stood either side of him. Jameson, the Sub, was aft with the Oerlikon there. Both Oerlikons were manned and so was the Lewis mounted on the bridge. Petty Officer Doyle was on the fo'c'sle talking to Beare. A leading-seaman was at the wheel because Ward was saving Doyle for the final crucial run in.

"There it is!" Joe lowered his glasses and pointed, "Fine on the port bow."

"Seen." Ward watched the tiny light through his glasses as it blinked in morse the letter M. It came from H.M. Submarine *Sturgeon*, acting as a navigational beacon, the marker for the start of the approach to St. Nazaire.

Joe said, "That was a swell piece of navigation."

Ward nodded agreement, "Green knows his stuff. Better him than me." The lieutenant, Commander Ryder's navigational expert on board the leading M.G.B., had brought them unerringly to this point on the dark and empty sea. And his job was not finished yet, not by a long chalk.

The escorting destroyers, *Atherstone* and *Tynedale*, turned away to start their patrol around the rendezvous point where the force would reassemble in the dawn for the return home. Ward wondered how many of them would make it. They sailed in the attack formation now, the M.G.B. leading with Ryder, Newman the commando colonel, and Green aboard. Astern of the M.G.B. steamed the disguised destroyer *Campbeltown* and on either side of her seven Fairmiles in line ahead. A single Fairmile and the M.T.B. brought up the rear. The M.T.B. carried torpedoes with delayed-action fuses. Wynn, her commander, had the task of firing them at the southern dock-gate if *Campbeltown* failed to ram it. *Phoebe* sailed between the columns and a cable's length astern of *Campbeltown*.

They passed *Sturgeon*, her hull submerged and only her conning-tower showing. Ward peered at his watch: ten fifteen.

Forty miles to go.

He looked at his watch again when the glow of searchlights and the flashes of gunfire lit the horizon ahead. The rumble of the barrage came rolling dully, distantly out to them. It was eleven thirty.

"That's the diversionary air-raid starting." Peter Madden cocked his head on one side, listening. Bomber Command had been ordered to mount a raid to divert German attention from the estuary to the sky. Peter muttered uneasily, "There's a hell of a lot of flak going up but I can't hear anything like a bomb-burst."

Nor could Ward. He looked up at the cloud ceiling and wondered if the bomber pilots were under orders only to try for specific targets so as not to cause casualties to the French? If so, then with this cloud the bomb-aimers would be helpless, able to see little or nothing below them. It's not going to work, he thought. All it'll do will be to wake 'em up and keep 'em on the alert.

The ships of CHARIOT were still at sea, the estuary of the Loire hidden in the darkness ahead.

Half past midnight. Joe Krueger said softly, awed, "Look at that! She must have been one hell of a big ship!"

Masts and massive funnels stuck up out of the sea to port and Ward said, "*Lancastria*. She was a luxury liner before the war." He had passed her wreck in the high summer of 1940 when returning to England in *Saracen* – with Catherine Guillard aboard.

The air-raid was over. The guns were silent, the searchlights doused, the drone of aircraft engines had faded away. Some bombs had fallen; they had seen the flashes and heard the *crump* of them. Ward knew that Catherine must be there now. Her duty lay in St. Nazaire, that was why she had returned there and would be in the town now. Under the bombs? Dead?

The voice of Doyle came up the pipe: "Coxswain at the wheel, sir."

"Very good."

Down in the wheelhouse the morphine and the dressings were laid out in readiness. The tiny *Phoebe* had no other quarters for her wounded: she was entering the mouth of the Loire and in just an hour or so from now . . .

Ward put thoughts of Catherine from him and went over it all in his mind again.

The port of St. Nazaire lay six miles up-river and on its western shore. The estuary was wide but mostly shallow and the only deep-water channel ran close to the western shore – and under the enemy guns. So the plan was to approach through the shallows, out in the estuary and away from the guns, and enter the channel only a mile from the port. That was why *Campbeltown* had been stripped and emptied so that she rode high in the water and drew only eleven feet.

Approaching up that last mile of the deep-water channel the outstretched arms of two breakwaters guarded the port's Southern Entrance with its lock, crossed by a swing bridge. That lock led to the St. Nazaire basin, with the U-boat pens on its left-hand or western side. Between the lock of the Southern Entrance and the channel lay the Old Town with its *Place*, the square looking out over the St. Nazaire basin. Another lock at St. Nazaire basin's far end led to the Penhouet basin which connected with the northern gate of their target, the giant Normandie dock.

The ships of CHARIOT, however, would keep to the channel past the Southern Entrance and on. From the river bank here the Old Mole jutted out into the channel, a stone pier a hundred yards long with a lighthouse at its end and a

232

landing slip on its northern side, and beyond that lay the Old Entrance from the river to the St. Nazaire basin, again with a lock, crossed at the basin end by another swing bridge.

North of the Old Entrance were gates directly on the river, leading into the Normandie dock, which connected via a further pair of gates with the Penhouet basin, thus completing the circular grid of docks and basins.

A winding-house stood on the left or west side of the Normandie dock by each massive gate. They held engines which opened the gates by drawing them back into recesses, closed them by pushing them out. Close by the southern winding-house was a pump-house, its pumps some forty feet below ground. To dry-dock a ship you opened the southern gate to the river with the northern one closed, brought the ship into the dock, closed the southern gate then pumped the dock dry.

So the route of the attacking force would lead past the Southern Entrance, past the Old Mole and then the Old Entrance to the southern gate of the Normandie dock. The commandos in the launches of the port column were to land at the Old Mole, those in the starboard column in the Old Entrance. Their orders were to capture and destroy a range of targets stretching from guns at the Southern Entrance, and the lock gates there, to the bridge at the north end of the St. Nazaire basin. And to secure the Old Mole as the point of re-embarkation of the force.

All these targets were important but the main one was the Normandie dock and that was for *Campbeltown*. Her commandos were to blow up the northern gate, the pump-house and the two winding-houses. *Campbeltown* herself would be used as a hammer to smash the southern gate. The gates of the dock were closed, it was pumped dry and held two ships under repair.

Ward was to take *Phoebe* into the Old Entrance hard by the dock and land Madden with his men. They were to cross the bridge over the Old Entrance and follow the road northward along the side of the St. Nazaire basin for some two hundred yards to the last building but one. They would find Dönitz there.

After landing them Ward would pull *Phoebe* out into the channel, then return later to the Old Mole to pick them up, with their prisoner, when the force was re-embarked.

He thought, And the catch?

There were twenty-eight coastal guns spread along the banks of the river and thirty-seven Bofors or Oerlikons, 40mm or 20mm guns, in or around St. Nazaire – or, Ward thought, the German equivalent, but call them Bofors or Oerlikons because the name on the gun didn't matter if the name on the shell was yours. Those thirty-seven guns were mounted on towers or bunkers and so were difficult to hit with gunfire from sea-level, a nightmare to assault from the ground. A flakship was anchored out in the channel opposite the Old Mole. The Penhouet basin held three mine-sweepers and there were five more in the St. Nazaire basin along with the five destroyers and the E-boat Ward had seen in the aerial photographs. Some might have left – or there could be more now; CHARIOT had kept wireless silence, heard nothing since they sailed. Small craft such as tugs were scattered about both basins and even these would mount weapons, if only machine-guns. Only? One machine-gun could be too much.

Five thousand men defended St. Nazaire and just six hundred commandos and seamen were to attack it.

Ward thought it did no good to dwell on odds.

He had his orders: Get Madden and his men in, and out again.

Peter Madden climbed to the bridge and said softly, "There's the land!" He carried his helmet now, swinging by the strap from one hand. Joe Krueger seemed calm as ever but Peter was restless, ready to go.

Ward made out the distant, low-lying smudge of the coast about two miles away off the port bow. In 1940 the Messerschmitts had come howling out of there, flying low over the estuary and he had shouted at Catherine Guillard to get below to *Saracen*'s wardroom.

It was quiet now but there would be eyes on that shore. Watching the ships of CHARIOT? The strung-out little squadron altered course marginally to 050 degrees. Then speed was reduced to ten knots. Ward knew that was because of *Campbeltown*: Beattie, her captain, had found that she settled by the stern at speeds over ten knots and drew another two or three feet. He might well need those extra feet under her keel because *Campbeltown* would soon be running into shoal water.

Patrick stood in the waist of *Campbeltown* with the other commandos in a shallow-breathing quiet. They looked out to the western shore of the estuary, a low, crumpled line cut dark against the night sky and they could smell the land. Their webbing equipment marked them; it was white and stood out more clearly in the darkness than their weathered faces. That was by Colonel Newman's order, so they would recognise friend from foe. For that reason also every man had a blue pencil-light taped to his rifle, Thompson or Bren. They stood between the protective steel barriers on *Campbeltown*'s deck, ready to drop down behind them when they came under fire.

Like the commandos in the launches, those aboard *Campbeltown* were divided into three types of party: Demolition, each man carrying a pack of up to ninety pounds of explosive and fuses. Protection, heavily armed to guard the demolition men who, because of their huge packs, were only armed with Colt .45 pistols. And assault, those thirty men led by Lieutenant Roderick and Captain Roy. Roderick and Roy: Patrick thought it sounded like a music-hall act, like Murray and Mooney. The two young officers were admittedly high-spirited, but there would be nothing comic about their performances tonight. They would be first ashore. Lieutenant Roderick and his men were to silence the guns on the right of the dock-gate, clear that area and hold it against any counter-attack until recalled. Captain

235

Roy's group had to silence the guns on the left of the gate, then seize and hold the bridge over the Old Entrance. That bridge would be the way back for all of them to the re-embarkation point at the Old Mole. If Roy or Roderick failed then God help the rest of them.

Patrick waited with nerves strung tight, knowing this was shoal water. In theory *Campbeltown* should slip over the banks but that depended on the height of the tide and the accuracy of Lieutenant Green's navigation. He had to be one hundred per cent right and who could be that, sailing strange waters in darkness? And this was no mere theoretical exercise. If *Campbeltown* ran aground then the German gunners would use her for target practice at their leisure.

She grounded. Patrick felt the shudder and it came back to him through the frame of the ship like a ground-wave as *Campbeltown* checked on the sandbank then slowly pushed over it. The shudder ran away towards the stern, faded and was gone.

Patrick let out his held breath and tried to think of other things. Sarah Benjamin. He had deliberately not read her letter until *Campbeltown* was at sea: it would have been all too easy to write back to her, comforting her, perhaps even reassuring her, and leaving all kinds of loose ends behind him. He thought now that he had been right, for once.

She had written: 'I can't do the little girl wronged bit and I'm not good at begging. But I wasn't playing fast and loose with you, even though you thought I was. I met my husband when I was seventeen and I loved him. He ditched me because he found another woman who could help him in his career and I couldn't – or maybe he just took her into his bed in London because she was there and I wasn't. I don't know, but it was all over long before I met you.

'That's all. I just wanted you to know the truth. Next time you're on leave perhaps we'll get in touch. I pray for you, my dear . . .'

So, all right, she had once called him a bastard and he was. The affair was finished, on his side, anyway. That was best, considering his occupation and its hazards. He was glad he had finally succeeded in painting her, finally captured the elusive fragility in her smile and the lost yet eager look in her wide eyes. Not bad, if he did say so himself. At least he'd have done a little good work if this trip turned out to be a –

Campbeltown grounded again, checked for a heartbeat then slowly slid on with the tremor running back through her again as she pushed clear of the bank.

Patrick swallowed. He was not afraid. All the way across, fear had lurked in the back of his mind but now it was gone. He had made no promises to Sarah and he was glad of that because it was unlikely he would be able to keep them. There were demolition teams below whose tasks were to blow up the northern dock-gate and winding-house. He was one of the party detailed to protect them as they worked. *If* they got the quarter mile to the other end of the dock from where they would go ashore. *If* they got ashore at all. *If* they were not all blown to hell before they got anywhere near the dock. Yet he was not afraid. Funny, that.

He demanded impatiently inside himself, Come on! Let's get on with it!

The time had dragged for Turner as he sat in the kitchen of the farmhouse. Jacques was continually in and out, keeping a watch on the road and around the house. Turner wondered if there were really German patrols about in the area or was Jacques just obeying an order given by the girl, and over zealously? Turner decided, from what he'd seen of young Jacques, that the latter was the case. Either way, Jacques' constant presence was a nuisance. It prevented the Englishman from getting away and seeking out a German patrol on his own account.

His job was almost done. He had only to make a telephone call, pass the name *Catherine Guillard* and claim his reward. Then soon he would be a power in the Party, sitting in the big, chauffeur-driven Mercedes. He looked around the kitchen and wrinkled his nose. He would have spacious quarters, probably a house in the country. There would be servants. Women.

He chafed. The old people went to bed but he still had a long time to wait before Jacques finally led him across to the loft by the light of his torch. The boy made one of his dramatic little speeches and then left.

Turner was glad to see the back of him. He prepared to go but, watching from the little window, saw Jacques still prowling around the house. Then the air-raid started and the boy stood in the yard to watch. Turner swore. He could see the criss-crossing of sweeping searchlight beams and the bursting of flak. Now and again he caught the distant drone of the bombers' engines but heard few bombs fall.

He fretted for half an hour before his patience gave out and he decided there was no reason to wait. He could see Jacques in the yard but the boy was obviously still intent on the raid. Besides, the noise of the flak would cover any sound Turner made. So he groped his way down the ladder, eased out of the door and worked his way around the yard behind Jacques then down the side of the house. Even the dog was no problem. It had yelped and whined ever since the raid started so that now, when it barked at Turner sidling past, Jacques did not even look round. Turner walked down the track to the road and turned right. One way was as good as another.

It was some minutes later that it occurred to Jacques that the airman would be awake; he would not sleep through this din. It also occurred to him that he might see more from the window of the loft than from the yard so he climbed the ladder and called, "*M'sieur!*" He switched on the torch and shone it on himself so the airman would see he was not a stranger. There was no answer. He swept the loft with his torch, scurried about it, tossing aside the hay, then paused bewildered at the head of the ladder.

The loft was empty. The airman had gone.

He remembered Catherine Guillard's warning, that the airman would become bored, impatient. But not so soon, surely! He also remembered his instructions and the tele-

238

phone number – but there was no telephone at the farm. He dropped down the ladder from the loft and ran out of the barn and along the track. When he reached the road he turned to the right. There was a doctor in the village only a half kilometre away who would let him use the telephone.

The air-raid was still in progress with searchlights sweeping the sky and sporadic bursts of flak. Because his attention was distracted he almost ran into the German patrol. He trotted round a bend, panting and flagging now, saw men standing in the road ahead and halted, darted into the shadow of the hedgerow. He could make out four soldiers, their rifles slung over their shoulders. The British airman stood in the centre of their group, bare-headed. The flak ceased momentarily and now Jacques could hear a man speaking vehemently. It sounded like the airman's voice but it was speaking fluent German so it had to be one of the patrol.

The group moved, the airman still at its centre, headed towards the village and Jacques followed, uncertain what to do. They came to the village, the soldiers' boots clattering on the pavé. Jacques trailed them to the house the Germans had requisitioned as a guardpost and when they went inside he crept up to the window. It was blacked-out so he could see nothing but he heard the voices, and all were German. The raid had ceased, the lights were snuffed out and the guns silent. He stood in the stillness right by the window and listened.

The patrol had understandably not believed Turner's story when he walked up to them. His German was good and his confidence huge – but a German officer masquerading as a British airman? More likely the airman was trying to bluff his way out of the trap he had walked into, so they took him back to the guardpost. The front door of the house opened on to a passage and a door on the left led to the office. The Feldwebel, Luger pistol in a holster on his belt, sat behind a table with a telephone. A chair stood before it and Turner sank into it.

The Feldwebel stared and one of the soldiers bawled in outrage at this insolence but Turner said, "I've told your boys already: I am a German officer on special duty and I must report to my superior. Telephone him and he will confirm what I say."

The Feldwebel hesitated. If this English airman was trying to make a fool of him – He asked, "Who is he?"

Turner told him and the Feldwebel's face tightened. He used the telephone and it took him a minute to get through but then he made his report, listened. "Yes . . . I see . . . of course." He handed the receiver to Turner. "Headquarters for you – *sir!*"

Turner spoke curtly. "I have the name. Yes, it was quick but they gave me a half-chance so I took it. The name? Catherine Guillard, Rue de Saille." His French was good enough to pronounce it correctly. He repeated it slowly, listened, said, "Yes. You have it right."

He hung up and smiled at the Feldwebel, now standing respectfully. The patrol were at attention. Turner said, "At ease. You were doing your duty."

The Feldwebel relaxed slightly, quickly produced a cigarette when Turner demanded one and lit it for him. Turner asked, "Have you got a drink?" Now he could have one; he reckoned he'd earned it.

"I have bottles of good German beer cooling in a bucket outside." The Feldwebel snapped at the soldiers, "Back on patrol, you lot!" He went out through a door to the rear of the house.

The patrol clattered out and Turner followed them to the door. "No hard feelings, boys. You acted correctly. Well done and good night."

They muttered their respectful thanks and tramped off up the street.

It seemed the air raid was over. The night was still, peaceful, though a red taint to the sky showed where a fire burned in St. Nazaire. Turner leaned on the door post and drew on his cigarette, feeling the tension draining out of him, elation taking its place. He had done it!

As he stretched his arms out, yawning, a young man – hardly more than a boy – appeared before him as if from the ground at his feet. He saw the pale face, wide eyes, and the sudden flicker of silver that was a knife.

Jacques had heard the name, *Catherine Guillard*, and the address, and had seen the respect of the German soldiers for his 'British airman'. Now he struck blindly, ignorant of how it should be done, but sick with shame that he had been duped and hysterical with rage. He held the knife by his side and thus chanced to drive it upwards so that its point entered below Turner's rib cage. The man gasped, stumbled back under the blow, Jacques stumbling with him, and when Turner's back hit the wall Jacques' forward-falling weight drove the knife in deeper. Turner slid down the wall and his deadweight tore the knife handle finally from Jacques' grip.

The boy turned and ran.

His mind was a blank. All he could see was the face of the airman, mouth sagging open and eyes wide, slipping down away from him. But he found himself at the doctor's house, had enough presence of mind to run to the back of it and hammer on the door there.

The doctor came almost at once; the raid had kept everyone awake. He stared at Jacques, whose hands and jacket front were stained with blood, and pulled him inside. "My God! What has happened to you?"

"I am all right. But I have killed a man, a German spy. I must telephone. Please!"

The doctor recognised a state of shock when he saw it. "Are you sure the man is dead?" There was the blood but he could not believe this boy had murdered.

Jacques nodded, put a red hand to his mouth as his stomach heaved, controlled it. His face ran with sweat but it was cold. "I must telephone. *Please!*"

"In here." The doctor led him along the hall and into his surgery, pointed to the telephone and Jacques seized it. There was shouting in the street, coming closer. The doctor muttered, "A moment." He went out of the room, opened

241

the front door and saw the soldiers hurrying up the street, carrying a loaded stretcher.

In the surgery Jacques heard a voice on the line and said, "I want to speak to Henri."

The doctor appeared behind him at the door of the surgery, put a finger to his lips, switched off the light and retired, closing the door. Jacques stood by the desk in the darkness with its smells of antiseptic, waiting in an agony of dread, listening to the tramping boots and German voices in the hall outside. He heard the doctor say, "No! Not in the surgery! Bring him in here! Put him on the table!"

When the bar closed the owner switched off the lights and went up to his bed, but he left Henri sitting in the darkness at a table by the telephone. The air-raid kept him alert but when it was over he dozed with his head on his arms. He woke when the telephone rang and grabbed it. He thought he recognised Jacques' voice but asked, "Henri? Who wants him?"

He waited for some seconds, hearing distant background voices, then came: "I am his nephew from the country."

That was the correct identification; it was Jacques. "This is Henri." Then a vehicle ground down the road outside, Henri thought it probably a fire-engine, and he put a hand to the ear not at the receiver to shut out the noise. "Speak up, for God's sake!"

Jacques raised his voice, "The mute is sick!" That was the code phrase for trouble and 'mute' was the cover word for an airman on the run who could not speak French. Then words spilled out of Jacques as the horror returned, all rules of security forgotten: "He told them where to find Geneviève!" He was shouting now. Sobbing. "*I killed him!*"

Behind him the door opened and the light was switched on. The Feldwebel stood in the doorway while out in the hall his soldiers were manoeuvring a stretcher into the opposite room. The doctor's voice came heavily, "But this man is dead."

The Feldwebel was a kindly man with a wife and a teen-aged son of his own. But he lived among a hostile people, aware of their hatred and he had seen a man bloodily murdered. He stared at the young man smeared with blood, his hand sticky where it held the telephone. Then he drew his Luger from its holster, flicked off the safety catch, fired twice and the boy collapsed over the desk.

Henri, standing in the dark and empty bar, heard the shots and let the receiver fall. He blundered across to the door, knocking over tables, and when he was out on the street he ran. But it was a long way to the Rue de Saille, and there would be German patrols to be evaded in between.

Hauptmann Engel sat behind his desk, chair pushed back and booted feet on the blotter. He gazed sightlessly past their gleaming leather at the window that looked out over the St. Nazaire basin to the U-boat pens, now covered by a black-out curtain. A sentry stood by the window with his rifle, at ease but unmoving, and the eyes under the steel helmet looked carefully away from Engel, stayed fixed on the opposite wall.

Engel had poured the glass of cognac an hour before when the air-raid started but it stood untasted. He had watched the liquid shiver as the few bombs fell and the shock-waves ran away under the building. He only moved to balance his note-book on top of the glass to keep out the dust the bombs set falling finely from the ceiling. The bombers had gone and it was quiet now, the surface of the cognac was still and the dust no longer filtered down.

There was slow pacing in the suite on the floor above. Engel listened to it and wondered if the Resistance would try for Dönitz. They should, and if they did he was ready for them. There was no sentry outside the locked front door but one stood inside it and another at the window of the room across the hall. Two men were with the Feldwebel upstairs, two more sat on the floor of the Citroën outside, with orders to see without being seen, and five lay in

243

ambush in the buoy-yard on the far side of the road. The massive buoys brought ashore for repair gave plenty of cover. Since the house was sandwiched between other buildings and its rear wall backed on to a warehouse, if the Resistance came their attack would have to be made head on. Engel had made his preparations and now he waited.

Private Pianka waited also, stretched out on a bench by the door, snoring softly, his cap over his eyes against the light. He woke when the telephone rang, lifted the cap and peered across at Engel, who reached out a long arm to the instrument. "Engel." He listened for only seconds then replaced the receiver and swung his booted feet to the floor, was out of the chair and limping towards the door. "We go!"

Pianka scrambled up and followed him. In the hall the guard there stamped to attention then hurried to unlock the front door. The Feldwebel appeared at the head of the stairs and Engel snapped up at him, "We'll be back soon! If they come just follow your orders!"

The front door slammed behind them and they heard the key turn in the lock. As they piled into the Citroën the two men in the back eased up from their crouched positions into the seats. Pianka started the car, switched on the hooded headlights and drove forward as Engel pointed. Pianka asked, "What's going on?"

Engel answered, "We were right about Turner. He sang to Grünwald." Pianka swore and Engel went on, "But our little bird sang, too. That was him on the phone. So hurry."

Pianka guffawed. "Two traitors are better than one!"

"Ours is saving his neck." Just twenty-four hours before, Horstmann had stood in the Abwehr office, handsome face working in panic as Engel read out in a rapid monotone the reports made by Grünwald's housekeeper on his affair with Grünwald's young wife, Ilse. Then Engel told him, "If Turner contacts your chief you will tell me at once, with full particulars. Or Grünwald gets this report."

They drove rapidly along the side of the St. Nazaire

basin, past the minesweepers and tugs tied up there, turned right and crossed the bridge over the lock at the Southern Entrance. The Citroën surged up the gentle gradient of the Place du Bassin and then the Rue Ville-es-Martin. The streets were dark, deserted, the sky tinged red from a fire in the port where a bomb had fallen. At Engel's order Pianka swung the car left and stopped in the entrance of the Rue de Saille. The street was quiet and empty: they were in time. Engel told the two in the rear of the Citroën, "The third house on the right. Get around the back at the double."

They scrambled out of the car and ran off into the darkness, rifles held across their chests. Pianka drove on quietly, then stopped when Engel said, "This one." They got out and Pianka lifted his fist to hammer at the door but Engel snapped, "We haven't time for that!"

Pianka set his shoulder to the door and burst it open. He stumbled in after it then ran up the stairs, his way lit by the torch held by Engel limping behind him. When Engel had first come to St. Nazaire he had put a tail on this girl and learned exactly where she lived and everything else about her – or so he had believed. That thought taunted him now. There were two doors on the landing and he went without hesitation to one of them. Light showed beneath it. Engel knocked, the door opened immediately and Catherine Guillard, fully dressed, looked up at him. Her face was pale but she seemed calm. No different, still with that look of cold hostility, even now when she must know her game was over.

He said harshly, "You've made fools out of us!" He stepped inside, lifted the suitcase that stood by the door and hefted the weight of it: full. He set it down, snatched the girl's coat from a hook and threw it at her. He told Pianka, "Hold her." He switched off the light, crossed to the window, ripped aside the screening curtain and opened it. He called to the men below, "All right! Go back on foot! And at the double!"

He limped out of the room and down the stairs, Pianka

245

hurrying after him, hustling the girl along by the arm. Engel climbed into the back of the Citroën, Pianka shoved Catherine in after him and slammed the door. As he slid in behind the wheel another car swung into the street, tyres squealing as it turned at speed. It raced down on them and halted with a screech of brakes. Grünwald jumped out and strode up to the Citroën, leather coat hanging from his shoulders, Horstmann at his back. Pianka started the engine as Grünwald stooped at the side of the car, peered in at the girl then glared at Engel. "This woman is Mademoiselle Catherine Guillard?"

Engel nodded. "That's right."

"Then she is my prisoner!"

Engel answered quietly, "No. She's mine."

That quietness should not have deceived Grünwald because he knew very well this tall officer with the cold eyes. But his own men were crowding around the car now in their dark overcoats and carrying their pistols, so he grabbed the handle of the car door and would have wrenched it open.

Then, still quietly, Engel leaned across the girl to place the muzzle of his Luger in Grünwald's face. The Gestapo man let go the handle and stepped back. "You wouldn't dare!"

The barrel of the Luger was rock-steady. Engel said, "I'm always having accidents with these things."

Grünwald was breathing quickly, and thinking. He demanded, "How did you know where to come?"

"A little bird told me."

Grünwald swore: "That treacherous swine of an Englishman!"

Horstmann's face was stiff with fear but Engel did not enlighten Grünwald, and told Pianka instead, "Drive on."

Grünwald shouted as the car pulled away, "I will go to the General!"

Engel answered, "You can go to hell! The sooner the better!" He sat back as the car swung round and accelerated away.

He was conscious of Catherine Guillard sitting stiffly in

the other corner. He did not speak to her. Pianka drove down to the Southern Entrance and across the bridge, along the side of the basin and so to the Abwehr office. The guard opened the front door and Pianka ran the girl inside and held her standing before the desk. Engel sat down behind it, took off his cap and smoothed his hair. He looked across the desk at the girl.

"You have two alternatives. If you talk to me I will pull some strings. I might be able to get you only a prison sentence, but I don't know. I honestly don't know. Or Grünwald will take you away and when he's finished you will talk to him. You will be glad when he shoots you."

Catherine Guillard could not talk, had to stay silent for as long as she could because the others, Henri and Jacques, needed all the time she could give them. She looked straight at Engel. "I don't understand. Why have you arrested me?"

Engel sighed. He had feared this.

Henri had arrived in the Rue de Saille with pumping heart and failing legs. He saw Engel's car stopped outside Catherine's apartment and knew he had lost his race, pressed into a doorway and watched Engel bring the girl out. Henri did not attempt a rescue; he was unarmed and he knew Engel. He saw the exchange with Grünwald, then saw Engel take Catherine away. Finally Grünwald and his men drove off at speed and Henri walked back quickly to his own apartment. Ironically, now that the crisis was past he met no German patrols: on his way to the Rue de Saille he had had to detour to avoid three. The sweat on his face and body turned cold. Once in his room his hands started to shake but he forced them to be steady as he set up the wireless again and strung the aerial around the picture rail. He sent the message again and again until London acknowledged: "Geneviève taken."

He packed up the wireless in the suitcase and lugged it down the stairs. In an alley at the side of the house was a lock-up garage where he kept the Renault van. He went in,

dumped the suitcase in the back of the van, then propped
the door open so he could see down the alley to the dark
street. He sat in the van and waited.

If he tried to leave St. Nazaire at night he would be
stopped by patrols so he would wait for daylight when his
papers would give him at least a chance. If Engel – or
Grünwald – broke the girl before morning and came for
him he would be awake, here in the van, and ready for
them. There was a window at the back of the garage that
opened into another alley and a safe house only two streets
away with a contact with a man who drove a lorry in from
Nantes to St. Nazaire and back every Saturday morning.
He would take the wireless if he could, because in the
Resistance such things were of great importance.

He tried not to think about Catherine.

Engel waited. He had told the girl about the traitor, made it
plain that she was betrayed, but she did not flinch. He had
shouted in her face, "You are a leader of Resistance with a
network of agents and a wireless to talk to London! I want
to know the names and where to find them!"

"I can give you no names. I don't know what –"

"When do the Resistance plan to attack this place?"

He had thought he saw reaction then but all she had said
was: "I know nothing of any Resistance plan." And she
answered his other questions, repeated again and again,
with silence or: "I know nothing of that."

So now he waited, trying with the silence and the coldness of his gaze to will her to speak. In the stillness he heard
the low voices of his two men returning on foot from the
Rue de Saille, reporting to the guard at the door, going into
hiding again in the Citroën. She had to tell him all she
knew. How long had she been an agent? What information
had she sent to London? Maybe she had caused the deaths
of good Germans, his friends. Maybe she deserved to die.
He shifted his gaze minutely. Nobody deserved to die as
she would in Grünwald's hands.

He was conscious of the glass of cognac on the desk, still untasted. He did not touch it.

This was not a soldier's work. The girl was very pale and he could see the sweat on her face and running down from her hair though the fire was dead and the room cold. The general would stall as long as he could because he too did not like the Gestapo, but Grünwald would demand his prisoner with the weight of Himmler, head of Gestapo and friend of Hitler, behind him. Engel thought he might have until morning, no longer, to make her talk.

In London they telephoned Quartermain at his hotel in Falmouth and told him of the wireless signal just received from St. Nazaire. It was the moment he had dreaded for so long. He thought that it was all going wrong and had a dread premonition of disaster.

Phoebe slid past the old tower of Les Morées standing out of the river. Only ten minutes left to go; less than two miles. *Campbeltown* and the M.G.B. in the lead were steadily increasing speed for this final dash and the launches were conforming. Green had brought them through the shoals, and so far they were undetected.

Ward could see the loom of the land to port, could smell it. He was no stranger to the tension before action but had never felt it so strongly as now. It was an atmosphere that pervaded the little ship, of high hope, excitement, and an apprehension thrust to the back of the mind.

Jameson the sub was aft with the Oerlikon. Madden stood by Ward, and his commandos crouched or knelt on the deck below on either side of the bridge. Each of them, Madden included, was armed with a Thompson sub-machine-gun and grenades. Joe Krueger, on Ward's other side, wore a Colt .45 pistol belted about his waist. Ward's hung from a hook below the screen, the spare magazines in the pockets of his jacket. He knew all of Madden's men by name from the last time, could recognise them despite the darkness. Sergeant Beare, his broad figure unmistakable,

249

little Jimmy Nicholl, Lockwood, Driscoll and the rest. He knew the names of his own crew as well, but little else about them. This was not *Boston* with her close-knit family, forged by long days and nights at sea. He might never learn any more of those men of the Fairmile. The thought brought a chill so that he shivered.

Joe Krueger glanced at him and said softly, "Maybe we'll make a home run?"

Ward did not answer. Was it possible they could slip right in without being detected? It was a dark and silent shore. Were the crews of the searchlights and guns stood down – or watching? At the briefing in Falmouth Joe Krueger had listened in silence as the port's defences were spelled out, the long list of guns. Afterwards he said to Ward, "From the moment they spot us we're ducks in a barrel."

Ward answered, "You heard Commander Ryder. We'll try to act like friendly ducks."

Campbeltown had been converted to look German, was now flying a German ensign, and Ryder had some other tricks up his sleeve. But would they work? If they did not –

To port a searchlight stabbed out a wide beam. The one beam was joined by others and they washed over the whole squadron as it forged up the placid river, M.G.B., German-looking destroyer with the German ensign flying and the long columns of launches. All of them were making big bow waves now as they worked up speed.

Peter Madden said, "That's torn it!"

A Bofors gun hammered from the shore by the search-light, its muzzle flash winking quickly, one-two-three-four; and again one-two-three-four. Ward saw no hits but a signal lamp was flashing from the shore and another in the darkness ahead, challenging. A lamp flickered in reply from the M.G.B. at the head of the squadron. That was Leading Seaman Pike, acting on Ryder's orders, able to send and receive signals in German and armed with a list of enemy callsigns and morsenames. He would be sending: "Proceeding up-river as ordered" – and the bluff was working. The guns ceased firing and some of the search-lights blinked out.

The exchange of signals continued, Pike sending and the lamp ashore flickering acknowledgment. The minutes were creeping by, the ships running on, every second taking them nearer their target. Ward had no thought of Catherine, Patrick, Quartermain, of anything but his ship and his task. The image of the port ahead, Southern Entrance, Old Mole, Old Entrance, Normandie Dock was stamped into his brain.

Gunfire burst out again but it was sporadic, hesitant and still no ship was hit. Pike was flashing his signal lamp: "I am being attacked by friendly forces!"

It worked again. The Germans were confused. The guns fell silent.

Ward knew, however, that it couldn't possibly last much longer. German ships would have stopped when fired on. He said clearly into the silence so that all aboard could hear him, "Stand by!"

The storm broke. The shore on both sides of the estuary, and the dark port ahead, were lit by gunfire. This time it did not stop. Ward bellowed, "Fire!" He saw the Oerlikons aboard *Campbeltown* open up an instant before those of *Phoebe*. The whole squadron was firing now and the weight of their fire brought a slacking in that from the shore.

Their briefing promised a flakship out in the channel opposite the Southern Entrance and now it rippled with muzzle-flame. The pom-pom aboard Ryder's M.G.B. hosed it from stem to stern and the muzzle flashes died away. Ward squinted against the glare of the searchlights. They almost blinded him, as had the lights off Devonport. But there was the Southern Entrance! *Campbeltown* swerved away from the breakwaters, racing on past them for the mole and the Normandie dock beyond, and still increasing speed. She flew the White Ensign now.

251

Engel's eyes left the girl briefly to seek Pianka as the gunfire broke out again, then ceased. "Find out what the hell is going on out there, but look out for yourself."

"I will." Pianka picked up his rifle and worked the bolt to ram a round into the breech. "But I don't reckon her friends are coming tonight. That'll be the guns firing at the RAF trying to sneak back in."

Out in the street he turned left and walked along close to the buildings, down to the bridge over the Old Entrance. He did not cross it but turned left again and went along the side of the Old Entrance towards the Normandie Dock until the estuary opened out before him. He paused, looking up at the sky.

Suddenly searchlights illuminated the water, guns opened up from both sides of the river and from the flakship anchored out in the stream. The Bofors on the pumphouse close by him burst into thunderous, flaming life. There was a destroyer bearing down on him in the estuary, flanked by lines of launches, all of them flying White Ensigns streaming in the wind, and all of them firing. He stood rooted for one shocked, stupefied instant then turned and ran.

The gunfire caused the dust to fall from the ceiling again but Engel ignored it except to raise his voice. Silence had not broken the girl so he would try another tack. "You had packed a suitcase. Where were you going?"

Catherine Guillard answered as if repeating a lesson: "To Paris. I have an elderly –"

"I know about her. I know you leave here to visit her but do you always *arrive*?" His memory stirred. "You were supposed to be in Paris at the end of last month, when the British attacked Bruneval and another base further along the coast. Somebody laid out lights to mark a landing ground. Were you in Paris then?" His hand went to the telephone. "This relative of yours is frail. I can ask people in Paris to get the truth out of her." Would he? It might not be needed, anyway. The girl's eyes had widened: he was getting to her. He pushed: "Well?"

252

He heard shouting, then boots pounded in the hall and Pianka threw the door wide open. "The British! They're on the river! A torpedo-boat and motor-boats! They're invading!"

Rubbish! Not invading! But after Bruneval just a month ago – another raid? Why here? Why tonight? There was a pause in the firing, brief seconds, but in that pause they heard the steps of a man crossing the room above, pacing quickly. Engel saw the girl's mouth twitch, her gaze flick up to the ceiling then return to him.

Now he knew. "You bitch! Somehow you found out when the admiral would be here and told them in London!" His mind harked back to that day when he proposed to Grünwald that the rooms upstairs should be fitted out for Admiral Dönitz to spend the night in St. Nazaire. He had told Grünwald, "You need have no fears for the admiral." The plan to trap the saboteurs had depended on the Resistance hearing that Dönitz would come here, so the men working on the apartment had been told it was for Dönitz and had naturally talked about him in the dockyard. It had also depended on the Resistance not knowing exactly *when*, so that they would be presented with the opportunity to attack but only at short notice. They would make their plans hastily and walk straight into the trap.

But now the British were *landing*.

"Guard!" His bellow brought the boots of the Feldwebel pounding down the stairs. Engel dragged open a cupboard and snatched the Schmeisser machine-pistol from the rack inside. He thrust his face close to that of the girl, speaking softly and his eyes holding hers, taunting her. The Feldwebel burst into the room and stood at attention. Engel barked at him, "Take the woman down to the cells! Then fetch in the others!" The men in the Citroën and in ambush in the buoy-yard, he wanted them in here now. "And quick! The British are coming!" He pointed at Pianka as the Feldwebel hustled Catherine Guillard away. "You take the car and drive like hell to the barracks." That was more than a mile away. "Tell them what you saw and that the

253

Tommies are making a landing. Then you stay there! That's an order! You try to come back here and I'll have you transferred, I swear to God!"

Pianka opened his mouth to argue but for once changed his mind in the face of Engel's stare. He pulled open a drawer of the desk, took a silver flask from it and shook it to make sure it was full then jammed it in the side pocket of Engel's tunic and muttered, "*You* look out."

Engel watched him tramp from the room then lifted his notebook from the glass of cognac on his desk. He drained the glass, gasped and hurled it at the wall. Then he prepared to fight for his life.

Phoebe and the long columns of launches chased after *Campbeltown* along the side of the eastern breakwater. The firing from the shore built on itself again. Gun flashes, interweaving streams of tracer, red, yellow and green, the beams of searchlights, all destroyed Ward's night vision. Then one beam seeking the ships picked out instead the end of the Old Mole with its lighthouse. Ward saw it as *Campbeltown* swept past it and marginally altered course. There was the bend in her wake and he followed it, "Port ten!" Beattie, her captain, had her on course for the last run at the Normandie dock gate.

"Meet her! Steer that!" *Campbeltown* was being hit, shells bursting on her sides and deck. So was *Phoebe*.

Joe Krueger bawled above the thunder, "Goin' to check on the wounded and damage!"

Ward nodded and Joe swung away, headed for the wheelhouse, the dressings and morphine. Ward saw him go from the corner of his eye, all his attention on *Campbeltown*.

The M.G.B. leading them swung away to starboard, getting out of *Campbeltown*'s way. There was the dock gate ahead of her and the black opening of the Old Entrance lying to port. She was hit forward of the bridge where her 12-pounder was now hidden in flame. Her narrow length was washed in brilliant white light from the searchlights in

which sparked the orange flashes of the Oerlikons firing
from their bandstands above the dock.

She seemed to stumble, hesitate and Ward thought,
torpedo-net. There was one laid outside the Normandie
dock gate. Then she surged on. Somebody lunged against
Ward and he glanced sideways and saw Joe back on the
bridge and gripping the screen by his side, eyes fixed on
Campbeltown. She swerved to port, Beattie making the
last fine adjustment so that she aimed straight at the gate
and also swung her stern to starboard to leave the way clear
to the Old Entrance for the launches of the starboard
column.

Now it was almost finished. In the glare of the lights Joe
Krueger's face was screwed up to take the shock as if he
were aboard the destroyer – once the U.S.S. *Buchanan*
that had patrolled the warm seas off Florida. Now she
roared in from the cold Atlantic to hurl herself at the gate
of the Normandie dock. She struck in a din of rending steel
and thumping concussion below as the bulkheads were
squashed in like a concertina. Her bow below was driven
back close on thirty feet but her fo'c'sle rode on to and over
the gate so that what was left of the stem overhung the
inside of the dock.

Campbeltown was still.

15

No Way Out

"Port twenty!" Ward watched *Campbeltown* as the head of the Fairmile swung away. The Bofors and Oerlikons on either side of the dock-gate were pumping shells into her from barely a hundred yards away. There were men already climbing down ladders or ropes from her crumpled bow to the gate, he could see them in the glare from the searchlights and from the fire on her fo'c'sle. They would be Roy's and Roderick's assault parties who had to silence the guns on either side of the gate.

"Meet her! Steady . . . steer that!" The Old Entrance opened before him, light reflecting on water between the stone walls on each side. He screwed up his eyes against the glare from the lights and the red tongues of muzzle-flame, from the Oerlikons aboard *Phoebe* and the enemy guns ashore. A cone of fire was concentrated on the Old Entrance, a spider's web of tracer, and Ward took the Fairmile into it. They were possibly forty yards from the steps on the south side though that was only a guess because they were invisible behind the glare. Ward sensed as much as he saw the commandos moving across the deck, getting ready to leap ashore. Then the cone of fire hit *Phoebe* and the Oerlikons stopped. He felt the launch lift under him, shudder and fall away to port. He shouted into the voicepipe, "Starboard ten!" There was no answer from the wheelhouse and the bow still swung to port. A fire broke out aft, the engines stopped and the Fairmile drifted.

Ward saw Joe Krueger now forward of the bridge and shouted down to him, "Man the wheel! See the Chief!"

Joe lifted a hand in acknowledgment and disappeared below the bridge.

Peter Madden's voice yelled from the deck, "The gun's a wreck!"

He meant the forward Oerlikon. Ward wondered about its crew and that of the gun aft, and young Jameson. The Lewis on the bridge was not firing. He went to it, stumbled over a body and came up against the place where the Lewis was – had been – mounted. There was nothing but mangled steel. He stooped to the body and felt enough to know he could do nothing for this man. He straightened and stepped up to the screen. He was alone on the bridge, like that time when the Messerschmitts hit *Saracen*, only this was much worse. He had never experienced anything like this.

Another launch was trying to fight its way into the Old Entrance and running into the same curtain of fire. His head turned. *Phoebe* was trailing flames from her stern as she drifted back down-river past the dock area of warehouses and towards the Old Mole. A Fairmile blazed near the mole and another was alight out in the channel. They were paying the price for having petrol engines. A gun fired rapidly from a blockhouse halfway along the mole. If the attacking force was to re-embark there then somebody would have to settle that gun.

A launch swung around *Phoebe*, headed in to the mole and slid neatly alongside the landing slip. Men leapt ashore and Ward thought he saw the wiry little figure of the young second-lieutenant in the demolition control party commanded by Captain Pritchard, one of the experts. There targets lay inland and they ran along the mole and out of Ward's sight.

Joe Krueger stumbled on to the bridge and bawled, "The Chief thinks he can fix the motors – but she's sinking! She's shot full of holes below and making water fast! Bowman's at the wheel – Doyle's dead!"

Madden appeared, demanding, "Put us ashore, Jack! You've got to get us in somewhere! *Anywhere*! I've lost half my men already!"

The engines started. Ward told Madden, "I'll do that.

Now get out of here." Madden could do nothing on the bridge and he might be safer off it, though God knew they had suffered enough casualties below. Ward bent over the pipe: "Starboard twenty! Full ahead!"

The Fairmile was sluggish but she answered the helm. They had drifted down past the mole now. Try again for the Old Entrance? But he could see launches burning there, and his own was aflame and going down. Madden had said 'anywhere'. All right. He turned the launch to run in to the shore downriver of the mole. The plans of the port they had studied showed a landing slip about forty or fifty yards south of it. They had been told not to attempt a landing on this side of the mole because of shoal water but now they had no choice. They went ashore here or not at all.

There was yellow light around them where petrol burned on the surface of the river and it stank in Ward's nostrils. The Fairmile was working up speed despite the water already in her and the holes in her sides that gulped in more. Fifteen knots? Maybe. It felt fast; they were charging in along the side of the mole and fifty yards or so from it. The bow pointed at the quayside ahead. A sweeping searchlight jerked its beam along the quay and he saw the angled line leading down that was the sloping concrete slip and they were steering straight for it.

The searchlight's beam jerked on, slid along the mole, jerked again and settled on *Phoebe*. It glared into Ward's eyes and he lifted a hand against it, grabbed hold of the screen with the other and braced his legs. He shouted at Joe Krueger, "Get down and tell them to be ready to swim for it! Tell Jameson to clear them from aft!"

"Jameson's dead!" Joe flung it at Ward as he turned to drop down from the bridge. "They're all dead back there!"

The quay rushed at Ward. He saw it through watering eyes, narrowed against the glare. It loomed above him and there was the slip. *Phoebe* was being hit again and again by the gun on the mole and another beyond the quay. There was an explosion aft then a *whooshing!* roar and the bridge was flooded in red light. It shook under him, jumped

258

beneath his feet as shells burst in the wheelhouse below. Then *Phoebe* struck and despite his bracing hand he was thrown forward and doubled over the top of the screen. She drove on with the way on her, riding on to and over the rocks and sand under her bow as *Campbeltown* had run on to the dock gate. She finally collapsed with her bow smashed against the quay and resting precariously on the slip.

Ward shoved himself upright and saw the commandos jumping from the bow, plunging up to their waists in water then struggling out of it and up the slip. Seven of them. Only *seven*? He remembered Madden: "I've lost half my men already!"

He fumbled the Colt pistol from the hook below the screen and belted it around his waist as Joe returned to the bridge. They were not being hit now because the guns had switched their target when the launch crashed into the quay but the din was no less. Joe shouted, "Come on!"

The stern of the launch was ablaze and they flinched from the heat of it. Ward asked, "What about the engine-room –"

"Finished!" Joe broke in.

"Bowman?"

Joe pulled at his arm. "I'm sorry, sir, but there's *nobody* left! Believe me! I went through her before I came up here. The commandos are ashore, what's left of them. Now come on, Jack! She's going!"

She was. As Ward followed Joe down into the bow the launch slithered astern, grinding on the rocks as the current tugged at her. Joe jumped, then Ward, but the bow shifted from under his feet so that he fell face down on the slip with the river washing over him. He spat it out, swearing, crawled out of it and up the steep concrete slope.

Beare waited at the head of it, down on one knee behind the low wall that ran along the quayside, his Thompson gun with its pencil-torch glowing blue held in one big hand. With the other he pointed across the quay. "See that alley, sir? In there."

Deed of Glory

To their right lay the Old Mole with its blockhouse and the gun in it still belching flame. The river was alight with petrol and blazing launches floated on it. To the left and ahead stood the Old Town, the jumble of its roofs serrated against the sky. Between town and mole was a rough square of quayside lit fitfully by the glare from the river and the sweeping searchlights, reflecting silver from the railway lines that traversed the quay. About two hundred yards away to the right and across the quay stood the high, square outlines of warehouses with a black valley running through them. Beare was pointing at the mouth of it.

Ward nodded, "Seen." Joe Krueger was trotting over the open ground and now he disappeared into the black cleft. Ward turned for one last look at his temporary command. *Phoebe* was twenty yards out from the quay and blazing along her length, the Oerlikons drooping and bent on their mountings, her deck nearly awash. She would sink in minutes.

Beare peered past Ward at the empty slip. "You're the last, sir?"

Ward answered flatly, "Yes." Out of a crew of fourteen he and Joe Krueger were the only survivors.

Beare straightened and started across the quay. He did not crouch but ran upright and so did Ward as he followed, jumping over the railway lines that curved along the quayside. Yelling came from somewhere to his left and a machine-gun fired. The tracer sailed down from high on the roof of a house beyond the Southern Entrance and passed over Ward's head, aimed at launches still trying to land at the Old Mole. Then he plunged between the tall cliffs of warehouses, the darkness there intermittently dispelled by the light from the launches burning on the river, a glare that washed in and out of the alley as the sea washes into a cave. He passed Joe Krueger and Beare, moved deeper into the alley. The commandos crouched against the foot of the wall, Spencer, Ryan, Driscoll, Lockwood and little Jimmy Nicholl. The pencil-torches made blue pinpricks in the gloom, the white webbing belts and ammunition pouches

260

were pale stripes against the khaki battledress that blended into the shadows.

He came on Peter Madden, standing with one shoulder leaning on the wall, Thompson gun and eyes trained ahead into the alley. He only glanced at Ward then away, but Ward saw his teeth show in a grin. Peter said, "This is a right bloody party."

Ward asked, "How many have you got left?"

"You've seen them: five. Beare and me make seven."

"There's two of us: Joe and myself."

Madden glanced quickly at him again. "Is that *all*? Just you two?"

"That's all." Ward thought the other launches would have fared little better and some of them worse.

Peter Madden said quietly, "My God." Then he called "Sergeant Beare!"

"Sir!" Beare came out of the darkness to stand beside them.

Madden said, "We'll move through here at the double and across Roy's bridge." Ward wondered if Roy or any of his men were alive. He thought he had seen them dropping down from *Campbeltown* but he remembered the awful fire concentrated there. Madden was going on: "I'll lead, you bring up the rear. Carry on."

Beare disappeared and they heard his voice relaying the order. Ward said, "I'll stick with you, Peter."

"Let's get on with it. We're late." Madden broke into a run, rubber-soled boots thumping softly on the pavé or concrete underfoot, racing through the alleys that wound between the warehouses. The darkness was riven again and again by flashes of gunfire and the fingers of searchlights overhead, that lit their way for a second then left the darkness deeper than before. They turned a corner, Ward loping long-legged at Madden's shoulder. Men crowded the alley before them and Madden fired the Thompson as he ran. The group dissolved, some swerving away, yelling, into another alley and out of sight, others falling. Ward ran around them as he followed Madden.

He tried to remember the lay-out of the area as he had memorised it from the model and the maps, tried to fix his position and heading but it was one thing to study a model, another to charge through a lightning-shot blackness. He thought they were close to the bridge . . .

They broke out on to a quayside, passing between a warehouse on their right and a tall building on their left. The Old Entrance lay before them, a rectangle of dark water, and *Campbeltown* on the dock gate two hundred yards away to the right. To the left was the bridge. Had Roy and his party reached it? At the foot of the landing slip on this southern side of the Entrance lay Ryder's M.G.B. So had Newman got ashore? Figures of men appeared to the left, crossed with the bands of white webbing and Madden shouted the password, "Weymouth!" He added his name: "Madden!"

They passed through. Ward thought he saw Newman and Terry, the Intelligence man – and a German soldier? A prisoner, hands held high? But he ran after Madden to the bridge and across. He needed to stick with the group: otherwise, in his dark uniform with no white webbing, he could easily be mistaken for a German. Roy and his men had taken the bridge and were holding it but Ward only saw the dark shapes of them where they crouched or lay and the spurts of flame as they fired. His boots thumped loud on the bridge, softened once across it. He glanced over his shoulder at the hurrying figures of the commandos. Beyond them, in the middle distance, were the squat minesweepers tied up to the quay but he could not see the five destroyers. He faced forward. The aerial photograph had showed the E-boat berthed just here by the Old Entrance but she wasn't there either.

Madden had not slackened his pace, intent on making up some of the time lost. They ran along a road. To the left was the basin with harbour defence boats and more mine-sweepers. Machine-guns aboard them hammered but their tracer slid towards Roy's party at the bridge, the men at the guns not seeing the racing figures of Madden, Ward and the others as they ran in the shadow cast by the buildings on the right of the road, an unbroken line of workshops and offices, each built on to its neighbour. About two hundred yards from Roy's bridge lay the office they sought, with the suite above where Dönitz could look out on his U-boats in their pens across the basin. Flame spurted from an upstairs window a score of yards ahead and the slug ricocheted, droning, off the cobbles of the road. Madden threw himself down close by the wall and Ward sprawled beside him.

Ward said, "That's the place." It was last but one of the buildings and those on either side of it looked to be some sort of stores with small windows set high. This was a three-storey office with a closed door at the head of a short flight of steps, ground floor windows on either side of the door and other windows above them. Those on the ground and first floors were open but the top ones were closed; light reflected from the glass. The firing had come from one of the open windows. There was a buoy-yard on the other side of the street. Ward could see the huge cylinders and cones of the buoys, eight or ten feet in diameter. They were in the yard for repair and some were freshly painted, he could smell it. There was a racketing din in the rest of the dockyard but no firing here because the men in the house could not see the two lying close by the wall.

Peter nodded agreement and lifted a hand. Beare sidled along the wall and Peter asked, "All here?"

"Yes, sir."

Madden gave his orders: "Covering fire, a plastic charge on the door, grenades at the windows, then in." That was all he needed to say; they had done this before.

Beare walked back, growling orders, and Nicholl, Lockwood and Driscoll slipped across the road and disappeared among the buoys in the yard. Ryan and Spencer came up, Joe Krueger with them and he crouched behind Ward. Beare moved past taking Ryan and Spencer with him and they waited ahead of Madden, pressed against the wall, watching the buoy-yard. All three had slung their Thompsons from their shoulders. Ryan and Spencer held a grenade in each hand, Sergeant Beare the plastic explosive in one hand, fuse, igniter and detonator in the other. The beam of a searchlight on one of the minesweepers in the basin slid across the faces of the buildings. It lit the upper floors but left the street below in darkness.

Madden said, without looking round, "We'll go in at the door."

Ward pulled back the sleeve on the Colt pistol, cocking it, and heard the double, oiled click as Joe Krueger copied him. He pushed off the safety catch and eased the hammer to half-cock. Now he only had to thumb it to fire.

The Thompsons opened up from the darkness of the buoy-yard and splinters flew from around the first floor windows. Beare and the other two moved quickly forward, crouched double to pass below the first ground floor window. Ryan in the lead jumped over the steps at the door and set his back to the wall by the further window while Spencer waited by the nearer. Beare worked at the door, moulding the plastic explosive over the lock, attaching the detonator and fuse. The Thompsons fired short bursts from the buoy-yard, sounding like a stick drawn steadily across railings, a solid hammering. The Thompson fired fat .45 slugs and was a man-stopper.

Beare pulled at the igniter and stepped clear of the door, his back against the wall. The Thompsons ceased firing. An explosion in the dockyard shook the ground and Ward wondered: a demolition party blowing up a winding-house? He took a breath and another, got his legs under him. Madden was on one knee, ready to go. A rifle barrel poked cautiously out of an upper window but was drawn back in as the charge on the door exploded. Timber scattered across the road and dust boiled out of the door-way. As Ward ran in behind Madden he saw Spencer toss a grenade through the ground floor window then step a pace out from the wall to lob another in at the window above.

Beare was first in at the door, leaping up the steps through the dust cloud and running inside, Thompson firing, Madden close behind. Grenades burst in the ground floor rooms in the space of two strides. One of those long strides took Ward to the top of the steps and the other into the blackness beyond.

The light came on and the bulb glowed yellow through the hanging dust above Ward's head. He was in a long hall with a door each side and stairs at the end leading up. Beare and Madden were crouched either side of the hall and a tall German officer stood at the top of the stairs, pointing a machine-pistol down at them. Ward saw this in the fraction of a second as the light came on then grenades burst in the rooms above, the flashes coming through the open landing doors and silhouetting the man at the head of the stairs. He staggered and a burst from his machine-pistol chewed plaster from the stair-well. Ward grabbed the electric light bulb and yanked it, flex and all, out of the ceiling. The hall was again as black as a chimney but the darkness was immediately ripped as Beare fired.

Into the silence that followed Madden shouted, "Ryan? Spencer?" There had been heavy firing in the rooms on either side but that had ceased now. Their ears rang but they could hear distantly beneath them a voice crying out or screaming.

Spencer called from the room on the right, "O.K. in here, sir! I'm coming out! Lockwood's with me!"

There was a long burst of Tommy-gun fire in the other room then: "Driscoll here, sir. I'm coming out." They heard the doors open, scraping on rubble, and Driscoll said, "I could hear somebody moving up there so I put a few up through the ceiling."

Madden warned, "Get against the wall!" He shoved Ward there. "The chap upstairs might try the same dodge."

He did. Plaster fell from the ceiling as a burst from the Schmeisser ripped along the floor of the hall. Madden asked breathlessly, "Where's Ryan?"

Driscoll answered, "Copped it, sir."

"Wounded?"

"No, sir."

"Are you sure?"

"Yes, sir. I used my torch to take a look."

The exchange was deliberately flat. Ryan had been a close friend.

Little Jimmy Nicholl still crouched out in the buoy-yard covering their line of retreat. In the hall they froze as the searchlight beam returned and the passing fringe of it swept in at the shattered door, lighting the dust-coated faces of the men pressed against the walls. High-pitched shouting, perhaps a woman's voice, still came up from below and as the beam slid away Madden called, "Joe! Find out what the hell is going on down there!"

"O.K.!" Krueger started to move along the wall, past the bottom of the stairs, searching for a way to the base-ment. Madden went on: "Driscoll! You go with him. Use your torch if you have to, but look out."

Ward felt Peter grip his arm. His eyes were growing accustomed to the gloom and he made out the pale smudge of Peter's face. Madden said, "I'll go for the stairs. Beare and the other two to cover and you follow up with them."

Peter was going alone because he was short of men. Ward said, "To hell with that. I'm coming."

"Bloody fool." But Madden accepted, "All right. Now!"

The Thompsons made an ear-shattering din in the con-fines of the hall, lighting it with their muzzle-flashes, satur-ating the top of the stairs with their fire. It ceased when Madden yelled and started for the black cliff of the stairs. Ward went with him, long legs hurling him up three steps at a time so that he was ahead of Madden when a light came on again, this time illuminating the stair-well above them. It showed him a landing with open doors to left and right, a length of corridor ahead. Then he threw himself down at the top of the stairs and a burst of fire from above and behind kicked dust and splinters from the wall close over-head, showering him. He squirmed back down on his belly, frantically trying to get out of the sight of the man with the gun and felt Madden hauling at his legs. He caught a glimpse of a boxed-in second flight of stairs leading up to his right and light spilling down them, then he was back under cover on the first flight and sitting up.

Madden's face glistened with sweat in the yellow light spilling from the landing and he swore: "Crafty bastard! The stairs leading up to him are behind this wall." He rapped it with his knuckles. It went up on their right and gave back the dull, solid sound of brickwork. "No shooting through that. The light's behind it as well. He commands this landing and anybody on it'll just be a sitting target."

Beare came up behind them and held out a grenade. Madden took it and stood up on the top stair, flat against the brick wall. "Squirt him – and the light, if we can." He pulled the pin from the grenade and the clip sprang free. He leaned forward, lobbed the grenade around the corner of the wall and up the next flight of stairs. It burst and the three of them shoved forward, scattering along the landing. Madden and Beare sprayed the top of the stairs with their Thompsons. The light bulb swung up there in drifting smoke, then went out.

Ward was on the floor, blind in the darkness. He rolled in through the doorway on the left of the landing and squirmed forward on his elbows, pistol held before him. Behind him another grenade exploded, the Thompsons hammered and then there was a ripping burst from high in the house. Silence. Outside the searchlight washed the face of the building and slid on leaving the room dark again but Ward had seen enough. He stood up and moved forward past the bed almost to the window but stopped short of showing himself there. Two soldiers lay dead close by the window, sprawled on their backs. There was no one else in the room.

He called Madden, who entered and stood by the door, breathing quickly. "I've checked the room across the landing. Nothing in there."

Ward said, "He's here." He lifted a German navy greatcoat from the bed and held it out.

Madden felt at it in the gloom; there was a faint glow

from outside where the searchlights made artificial moonlight. The braid on the coat showed yellow and was stiff
under his fingers. "He must be with the others on the top
floor." He paused, then: "I said 'others' but I think there's
only one left, well back from the top of the stairs and out of
reach of grenades. We chucked one up but he's still active;
he probably rigged some sort of barricade up there. I think
he knows what he's doing. Tricky."

An explosion shook the building through its founda-
tions, the sound of it coming like a clap of thunder. Shards
of broken glass still hanging in the windows fell and
smashed on the floor. Plaster cascaded around them, the
dust setting them coughing and Ward said, "That could be
the north gate."

"Sounds good, anyway." Madden called, "Sergeant
Beare! Anything moving up there?"

"Nothing moving, but he laughed just before that charge
blew."

"What?"

Then a chuckle came again from the landing above and a
voice echoed in the well of the stairs, *"Komm', Tommi!"*

Beare said, "We've got a right one here, sir."

Madden answered, "Let's go and get him."

Joe Krueger called from below but his words were lost in
a burst of firing out in the basin. He shouted again: "Better
come down an' see what I've got!"

Madden demanded impatiently, "Can't it wait?"

"No!"

Ward and Madden exchanged glances. They had been
late getting ashore and racing against time ever since. If the
commandos from *Campbeltown* kept to their timetable,
and the explosions suggested so, then they would soon pull
back across Roy's bridge. Then every minute Roy held on
waiting for Madden was another minute his men would be
exposed to that murderous fire. But Joe must know all that
. . . Ward nodded, then Madden in reluctant agreement.
They slipped out of the room and along the side of the
landing to the top of the stairs. Beare was down on one

knee in the cover of the opposite doorway, Thompson pointing up at the landing above.

The searchlight still swept the street, spilt in at the empty frames of the downstairs windows and over the wreckage in the entrance hall. It lit Joe Krueger and the woman he held at his side. Her hair hung tangled about her face and she stared wide-eyed up at Ward and Madden, anonymous shapes in the dim light above her. For a moment Ward did not recognise this woman as the girl he knew. Then he did.

Peter Madden whispered, "My God! It's the same girl!"

Joe Krueger said, "There are cells down there. We found her in one of them and the keys hanging on a board. Nobody else." He finished with an edge of doubt, "She claims she's a British agent."

"She is!" Ward ran down the stairs, Madden at his heels.

Catherine Guillard peered up at him. "John?" She was not surprised to see him. She had been afraid but now was free and felt a great surge of relief. Surprise might come later; she could not feel it now.

He held her by the shoulders. "Did they hurt you?"

She shook her head and sagged against him. "Just questions." Then she pushed away and lifted a hand to brush the hair from her face. "Dönitz is not here. He never was here."

There was a stunned silence. Madden broke it, refusing to believe her. "How do you know? You were in a cell. We found his coat upstairs!"

Catherine shook her head. "Engel told me. He is the Abwehr officer who arrested me. He said it was his idea to pretend the admiral would stay here tonight. A friend of mine watched and thought he saw Dönitz come here but it was only one of Engel's clerks, probably wearing the coat you saw. It was all a trick to draw the Resistance into a trap . . . and I believed it. I told London that Dönitz would be here tonight . . ."

Madden argued, "This man could have been lying."

Ward did not want to believe Catherine either, but: "How many men were there in here, Peter?"

They all compared notes, then Madden said, "I make it

269

thirteen: eight down here and five upstairs. Then there's the one still holding out up there. Maybe more than one, but I don't think so."

"Not many for an admiral's guard." Ward frowned. "And no flag-lieutenant, no naval personnel at all."

Joe Krueger muttered, "That doesn't add up to Dönitz being here."

Catherine said, "He is at the Château Beauregard, where he usually stays when he comes to St. Nazaire. It is five kilometres from here."

He could as well have been on the moon.

Quartermain's months of watching and waiting, *Phoebe*, the dangerous work of all of them here and the men killed, all for nothing.

Madden took a deep breath. "Well." He looked at Ward, "We might as well get the next bus back."

Another thumping explosion shook the house, more glass shattered and fell, dust swirled around them in the hall. Madden said, "That could be the northern winding-house."

Ward explained to Catherine, "Taking Dönitz was just one part of the raid. The main target is the Normandie dock."

Madden took off his steel helmet, ran his fingers through his hair and replaced the helmet, settled it on his head with the strap under his chin. He called up the stairs, "Did you hear all that, Sergeant Beare?"

Beare growled bitterly from the darkness above, "Enough, sir."

"Come on down. We're going home."

As Beare slipped across the landing to the stairs he called, "Next time, Fritz."

He got no answer.

Engel heard the voices below, the girl's among them, but only faintly and he did not understand a word.

He sat in a room five paces from the head of the stairs. His back was against the wall and through the open door he could see the cupboard he had dragged out across the landing as a barrier against grenades. It stopped most of the steel splinters and the others ripped on down the corridor past the door. There had not been a grenade for some minutes, boots had receded softly down the stairs and the voices had ceased.

The Schmeisser lay across his thighs while he tied a handkerchief around the gash in his left forearm. It was bleeding badly and he felt sick. Those Tommies had over-run the house like a battalion, though he would swear they were out-numbered by at least two to one.

He thought they might be waiting for him to go down so he would sit here for a while and stay alive. There was always tomorrow. He wished he had a drink and then remembered the flask Pianka had given him, worked it out of the pocket of his tunic and took a long swallow of the cognac. That was better. He hoped Pianka was all right. The man was a very old soldier and could surely take care of himself – but tonight things were unpredictable and he might take chances to come looking for the man he had saved once before, in Russia.

He said softly, "Sit tight, Pianka, you old bastard. I need you."

He was lucky to be alive. Would they come up after him? They? Only briefly-glimpsed, quick-moving shadows except when he switched on the light in the hall and saw the tight little group of them coming in fast. Then that bloody grenade blew up, the light went off and one of them down there sprayed the landing. He thought he was dead, then, but got away with only the gash in his arm. The second time, when he lit the upstairs landing, he glimpsed a dark uniform with the gold rings of a naval officer on the cuff, and a broad back that dropped to the floor so the burst from the Schmeisser missed, but a very big man, tall as himself.

He knew he had to watch the stairs but no one came. The gunfire kept on and on all around the dockyard, deafening, maddening, while the searchlights lit the house through the shattered windows and ripped blackout curtains, then

271

swung away to leave it in darkness. The house itself was silent as the grave.

He liked that Guillard girl, in spite of everything.

He wondered about her, if she was safe.

Oh, mother, I feel bad.

He fainted away.

Patrick stood on French soil again after nearly two years but did not pause to savour the moment. He had seen some wild parties in Montparnasse but never anything like this. Brilliant light laid the dockside bare for an instant, showed the solid cubes of winding-house and pump-house, the gun on it silent now, wrecked; Roy's men had done that. Cranes towered, each like a huge gallows with its outstretched jib. Railway lines ran along the quay – Then sudden darkness as the searchlights swept away, blackness he could feel like a sack pulled over his head. Patrick tripped and fell, elbows saving his face, but painfully. He swore and scrambled up again. It was a quarter mile along this bloody dock. He ran.

Firing came from ahead and to his left and then the Thompsons of Lieutenant Denison and the others in Patrick's protection squad were racketing in front of him, grenades bursting. One man in each protection squad carried grenades and a pistol. The firing ceased. He was almost up with them and could see Denison's burly figure now and another crane looming, firing again from the other side of the crane, Denison taking it on with his Thompson and the other two hurling grenades. Patrick was up to the crane, steadying, getting a good grip on the Thompson. The grenades burst, the firing ceased and they ran on. Soft thudding of rubber-soled boots, panting breathing, pale flashes of white webbing. Ships in the dock. Two of them. Tankers? Passing the second of them now. Another black cube standing out of the night to the left and the glint of water ahead – the northern winding-house and the water of the Penhouet basin on the other side of the north gate of the Normandie dock. They were there.

Get down in place in the screen to cover the demolition men, behind this stack of timber! Its resinous smell mingles with the cordite reek of the Thompson trained out over the top of it. Eyes searching: anybody without a blue light, anybody banging about in ammunition boots instead of rubber soles, let them have it. Gulping air after the run but hearing above this panting the boots of the demolition parties coming up, covering the quarter mile at the double under the packs of explosive, up to ninety pounds a man.

Whip-crack of slugs overhead, spit of fire out in the darkness. Give it a burst. Move to a new position. Another burst. Move. Change the magazine. A jerking shadow in the middle distance, crossing from one patch of dark solidity to another and seen against far-off light. Cover it, lead it, squeeze. The jerking shadow falls. Move. Fire. Move. Howling ricochet off the timber and pain, wiping at the blood on one cheek and splinters of wood coming away. Move. Fire.

Gun jammed – blast! Watch the front, hands can deal with the jam and the gun's invisible in this darkness anyway. Cock it. Magazine off. Thumb out the jammed round – magazine in.

Hell of an explosion away down at the southern end of the dock. Smalley's party has blown the winding-house there. A while ago Corran Purdon and his four corporals smashed in the door of the winding-house at this end and disappeared inside. They would be setting their charges now. The others are working on the gate. Chant and his party were to deal with the pump-house –

Christ! There it went! A booming roar and the ground lifting.

A closer blast from the gate nearby but a much smaller charge. Were they trying to blow their way into the inside of the gate to set charges there?

Oerlikons opening up from the other side of the Penhouet basin and shells bursting all around. Small-arms fire from the tankers in the dock. Shadows of the gate demolition party running to the side of the dock and taking on the leading tanker with their pistols. Another two with Thompsons scurrying back towards the second tanker. Time to get out, follow them, belting at the double along the dockside and down the tanker's gangway. Aim the Thompson along the deck and fire the magazine off, all twenty-odd rounds of it. Back up the gangway, nobody firing aboard the tankers now, change the magazine and drop into the covering position again, breathing wide-mouthed.

Fire. Move. Fire.

Deafened as they blow the gate. The demolition party moves back from there. Teeth-jarring concussion as Corran Purdon fires the charges on the winding-house. It lifts clear of the ground and falls back in a pile of rubble.

All done. Both winding-houses, the pump-house and the gate; whacking great holes in that, the water roaring through.

Can't see how many blokes are left. Can't see *anything* most of the time! But there aren't near as many as came up.

Pulling back along the side of the dock, heading towards *Campbeltown*, Roy's bridge and then the re-embarkation area by the Old Mole. Try to scrounge a lift from cousin Jack.

They slipped out of the wreck of the Abwehr office one by one in a spaced file, Madden leading and Ward behind him. The searchlight still swept across the buildings so they moved in short dashes, dropping down close to the wall when the beam came seeking. Broken glass and rubble crunched under their feet when they moved.

Madden held out a spread hand, signalling a halt, then went on alone towards Roy's bridge to shout the password and clear the way for the rest of them. Ward waited, down on one knee by the wall, and glanced back at the crouched men behind him. Catherine Guillard was somewhere among them. Pinpricks of blue light still marked the commandos. He looked ahead. The swing bridge was only fifty yards away and under fire, from ships in the basin and guns mounted on the U-boat pens on the other side. Stray bullets pecked at the wall above the waiting group and bursting shells showered them with dust and débris.

Madden returned and shouted so all of them could hear, "Close up and follow me!" The huddled figures rose. Ward trailed Madden and heard him call the password, "Weymouth!" They trotted past a man behind a Bren, firing bursts of tracer at one of the minesweepers in the basin. The Bren magazines were all loaded with three rounds of tracer in every five.

Madden halted near the edge of the quay and in the cover of a wall. "Roy's lost half his men but he's still holding! Only Roderick's group to come through now! Go *under* the bridge!"

They saw the point of that. When they crossed the bridge before it had been under sporadic fire, but now it was swept continuously by machine-guns. Crossing underneath it they would have at least some cover. Its underside was a lattice-work of steel girders, its seating in a well cut out of the quayside below them. Beare went first, then Lockwood. Ward lowered himself down the six foot drop into the well, seized Catherine Guillard around the waist as she followed and set her on her feet. He pointed to Lockwood working his way along between the girders under the bridge and shouted above the din, "Follow him!"

She nodded and swung out over the black water to edge her way across using hands and feet. Ward went after her, keeping close, ready to hold out a steadying hand. The firing from the basin clanged and howled off the bridge above and from the meagre shelter of the girders around them. Beare hauled them in on the far side and shoved them towards the cover of a warehouse wall.

Madden, last across the bridge, came to them and softly called the roll. "Nicholl, Lockwood . . ."

Answers came out of the darkness, all but one and Beare said, "Spencer was hit on the bridge, sir. Machine-gun. Just after Mr. Ward came over."

Ward thought it could easily have been Catherine or himself. Spencer was a quiet young man. He had been with Madden on the raid to bring back Peyraud.

Peter Madden said, "Roderick's group are coming through now and Roy will be pulling back. Colonel Newman is regrouping on the quay by the Old Mole and Roy says the whole area is alive with Jerries – so look out!"

He led on and they worked through between the warehouses, threading the narrow canyons. Twice they ran into parties of the enemy and fired savagely at point-blank range. Ward kept ahead of Catherine, Joe Krueger behind her. He emptied his pistol into dark silhouettes that screamed or groaned, fell or ran, then changed its magazine and emptied it again.

They came to the assembly area where the survivors of CHARIOT, less than a hundred and a third of them wounded, held a loose perimeter. They had the cover of a few railway trucks where the silver criss-crossing lines made a big triangle a hundred yards to the north-east of the Old Mole. Madden shouted the password and led his party forward.

Patrick, crouched behind a truck, saw Ward's tall figure stride by. Back in Falmouth cousin Jack had joked, "Don't be so bloody rude or I'll leave you to walk home." Now, by the look of things, they would all be walking.

Ward stared out at the Old Mole and the Loire. The river was on fire where petrol floated and flamed and on it drifted the blazing wrecks of Fairmiles. The gun on the mole still fired at some target down river and the searchlight at the end swept the estuary. The enemy held the mole so no one would re-embark from it. Besides – He turned to Catherine and told her, "There are no boats to take us back."

But there was no time to dwell on that. Madden's little group was sent to plug a hole in the defence around the perimeter. There were many gaps and not enough men to fill them. This was no safe haven – the Germans were closing in on all sides except from the river. It was more of a shoal, the enemy swirling into and out of it like the tide, defenders mingling with attackers and all in the dark.

On the river side there was the glare from the burning petrol. In its light Ward saw Colonel Newman standing in the dubious cover of a railway truck with his second-in-command and adjutant. Madden went to report to Newman, stood rigidly at attention and saluted as if on parade.

Ward lay behind the wheel of a truck with Joe Krueger, Catherine between them. She looked at the river – close to the shore it was not on fire. She had decided that when the soldiers had to surrender then she would go that way. She was a poor swimmer so the chance of escape was slender but the alternative was Grünwald.

Ward knew these men would not surrender. He changed the magazine of the Colt again and as he did so looked across towards the little group around Colonel Newman. A German stick grenade wobbled across the red-lit sky and fell close to Newman's feet but when the smoke and dust blew away he still stood.

Peter Madden came to crouch by Ward: "We're breaking out into the country and going home through Spain and Gibraltar."

He allowed this to sink in, then went on, "They're organising parties and I said there were enough of us for a party on our own. We're going out across the Southern Entrance. The nearest bridge is only a couple of hundred yards from here across the dockyard but it's all open ground, so to get to it we're going back through the warehouses to Roy's bridge. The ships in the basin have hauled over to the U-boat pens so it should be possible to get along the quay to the outer bridge over the Southern Entrance. That way it's about six or seven hundred yards."

Ward, watching his front, squeezed off a shot at a moving figure and saw it go down into the darkness. He asked, "When?" Because the firing around them was growing even heavier, and besides –

"Very soon." And Madden spoke the thought in Ward's

mind, "It's getting too hot here and ammunition is running low. How much have we got?"

Ward said, "I've one more magazine and five left in this one; fifteen rounds altogether."

Joe Krueger said, "About the same."

Madden scowled. "Sergeant Beare?"

"Just checked, sir. Grenades all gone and about thirty rounds a man remaining."

Joe said quietly, "So we go soon or throw rocks."

They started a few minutes later, at just after three in the morning, the break-out parties tagging one behind the other, with Roy and Newman in the lead. Ward was at the tail with Madden's party, Catherine in its midst. They wound again through the dark clefts between the warehouses, checking briefly when the head of the column ran into the enemy and bombed or shot its way through, then hurrying on. At the tail they heard the clamour of that fighting and had their own minor actions when they were fired on from alley-ways alongside. That took more of their dwindling ammunition but no one was hit.

They came to Roy's bridge, now hopelessly enfiladed, and turned left to run along the quayside between the blank walls of warehouses and the St. Nazaire basin, glinting under the moon now shining through scattered clouds. They came under fire from the guns mounted on the U-boat pens across the basin but they were halfway to the bridge and running hard when little Jimmy Nicholl was hit. They halted while the rest of the column ran on. Ward and Joe Krueger lifted Nicholl and carried him to cover in the darker shadow by the nearest wall. Madden and the others closed around and Beare examined Jimmy with Catherine by his side.

Madden asked, not turning, still looking along the quay towards the outer bridge where the column had halted, just short of the Old Town Square, "How is he?"

Beare answered heavily, "He's unconscious, sir. He's got a nasty chest wound and probably others."

Ward peered over Madden's shoulder. There was scourging rifle fire from the far side of the bridge and machine-guns hammered there, set high on some building at the Southern Entrance.

Madden said quietly, bitterly, "There's no way out across the bridge."

Patrick waited with the rest of the column in the cover of the warehouses by the Old Town Square, looking across its hundred yards of open ground to the bridge that spanned the Southern Entrance, bathed now in brilliant moonlight. There were a score or more of German riflemen lying prone on the quay on the far side. He could not see the men but the flashes of their rifles firing showed where they lay. There was a machine-gun in the concrete pill-box on the other side of the bridge and to the left of it, others high in houses or on roof tops.

This bridge was the way they had to go. Patrick wiped his hands on his trousers and took a better grip on the Thompson. His last magazine was loaded and half of it already fired. Sergeant-major Haines was setting up a Bren to give covering fire. Patrick was ready to go, could feel a coiled-spring tension in the men around him.

The Bren opened up, Newman shouted an order and ran at the bridge with Roy at his side. Patrick and the rest charged after them. He heard the *whip-crack* of firing passing close over his head, ricochets shrieked off the suspension girders of the bridge, rubber-soled boots pounded on its hollow steel frame like a drum.

The German riflemen melted away from the charge, scrambled to their feet and scattered. Patrick was over, saw Bill Copland rush at the pill-box, fire through the slit and silence the machine-gun inside. They ran up the road in a ragged column and a motor-cycle with a sidecar carrying a machine-gun swerved out of a side turning. Patrick and every other commando fired at it and the motor-cycle skidded, crashed into a wall.

An armoured car appeared in the street ahead, machine-

279

gun firing from its turret. Patrick swerved to the right, away from the machine-gun and out of sight of the man behind it. He found himself in a side street and realised the others had swung left and he was alone. He could hear the engine of the armoured car growing louder so he went on up the street at the double. In fifty yards he came to a cross-roads and ran full tilt into a German patrol.

There were three of them, two armed with rifles, one carrying a pistol, and Patrick thought he was probably a non-com. The Thompson was empty so he grabbed it by the hot barrel and swung it like a club. The shock jarred up his arm and one of the riflemen reeled away and fell on his face. The other tried to defend himself with the rifle held out before him but Patrick smashed down the guard and the man behind it. The non-com pointed his pistol. The stock was broken from the Thompson but Patrick hurled what he had left, barrel and chamber. The non-com ducked away from the flying chunk of steel and his pistol fired but at the ground, then Patrick was on him. He grabbed the man's arm, twisted and broke it at the elbow so the pistol fell, smacked the edge of his hand into the shouting face, silencing it. Then he left the man lying, ran on up the street and halted at the end where it was crossed by a broader road.

His side of the road was lit by the moon, enough for him to read the plate almost over his head: Rue Henri Gautier. Shadow lay along the opposite wall. To his right the road lay wide, straight and empty, pointing roughly north and that would be a way out into the country. There was sporadic firing coming from the direction of the bridge behind him and no point in returning, weaponless, to the others. So he was on his own. All right.

He trotted across the road and headed north in the shadow cast by the wall, passing houses where people lived, ordinary Frenchmen, awake now and perhaps watching anxiously from their windows. He could perhaps seek shelter in one of their houses but not for long – Jerry would certainly mount a search in the morning. He checked when he came to a narrow side turning, peered into it, saw only darkness, and decided it was a blind alley. He had just started across it when another German patrol spilled out into the street from a cross-roads a hundred yards ahead. He side-stepped into the alley and watched. This was not just a patrol, he thought, but reinforcements headed for the dockyard. There were already around thirty men advancing towards him and more still poured out into the road. They were spread right across it as they hurried towards the sound of the firing.

He swore under his breath, turned and moved quickly, soft-footed, deeper into the alley. There was a shed of some sort blocking the end of it, with double doors and one of them ajar. He slipped around it and in. A window at the back let in moonlight that showed him an old van. Transport? He slid along the side of it, then froze momentarily as he saw the figure of a man sitting inside it, behind the wheel. Patrick yanked open the passenger's door and dived in, left hand clamping around the man's throat and the other whipping the commando knife from its sheath on his thigh. He jabbed the knife against the side of the man's neck until he winced as its needle-sharp point pricked his skin.

Patrick held him thus and watched the end of the alley through the half-open door. The troops passed in a noisy stream, then a trickle . . . that ceased. The alley was quiet again except for the distant firing. Patrick said hoarsely, quietly, *"Silence! Oui?"* The man nodded fractionally against the clamping hand. Patrick released its pressure but did not take it away, nor the knife. In the moonlight that filtered in through the rear window he saw his hands were black with blood from the earlier fighting.

Henri whispered, "You are English." And when Patrick nodded: "I am of the Resistance. You understand? I have to leave St. Nazaire, also. There is a way for us."

Patrick asked, "In this?"

Henri shook his head. "One of us was . . . taken last night, so my cover may be worthless. I dare not risk being stopped." He explained about the truck from Nantes. "In

281

the truck we can keep out of sight. It is a chance at least. There is an old suit – overalls, yes? In the back, here. You wear those."

Patrick took away his hand, then the knife. He had understood Henri easily enough, still remembered the French he had learned in Paris. He sat back in the passenger's seat, suddenly very tired. For the first time since he had stood on the deck of *Campbeltown* he thought of Sarah. Not of their nights together, not of her body, but of Sarah herself. He hoped she was safe and happy, but that she would be glad to see him when he got back. He would get back. Nobody would stop him.

Henri rubbed at his throat and looked at the tall man now easing himself back in the other seat. His soldier's helmet was missing and a lock of black hair hung over his brow. His eyes were dark and determined in a face that was filthy and streaked with sweat runnels. His hands were big, strong and seemed to have been dipped in blood. His grip on Henri had been like iron, and there had also been the knife.

Henri said, "I thought I was close to death, then."

"You were."

A flat statement. Henri believed that this man would kill anyone who stood in his way. He said in careful English, "I was in England a little time. I learned to speak, a little. You are a commando?"

Patrick grinned at him. "Me? Don't you know a bloody artist when you see one?"

Ward watched the incredible charge across the bridge and Madden said, "They made it!" And then softly, "Oh, hell!"

In front of them the Old Town Square had filled suddenly with German troops, barring the way to the bridge. There was no hope of escape across it for Ward, Madden and the rest.

They fell back towards Roy's bridge, stealing along in the darkness close against the warehouses. The firing on

the other side of the basin faded into the distance. Ward
wondered how Newman and his men were faring.

Lockwood and Driscoll carried Jimmy Nicholl between
them, limp and unconscious, his legs dragging. German
voices shouted all around them, from the ships in the basin,
from beyond the warehouses that briefly sheltered them,
from behind them on the quay and ahead, from the other
side of Roy's bridge.

There was no crossing it so they turned the corner and
were back in the area of the Old Entrance. Madden, in the
lead, halted at the open door of a warehouse. He and Ward
stood for some seconds listening, and Ward looked across
the quay to the black water in the rectangle of the Old
Entrance. The skipper of that E-boat sneaked in here
ahead of the destroyers . . .

Madden muttered, "Sounds empty. It might be a place
to hide – or a death trap."

Catherine said, "There is a loft. A ladder leads up to it."

Madden advanced a step. "Is there, by God."

He hesitated but Ward had already made his decision.
"We know there's no way out by the river. We've got to lie
up during the day then try to get out overland tomorrow
night. There's no chance now. Come on, you and me first."

Madden nodded, glanced around, saw Beare lurking
close and told him, "We'll take a look. Wait here."

He went quickly through the door, moving right and
Ward followed, moving left. A few paces inside they halted,
accustoming their eyes to the deeper darkness. Ward
made out alleys running between huge stacks of crates
piled high above his head. Beyond lay blackness and silence. If there were windows in the warehouse then they
were blacked out because none of the glare from the fires in
the dockyard and the sweeping searchlights penetrated
into this black cavern. There was only the faint, grey
rectangle of the door.

Madden called, "O.K., Sergeant Beare, get 'em in."
And when they were all inside: "Where's that ladder?"

They followed Catherine as she walked cautiously between the piles of stacked crates, hands outstretched before her, until she came to the wall. She worked along it slowly then said, "Here."

It was a steel ladder, clamped to the brickwork, vertical. Madden climbed it and passed through the square opening at the top into the loft. Beare followed with Nicholl, wrists lashed together with a handkerchief and around Beare's neck, hanging on the sergeant's back. The rest followed and Ward was last.

There was room to stand under the roof. The timber floor was solid and did not creak. Faint light entered through wide, shallow windows like horizontal slits that overlooked the Old Entrance and were not blacked out. Well-filled sacks were piled all around the entrance to the loft, to the height of a man and right up to the windows. They seemed, from the smell of them, to contain greasy cotton waste or cleaning rags.

Madden set a watch at the head of the ladder and another at the window overlooking the Old Entrance. "But keep your heads down. Don't be seen, for God's sake."

They made a nest among the sacks close by the ladder for Nicholl and those not on watch. Beare and Catherine worked on Nicholl, Madden collecting the field dressings that every man carried. The most obvious wound, in Nicholl's chest, had been hastily dressed before they moved from the quay, but now they found the others. Catherine and Beare did all they could but it was hopeless. Little Jimmy Nicholl did not regain consciousness and died very soon after.

Madden said with bitter self-recrimination, "I should have left him on the quay. They might have got him to a doctor and saved him."

Catherine shook her head and Beare said, "No." He had seen wounded before, too many.

Catherine stayed kneeling beside Nicholl and prayed for the soul of the young man she hardly knew. Then she lay down like the others, and tried to sleep. But, tired as she was, she remained wakeful.

The men took it in turns to stand sentry for an hour at a time. When Ward was not on guard he slept the sleep of exhaustion, but fitfully. Catherine watched him. Once when he half-awoke he found her close, her arm around him. He put up a hand to touch her cheek, then closed his eyes and slept again.

The small-arms fire went on intermittently through what was left of the night but it had moved away. Catherine thought the Germans must be hunting down the commandos who had broken out over the bridge. With the dawn the firing ceased and Madden woke them all. They stood to as the light grew.

16

CHARIOT OF FIRE

Pianka came looking for his officer in that first light.

Engel still sat in the room on the top floor, watching the stairs. He had woken in the last of the night and heard the swift scurrying of booted feet as men ran from cover to cover. Listening to them, he could see them with his mind's eye, moving in dashes with heads turning nervously. He heard the fighting ebb away into the distance and now the booted feet moved more slowly but still with pauses when they halted, reluctant to break from cover until a growled order started them.

He did not feel so bad now. The arm was stiff and sore but he was alive and here was another day.

Pianka's voice came from the road outside: "Hauptmann Engel?"

Engel answered, "Wait! Is anybody with you?"

"An N.C.O. and ten men."

"Send them in. Tell them to be careful. I think the Tommies have gone but you never know."

Engel heard them enter, cautiously. With a grunt of pain and muttered cursing he climbed to his feet, dragged the cupboard aside and descended the stairs. Pianka stood at the foot of them, scowling with a mixture of relief that Engel was alive, and concern at the sight of him, filthy and with a bloody rag wrapped around his arm. Pianka started, "You'd better go to the dressing-station –" Then stopped as he caught Engel's eye.

Engel asked, "Did the ships take them away?"

Pianka spread his hands. "I don't know. I heard they couldn't get off from the Old Mole and tried to fight their way out through the town but that's just rumour. It is very confused."

Engel said grimly, "I'll bet it is." Then: "They took our prisoner. I heard them talking with her." He turned to the N.C.O., "You and your men come with me."

The corporal stood to attention and protested, nervously because he knew about this eccentric officer, "I have orders to search –"

Engel cut him off. "That's exactly what you're going to do: search. Come on."

The N.C.O. swallowed his objections and obeyed.

They worked through the buildings along the side of the basin and crossed Roy's bridge. There they met a Feldwebel who told Engel that prisoners were held in a café on the other side of the Southern Entrance. "A hundred of them charged across the bridge. God knows where they thought they were going. Maybe they had gone mad because their boats had burned. We only captured them because they hadn't a round of ammunition."

Engel looked at him sharply. "Were all the boats sunk?"

"I don't know, but many were; maybe all."

Engel went to the café, looked over the prisoners and there were some young naval officers among the commandos but not the tall man he had seen. There was no Catherine Guillard.

He took his men searching through the town and back past the U-boat pens, then crossed by the bridge to the other side of the basin and combed the area around the Normandie dock. The devastation there appalled even him. He stared at the wreck of the northern gate, *Campbeltown* rammed into the southern, and the heaps of rubble that had been the pump-house and winding-houses. He whispered, "My God! It will take a year to get it working again!"

He recognised a major of engineers standing on the deck of *Campbeltown* and bawled up at him, "Do you want a corkscrew to get her out?"

The engineer stiffened at sight of Engel but answered, "She'll come out and the gate will be all right after some work. We looked for demolition charges but the Tommies didn't manage to lay any here – I'm glad to say." He grinned as relief relaxed him. "They filled up her bow with concrete so she'd hit the gate like a hammer but they got their sums wrong and it wasn't enough, it didn't work."

Engel shrugged and went on with his searching. Twice Pianka suggested Engel should go to have his wound dressed and was cursed for his temerity. It was close to noon when they passed Engel's office again, heading towards Roy's bridge and Pianka said, "Maybe they got away."

"No!" Engel knew that abrupt denial came from instinct, not reason. Or was it bruised pride because he had lost his prisoner? No matter; he felt in his bones that the girl and her rescuers were still here in St. Nazaire. He would find them.

Pianka tried again: "The dressing-station is not far –"

Engel sighed with exasperation, "For Christ's sake! Can't you shut up? You're worse than a nagging wife!" He paused, glaring at Pianka's stolid, square face. Pianka was looking weary, he was too old for this game now. Engel said, "Go to the dressing-station and fetch a medic. When you catch up with me he can do the job."

Pianka knew he would have to settle for that, turned and hurried away.

Engel limped on towards Roy's bridge again, his Schmeisser carried loosely in one hand.

Ward lay on watch at the window in the loft as the dawn broke. Joe Krueger, come to relieve him, lay at his side. They, with Madden, were taking turns at keeping look-out from the window, an hour at a time. Beare, Lockwood and Driscoll did the same duty at the head of the ladder. The light grew slowly that morning because of the smoke from fires still smouldering all over the dockyard that rose to hang like a false cloud-base above the port. But the day came and from the narrow window, the glass blasted from it by the demolition charges of the night, they saw something of the area around their end of the warehouse. Their angle of vision was a semi-circle from Roy's bridge and the St. Nazaire basin on their left, past the Old Entrance like a small rectangular inlet right ahead of them, to the southern gate of the Normandie dock. The gate was buckled so that the rising tide washed into the dock and *Campbeltown* rested on it like a stranded whale, with her bow projecting a foot or more beyond the gate and over the inside of the dock.

They could see on the other side of the Old Entrance the rubble of the pump-house and southern winding-house and they caught glimpses of the traffic on the river, for the most part launches on patrol. German troops, armed sailors and marines picked their way edgily through the litter of the shattered dock. But always *Campbeltown* drew the eyes of Ward and Krueger. As time went by men climbed aboard her, soldiers and sailors, officers among them.

Joe said disgustedly, "Fritz is looting her!"

Ward left him on watch and crawled back to the nest in the sacks by the head of the ladder. Lockwood was on watch there and he had fashioned a peephole through the sacks so he could lie inside their cover and still see through the open trap at the head of the ladder to the floor and the entrance of the warehouse. The commandos not on watch were sleeping, huddled down in the gloom.

Ward sat down by Catherine's side. They talked little and it was not about her capture or his rescue of her, but of the few hours they had spent together in London and on the Hampshire coast. That was something to look back to. They did not talk of the future.

The morning crept on. There were bursts of firing now and again, but most of it distant. Ward stood another hour-long watch at the window. Catherine went with him and at the end of it they returned to the refuge among the sacks. Once Madden came from prowling the loft and said, "The ladder we came in by is the only way out, so we're done for if we're found. Still, nobody seems interested in this place. We might get away with it."

They had all cleaned their weapons. Ward had five rounds of ammunition left in the Colt while the others had between five and ten rounds. He knew in his heart that Madden was only trying to keep up their spirits with talk of escape. The Germans would be bound to search this place before nightfall.

It was close to noon when he crawled over the sacks to the window to relieve Madden. Joe Krueger was already there, staring out at *Campbeltown* and Catherine went with Ward again so the four of them lay side by side but well back from the window. A breeze came in off the river, tainted with smoke, and cold. Catherine shivered and Ward pressed her hand.

The scene below had changed little except that *Campbeltown* now swarmed with men. Joe said, "There's more aboard her now than she brought here, I reckon three or four hundred."

Madden started to move back but stopped as Joe went on: "Huh-uh! This could mean trouble!" He pointed left to the bridge Roy had held for so long under murderous fire. On the far side a group of soldiers were halted. The officer commanding them was bareheaded but he topped them all. He stood stiffly erect, looking down at a man in a slouch hat with a long leather coat hung over his shoulders like a cape. Another man, tall and blond, and a young woman in a fur coat, walked on quickly towards *Campbeltown*.

Catherine said softly, "The tall officer is Hauptmann Engel. He is the one who held out to the end in the Abwehr building. He is talking to Grünwald."

Ward felt her tremble and knew this time it was not from cold. He asked, "Grünwald?"

Catherine said, "He is Gestapo. He came for me but Engel arrested me first. If Grünwald had taken me I would have gone to Gestapo headquarters for – interrogation. I would have been better dead."

Ward watched them. They were good targets and with a Thompson – but there was no ammunition to spare for vengeance. They would need it all at the end and that would be soon. He thought that Hauptmann Engel was hunting them and would seek them out. He was sure of it.

Catherine said, "Those two men hate each other."

Engel said, "What brings you down here when you could be in your warm office with your files? Did somebody tell you the fighting was over?"

Grünwald had halted because Engel stepped in his path. He saw his wife Ilse and Horstmann hurrying on without him. He was impatient to follow but he smiled at Engel, sure of himself now. "My sense of duty calls me here, the same sense of duty that will make me write a report on the way you took my prisoner from me by force."

Engel smiled back at him. "It will be quite a report. You've been a lying swine all your life and you won't change now."

Grünwald's smile became a grimace. "You will regret that!"

"No, I won't. My only regret is that the Tommies didn't catch up with you, but no Tommy could run that fast."

Grünwald looked past Engel to the soldiers grinning behind him. He edged around Engel and started off along the quay.

Engel rasped, "You're going to the ship?"

Grünwald turned his head but did not stop. "So? There may be valuable information on her." He walked after his wife and Horstmann.

One of the soldiers muttered wistfully, "I heard there could be food and cigarettes aboard."

"So did he," Engel said shortly. Then he snapped at them, "But you lot are here to hunt Tommies, so keep your eyes open!"

He watched Grünwald hurrying, almost running down to the old destroyer. Then his eyes moved on to the other destroyers now anchored out in the channel about 400 metres away, *Jaguar* and the other boats of Schmidt's Fifth Flotilla. A *Schnellboot* was slipping into the Old Entrance on the tide and tying up to the steps opposite him. She was about thirty-five metres long, low and narrow, with an open bridge over the little wheelhouse. A 20mm Oerlikon was mounted forward, another aft. He could see Rudi Moller, her captain and his friend on her bridge, but he would have recognised Rudi's boat anyway from the death's-head painted black on the superstructure. Engel rasped, "Come on!" He limped towards the bridge at the head of his men.

Joe Krueger said softly, "Well, I'll be God-*damned*! It's Dirty Bill!"

Peter Madden, helmet removed for his time on watch, ran his fingers through curly hair matted with sweat. "Who?"

"The E-boat. We've met her before."

"Ah!" Madden was uninterested. The time for decision was almost on them; that was a German search party approaching on the other side of the Old Entrance. He turned his head, saw Beare watching him, and beckoned. He asked Krueger absently, "Why d'you call 'em E-boats, anyway? What does the 'E' stand for?"

Joe shook his head. "I don't know and I've never met anybody who did. Jerry calls 'em S-boats, *Schnellboot*, *schnell* meaning quick. They're that, all right; cruise at thirty knots and can hit forty."

Ward did not take his eyes off the boat. Back in Falmouth Quartermain had said the E-boat went to sea and returned by the Old Entrance. And so she had . . . Here was a slim chance – if he could take it. And this was an old enemy.

As the boat was made fast the rumble of her engines died away and her engineroom staff came up from below, the coxswain and the wireless operator from the wheelhouse under the bridge. Her captain climbed the steps to stand on the quay. He and all his crew stared across at *Campbeltown*.

Joe muttered, "More of them to loot the old girl."

292

CHARIOT OF FIRE

Catherine asked, "Does it matter? She's done her job."
Ward said, "She's not finished yet."

The tall man, Engel, limped across the bridge, his soldiers behind him. He looked at their warehouse but turned to head towards the E-boat.

Beare had come up and Madden whispered, "Tell Lockwood and Driscoll –"

But Ward shoved back from the window and took command: "Quick! Everybody! Never mind the look-out here!" He scrambled back into the refuge among the sacks, the others following. They were all there, huddled down, Driscoll with his eye to the hole through which he could see the warehouse below.

Ward said rapidly, "A search party is coming this way and they'll be in here any minute – but there's an E-boat outside and I propose to take her. Mr. Krueger here can make her go. Right?" He glanced at Joe, who nodded. Ward went on, "We ambush the search party but not when the first one comes in at the door; we wait till we can get a few of them. Then across to the boat."

He paused and looked at Madden. "All right, Peter?"

"Sure." But Madden avoided his eyes.

Ward knew why: Peter was too aware of the odds. They might ambush some of the soldiers but the rest would be waiting outside and the E-boat carried a crew of twenty or more – and machine-guns. Ward said, "If we surrender, then we'll be prisoners of war, but Catherine won't. She'll be treated as a spy. So I'm not surrendering, I'm giving this a try. The chances are poor, and any man who wishes can stay behind and give himself up afterwards. No disgrace. I only ask for his ammunition. In my eyes you're all heroes and nothing can change that. So, who's coming?"

Eyes stared distantly out of drawn faces shadowed black by dirt and stubble. Ward glared as madly as any. He looked around the little circle and saw every man with a lifted hand.

Engel walked past the warehouse and halted by Rudi

293

Moller. "What brings you here, old friend? That drink I promised you?"

Rudi glanced around, "Franz!" Then his eyes widened as he took in Engel's ripped and dirty uniform, the blood on his sleeve and hands. "You've been in a fight."

"One of those nights. Where were you?"

"At sea, with *Jaguar* and the flotilla, hunting down the Tommies' launches. I usually slip into the basin this way – it gets us ashore quicker. But there'll be no going ashore for us today. We've topped up with diesel and we're waiting for orders here where we can see signals from *Jaguar* out there in the channel; our wireless has broken down."

"Tanked-up? What range does that give you?"

Rudi shrugged. "Around eleven hundred kilometres at cruising speed."

Engel said ironically, "You're going to chase them all the way to England?"

Rudi shook his head. "No more hunting. But after what happened last night I'm going to be ready for anything."

"Did any get away?"

"A few, in the first hour."

"And afterwards, after the demolitions?"

"None." That was said with flat certainty and Engel thought that his instinct had been right: his quarry was still here in St. Nazaire. Moller went on: "But I tell you one thing – there's something bloody funny about *her*." He nodded at *Campbeltown*.

Engel could see Grünwald on her deck now with Ilse and Horstmann. He asked. "What d'ye mean, funny?"

Rudi Moller jammed hands in his trouser pockets and scowled. "They're not mugs. They'd know they couldn't smash through the gate with an old destroyer like that."

Engel said, "The engineers aboard her now say the Tommies packed her front end with concrete to give her more punch."

Rudi shot a quick glance at him. "What about an explosive charge?"

"None. Just the concrete."

Moller shook his head, not satisfied, then: "She's one of the old American flush-deck destroyers that the Yanks sold to the British. One just like her gave me a hell of a scare a few weeks ago and this one scares me now."

Engel said, "I have work to do but remember to come for that drink." Moller nodded but did not answer and Engel turned away, left him staring across at *Campbeltown*.

Ward looked round at the faces shadowed in the half light that filtered down to them where they lay at the bottom of the nest of sacks. "Thank you." Then he gave his orders: "I'll lead, then Captain Madden, Lockwood, Driscoll, Sergeant Beare." All the Thompson guns.

Catherine whispered, "You said the ship was not finished. What did you mean?"

Ward checked that the Colt was loose in the holster. "Two explosives experts, Lieutenant Tibbits and Captain Pritchard, packed a four-ton charge in her bow." *Campbeltown* was a chariot of fire; CHARIOT was no haphazard choice of name for this operation.

Catherine's eyes widened. "*Four tons!*"

Ward nodded, "Twenty-four depth charges set in concrete, with small holes left in it to drop delayed-action pencil fuses down to the charges. I don't know whether Tibbits slapped some cement on the holes afterwards but maybe he did because the way *Campbeltown* is crowded means Jerry hasn't found the charges or even suspects they're there."

Then Driscoll interrupted him. "Search party!"

He eased aside so Ward could peer through the peep-hole. The tall officer was framed in the rectangle of the doorway, a submachine-gun in his right hand. Ward could not see his face, silhouetted as he was against the light, yet something about the way the man stood, the turn of his head, stirred memory. But it eluded him, was gone as the man limped forward with a peculiar stiff swinging of one leg. Ward had drawn his pistol and it was cocked, trained

295

on the man below, set safe with Ward's thumb on the catch. Not yet. They would have to ambush the search party from up there then fight their way out. The man looked up, eyes searching the darkness of the roof and Ward pressed his face down into the sacks so the white of it would not give him away. Not yet. Count to ten, give him time to come on to pointblank range. One . . . two . . .

Engel was some yards ahead of his men who were still outside on the quay. He stood in an alley between crates stacked high above his head and peered up into the gloom above the crates, the lifted barrel of the Schmeisser following the line his eyes took as they searched. Had there been a flicker of movement then? Nothing now. If he found the girl, would she betray her friends? He knew she would not. So she would go to Grünwald.

Engel wondered if he really wanted to find her –

The blast sucked the air from his lungs and hurled him down the alley. He was unconscious before the flash lit the inside of the warehouse brighter than noonday, and knew nothing of the stacks of crates blown inwards like leaves on the wind to fall on and around him.

In the loft they were well away from the front of the building and sheltered by the bags of cotton waste, so that, although great sections of the roof tore off and spun away, and they were all rolled along the floor, none of them lost consciousness. They screwed up their eyes against the searing flash and winced at the thunderclap that deafened them – all in a split second – then lay, alive and aware but numbed by shock, deafened, blind, and uncomprehending.

Ward, alone among them all, understood what had happened. *Campbeltown* had blown up.

Like *Boston*, *Campbeltown* never let you down when it really mattered.

Now it was up to them. He climbed to his feet and stooped to reach out a groping left hand, realised he still gripped the Colt in his right, found Catherine and pulled her up to him. Her lips moved but his ears still sang and he shook his head, shrugging. A breeze was sucked in through the shattered roof and the dust cleared enough for him to see Madden, Beare and the others getting up from where they were scattered along the floor. He waved at them with the pistol, gesturing towards the ladder.

Joe and Peter went with him across the now sagging boards while Beare herded the others ahead of him.

The ladder was still there and secure. The concrete floor from the foot of it to the door was littered with rubble but swept clear of the crates, now piled high in the rear half of the warehouse. Ward dropped down the ladder and stood at its foot as the others descended. One by one he urged them on their way, Catherine included, with a shove towards the door. Last down the ladder was Lockwood and Ward was about to follow him to the door when he saw movement from the corner of his eye. He turned and saw the piled crates shifting, settling, looked into a narrow valley in the mountains of them and saw Hauptmann Engel, wedged and helpless. This was his enemy. This was the man whose Dönitz masquerade had out-witted them. This was the man from the house along the quay, the man who had laughed. And this was the man who had captured Catherine.

Ward lifted his pistol, aimed it carefully.

They peered at each other in the gloom, scant yards between them, closer than they had been on that day of high summer in 1940, and recognition came to both of them. It stayed Ward's hand, long enough for the white heat to go from his anger. He was no more able to kill this man now than he had been in 1940. He lowered the Colt and turned away. Catherine Guillard was at the door, peering back into the dust-hung dimness of the warehouse and he ran to her.

Engel watched him go. With the shifting of the crates he had become blearily conscious, just in time to see Ward at the foot of the ladder and turning. Then Engel had stared again into the muzzle of this Englishman's gun, even as he had stared two years before. But today there was a differ-

297

ence, for today he too was armed. Ward could not see it, in the gloom and behind a screening box, but he still held his Schmeisser and it would only have needed a twitch of his wrist and a squeeze of his forefinger –

But the Schmeisser had sagged under its own weight and his weariness with killing, and he watched, only half conscious and deaf as the Englishman turned away and went quickly to the door. Engel did not hear the rumble of the crates as they shifted again but he saw them as they toppled in an avalanche and buried him.

Ward grabbed Catherine's arm and they ran across the quay with Madden and the others, stumbling through the rubble. *Campbeltown* no longer rested on the dock gate. The gate had been blown to fragments, so had the fore-part of *Campbeltown* and her after-end had been washed inside the dock and lay there on the bottom. No one aboard her had survived, nor had anyone caught in the open within hundreds of yards of her. The soldiers on the quay and the crew of the E-boat had gone but there were butcher's-shop traces of them.

Ward led his party down the slippery steps on the side of the Old Entrance wall and aboard the E-boat. He saw she had lost some paint where the blast had hurled her against the quay, despite the fenders slung between her side and the wall. But the German ensign still flew over her.

He went to the wheelhouse with Catherine while Joe Krueger dropped down into the engineroom. The engines started a moment later. Ward felt the powerful beat of them in the deck beneath his feet; Joe had come through. Madden and Beare cast off and Ward took her slowly astern and out into the stream, turned her and headed down river. The soldiers quickly took cover below, Madden crowding in with Catherine and Ward. Peter said, "Driscoll knows a bit about engines so he's gone to see if Joe needs help and he can relieve him later."

Later? Madden's voice came distantly; Ward's ears still rang and he felt numb, acting only on instinct and trained reactions. As they slid past the Old Mole he thought they had a hell of a long way to go and Peter's talk of *later* was a bit optimistic. Then he remembered the German ensign that flew over them, and that the E-boat with the death's-head on the superstructure would be a familiar sight on this river. The destroyers anchored off the Old Entrance had not challenged. There was a chance.

And Quartermain had wanted an E-boat as much as he wanted Dönitz . . .

When Engel awoke he was in a hospital bed, his head bandaged and Pianka sat on a chair a yard away, hands on knees. He was coated in dust, nails broken and fingers bloody, his square face anxious, watching Engel. Who thought back and said, his voice a croak, "You dug me out." And when Pianka nodded, still anxious, Engel said, "You would." Then: "Did you see them?"

"Who?"

"The Tommies! The naval officer! The Guillard girl, you dummy!"

"No need to shout!" Pianka was relieved. They were back to normal and this was the old Hauptmann Engel talking. "No, I didn't. There was one hell of a bang that threw me and the medic across the road when we were still nowhere near the place. When we got to the warehouse there was – nobody, just a lot of blood and – bits." He swallowed. "No ship. No dock-gate. We found you after about ten minutes and nobody else showed up for another ten."

Engel asked, "What about the *Schnellboot*?"

"Ah! *That* I saw. It was out in the channel, Rudi Moller was taking it out to sea."

"No, he wasn't." Engel thought back. Rudi had been on the quay and no one there could have lived. "How long ago was this?"

"Just before noon." Pianka cocked an eye up at the clock on the wall, "Three, maybe four hours ago."

They would be at sea by now, clear away. Engel swore and Pianka asked, "What's the matter now?"

Engel told him and Pianka grumbled, "So? You could have been a dirty mark on the dockyard wall. You should count your blessings."

Engel lay silent and thought that wasn't a bad idea. He was alive and Grünwald was dead. The Guillard girl had escaped but that meant he did not have to do anything about her, would not have to hand her over to Grünwald's successor. Then there were the orders that had arrived all those weeks ago, on the morning of the day Grünwald came to the office and Engel proposed the trap baited with 'Dönitz'. He had promised Grünwald all he wanted but with tongue in cheek because the orders in his pocket meant the transfer of himself and Pianka to Spain, to be attached to the Embassy there, at the end of the month. So that Grünwald would have had to begin his little empire-building all over again, with Engel's successor.

Engel rasped, "Count my blessings? Anybody else would get a sexy little nurse but I draw you. Get back to barracks and start packing my kit. In a day or two we'll be on our way."

Pianka got up, grinning. "We can watch the British agents in Madrid and they can watch us."

Engel said, "Get me a drink. Never mind what the medics say, you fetch me a bottle, or I'll have you sent back to Russia." He relaxed against the pillows. The old bastard wouldn't bring a full bottle but he would smuggle in a drink. In Spain there would be sun to soak the ache out of this damned leg, lights in the streets and girls. With any luck at all, he and Pianka would live out this bloody war.

The truck pulled off the road three kilometres outside of Nantes, drove down a muddy track and into a farmyard. Henri and Patrick, shapeless in dirty blue overalls, got down and the truck drove away. A woman came quickly out of the house, embraced Henri and they talked rapidly. Patrick understood every word. He looked around him curiously, but unafraid.

Henri said, "There are clothes here for you. There will

300

be papers and I have money. This is a way we have used before for airmen and it is safe."

Patrick nodded. He knew it would be all right. He was on his way.

Quartermain waited in the Headquarters that Ryder had set up in the house on the cliffs above Falmouth. At two in the morning of the twenty-ninth HQ Plymouth telephoned to say that Ryder and some survivors had returned. The raid had been a huge success, its main objective accomplished, but the launch *Phoebe* had been seen, blazing like a torch and sinking near the Old Mole under heavy fire.

There was an air of celebration at the Headquarters but Quartermain did not stay. He went out to the Daimler and Leading Wren Jenny Melville drove him down through the darkened streets to his hotel in the town. When he climbed stiffly from the car he told her, "You won't be needed again tonight, but you'd better come in and we'll find you a cup of tea."

The girl asked, "Is there any news, sir?"

Quartermain answered, "They aren't coming back."

He went in and asked the night porter for tea.

"There's nobody in the kitchen, o' course, sir, but I expect I can find something."

Jenny Melville said, "I'll see what I can do, sir."

She walked quickly past Quartermain, who asked the porter, "Will you fetch me a scotch, please? A large one."

Scotch was scarce and officially the hotel had none but the porter went to the hidden bottle.

There was a fire in the hearth and Quartermain sank into a chair before it and stared into the flames. He felt old and tired, chilled to the bone. All gone. Catherine Guillard, John Ward, Peter Madden, Joe Krueger, and all the good men with them. He, Quartermain, had sent them. The porter brought him whisky in a thick glass and he sipped it neat, remembering them. The young ones had died and he was an old man.

He sat there for a long time. Now and again the girl came

301

quietly to the door behind him, watched him for a minute or two with her teeth in her lower lip, then went away.

He was remembering Catherine Guillard saying, when she was still exhausted after the raid to bring back Peyraud, "I will return to France." She had said it calmly, knowing the death that might well await her there. And Jack Ward at Harwich, unshaven and hollow-eyed, bitter at the escape of *Scharnhorst* and *Gneisenau*. Quartermain had asked him, "Ready to go again?" And Ward had answered, "Any time."

It was close to morning when Quartermain stood up and Jenny Melville came in from the kitchen. He said, "Find out the time of the first train to London, will you? I'll go back alone and you can have a day's rest then come on tomorrow with the car." There was work for him to do; he was not finished yet. He would see this war through to its end, or his.

The Leading Wren went to the reception desk and the telephone there. It rang as she reached it and she lifted it, answered, then held it out to Quartermain. "For you, sir. Headquarters."

He took the instrument, noticing that the girl was red-eyed as if she had been crying. "Quartermain . . . I see . . . Yes, thank you for telling me."

He went out quickly to the Daimler and Jenny Melville drove him down to the harbour where the motor-launches berthed. As they went he told her, "They're coming in. I asked Ward for an E-boat so he captured me one . . . God knows how, but its wireless didn't work so they couldn't tell us. They've just met a destroyer on patrol outside and she sent a signal that she's bringing them in."

A Fairmile waited for them at the jetty, slipped as soon as they were aboard and ran down river in the cold dawn. Quartermain stood at the side of the captain, a lieutenant R.N.V.R., the girl a pace or two behind. As they left the harbour and met the sea the Fairmile pitched to it. The girl put out a hand to hold on but stared ahead.

There was a mist on the water and the E-boat came out of

it quietly, slipping along slowly with only a ripple at her bow. The Fairmile slowed and started to turn. As the E-boat stole past, Quartermain made out the face of the American, Joe Krueger, at the helm in the little wheel-house. Jack Ward stood on the bridge above, Catherine Guillard at his side. Quartermain could not believe it; her 'pianist' had reported her taken by the Gestapo. She wore a German naval greatcoat that hung around her in folds and her short fair hair was blowing in the wind. He thanked God that Ward had brought her, not Dönitz, out of France.

Peter Madden was in the waist and he lifted a hand, grinning. Quartermain saw Jenny Melville waving back and crying openly now. He thought that he'd been slow, not to have seen that going on right under his nose.

The escorting destroyer turned away to head out to sea. She was a flush-decked, narrow ship with four upright funnels, old, rust-streaked and hard-worked. She might have been *Boston* or *Campbeltown*.

Quartermain saluted them all.

Epilogue

Lieutenant Wynn in M.T.B. 74 fired delayed action torpedoes at the lock gates of the Old Entrance and they exploded forty-eight hours after *Campbeltown* blew up, creating further chaos.

This book is not intended as a history of the St. Nazaire raid, though I have tried to set my story against the background of the time and stuck to the facts so far as I could. There was no Alain Peyraud; the staff of Combined Operations collected the essential information on the construction of the Normandie dock. Where I have named real people it was because they were integral to this story. It would take another book to describe all the individual feats of bravery that night. The men of CHARIOT won five VCs 'before breakfast'.